Jack!

Tova Dian Dean

Copyright © 2013 Tova Dian Dean
All rights reserved.
ISBN: 1490338322
ISBN 13: 9781490338323
Library of Congress Control Number: 2013910294
CreateSpace Independent Publishing Platform,
North Charleston, South Carolina

Para Sergio, el latido de mi corazón,
los huesos de los dedos

Chapter 1

The door on the small desert house opened a wedge. Jack noted the usual predawn smell of wet bamboo and gently blowing sand. It was an hour before sunrise, so the horizon had that fading, navy-blue quality, and the stars still littered the deep bowl of the sky with a thousand dots of light. Jack angled his body sideways to slip out of the house soundlessly. He didn't care to wake up his mother; she'd gone to bed the night before agitated; all angle-eyed, and ready to blow over the broken-down car. There was a good hour to get it fixed before the day became unbearably hot, and she got up.

The rickety old porch was a flat deck, uncovered, and made of wood planks that were warped from the sandy wind constantly passing over while the sunlight baked it. The night air had cooled it to the temperature of cold stone.

Gripping the side of the house, he swept a foot in the air until it banged into his boots. Once he got hold of them, he slammed the heels together several good whacks to be sure anything alive was completely evicted. Jack dropped them to the ground and worked his feet in. The laces were gone; both tongues hung out as if they were swollen and desperate for water, but the boots felt more like home than his bed. He crossed the face of the porch in three long strides, stepping down into the sandy yard without a sound, hurrying toward the shed to get his toolbox, car parts, and buckets of water.

He had to work quickly before the sun rose and the desert heat began baking everything, especially him. Once this happened he would be forced back inside until sunset. Oh, he looked forward to that to be sure—lazily wearing out the day, comfortably embedded inside the soft contours of the old sofa in the living room—but that wouldn't get the car running.

He lumbered in a rolling gait to his mother's old car, where he set the rebuilt part and his toolbox on the worn but sturdy workbench. He threw an old wool blanket over these before going back to the shed to get everything else he'd need to fix the car. Picking up all the buckets with both hands, he made his way out of the rickety shed, knocking over a couple of old brooms and finally banging his foot into his old childhood wheelchair, that undersized chariot of small metal bones, where he, as a scrawny kid, had passively sat for some very uninformative years that had set the tone for his entire life, it seemed. The memories stung. Jack filled the buckets with water from the outdoor spigot, hardly noticing the sulfuric smell.

This place he grew up in was a miniscule desert boondocks made up of only a couple of dozen inhabitants living in all types of creatively fashioned housing built on the homesteaded land, free of building codes, randomly situated within some loosely set boundaries optimistically called *Foison Surrounded*. One crumbling strip of highway—a paved mule train corridor—sliced the town in half and connected it to the outside world, east to west. An ancient lake used to be a major part of a transportation system, but sometime in the early 1900s the water was sold to distant Los Angeles, and they took it all, leaving a glaring white, sulfuric, dry lake bed that cracked and flaked.

A decade or so after World War II, when the highway shifted to a more efficient desert corridor, the town found itself in the absolute middle of nowhere. Occasionally people still arrived for the spiritually healing effects of what was known as the Numinous Vortex, a winding valley of natural cathedrals created by extraordinarily fashioned *tawls* that jutted into the sky like gigantic rock castles. People liked to visit during the windiest time of year, providing a variety of amusements, and sometimes a little extra cash, for the locals.

There was underground water. The townspeople all tapped their own wells, or bought water, and stored it in tanks, or both. They had septic tanks and propane. Vern had a windmill that generated free energy, but he was the ingenious one in Foison. There were plenty of yucca and mesquite trees and other tenacious shrubs, sand, shards of rock in every imaginable color; heat in the summer; miserable, inescapable cold in the winter; springtime could be dazzling but was here and gone in a quick explosion of desert blossoms, then back to bleak.

Daylight had arrived by the time Jack opened the hood to the car, arranged his tools and buckets of water, and got situated under the corrugated awning. This piece of the western desert was partly ringed by the nearby mountain range, the ancient tawls, and possibly sunken into some sort of ancient meteor impression. The sunlight emerged as a vague glimmer, and then it lit up the world with a *wump!* Cold air began to steadily rise from warm to blazing. Sweat began skidding down his forehead into his eyes so that he had to tilt his chin up and grimace just enough to use his eyebrows as sweat gutters, diverting the water from his eyes to the outer corners of his cheeks where it sloshed down to meet at his chin, which he wiped on his sleeve.

Jack took his head out from under the hood to move his wrenches into one of the buckets of water. The sound of an engine starting somewhere in the little town caused him to look up. It was Evonal's truck; she was up early, he thought, wondering where she was off to.

At some point, round when he was about six, the inhabitants had pitched in their money to build a concrete landing pad for UFOs. Jack liked to think he kept an open mind on all things, but he never really believed in anything, except that he could get this antique car running every time he needed to. The desert now smelled of scorched dew; his sweat stank like heated, salty ammonia.

Even though he was under shade, the heat of the sun was using his own clothes to burn his skin; it felt like an iron being pressed on him. He worked quickly, steadily, mechanically even, breathing heavy with the effort to get it done in the rapidly rising heat. When a breeze blew over him, Jack went cross-eyed from the momentary sensation of cool relief.

"It's getting too friggin' hot. Come on, old woman, don't make me suffer," he pleaded with the old engine, but he gently, gently pulled on the wrench.

This is where Jack Stanger found himself some thirty-odd years after his own birth, still living with his mother, disappointing her most every day, though he hated to; he didn't seem prepared to do anything else. Jack leaned in, digging into the very heart of the old heap—a 1929 Mercedes Benz Gazelle, always poorly running and in very shabby condition—a car that she once dubbed her best son, not that he blamed her—but it certainly could not fix itself.

The front door opened and slammed. His shoulders pinched.

"Jack, we're down to a lump of peanut butter and the heels of bread," cried his mother, Mavis Stanger, her alert that some financial emergency had again inserted itself into their lives.

A child of that particular generation, he preferred snacks to real meals, but he didn't try the joke. Jack continued to work, bracing for the emotional storm.

"JACK!" his mother called again. The unstable note of his name warbled before snapping closed; he tried not to flinch, but he didn't want to look up.

"JACK!"

"I hear ya'." Jack let go of the engine and turned to face her, glad to be squinting from the full sun at her back. From the quivering of her body it was obvious that his mother was in her quiet frenzy mode.

Mavis Stanger was a tiny slip of a woman—a pennaceous feather—who seemed fastened to the earth by some extra pull of gravity. As a small boy he feared the wind would capture her and sweep her to another place, and there she'd be: better off without him. The most surprising thing about her was that she was quite pretty, something wasted in this bland desert. There were no prospects here for her romantically; her head was always bound in a scarf; she kept her hands dropped firmly in her apron pockets, shoulders folded in, like a wounded bird.

"I just finished the job for…"

"Sell the car!"

"I got a couple hundred dollars…"

"Sell the car," she cried. "Just take it over to the Car Spot in Edgecrest and sell the car. I put the call in already this morning. They're expecting you. We gotta have the money, Jack."

Jack knew she was in a certain kind of mood, and it was always best that he just wait for her to blow it all out, hoping the car would eventually be spared at the end of this Thursday maelstrom. It would be foolish to press his cash on her. The temper she was in, she'd chop it up and make it into a salad garnished with cactus needles.

"I know you're thinkin' I'll change my mind, but I can't. Vern says the house is rotted away right down the middle. It *sways* in the wind, if you haven't noticed. If we don't do something soon it's gonna split into pieces and *shred*. Vern's own words. And we can't eat the shred, Jack. We can pitch a tent, we can drink the well water, but we gotta have food."

Jack studied her resolve. It seemed fixed. All of her life she had said the day she had to give up her car was the day she was to die. Although he didn't believe she would die from the loss of it, he sorely disliked the responsibility of selling the old car, mainly because of its unpredictable aftermath. And good-natured Jack hated anything having to do with negotiation. Mavis Stanger didn't like to part with anything, and eventually she'd probably demand that he go get it back, a feat that would be impossible in the used car world, and a fact she would not accept as an excuse. It wasn't very valuable, especially in the shape it was in—sickly, weatherworn, an engine so old few people knew how to work on it, let alone get parts. His posture shifted.

"Don't you think you can talk me out of this. I can see your foot tapping."

Jack pushed his feet into the earth, thinking how he certainly didn't relish the thought of a break down in this heat, but thoroughly savored the prospect of getting into a familiar city to loosen up and kick up his heels a bit. He knew he could pick up a couple of repair jobs at Blick's garage; he was always begging him to take on more work. It'd come about by accident that Jack was a surprisingly adept mechanic. The old car could be stashed there until his mother demanded he get it back; he'd have pocket money enough to fool around for a few days while Mavis's mood shifted. He'd bring home groceries for a month.

"I won't change my mind, Jack, so don't think stalling is gonna save it. Get it done, quick and clean. And you'd best get out'ta this heat, son. Why look at this day. That sun's just two slim fingers off the horizon, and already it's blazing to kill. I'm going back in. Gotta be crazy to stand out in this heat. For any reason."

By the time he looked again, his mother had vanished back into the house. A careless move caused his hand to brush across hot metal. "Jeeeez USSSS!" he cried, shaking it to cool. "You're done, old woman," he declared. He wrapped his shirt around his hand before slamming the hood shut, punctuating the sentence on the old car.

■ ■ ■

Chapter 2

Crystal was a gleaming white gypsy woman with short reflective hair shaped to her head like a platinum swim cap. Nothing like the gypsies of the Hollywood movie sort; those seductive, dark-haired beauties, backs bending, arms slithering like poisonous snakes to bring down the sky. Crystal looked like a cotton-candy girl next door, but her soul, her soul: wicked free, wrapped in loose colorful scarves, winding out in the wind, all cruel, unpredictable gypsy heart. Naturally, Jack had always found her irresistible.

The motel room was dingy even with the door flung wide open. "Good enough," she'd said, leaping in, pulling her clothes off, and going boldly naked right to the bed. Once his clothes covered hers, Jack stamped his footprints into them on his way to the bed.

Before he could make his big move, she had him straddled, pinning him to the mattress with those shimmering legs bent at the knee, a cloud pinning a mountain to the earth. One long slender arm propped open the distance between them.

"Come closer, Crystal!" he pleaded.

"Before you get anything more, say you surrender. Say it right now," Crystal whispered in that low rasp, the voice that hid all the cactus needles. Cupping his chin in her palm, she turned his head sharply and stuck her lips into his ear.

"Say it."

"I surrender," he cried.

"That's a good boy. And now I have something very special for you. Better than anything you've ever tried before." Crystal flashed a small envelope, like the kind flower seeds come in, only it was a shiny black with no writing. Her smile was huge, seductive, but Jack shook his head.

"None for me, thanks," he said, and they eyed each other. The room became stifling hot for those few seconds, his feet banged together like they knew it was best to get going, but Jack had no intention of leaving.

"More for me!" she finally said before the crook of her arm hid her face while she wiped her lips on the smooth hump of her bare shoulder. After taking a beer off the nightstand—a movement Jack loved because her nipples brushed against his chin and shoulder—Crystal cracked it open, taking a long pull, before she tipped the envelope to her mouth, shaking it lightly as she gently sucked. Wadding up the small envelope, she threw it to the floor before dropping her wet mouth on his, pressing whatever was on her tongue onto his. The bitter seeds burned the roof of his mouth, a taste that quickly swelled into his nose. This time he grabbed the beer and emptied it into his gullet, tossing the can into the air as he fell heavily into the pillow.

"What the fuck was that?" he wheezed.

"You're gonna love this, Jackie," Crystal promised, laughing.

The effects seemed to be immediate. As his cerebrum dulled, all sense of intelligence quickly left him; he couldn't open and close his own hands, couldn't speak, only grunt. The occipital lobe was on very shaky ground; his eyes were rolling around in their sockets. Both the temporal and parietal lobes seemed to unite and intensify their function, all sounds. For several anxious moments he thought he was in deeply in love with Crystal. Rolling off him, she laid back into the mattress; unfolded. Together they went wild.

"That's right, baby just like that, baby. Now put a jimmy on it and let's get to it..." The condom seemed to appear in her fingers, pulled from thin air. The wrapper of the jimmy easily ripped in half with her one quick motion. She dangled the filmy balloon for him to take, but he couldn't imagine how to grasp it; his hands were swelling into fat mitts. He shook his head. "Help me!" he cried, making her laugh crazily, like she'd accomplished something important. And then she flattened him back into the pillows, wrapped him in protection, and straddled him.

"I'm so gonna make you pay for that last time we were together. Do you remember that, Jackie?" She laughed.

A sliver of Jack's cerebrum perked up, and he half sat. Through the haze he vaguely recalled their last fight. A huge scene at the outdoor produce stand at the Hunt & Gather, over a dark, buxom girl named Vida. Fruit flew, whole watermelons hitting the sidewalk, splitting open, ruby red; the shiny black seeds glittered like sequins in the hot bright sun. At that point he'd run, his thick boots slamming on the pavement, while his shoulder blades pinched together, protecting his spine from whatever fruit bomb might explode there.

Crystal grabbed his chin and shook his whole head. "You want it, Jackie, you gotta pay. You willin' to pay, Jackie? If you take me, I promise to make you pay!"

Vindictive Crystal wasn't someone to make a promise she wouldn't keep. Thinking maybe he'd best get out of there, Jack leaned his weight toward the foot closest to the floor. Taking both of his hands, she fastened them to her breasts and breathed heavily.

"Well? You ready to pay?"

Stoned or sober, it would always be the same answer.

■ ■ ■

Chapter 3

Jack was awakened by his own pulse hammering into the bones of his skull, a full-blown *katzenjammer* pounding him facedown into his mattress. Pressing a hand into the bed, he lifted up his shoulders, but his head stayed a dead weight too heavy to lift. With extraordinary difficulty, he rolled onto his back. The cracks on the ceiling outlining the map of the Old World shattered by hundreds of bolts of lightning were still there. He had absolutely no idea how he'd gotten home, but of course he knew Crystal had stolen everything. The taste in his mouth was bitterroot and the deepest parts of Crystal's body; together it created a terrible, dry musk mouth.

All at once, his stomach punched a warning. Bolting from the bare mattress, he barely got his head outside his window before he vomited so hard he felt his eyeballs pop. Temporarily blinded, but still retching, he dug his thumbnails into the sill, leaning out as far as he could, while his body rocketed out the contents of his stomach. And then when the spasm let him go, he fell exhausted across the sill, his arms hooking his upper body over the ledge. Spent, his lower body went slack, pegging his knees against the wall. Jack passed into some sort of head pounding haze that left him awake, but helpless to save his upper half from the scorching sun. And then the hammering in his head also became hammering on his back, but more pointed, and although he didn't think it possible, angrier.

"Jack! Jack!" his mother screeched. "Wake up! You tramped tumbleweeds into the front room and left the door open! The house is full of lizards! Good grief! Wake up! I don't see the car, and I know how you spent the money. I can smell it coming out of your pores. Don't bother to lie. Wake up! You sorry jackass! Wake up! You're being cooked alive," his mother called loudly and directly into the back of his ear while slamming her fingertips into the soft meat just under his right shoulder blade. Tiny as she was, she somehow wrenched him from the sill. He was too stiff to do anything more than fall onto his back curled just as he'd been over the windowsill, a disfigured human question mark. His mother's softly wrinkled face, framed by the worn paisley scarf, looked madly down at him, the inner tips of her brows plunging to the center of her small nose. After a moment's pause, her eyebrows lurched away from each other, her mouth gaped open. One hand delicately covered her throat.

"What in this world have you done now?" she whispered meekly. Speech had left him, but it wasn't because his tongue would not work. True, it was a bit swollen, but not abnormally so; he was breathing, and as dry mouthed as he was, he could still swallow. The back of his neck and arms were cruelly sunburned from his time out the window; already he could feel the blisters burning into his skin. He told himself if he survived this hangover he would get a steady job; wherever that took him, he would move there, settle down and stop fucking around with wild-ass women.

The face of his mother disappeared in a blur of soft colors, leaving the peeling, yellowed ceiling above. A few regular heartbeats reassured him that he would live. The pain in his head was lessening. He relaxed into it, prepared to endure until it was gone. And then his mother was back.

"Your eyes have turned strange! Jack, what have you done this time?" A mirror flashed close to his face; his mother's bony hand shook as she held the edge of its cheap frame. Jack peered at himself.

"They're not green now. They're both uh—golden. Like a cat's," Mavis whispered.

Jack looked hard into the mirror. Both twinkled back at him like they had a life of their own. With the grunt of an animal, Jack managed to roll to his side, still frozen in his slightly twisted fetal position. He squeezed his eyes shut and plunged into a heavy, painful sleep.

The seeds Jack vomited into the hot desert slipped down easily through the burning sand. They were well coated with the acid of the human's stomach, at last weakening the hard shells that had kept them in hibernation. Ancient seeds. When an allergic animal vomited them, they were properly prepared to germinate by the bile in the stomach. If they passed through the body, they were destroyed. Thanks to Jack's carnal night with Crystal, they were ready to take root.

These seeds had an outside veneer that was harsh and bitter, repulsed insects, attracted most animals. Now that they were fertile and hatching, they repelled all insects, and scared animals off with their frightening, deadly scent.

There were seven seeds in all. Two were genetically impotent, had always been. Two of the remaining seeds did not have the biological oomph needed to realize fruition in this harsh climate. A third remained in that mysterious slumber Mother Nature sometimes provides—a sleeping beauty, as it were. The sixth seed found the old town well, and let itself in through a side chink of the rock lining. It took only a few moments to reach the bottom and settle in. The water was richly sulfuric, which made it full of a type of bacteria that uses the sulfur for energy. Malodorous when it hits the air, it is harmless to the animals and humans that drink it. It would force the vine to produce fruit at a rate much faster than normal, which could both weaken it and spread its influence faster. Once the well was sucked dry, the vine would slowly die too.

The vine that grew from the seventh seed continued to unfurl, seeking clearer, sweeter water as it aggressively snaked beneath the hot dry sand, far below the surface, where life actually thrived. South of its germination point it detected an abundance of water deep beneath, but the layered sheets of volcanic rocks made an impenetrable seal over that source. By changing course, to the opposite, more northerly direction, it quickly found another source. This underground river was feeble, but steadily flowing under the arid desert. This phenomenon of water was created by an ice age, and a drop in the desert floor at the point where a convergence of several veins of deep natural rivers met and rose close to the surface, creating a miracle of life along the surface. To avoid the fence of roots these oasis trees have shot down, the vine went along deeper until it found the very cool, dark chamber that was now an old, abandoned vertical mine shaft; a place where water naturally pooled, trickling in and out of a sustainable source. Once it had sunk deeply into this sweet, silver-laced spring, it dropped its permanent taproot, pumping the life-giving water through its veins before beginning its majestic climb through the earth and toward the sun.

■ ■ ■

Chapter 4

Sam Skookum, an old miner who had lived for years on the highest pinnacle of a tawl right above Foison Surrounded, was a big strong man harshly weathered by the desert climate. He was also a cranky man, and although some thought that he was a man of short intelligence, this was a guise he had carefully constructed. The huge, thickly skulled head was a cache of excellent brain matter, and he knew it. Sometimes he could feel it working—this was always a good feeling, and he'd always been clever with his hands; could fix anything.

"Let stupid people think what they think, and use it against 'em whenever possible," he liked to tell his old dog, Kept, while stroking its bony head with the palm of his hand. At the top of his own head grew a thatch of dull, curly hair that he chopped back with the sharp edge of his own pocketknife, a stalk at a time. His eyebrows grew wildly across his forehead, each pointing toward one large ear. Sam Skookum had killed many living things during his lifetime, both animal and human. Some he liked to think about, some he didn't mind thinking about, while others nearly destroyed him. Smash into a man's gut with a smoothbore musket at close range—well, it wasn't something to dwell on no matter how foul your mood.

When his stomach rumbled, he took a swallow of the bitter black coffee that nearly boiled in the thick mug he held before pulling his binoculars to his eyes. From where he stood, one foot atop a rock, the other a slight vertical slant on the uneven ground, he could see much of the corrugated steel rooftop of Vern's place and most others in the daft town. His eyes were squinted against the brightness, muting all the colors in the deep sunken patch of land below. Above him the sun burned hot and bright against the brilliant blue sky. Great bunches of white clouds slid along, collecting overhead to prepare for their regular deluge. When the gray bottom clouds covered him in a deep shade the colors before him became vivid in their hues. People never realized how much color a desert held, but all his life they was all idiots, so why should it be a surprise to him just now?

Down below he heard a cock's crow. Someone always kept chickens, and *gawd* how he used to love it when he could sneak down there, steal hens, swipe some of their stuff, rile up them paranoids, but good. His was a true vantage point in every sense of the word, he thought, swishing the coffee around his teeth before swallowing it in one great lump of hot liquid. Coffee was something he enjoyed in the mornings, and he had enough green cans of MJB stored to last several years, if he wasn't careless. And if he ran out, there was the dried berries that brewed; he was smart enough to figure a way back down to steal some more. *Ahhhhhhhh*, he sighed; he'd broken harder habits than coffee; tobacco: that was hard to get over. He put the enormous binoculars to his eyes for another look at Foison.

Sam had always thought that the town looked sunk into a crown of thorny rocks. A big crown, a giant's crown, one pulled off its head and tossed away, discarded, useless as it all was. The old highway ran right through it. He remembered how they tore down some rock houses to put it in; modern efficiency, he thought bitterly. Just outside the crown someone once had the idiotically brilliant idea to drag in an old ferryboat to make it some sort of bed and board for the old miners that used to need a place to collapse after spending everything they had to fill their bags with nothin'. Old Sidus took up residence in it; had been living in it now for several decades. The thing was kept shipshape, painted every year that glaring white, anyway. Just southwest of it, and inside the crown, there was the roof made of metal sheets and then covered in broken glass, he knew the house's walls were made of thousands of wine bottles stuck together in stacks by some sort of hard clay they dug out of the ground down there. It looked like a house made up of drunken polka dots, he thought. Some hippie candle maker or some such took it over from the family what moved off. There was now a thick garden of succulents and cactuses stretched out along the back door. Probably kept out intruders too, now that he'd thought about it. There was a tiny church made of bottles too, only the builder had stuck the necks to the outside so it sang and whistled in the wind, like an idiot crying for help after he'd bricked himself in. The moans spooked ordinary people, but he liked the moans. Over 't yonder beyond the polka dot place was Vern's whirligigs—flat-wood cutouts of half-sized humans, engineered to do some mindless task like saw an imaginary tree in half when the propeller turned the crank using the wind—these were always moving like so many idiots working for nothing. His large windmill turned slowly day and night. Skookum did not know its fool purpose.

Skookum slid his point of view over to Silver Sylvia's, as it was his habit to check on the old gal every time he took a look down there. The world had never done that aged beauty right, but she held up to it; knew right from wrong, was stubborn about that. Had those two bad boys what were always after her gold, but she'd die before she let 'em get it. And they'd tried plenty enough. She was tougher than anyone ever guessed. Not even Skookum knew where she'd kept her stash, but that was her prerogative. Things looked all right there, today though—not that he could get down there and raise a rifle to help, like he used to—so he looked on.

The UFO landing pad made him snort with contempt, the only thing that landed on that was bird shit, and when they started in with their fireworks and their hippie-dippie dance jags, he wanted to shoot them down to save them from their embarrassing stupidity. He spent several minutes fuming over this until his attention shifted to the one spot he never wanted to look for—but always did. He steadied the binoculars. When Mavis Stanger came into view, and really from where Sam stood, it was like watching a little bird moving along the ground—he stood stalk-still to focus on her feathery movements. Even with his powerful binoculars he could not see any detail of her, but his mind worked on filling in what it could not see and wasn't freed until she disappeared. Once the spell was broken, he dropped the binoculars so they dangled around his neck, and moved the rim of the cup to his lips to take another hot gulp. It was with enormous satisfaction that he could see everything from up there. The thickly brewed coffee only made it all the better. Yes, he could see absolutely everything he needed to in order to take full advantage and guard his treasure of secrets, his bags of gold.

When the thunder boomed and the lightning crackled, he looked up excitedly; he held out his arms as a lightning rod. He liked the occasional jolt of lightning, it put a new snap in his step and reawakened parts of his brain that he felt were trying to slough off. Lightning crackled overhead, long branches of hot white, so he stood atop a rock, extending his arms over his head, and was rather disappointed when the electrical storm passed over without bothering with him. When the rain began to gently fall, Skookum was still feeling smug as he turned to get his meal. He kicked a cactus with his hard boots; watched the big dog put its nose to the ground to root something out; and surveyed his unreachable, remote land with great satisfaction.

What Sam Skookum couldn't see even with his powerful binoculars was the vine settling into the secret well of sweet, hidden water at the bottom of his tawl. Settling in and sending down its permanent taproot to take full advantage of its own lucky find; settling in to create its special floral ladder, one that would soon connect earth to sky, north to south, Sam Skookum to Foison Surrounded, unconcerned as only a plant is with the vagaries of these dull humans.

■　■　■

Chapter 5

Jack found himself awakening from his stupor on the sofa, in the same position he'd fallen asleep while trying to make his way to the kitchen sometime during the dark of night. Both arms were tingling painfully from sitting upright with them folded across his chest; his knees ached, his feet were still numb. Bright daylight flooded the small room. There were the voices of several women coming from somewhere in the same room where he now sat—some type of gathering that had nothing to do with him, he hoped. Hanging in the air in thick swaths were the smells of dust, patchouli, burnt cinnamon rolls, and the leavings of several cups of strong, black coffee, finished long ago, and so many other indigestible things that his stomach blanched. He gagged a small, dry heave and thought he tasted his intestines, which made him gag a little harder.

This started a caca-racà from the flock of human female *Gallus domesticus* gathered at the window.

"Shhhh! Is he awakening?"

"I'm not sure."

"Well did he stir?"

Cluck, cluck, cluck.

Jack let his head fall back. He opened his mouth and pretended to snore until nothing more was said about him. The last thing he wanted was to be the focus of any conversation held by this flock of hens, especially when he was still feeling this far under the black cloud.

"We had some rain just last night, but those yuccas do look tired, like they can barely keep their arms up," his mother said, each word drawn from her body as if it were stealing real time from her life. Hen tongues clucked, and *teeched-teeched* in chorus.

"It's gonna be a hellacious summer before it's all over."

"Hot, with not much rain at all, I'd bet. Just look at them little cactuses, shrunk dry as an old apple core. Who ever saw such a thing?"

"Something deep down is taking the water." Astrid Lake's voice crackled like it was shot through with static electricity, a common feature in their arid desert.

Jack shifted uncomfortably. He wasn't entirely sure why they were there. It was unusual for his mother to have anyone over, but as his head cleared, he had an idea that he was probably the reason for this gathering. Opening his eyes a crack he could see their purses were set around him, sharing the sofa. The one that was slouched on the back, at his eye level, was littered with a collection of slogan buttons. *GREEN PEACE!* the brightest one admonished. He had no idea what this meant, and yet he wanted to get as far from it as he could. He tipped his head back to peer around under his lashes. The women were a blurry bunch of dull colors standing at the window. As a group they blocked out the wall with their backs to him. As soundlessly as possible he carefully eased his butt to the edge of the sofa, planning on getting to his room in a near crawl if that was what it would take to get away unnoticed.

"Oh! He's awake!" someone said before he even broke contact with the sofa.

"I'll just be getting back to my room," Jack said, starting to stand. "Leave you all to your gathering here."

The women just shook their heads sadly at him, crossed their arms, and together made a fortress of disapproval that he could not get past. All but two of the woman from Foison was there, and their collective scent was syrupy and menacing. He sat back down to see if he could wait them out.

"You're right about his eye color, Mavis." Each shook her head at him, gravely, eyes narrowed, mouths shut, hard lines drawn across disapproving faces. Hens after their bug. His mother was the only one who didn't have her arms crossed. Both her hands were dropped into the depths of her apron pockets, making hard knots at the bottom of each. The scarf on her head was drawn down so tightly he could not see her eyebrows.

"We'll wait for you outside, Mavis." One finally told his mother, breaking rank.

The purses were gathered, the front door opened, the women moved out slowly in one protective clutch, keeping their kind eyes on Mavis, while shaking their heads at Jack.

Mavis leveled her gaze on him and, for the first time in his life, seemed unable to speak. They watched each other for several minutes, but instead of working herself up like she usually did, she seemed to be winding down, all her hinges folded some, even her ankles.

"Are you OK?" he asked.

"You have just finally sucked the life out of me, Jack. It's gone for good, I can tell. I'm only able to take in half breaths. I'm sure the desert air will suffocate me, what with all the blowing sand being kicked up by the air travel these days. Look at…"

"Why do you stay here?"

She looked taken aback—her feathers ruffled—her shoulders pulled toward each other. After a few moments of glaring at him she finally whispered, "All my bits and pieces." She razzled the air with her tiny hand, as if screwing an imaginary light bulb out of its socket before dropping it back into her pocket. "I like to keep track of all my bits and pieces here." And then, she drew herself up, took her hands out of her pockets, turned her back to him, and stooped over. When she stood up again and faced him, both of her hands held the handle of a small suitcase that must have been waiting by the door. Although she still looked small and defenseless, her expression was harder, more resolved than he'd ever seen it. There was no wild-eyed anger with the flaring nostrils that usually preceded one of her full-blown tempests.

"The place needs a new foundation and roof, Jack. There's no food, the barrel garden is all that's left and it needs watering and tending to live, but you'll have to find a way to buy an order of water or switch it over to the well. You do it if it matters to you. I'll be over at Telly's until you fix the problems.

And you're gonna have to fix the problems, Jack. Like a grown-up man. Once and for all. Grow up." At this last part her chin tipped up in defiance, like she'd been rehearsing this over and over in front of a mirror. Just outside the door the women were gathering force. Their applause, he thought, overly dramatized the situation. His mother continued to stand there, awkwardly. It wasn't like he wanted to live there, but whenever he tried to leave she found a way—the threat of cancer, an ailing heart, a foreign blood disease, something life threatening—to pull him back. Until this moment, Jack always imagined that she understood that he was the one taking care of her and that somewhere deep down in that tiny, irregularly beating heart of hers she needed him. The silence slapped at his ears, painfully, lasting until he just couldn't take it anymore. When he looked up he realized his mother had already slipped out. The door was closed. Jack was alone. Dropping back hard into the sofa he let his head fall into his hands and halfheartedly tried to fight back his enormous sense of relief.

An hour or so later, while Jack was considering if he could stand the needling water of a shower, he got an inexplicable sense that he was supposed to be somewhere very specific and very soon. Feeling a sudden, great surge of vigor, he quickly roused himself from the sofa, took a meager shower so the town dogs wouldn't bother him, and left the house, still buttoning his shirt. Odd as it was, when he found everyone in town gathered around the power pole across the highway, he was not in the least bit surprised. Foison was a town of odd people, easily fascinated by ridiculous occurrences. Keeping a low profile, Jack scooted over and stood at the fringes, listening to them voice the obvious.

"There's a green Hawaiian-type vine wrapped itself around the power pole."

"It's alive."

"It ain't from the desert neither."

"It's *not* from the desert *e*ither," someone corrected; it sounded like Old Sylvia, the old bag, know-it-all, Jack thought acidly.

"And you did hear me say *Hawaiian*-type vine, because I certainly know it's not from the desert. Just study the size of them leaves for a minute."

"Look! It has fruit on it," someone said.

"Already."

"Pick it."

"You pick it."

"Wait! It's turning color."

"Is it still growing?"

"No, ripening. No one touch it yet."

No one moved toward the plum-sized fruit that had turned a golden color in the time it took Jack to get his shirt buttons straightened out. Everyone seemed cemented where they stood, their eyes fastened to the plant.

With two exceptions, the people of Foison blended in to their environment as if they were also indigenous plants, sprung from seeds there in the desert sand. They all wore the same washed out blues, grays, and dull beiges of the ubiquitous desert sand; their hair was styled to keep out the sand and the wind. The two exceptions, the tropical flowers among the desert shrubs, were Astrid Lake, and her younger sister, Linda. Astrid, a tall bone-thin woman always dressed in layers of sheer, colorful fabrics was about his age, he guessed. That morning she stood with the crowd, her arm protectively draped over her younger sister's shoulders. Unlike her sister, Linda wore tight, short clothes in bright colors, a bouncing camp leader at a tropical summer camp for enlightened children. She was just entering her twenties, he figured. The sisters were the newest residents of Foison, and like everyone else there, they came with some cloud hanging over them, something no one ever really talked about. He avoided them. Still, on any other day Jack would take his time working his eyes over the hard curves of Linda's plump bottom, but today Jack couldn't get interested. Instead, he slipped away from the gathering, walking steadily toward the easternmost tawls. Although it was hot and his feet burned even through the thick soles of his boots, the traveling made him feel weirdly elated.

After a few minutes Jack found himself studying the sign that directed interested parties to the old Pentecostal Church by a red arrow and the faded words, *150 Steps The Right Way, That Way.* The church was no longer there. Sold at auction, the building had been moved as a landmark edifice to a faraway city. Jack stood in its empty spot and waited to get his sense of direction by pivoting until an impulse started up his feet again.

Once he got past the three-dimensional, fifteen-foot metal coffee cup with the sun-blistered words, *Hot Coffee* stenciled in faded red over the burned-out cream paint, he again stopped to get his bearings. Sweat rained off his forehead. This he swept away with his thumb and tossed it to the ground in one salty sheet of water. From there, he headed due north and kept a steady pace, noting that the wilted cactuses seemed to be like markers pointing the way. Jack noted the devil's slagheap that loomed to his left. Like everyone else in town, Jack cut a wide swath around the gigantic mound of leavings from some past government project. It looked like a gigantic dead animal encased in something solid that was now coated with thick grainy sand.

At the base of the sky-high tawl, which was one of several local monuments to the ancient volcanic spews, the earthquakes, and the grinding force of the last ice age, he took an easterly course, skirting the edge until he spotted what he was after, the thick green rope of vine that grew from the base of the tawl, providing an easy ladder up the heretofore unscalable, wind-blasted walls.

Against his very nature to avoid such things, Jack stuck his foot into the first heavy leaf and began the long climb. Once Jack reached the top he put his left foot out to tap the ground, checking for firmness before he took his weight off the vine and planted it on the dark orange earth. The soil looked hard packed and clay-like, but felt springy, like stepping on a dry sponge. Just like the desert below it was littered with rocks of all shapes, sizes, and colors—oranges, purples, black, browns, beiges, whites—every color of planet earth, it seemed like to him.

"Jeez," he sighed. "Is this it?"

The tawl was somewhat flat with hilly mounds of craggy, but colorful boulders of different sizes. Deep green shrubs clumped and clustered everywhere, but huddled close to the ground, giving him the sense of high winds crushing at this mountaintop, but not even a whisper of air passed by as he stood there. Rain had to fall there regularly; it was too green without it, but the sky was now the same blue sky he saw from down below, and just then, cloudless. Far off on the very distant horizon a bank of clouds rested against more blue sky, but they seemed miles—no worlds—away. He turned his back on them.

All in all, the plateau was just like the smaller ones Jack and his friends used to climb so they could freely guzzle beer until some assclown was willing to parachute off it with an old sheet. Bones were occasionally broken, but no one had ever really suffered a permanent injury. Peering over the edge, Jack decided that this tawl could be safely parachuted off, and although he wasn't an expert, he thought a chute could open twice; it was that high. Since he didn't have a parachute and the distance to the bottom promised a certain death that he would clearly see coming, he took several giant steps away from the edge.

This tawl was much larger than any he'd been on; he could not see any other outer edges from where he stood. There was water somewhere and lots of it; he thought he could actually smell and taste its purity too. But pure water was not a reason he would ever climb that vine. A few drops of rain landed on him. He was surprised to find that there were now clouds far above; he had expected to find them moving in around his feet at this altitude. The rain moved off with the clouds.

He walked a few strides to stand atop a small hill for a better view. Far, far below he could see the scattered buildings that made up Foison—the roofs of every building in town, the ruins of the old rock houses, and the foundations of others that were now long gone. If you considered the old foundations, the town was far more symmetrically laid out than he ever realized, like a giant H but crossed through twice. It was the highway that had skewed it in his mind, and it ran at a diagonal, more like southeast to northwest instead straight arrow east to west, as he'd believed. The people below looked like moving lines, but he swore he could still recognize each one. The sight made him feel nostalgic, vulnerable, and protectively tender for the place that he hadn't felt anything for since he was a boy. It *was* actually a place on earth, he thought, his place, and he wished he were home in bed right now sleeping off his hangover. So why was he here?

Jack turned his whole body in circles several times, but his sense of searching for something became vaguer with each turn. He began walking. Behind one of the larger rocky mounds he found what he thought might be old mining equipment.

"Well, well," he whispered to himself. There was a concrete slab with a date deeply etched into it: 1895—about the time of the futile gold rush around Foison, when that rumor of gold caused a minor stir, the first birthing of the odd town, and all the inspired legends of lost gold. Now he wondered if there wasn't something to it. The signature next to it was a vicious downward scratch and then a deep, back slash, unreadable. On top of the slab there was a rusted wheel with teeth, the remnants of the bolts that had held something heavy to it, scattered rocks that were too big and heavy not to have been deliberately heaved onto the slab by someone or something. Growing out of the cracks were slender tresses of long grass, the color of honey. Jack couldn't decide how the original rig was used, but guessed it must have been some kind of block and tackle bolted to it, a rig that was meant to move a ton of weight.

"Some wizard got all this up here." He whistled low, impressed. There were lots of abandoned mines in the hills and tawls around Foison, some with shafts hundreds of feet deep. It's possible this had one too, somewhere, but how people got up there in the first place was a mystery he might like to solve someday when he had company, say Vern with his big rifle, along.

Without fully standing, he moved around the thicket of low-growing brushes, disturbing them as little as possible. He'd never seen this one particular shrub around his desert, and the scent of it made his gums burn. Of course he was cautious of stinging insects, snakes, and easily angered women. This brought back the memory of Crystal and those seeds—started him thinking about the chain of events a bit. The huge vine had seemed so natural to him; he hadn't once questioned its unusual size or the ease with which he climbed to the top of it. Jack planted his feet, tilted his face to the sky, and drew in a deep nose full of air.

Like all desert rats, he could smell the water over everything else, but there was definitely the odor of an old campfire, the smell of lizards in the greenery, and he thought there was a dog too. He sniffed at the air again. The distinct stench of rotted meat made his insides quiver uncomfortably. Jack stuffed a hand in his pocket and took inventory: a wadded-up twenty-dollar bill, a few coins, a strip of wrapped gum, and a pocketknife. Somehow he felt all these things woefully inadequate in any situation, but might even cause his death in this one. But why?

After another full turn, he smelled a snake and froze. A rattlesnake had once mistaken his big toe for a mouse; the aftermath left him keenly aware of them too. Edging along the brush cautiously, he went until he saw the small snake sunning itself on a flat rock. It wasn't poisonous, but he retreated anyway. Other near-death experiences began to flit around in his mind, but before he could figure out how these loosely tethered thoughts might connect him to his present situation, something else caught his eye. Smaller than a playing card, it lay on the ground just a few feet from his right knee, and winked at him using a bit of sunlight. He stayed low and went to it. It was some sort of women's pin that immediately reminded him of his mother, although he did not know why. Picking up the delicate filigree pin, he turned it over in his hand—the clasp was broken so no wonder it fell, he thought, pocketing it. From somewhere nearby he heard the plaintive wail of a dog, so he'd been right about that. He tensed and waited and wasn't disappointed; saw something flash bright yellow within the green brush, thought: a car-sized, *yellow* dog?

Without warning, the yellow flashed into a gunshot, and then a fierce dog was snapping in his face, its giant paws slamming into his chest, throwing him back. Jack scrambled on one hand and two feet like a crab, but butt down. The dog's teeth snapped; its breath was harsh and powerfully doggy. In some sort of Russian dance escape maneuver, he tried to fend off the dog by kicking at it with his enormous feet, using his hands to scuttle away when suddenly he went from solid ground to falling and then slipping down an earthen shaft. As soon he banged into solid ground, he spun around so he could use the soles of his feet as shields, shocked he had such presence of mind. His heart slammed against his sternum, flattening his lungs. A few more heart slams passed, and it must have been the blood pumping hard into his brain, but his thoughts centered around his bitter disappointment that he would not live to be a very old man, as he'd always believed. And then he thought of how no one would know he was gone except for his mother who would never ask anyone to put themselves out to search for him. Mavis may never think to look for him.

Jack realized he would live only if he got himself out, so he braced against the wall planning to spring hard at his opponent (hopefully flying over it, or diving under it, but not directly into it). Jack tensed and waited. And waited. And waited. Then he realized he could no longer smell the dog, and there were no sounds of snarling or barking or anything. After a time, he shifted his position from the crouched, cramped one to something more comfortable; soon his butt rested fully on the floor. After more time passed quietly, he even stretched out a little. By the time Jack's heart was beating soundlessly again, the ringing in his ears had turned into a soft blur of noise. A few more minutes passed in contemplation, in which he examined the walls—this was obviously a hand-dug shaft—he realized that with the meager sunlight that made its way in. Perhaps because of his newly wrecked eyes, his vision became perfectly adjusted to the darkened cavern.

Jack leaned comfortably against the dirt wall to take a better look around. Obviously someone once used this place regularly. Dug into the walls at regular intervals were stubs of old half-burned candles. Crawling on his hands and knees, he lit these, but the soft amber glow only gave the place an even gloomier look. This was certainly not the place where he wanted his carcass to turn to bones, but of course he couldn't imagine such a place anywhere. There was never a time when Jack wished to die. He took a couple of deep breaths. Someone had fortified this tunnel with the typical sturdy beams found in all the old mine shafts, but it was too small for much more than crawling through, he decided. The smell in there was oddly metallic and dank, and it gave him a terrible thirst for beer—and then, for no particular reason, he had the strong sense that he would get himself out of this. It was within this thought that he caught the first scent of a peculiar, yet delicious odor. Sniffing greatly, he easily discerned a dozen subtle scents from the earth that surrounded him, including his own sweat in damp clothes, but above it all, was an irresistible, mouthwatering tang. Forgetting everything else, he began to move toward it, which was easy just by following the line of old candles. He lit those that would take hold of a flame on the first touch of his lighter. His stomach rumbled, yet it wasn't hunger that he felt; it was more like a horny yearning, but much, much more complicated, higher up in his gut, and deeper. Jack continued crawling with determination, spurred on by this odd lust.

Eventually he found another tunnel to his right, but he didn't know how deep it was, or if it led anywhere, but the delicate, delicious odor seemed to waft from there. The scent grew a bit stronger as he crawled along, and although he did not believe in ghosts, he felt them all around him, but he was no longer afraid. Anyway, nothing could have deterred him; this impulse toward this unknown scent was why he came. When his back cramped from crawling, he simply flipped over to rest, patiently waiting for the pain to ease. Eventually, he came to a place in the tunnel where he was sure the scent emanated from. It was larger there; a small person could stand, but he would have to stay down to keep from hitting his head on the ceiling. Whatever he was searching for was right there, but it was too dark to see where it was coming from. Feeling his way for the scent, his fingertips moved up on the dirt wall until he found an opening. Getting to his knees, he found a deep portal. Inside was a nice supply of fat candles. Once it was illuminated, he was surprised to find it was a miniature shrine. There was what looked like an old ivory hand mirror, a pair of earrings that again brought to him thoughts of his mother, like a strong dank draft—a sensation he didn't enjoy. Jack thought for a minute before taking the filigree pin out of his pocket and setting it next to the earrings. They matched, so he left them together and looked at the rest of the dust-covered junk.

Set inside a small vase was what looked like an intricately carved miniature flute. Scattered around the dirt shelf were a few other small items, among them something flat. Although it was dirty, he knew this was the tantalizing something he was searching for. When he picked it up he was surprised at its heft. Even though it was covered in a thick layer of dust, he could smell the gold—because that was what it was—without holding it to his nose. Taking up the slab, his fingers could not stop rubbing it. Soon he knew it was not only cold and heavy, but intricately carved. Jack wiped and blew the dust off, until he found a gold ingot clearly stamped or maybe formed in a mold with images he guessed had some special meaning to someone, somewhere. Without pondering everything further—he was no poet, he knew he would never unlock these mysteries alone—he dropped the ingot into his front pocket. The weight of it felt just right there, he liked the feel of the golden slab warming his leg. Jack had no guilty conscious about taking it, not a bit. Somehow it felt right that unguarded gold belonged to whoever could swipe it. The original golden rule: finders keepers, he thought gleefully.

Now, he thought, pinching his stubbly chin between his thumb and forefinger, he would just have to get out alive with it. This single ingot, dust covered and long forgotten, was a fluke find taken from a hidden place that someone, long ago, made for personal reasons, like the crap Jack had thrown in the bottom drawer of his dresser since he was a kid. He patted the ingot, and stuffed two candles into his back pocket. "Bird in a hand!" he told the rest of the things on that earthen shelf before he blew out the candles, let his eyes adjust the best they could, and began crawling with the thought that he'd either hit a dead end or an exit.

Using the touch-and-go method of first feeling and then moving gingerly for fear that the floor might fall out from beneath him, or the walls might fold in, he kept moving as long as his hand hit solid ground and empty space in front of him. After what seemed hours he smelled the undeniably pungent scent of bruised creosote leaves and the cool, fresh night air. The exit was only a few feet away, but Jack hesitated. Someone shot at him, so there was at least one person, one weapon, and a big, angry dog. Rubbing his face and hair with dirt he cautiously stuck his head out. The night air was fresh and still, alive with a thousand scents of familiar desert life, but also much more. The ground was wet. A fat, full moon hung overhead, a glowing pale amber ball that seemed close enough for him to sign his name across in large letters: *Jack!*

Somewhere just beyond him, there was a roaring fire burning, he could see the flame curl into the sky before its brilliant edges curled, sparked, and then vanished into smoke. It wasn't a creosote fire; the scent was clean, like it was fueled by something that didn't stink. There was a loud, man-size burp, the clinking of a bottle hitting a rock, but not breaking. A man cried out, sang a piercing, mournful ballad of betrayal, and then went silent mid-verse; all signs of a man drinking heavily and alone, Jack thought. He didn't hear the dog at all. Then the breeze shifted, and the stench of the man cut through the air as cleanly as the point of a sharp knife slicing off his nose. "Awk!" he whined. Tears clouded his vision.

Jack rolled away until he found a patch of clean air. Fingering the flat, soft ingot, he took in a few whiffs of clean air. By the fourth nose full he was certain he could smell more gold, just like he imagined when he was underground, but it smelled much yellower, deeper, raw, and more delicious than what he had in his pocket. Jack thought about that perpetual rumor of gold that people had been talking about for years in Foison Surrounded. The most popular tale was about a small gang of high-grading pirates, thieves who had looted as much as they could out of dozens of mines, before the owners could run them off. This was a common type of theft with gold mines; such stories abounded. Legend had it that an especially successful gang holed up near Foison, but while the gang narrowly escaped, the gold was never found. It was a well-worn story in any territory with gold mines, and Jack never paid any mind to those old tales; to him they were just talk he had to put up with for free beer. But now he was certain this was an old mine or a hideout or both, and all that stolen gold was right there. The only mystery was how they got up and down the tawl, but he hadn't seen it all, so maybe it was no real mystery at all; it was likely there was a hidden passage somewhere.

Only an idiot wouldn't consider trying to locate and steal everything that was there—imagine the life he could live.

There was also no doubt in his mind that somewhere on that tawl there was more gold; he could taste the density of it all now that he had some in his pocket. If there was a fortune in gold, and he was certain there was, it was well guarded by the occupants of this tawl, with their fiercely aggressive, enormous dog and loaded shotgun. And, gold was heavy. Even if he found more, it wasn't like he could sling a bag of it over his shoulder and romp back down that vine with it. To steal it demanded keeping a steady head under pressure and careful planning—two skills he did not possess. What he owned was in his hand and this, he felt certain, he could get away with, so he got on his way.

Because his knees felt bruised, swollen, and rickety, he crawled facedown and straight-legged along the ground until he reached the top of the vine. Standing very slowly, he let his knees settle in and stop quivering. Before taking a step, he shook his leg to be sure the ingot would not drop out. Its weight dragged down the waist of his pants to just under his right hipbone, but everything else stayed in place.

Jack wasted no more time. Wrapping an arm around the thick axis of the vine, he stepped deeply into the leaf axils and tested his weight with a conservative bounce. Once he felt relatively sure he could descend without slipping, he slowly worked his way down several feet before he stopped, clung to the axis and panted heavily. He needed a breather, but more than that he wanted to examine the gold by the cold light of the full moon.

The gold ingot was like nothing he'd ever had in his hand; he turned it over and over. Just the feel of it made him taste gold in his mouth as if he were chewing on it, like a luscious candy bar that softened from his body heat but never dissolved. Patting it again and again, he kept thinking gleefully that he hadn't dreamed this; it was real. Once he felt rested, he dropped it back into his pocket and worked his way down until he hit the sandy part of earth that connected him to his own small corner of the world. He'd never felt such a sense of relief. Starving, filthy, dirty, elated, and somewhat terrified that he would still be caught, Jack slapped the bottom leaf an exuberant high five and began to make his way home. The ingot in his front jeans pocket hugged his body with a closeness he'd never felt to any human.

During his trek back through the dark desert, he pulled bits of stuff—weeds, small stones, and a very fuzzy leaf—from his matted, curly hair with one hand while fingering the ingot in his pocket with the other. The day he'd secretly learned to ride a bicycle was close to the feelings of jubilance and terror that were spiriting him along that night. He had no idea what time it was, but he was thirsty and needed to get home quick. The sand was already quite cool, and he kept a weather eye out for any unusual movements. Flash floods and the random tourist in a quad were a real threat at night. First, he checked the heavens for that telltale bank of ominous clouds with their cracks of thunder while listening for the ripping sound of a two-stroke engine. He moved quickly, occasionally ducking behind a cluster of rocks to catch his breath and take a good look around, trying to decide if he was being paranoid.

Jack thought he'd feel safe as soon as he spotted his own house. But once he saw the familiar outline of his place—the hipped roofline, the rectangular box that sat under it flanked on the one side by the old sagging porch—he hesitated. If someone knew it was him that'd been up there, well, this would be where they'd be waiting. But, who would know? And he wanted to go home. Once he crossed the front porch, he went on in the front door the same way he had all his life, except he didn't turn on the light. Inside the small living room Jack sensed changes, but nothing threatening. Some of his mother's layers were gone, quilts, pillows, the lacey things, and such, which he found a relief, really. It meant she wouldn't be back for a while. His hunger drove him immediately to the kitchen where he located the near-empty jar of peanut butter and two heels of bread by smell alone.

Jack leaned into the cupboard so that the ingot was trapped in his pocket, secured there between his leg and the knob of the drawer. His big hand covered the top of the jar like a mitt. It took one good turn to get it off and flip it into the sink. Using the first bread heel, he scooped out as much as he could get inside the fold without tearing it, and shoved this into his maw, chewed only enough to make room for water. This he drank directly from the tap, twisting his head enough to get it to flow into his mouth without losing anything to the sink. It had that dusty-tin taste, like it'd sat in the pipe all day, but he didn't care. Once that first mouthful was down, he used the second heel to scoop out as much as it could hold before gulping it down. When the last of the bread was eaten he dug the slippery, oily peanut butter out with his bare hands. When there was only a thin film of peanut butter left clinging to the smooth surface of the inside of the jar he scraped it out with his index finger, shoved this into his mouth, sucked it off, and could not stop until the jar was scraped clean as new.

Still starving, but no longer able to stand the smell of himself—and there was no more food, anyway—he staggered into the tiny bathroom and turned on the shower. Holding the ingot, Jack surveyed every surface trying to decide the best place to set it, but after thinking it over several minutes, he just could not bear to set the ingot down so he undressed and showered with his treasure clutched in one hand. This he found surprisingly easy, and if the heat softened it some, it didn't matter to Jack. It was like holding a bar of soap, only not at all slippery; it seemed to stay almost magically in the palm of his hand. For good measure, he rubbed it all over his body and felt rejuvenated by it. Once out and toweled off, also still using only one hand, he again couldn't decide on a suitable hiding place for his own little private gold mine (as he had come to think of it), so he took it to bed with him, tucking it deep into the pit of his arm where it hugged him back. After working his head into the thickest spot of his old, battered pillow, Jack waited to slide easily into sleep, but just as he was drifting off he began to think thoughts that both surprised and disturbed him.

The people of Foison Surrounded, he thought heavily, might be under some kind of attack from that weird vine. These were not people equipped to fight against anything real, he thought dreamily. First thing in the morning he would get up and hack it out. Outside there was the familiar and comforting hoot of an owl; he could hear the bats fluttering after moths. The air stirred, grew colder, heavier. And while his exhausted, aching body felt as flattened to the bed as the old sheet that covered his mattress, his mind began racing. He was certain he could smell that tawl, that rare damp earth, the snapping fire, the tantalizing scent of the dangerous, raw gold hidden there. And then the cool night wind shifted again, carrying in the familiar scents of Foison, all of which settled on top of him like a thick, blanket of hair. "If I ever wanna knock off, I'm gonna have to get up and close that fucking window," he told his ingot. And then he slammed into sleep.

About the time Jack was rolling over in bed for the forty-third time, the new morning rain was spirited enough to rouse Skookum. Wobbling, he dragged himself up off the ground where he'd passed out. Because he made his own booze and the bottles were a pain in the ass—well, impossible to get now, he took a cursory survey of the area to see how many he had broken. Any made him murderous, which he took out on Kept, so fortunately for the dog, they were all whole. On his way back into the shack that kept his bed and whatnots, he kicked the shotgun, sending it spinning, but didn't bother to pick it up. Next, he knocked over something that rattled when it hit the ground. With each step he slammed his hard boots into the ground, sending up dust and crushing everything that fell under his thick soles. The dog lay still, watching him through half-opened eyes. When Skookum passed, it got up and crept after him from a good safe distance behind, watching as always, waiting to react.

The vine was also responding to the new sunrise, taking a stretch. Ancient DNA allowed it to color itself to match the burnt orange, deep reds, browns, and purples of the mountain it now depended on. It kept its leaves close, put more energy toward producing more twining modified stems, and the adhesive pads that kept it firmly attached to its new host were, of course, a priority. It was surprisingly easy for the rare plant to adapt to this desert. The vine took a southerly route; once it found more water on the mountaintop it could eventually weave itself into the tawl and live forever. Soon it would make its rare fruit. This was its purpose: to take in nourishment, sunlight, and air, reproduce, and grow however it must to survive, to create more of itself, as all living things must do. So was the natural order.

■ ■ ■

Chapter 6

The echo of voices bounced through his dreams. When he got one eye half opened he thought it sounded like Vern having a look around the foundation of his house. Jack awoke thinking Mavis had called him over, so he lay still in case Vern could hear him moving around. And then he remembered everything. He noted he was still alive, it was the next morning, his gold was still safe in his armpit. Somewhere in Foison a barbecue was being lighted. The voices were echoing from downtown, and not near his house.

"Vern!" he hollered over and over, even leaning out the window. His voice echoed across the flat plain of the desert, and when no one answered it made him feel sheepish, like he was calling for his mother. After that Jack searched his tiny house to be certain he was alone, before he went in and closed the bedroom door. Satisfied he was alone, he quickly dragged the frayed curtains across the blinding ray of sunlight. Although it broke the one strong stream of light into dozens of small splotches that fell on the floor, and did little to darken the room, it satisfied Jack that he was alone and hidden. With his mother gone, there was nothing stopping him from nailing the old blanket over the window, but he didn't bother. He pulled the gold from the pit of his arm, where it had softened like sweet butter.

The ingot had beautiful, unusual markings molded into its delicate flat surface. He knew it was worth a goodly pile of money, although he had no idea what size pile: the couple-of-thousand size or the few-hundreds size. Either one would suit him. Any amount would be that much more than he had on hand at the moment, and he needed a car if he was going to get a job and out'ta Foison. Jack looked at his hands. They still smelled of peanut butter even after his shower, and his stomach rumbled like crashing freight trains. He turned the ingot over in his hand thinking. Something deep inside still made him yearn to go back to that tawl, but Jack knew he never should. This piece of gold had to be enough. He turned it over in his hand again, thinking.

The ingot was obviously an extraordinary thing to own, especially for someone like him. Anyone would make the natural assumption that he stole it, and although Jack was clear on the finders keepers law, he was confident the good people of Foison held fast to the same rule. The big worry was if anyone got wind that gold was found in Foison Surrounded, that sky-high tawl and every other natural edifice in the vicinity would be leveled quicker than a rickety shack. If there was ever a thing Jack must keep secret, it was this gold and that tawl. Never very good about keeping anything, he was certain that he would. His stomach roared. Even with the window shut, he could smell food. Somehow, Jack had to figure out how to sell the ingot.

After some chin rubbing, Jack sprung off the bed, grabbing his clothes with his one free hand. Buttoning a shirt was too much trouble so he forced his head through the neck opening of the cleanest T-shirt he could find, wrinkling his nose at the sour smell. To try to cover it some, he pulled a shirt over that, leaving it unbuttoned. Once dressed, he ran the fingers of his free hand through his matted hair, dragging out something dry and unpleasant that he flicked to the floor and hurried away from. After catching a glimpse of himself in the mirror he almost decided to go back for a comb, but then he went for the door instead. His clothes were crooked, wrinkled, and he couldn't manage socks—he rarely bothered with them anyway, but he'd never felt better.

Once Jack stepped from the porch into the soft sand he stopped and looked toward the tawl. It could not be seen from his porch, but it was as clear in his mind as if it were right there outside his own door. There was such a strong pull to return that only great self-control and his ferocious hunger kept him from running there. The morning heat covered him like a coat, sweat filled his pours, his muscles burned, his joints squealed when he moved, and still he stretched and yawned with small shocks of ecstasy. Everything seemed brighter, clearer, and even piercing to all of his senses, but most especially to his sense of smell. In one great inhale through his nostrils, the entire town came to him. And surrounding this was the tantalizing aroma of barbeque pork loaded with plenty of honey sauce.

From across the highway it looked like the clutch of townspeople had gathered under a new green shelter they had erected between two of the power poles. It wasn't until he got to the very edge of the highway that Jack realized that the shelter was that weird vine growing up one power pole, across the power lines and then around the next power pole, creating a thick canopy between the two poles. Its growth had been fast and now those globes of brightly colored, shimmering fruit hung at dozens of points across the vine like a giant's Christmas lights strung along with the green leaves. Jack hesitated while his stomach roared.

"Hey there, Jack, come on and join us for some eats!" Vern called, scooping his whole arm through the air. Jack's stomach propelled him forward.

"I'd like that, Vern!" Jack called, hurrying toward the food.

Everyone was laughing and talking under the plant canopy, the battered metal barbeques rested on their wobbly tripods just outside the natural awning. Several people tended the cooking meat, whacking it down with spatulas as the smoke wafted up dark and gray and then at once blended into the rest of the clear air and vanished.

"What is that thing?" Jack asked.

"Nature's best shade it could provide! It's growing! Step inside, Jack, you're in for a real cool surprise."

Although he was never keen on surprises of any sort, and he was certain that just like the past few days, this day would be overloaded with more unpleasant ones, Jack went.

Once he was under the plant canopy, the temperature dropped to a surprisingly tolerable level. There was the usual assortment of odd-sized tables pushed together to make one long stretch that hosted huge bowls full of chips and such, the usual outlay for the town's barbeque. Chairs were everywhere, but no one was sitting in them so neither could he.

"Is it real?" Jack asked, studying it.

"It's real as real! We're celebrating it."

"Well don't mind me!" Jack said, wanting to blend back in.

"Grab a drink, Jack! Relax!" someone called.

There were stacks of drinks that Jack already knew were warm, ice was a precious commodity no one much bothered with. Once outside, anything liquid was warmed to the temperature of tepid bath water within fifteen minutes or less. Everyone was used to drinking warm beer, soda, and water. The only thing amiss was the way they were actually talking to one another. Of course they spoke to one another during gatherings—that was the whole point of a get-together, but in the past those discussions would get very heated—it was like a rule—they all had to disagree on most everything, but today the entire group seemed oddly chummy.

His heart rate sped up, blunting his hunger. Everyone smiled and nodded to Jack like he mattered, causing him to wipe at his chin like he might pull the skin from it. He knew they must all be high, but then he also began to feel mildly paranoid that they were able to detect his gold. It took conscious effort to keep his hand off the ingot. He knew better than to touch it and began chewing at his fingernails just to keep his hands off it. A knife of hunger stabbed at his belly, but his feet were trying to pull him away.

"Don't be shy, Jack. Get some eats!" Mackson, a tall, rectangular-shaped man with a pom-pom of black hair spraying off the top of his head, waved a dripping spatula in the direction of the tables before putting it back over the smoking meat.

The cooked food was being loaded into bowls and onto the table in trays. His stomach roared, but he began to back out from under the canopy.

"Grab a plate!" Mackson said. "We got chips, chicken, hot dogs, beans, the usual surprise casseroles, and now, thanks to the vine, fresh fruit grown right here in Foison! Go on, dig in!"

"Try some of the fruit!" someone else called. "It's fresh from our vine!"

"Great!" Jack cried, but he couldn't move toward any of it.

For this group of desert-hardened, suspicious anchorites who were very, very particular about everything, to be eating the strange fruit seemed more unnatural than the vine itself. He had the uneasy feeling that the monkeys had escaped the zoo.

When, at last, someone put a plate of chicken and tortillas in his hands, he began wolfing it down by holding the plate to his face so he could shovel the food into his maw with a simple plow of the flimsy plastic fork. Once Jack got it in, he chewed hard, slamming his teeth together hungrily, eating the soft meat, bones and all. The grease made it easier to swallow large chunks, he realized, slowing down enough to begin tasting it. The tortillas were fresh and homemade, soft as buttery bread. They went down like strips of floury, nicely charred silk. Jack could not remember ever taking such pleasure in food. Every bite tasted better than the last and each time a mouthful landed in his stomach a feeling of tingling warmth and well-being shot through his entire body. Even the tips of his fingers seemed grateful. Every muscle in his body felt strong and ready to work; his joints were again agile and silent.

"Slow down there, Jackie!" Evonal laughed, taking the empty plate and giving him another. "You're gonna get the hiccups." Evonal was the only one left in Foison close to Jack's age. Like Jack she grew up there, but her parents had been a dead a good long while.

Jack swapped his cleaned plate for the loaded one Evonal was holding out to him. When he dropped his fork, he snatched it off the ground and wiped it off on his pants.

"Here try it with a clean fork," Evonal said, taking the dirty one before he could get it in his mouth. The minute he took it in his hand he tasted the metal: real silver. Jack examined the fork, felt its weight, turned it over to see the hallmark. Yes, silver.

"You got another fork, Evon?" Jack asked.

They'd gone to school together, although he recalled she graduated before him. She wore funny dresses that had pockets sewn all over to carry her troop of miniscule, yappy dogs and other such things that she might need at a moment's notice. Although they were always covered up, he knew her legs to be shapely and muscular like the rest of her body. Otherwise, she was tall and strongly built, with long brown hair, small eyes, but full lips, and exceptionally free spirited those couple of times they'd had a meeting in her bedroom.

"Try this one, Jackie Boy," she said taking another from one of her many pockets and offering it to him.

Jack set the first one on his plate to lick it. Aluminum. He handed it back to her with a grimace. "This one tastes bad, I'd throw it away. Got another?"

She handed him a large fork with three sharp tines, shaped like a pitchfork. He stroked it with his thumb before touching it to his tongue, tasting various other metals that he couldn't name, wishing he'd paid more attention to the periodic table in high school.

"I'll use the first one," Jack told her, taking it back into his hand just to rid his mouth of the astringent taste. He sucked on the dull tines until his appetite returned. He could taste metals now, he thought between bites. Jack wondered if he was getting superpowers. Not so farfetched; he could see perfectly well at night, could smell gold, and now he could also taste metals just by licking them. Taking his chin between his fingers and stroking an imaginary goatee, he thought about how unlikely it would be that he would ever become heroic at anything, even if he could.

"If you don't need anything more, I'm going on now, Jackie. See ya later."

Jack watched her walk away, noting how her dark brown hair hung as far as the bottom of her ass, covered her back like a cape, and it shimmered in the sunlight. The hem of her dress rippled around her strong calves, and he started to wonder if she might be the one to help him. Evonal had a truck. She was weak-minded enough for him to be able to distract her—send her on some frivolous errand so she wouldn't be aware of the transaction at all. Of course she would get ideas, probably want to have sex again. This caused him to pause. Sleeping with her had always been rewarding, but three times might make it really hard to get along in this town if she wanted to nurture plain sex into something more complicated. He looked over the townspeople again. Foison Surrounded seemed to lack people with enough integrity to keep a secret, he thought. His attention wandered back to Evonal who was busy stacking trash into bags, like she was also trying to avoid being drawn into the various conversations. Neighborly, but maybe not a 100 percent willing participant. *Huh*, Jack thought.

Someone came by with a bowl of the fruit and passed it under his nose. The scent made the back of his throat close. "Thank you, no. Not a fruit eater." Jack returned to his own plate, shoveling the food in, feeling as if he could never get full.

"Hey, Jack!" someone else called. "If you won't come talk to us, at least sit down and eat properly!" Jack nodded, but didn't take a chair. Instead, he went out of his way to find a suitable rock where he could study them; low enough to drop out of their line of sight and go unnoticed. It had to be Evonal, he thought. She was probably the only one who would take him anyway. A faint shadow at his feet cast a sense of caution. Jack lifted both feet out of habit, but when he looked down, it was his mother's two tiny black shoes pointing at him.

Jack looked up at her, squinting from the harsh sunlight. She stood with her arms wrapped across her waist as if she were holding her very core together.

"Ma," he said. "I'll make everything right. You can stop worrying. I can promise you—"

She stomped painfully on the arch of his left foot before turning and walking away. Gasping, he'd had to hold tightly to the plate so he wouldn't drop it. Crossing his right foot over the injured foot, Jack dropped his chin to his chest and worked on getting his breaths to come out evenly. A breeze wafted past, carrying a certain scent that made him feel instantly joyful. He thought of the tawl, and he wanted to go right then. From somewhere far off he could hear a rattlesnake shake its warning. Jack stood up, laid the plate on the rock and went to speak with Evonal. The time to get things right couldn't wait any longer. Once that was settled he could do what he wanted with his one, feeble life, finally free of feeling any responsibility to anyone.

Jack found Evonal stacking plates, whistling softly to herself.

"Evon, can I talk to you a minute?" Jack asked. She looked up in half surprise, as if she'd completely forgotten where she was.

"I'm not interrupting your thoughts, am I?" he asked.

"Naw. Thought I'd haul these burnables to the incinerator," she replied, taking up two trash bags. Walking away from the crowd, she beckoned him with a swivel of her flat palm. "Grab a sack," she said quietly. Jack took up two more sacks, wrinkling his nose, and followed her.

"Yes?" he asked when they were at the rusted metal trash box next to the incinerator.

"Didn't you want to speak with me?" Evonal asked, taking the garbage and shoving it into the enormous brick oven with its fifteen-foot chimney.

"Right!" Jack coughed, tugged his chin, and then finally got to the point. "Listen, Evon, I need a lift. It's important, or I wouldn't ask."

"Where to?"

"Can I tell you on the way?"

Evonal let her arms dangle at her sides, before she shrugged. "Ok. Let me get my purse. Can you tell me how long we'll be gone? I have to fix my dogs."

"It's gonna be about six hours. I can reimburse you for the gas on our way back home."

"Aw, it's fine, Jackie. I got nothing to do just now anyway, and I could use a distraction. Just give me a few minutes to get ready."

Twenty minutes later she rumbled up in her battered, but sturdily running truck. To his relief she didn't bring any of her annoying, yapping pooches.

When she'd first asked, "Where to?" as he got into the truck, he'd only said, "Head east." She'd followed that with an "Okeydokey, buckle up," and nothing more. For the first few minutes he sat tensely belted into the truck, but relaxed as soon as he saw how effortlessly she wrestled the large steering wheel to get that obdurate truck around the broken concrete, all the gashes and dips, and the debris that'd blown onto the old highway—while smoothly shifting gears. Once they got to motoring on a more or less straight and free line, Evonal pushed a disk into the player, and settled in.

"Sing to me, Janis Joplin!" she called. After that she didn't press him for conversation, seemed content to sing along with the Janis Joplin, steering him east, as he'd requested. Jack often worked on this truck and was pleased at the smooth machination of its transmission and engine working in sync.

"It's running well," he said over the normal old truck noises.

"Yeah, I had to get a tire changed up yesterday after I got stuck in Chrysopoeia. On the way home it had a couple of hiccups after I bought gas. I thought I'd have you look at it if it kept acting up."

"What were you doing way over there?"

Evonal shrugged, went back to her singing. The world outside rushed past, forcing the heat in through the open windows. For such a blistering hot ride, he felt surprisingly good.

"Where to now?" Evonal asked again when they were almost to the point where the old highway joined the new four-lane. They'd have to either go north or south or back to where they came from.

"Tromvia's," Jack said as matter-of-factly as he could. Then he drew his lips into a tight line, as he crossed his arms over his broad chest. Her eyes rolled comically, as if he was being overly dramatic, but she wheeled them north and said not a single word until they parked near the store. As he was opening the door, she tapped on his shoulder until he turned to look at her.

"Listen, Jackie, whatever it is you got to get rid of, don't tell Trong Tri where you got it. Don't bullshit, don't tell the truth. Just say nothin'. He'll respect that. Got it? Anyway, nice shirt. Let me fix it up some here though. Hold still." Then she quickly buttoned him in, giving his shoulders a quick ironing with her palms before laying on two firm pats to let him know it was all over.

"Quiet's the key word here, Jackie. This remark is going to sting, but it's easy to tell when you're lying," she said quietly.

The remark inflamed him, the tips of his ears smoked, his tongue tasted like burnt toast. He hadn't told her anything, and he hadn't asked her advice and he'd also just spent the last three hours thinking up his whole, detailed, believable story. People always said the more details the story had, the less the lie it seemed. Jack considered himself a polished liar.

"You OK there, Jackie?"

"I think I got it here, Evonal, but thanks." His tone was sarcastic and biting even.

She just blinked back at him, moonfaced and faintly freckled, revealing nothing of her thoughts. When he narrowed his eyes back at her, she gave him a neutral smile—a demure crescent, and simply waited. Jumping out of the truck he slammed the door hard, took three giant steps toward the store before he stopped, turned, and hurried to her window.

"You coming?" he asked, tugging her door open. Her left shoulder lifted as she nodded and then stepped out of the truck, her skirts swirling in the breeze. Evonal didn't bother to lock her truck, or even roll up the window, and she didn't carry a purse. He supposed that since she had a pocket for everything, she didn't really need one. She dropped her keys into the one nearest her hand.

Evonal easily matched his stride, keeping a pleasant but neutral expression, looking around at everything as if they did this kind of thing all the time. In his pocket the ingot seemed to grow hotter. Maybe it was only in his imagination, but it seemed to wrap tightly around the curve of his thigh. When the front of the store came into view, his leg began to burn. Chewing his thumb he reminded himself again and again why he had to sell it.

Evonal squeezed his hand, and said, "Looks like he got a new sign."

Tromvia Vietnamese Grocery and Virtually Everything Else was aptly named. From the outside it appeared to be a modest wood-frame building with a steeply pitched roof, like in the old era of clapboard stores with a deep wood porch and hitching post out front, but once inside it seemed to cover several blocks.

The store was a phenomenon of inventory, and a model of organization. Everything was boxed, stacked, or tucked into clearly labeled pullout drawers. There were freeze-dried bags of whole meals, popular with the diehard hikers who frequented the famous nearby mountain range. The canned food section was a monument to the industry's ingenuity; virtually anything sealed into a can could most likely be found there. The meat counter sold frozen-only cuts from the deep meat lockers behind the counter. Customers chose the cuts from a plastic mat of colorful pictures and got the meat delivered to them in see-through freezer bags. Overhead, birds flew around in the top eaves, carefree. Trong Tri, the owner, was a man known for his hand-carved saddles, homemade cough drops, and discretion.

"Ah, Jack," Trong Tri spoke softly and, in contrast to his drab outward appearance, with an educated, somewhat British accent.

When Jack flashed him the ingot, Trong Tri nodded only a little, but also beckoned him to follow.

Trong Tri's office felt small and close. It wasn't a place where Jack cared to linger. Everything seemed to be some shade of depressing gray, giving an aura that struck him as being rather dusty, though it was immaculate. There was one thick, dark desk with oddly shaped lamps set at each of the outside corners and a computer in the middle. Behind the desk was a bulletproof glass window set inside the thick, strong wall. Jack assumed there was a room-sized safe behind that wall and one impervious to anything but a nuclear bomb. Of course, he could be wrong; he used to spend a lot of time leafing through comic books. Still, there was no doubt that Trong Tri was a smart businessman and would know how to avoid theft, Jack thought, turning his thoughts back to his precious bar of gold. The thought of giving it up now caused him to break out into a cold sweat while his gut wrenched.

Evonal handed Jack a tissue and then positioned herself just out of Trong Tri's line of sight, but where she could look directly into Jack's eyes. He found her presence comforting, but couldn't wait to get away from her either.

The three of them stood in the approximate center of the room expectantly.

"Go ahead and show it to him, Jackie," Evonal eventually said, but there wasn't a trace of expectation or curiosity in her expression.

Jack drew it out of his pocket. Showed it to them both shyly—like he'd just admitted a little too much over beers.

"It's a gold bar," Jack said to cover his embarrassment.

"Hmmmmm, interesting," Trong Tri said, but didn't reach for it.

"Just the one?" Trong Tri asked. Jack shrugged. Nodded.

"What can you give for it?" Evonal asked pleasantly. Jack just gave in, and let her at it. It was probably better anyway. He could trust her better than himself.

"Well, it's a shame it isn't a gold nugget," Trong Tri responded. "They're worth more."

"Why so?" Jack asked, a bit indignant.

"Rare. A one-ounce gold nugget is rarer than a five-carat diamond. Rare and considered a gemstone. Also, tourists love them. They can tell people they found them out in the hills. Of course coins are the most desirable, efficiently minted, a form to be trusted. Easy to collect, display, and legally sell.

Good investment if you believe in gold. But this is a work of art, isn't it? May I hold it, Jack?"

Jack tried not to flinch when Trong Tri put out his hand, but he didn't open his hand either. Trong Tri's eyebrow raised a pointed question. Evonal watched him patiently, as if she was surveying a hatching egg. He was trembling. Every drop of moisture in his mouth vanished, making his tongue so rough it felt like sandpaper scraping the roof of his mouth.

And then he dropped it into Trong's hand. The conversation went on between Evonal and Trong Tri, but it may as well have been in a foreign language, Jack couldn't take his eyes off his beautiful ingot, wondered if he really needed to sell it after all. Hadn't he been poor just fine all these years? Trong Tri and Evonal consulted the computer their heads stuck together at their ears. Jack could not control his trembling.

Trong Tri spoke softly, still reading the computer screen, "You know, Evonal, this ingot has a rare marking. Listed here as from a cache of stolen ingots taken from a Japanese family during the internment camp period of World War II. There's a reward offered too."

"Did you hear that, Jackie Boy? It might get back to its rightful owner. In'nt that just so right?"

Although Evonal tried to include him in the discussion, he could only flag a limp-wristed hand whenever she asked him anything. In the end he watched a stack of cash go to Evonal from behind the darkened window. Evonal counted it twice and this took some time. This was more money than Jack had ever had at once in his lifetime. Which was no consolation whatsoever. Evonal callously put it away in one of her deep pockets, took Jack by the arm, and steered him away. The walk out of the store was a blur, but once they were outside, he wondered if he could go on another step without dropping where he was and sleeping it all off.

"It's so pretty here and smells good too," Evonal remarked happily, waving her hand at the stand of the smooth, green-barked trees that grew behind the store. Jack had no idea how they'd ended up behind the store.

"Come on, Jackie, you can make it," she coaxed.

"I need water," Jack replied weakly.

There was a steep, deep stream that ran through this town, from entrance to exit and beyond, far beyond; it tumbled down rocks and boulders for many miles. Feathery trees grew along the banks of the stream, only the leaves did not droop; they sat upright on the branches, pointing thousands of bright green fingers at the sky.

"I need water!" Jack cried, heading toward the river where he intended to throw himself in and soak it up through his pores too, but Evonal held him back.

"You can't drink from that. It has that cow poop germ in it." Evonal produced a bottle of water from her skirt and twisted the top off. Jack guzzled it down.

"Don't never eat the catfish from that stream neither," Evonal advised seriously. "It'll do things to your mind, I promise you."

Jack guzzled the second bottle of water she handed him, his spirits, at last, reviving.

"What kind of things?" he asked, putting the empty bottle into her hand.

"Probably all the kinds of things you'd just imagined," she responded. "Just don't say you weren't never warned, Jackie Boy. I think you need something to eat. But first, do you want to go to the bank and put some of that away for safekeeping?"

Jack found himself chuckling, giving Evonal the once-over again. Here was a kind, kind woman, he thought. The clothes she wore were downright insulting to the type of person she really was. And she was a great deal smarter than he'd ever credited her for. He followed her.

The Bank of WAQ Mutual was a small, indistinct brick building that shared the same piece of property as the courthouse, police station, and town jail. There was a strip of bright green lawn separating each building and a dry fountain in the center courtyard where nervous pigeons milled like royalty at a public hanging. Evonal took him directly inside, and walking in as if she'd done this a thousand times, she went to the only window, greeted the teller with a polite, "Good day to you," before telling her that Jack was going to open an account, and he'd be needing a debit card. She informed Jack they had a branch in the two nearest towns to Foison. She counted out a thick stack and handed it to Jack, instructing him to put it away in his wallet.

"You'll have to give the teller here your driving license," she instructed him.

Jack felt his back pocket, relieved his thin wallet was there.

Evonal set the stack of cash on the counter, discreetly moving her body to shield it from view. The bank was empty, except for the three of them right there at the window, but Jack was touched by her caution.

"It's a lot of cash," the teller whispered.

Jack's mouth opened, ready to deliver his story. Evonal put an end to that by dabbing her fingertip on her upper lip like she was wiping something off it. And then she took her finger away just as fast as she'd brought it out.

"I'll just sit over there and wait," she told him.

After he signed everything and watched the clerk count out the cash, and then disappear with it, he was left alone at the window with a clipboard, a form, and a pen.

Jack went to the sofa and dropped into it next to Evonal. The two of them made the sofa creak. Evonal seemed comfortable with both feet settled politely on the floor, side by side. His own knees came up to his chin.

"Why all the signals for me to keep my mouth shut?" he whispered to her, holding the clipboard up to hide that they were talking, even though they were still alone in the bank.

"Never say no more than you need to," she whispered back to him. "To anyone, for any reason, especially when it concerns money. You've got my arm trapped." They each made adjustments until Evonal was able to drag her arm out from between them. She dangled it as if to inspect it for damage before letting it drop onto her knee. Every one of her fingers and both her thumbs had a lumpy, turquoise ring shoved past each knuckle. This bothered him; he thought it made her look indecisive when clearly she wasn't.

As Jack labored to fill out the form, Evonal patiently laced her studded fingers together and covered a knee with them. There was mildly obnoxious music playing quietly from somewhere overhead. The more he scribbled his business over the form, the more he thought how that pile of money seemed to shrink smaller and smaller. The first thing he'd have to do was give his mother a goodly chunk of it, something he wanted to do, but he knew it wasn't enough to sustain either of them for long. This thought put in his mind the whole place up there, at least the little bit of it that he'd seen. Evonal yawned, turning her face to her shoulder to hide it.

"Evon, exactly when was the World War Two that Trong Tri was talking about?"

"Aw, that German Hitler started it in Europe in the 1930s. We joined in 1941, after the Japanese bombed us in Hawaii. The two wars got merged. It all ended in 1945 with two big bangs. All of it gruesome."

He reappraised her.

"Trong Tri said it was stolen from some Japanese family. I don't get it." Jack didn't mind appearing stupid, because that was pretty common knowledge.

"Our government just shamefully rounded up all of the Japanese citizens and put them in camps starting in 1942. One of those camps is pretty near Foison, within driving distance anyway."

"Aren't you in the least bit curious where I got it?" he asked her.

"Nope."

"It's a pretty cool story," he wheedled.

"Tell it to yourself, Jackie. It's probably something I never want to be asked about, in't it?"

"Yeah," he replied, and sulking, he signed his name and let the pen drop.

"Gawd, I'm really starving now the excitement has worn off."

"Evon, how long do you think this kind of money can last?"

"How fast do you plan to spend it? Just count up how much each and every day you usually spend and then divide," she replied seriously.

A familiar gloom began to drape itself around Jack. Even with money in his pocket his constant poverty was like an undersized, heavy coat he could never remove for long. With what he had in the bank he could easily get a good reliable truck, take that full-time mechanic's job, and settle down to the life he'd always believed he really wanted. Fixing engines was something he liked. Independent of his regular thinking brain, his mind began examining the future. Eventually Jack had to admit to himself that he would never settle for that now. There had been talk enough of the disease he'd caught up there on that tawl. He had gold fever and there was no cure for it but more gold—or death. And oddly enough, this seemed to be the one way he wasn't afraid to die.

It was deep evening when they put wheels inside the boundaries of Foison, but it still was like dusty daylight to Jack. When they came to Framers Juncture, a narrow dirt road that intersected and crossed the highway, Evonal braked to a stop and flicked up her high beams. Craning over the steering wheel so far her butt came out of the seat, she looked right and left and then right and left again. A dangerous spot, this one, where tourists would come firing out as if everyone driving crosswise should be expecting them.

"No one's coming, Evon. I'd of heard 'em by now."

"I'd hate to hit a jackrabbit, Jack. You know how they're drawn by the headlights. They make such a terrible pop when they're flattened by the truck wheels."

Jack always considered them suicidal. It was like they waited until you got there and then ran under the tires deliberately. When he said this out loud, Evonal said, "They're just dumb bunnies, Jackie, just brainless little creatures. I'd like to just give 'em a minute to get on their way without getting squashed, because I can."

Nodding, Jack settled back and waited, taking a good look around. The thick, acrid tang of cold barbecue soot hung in the clear night air so strongly though, the townspeople must have concluded the eating fest within the past hour, but he didn't hear anyone. The thousands of stars now appeared to Jack as twinkling, crystal ambers. He watched one slip through the sky and vanish. Evonal stepped on the gas, and they lurched along until the old truck picked up enough speed to smooth out. The closer they got to the center of town the more anxious he was beginning to feel. Jack tried to keep his head from turning toward the tawl. Evonal, it had become apparent, was intuitive and perceptive, and worse, she seemed to know quite a bit about his natural inclinations. She would know he was up to something, and even though he was certain now that she would never mention it to anyone, she would still know.

"Almost home." Evonal sighed, but he couldn't tell if it was from relief, or regret. He understood completely.

The day with Evonal was winding down and he found himself regretting that, but now that he was back in Foison Surrounded, the longing to break free and return to the tawl became so intense he thought he went blind. When Jack could see again, Evonal had maneuvered the truck into her spot under the newly built wooden carport, and turned off the key.

"You comin' in, Jackie?"

"Are you gonna want sex, Evon?" he asked bluntly.

"I wouldn't kick you out of bed."

He pulled the handle and shoved the door open with his body weight. "Let's get to it then, sweetness," he said cheerfully. Before they even got to the porch he could hear her little yapping mutts whining and barking. He followed her into the house anyway.

"Make yourself comfy, so I can see to the dogs. Want some coffee?"

"Yep."

Inside her small house, she stopped him in the middle of the front room and pointed a finger.

He went and stretched out on her bed, listening to the sound of those miniature Chihuahuas going wild in the room next door. She made clicking noises, cooed, and sang to them, but this did not seem to calm them in the least.

"You're not going to let them out, are you?" Jack called to her.

"Naw, Jackie, they'd just bother us. You're not laying on my clean bed with those dirty boots on, are you?"

"Off," he told his boots before he sat up and kicked them off. One after the other they hit the floor with a thud, bringing a reinvigorated racket from the mutts in the next room.

Jack wondered if she was letting them lick her face and resolved to talk to her about it before any kissing started. There were other sounds, ones he couldn't identify, and then the door opened and closed. Her footsteps were small and light, but discernible all the way to the kitchen. The rich aroma of coffee floated to him as soon as she opened the can, a scent that just then seemed almost sacred. He hoped she had lots of sugar. On a small table near her bed was a row of wooden drawer knobs surrounded by her paints and slender brushes with just a hair or two in each tip. Jack recognized two of the miniature portraits she had completed on two of the knobs. One was Juanita, the other Vern, but there was a series of knobs painted of the same man, just at different angles of his face. A stranger to him, but someone she must have known well, because every angle caught him like a photograph. In fact, when Jack took his eyes to the beginning of the row and rolled them down each portrait, it was like a moving show. It looked as if the man was turning his head to look over to him. The last one, the face that should have revealed the most emotion—because they all seemed to be leading up to that moment when one loved one turns to greet another—was startling in its rawness. Smiling lips, sure, but sharklike, measuring eyes. No love there.

When she entered the room, their eyes met. He wanted to tell her that her talent astonished him, but he didn't know how.

"I'm gonna take a shower, Jackie. I use the stinky well water for showers and washing, but the coffee is bottled," she said, moving to the table and laying a clean rag over the small works of art. "You want in?"

Before he answered, Evonal began taking her clothes off, inspecting each piece methodically. Some pieces she folded carefully and placed over the back of a chair; others she tossed into the clothes hamper. He liked the way each part of her body was slowly revealed to him, and she undressed as if there was no one else in the room. Evonal was a big-boned girl, with nice tits that were slinging down some. Her belly button was a deep oval, and sexy; her shape was solid, curvy, and fine with him.

Jack found that he wanted to shower with her, wanted to let her wash him. He felt like being babied by her; his burning muscles could use a massage. He undressed quickly, following her into the bathroom. Inside the shower though, she was all business—washed herself with a bar of soap and limp washcloth, as if he wasn't there at all. While this was a terrible disappointment to Jack, he consoled himself by watching how when she dipped her head back under the shower spray, her hair became a dark, dense curtain with droplets forming along and then falling away from the very edge. And then he said: "*Like Rain it sounded till it curved, and then I knew 'twas Wind.*"

"Emily Dickinson," Evonal said, pouring shampoo straight from the bottle onto the part in her hair.

"How the hell would I ever know that?" he asked her, a bit shaken.

"Ninth-grade English. Mrs. De Zeet. See? Some things stuck in there, Jackie."

"Let me wash that for you," he said. He helped her shampoo the mass of hair, but Evonal seemed to be alone in there. Once dried off and back on the bed, she didn't seem all that interested in him there either, not the way he expected. The last time she leaped on him like a hungry tiger and they wrestled for the top. Jack reached for her and she let him feel her up, but her face was all hard lines of concentration, like this was going to take some effort on her part.

After a couple of minutes she flipped him onto his back, climbed on top of him, grabbed both his wrists and pressed them over his head.

"I heard you liked being handcuffed," she said, but it was rather halfhearted, he thought, and she let him pull his hands free without so much as a playful tussle. Her own dropped limply to her sides and hung there.

Jack rolled her off him took up a bundle of her hair and pretended to paint her face with it. "You were great today, Evon. You surprised me, and I can tell you honestly that I don't think I would have done so good without you. It was a great fuckin' day, thanks to you."

Evonal laughed dryly. "Put the cap on, and just give it to me, Jackie."

"You don't seem all that interested, Evon," Jack said.

She waved her hand over his lower bits before dropping it to his belly without touching the obvious.

"Is it your age thing?" he whispered.

"What age thing?" she asked quietly, but her eyes narrowed in that way a man never likes to see a woman do, like she was getting ready to spring a trap he should've easily avoided if he'd a just remembered to never ever speak during sex.

"I just heard that when women reach a certain age…"

"We're the same age, Jack. And you're hard as ever. What makes you think I'm any different?"

"You're older," Jack insisted, crossing his legs at his ankles.

Evonal laughed out loud. "We're about two months apart and you're older. You're July and I'm October. The thing is, Jackie, you think everyone is older than you because you haven't realized that you've been aging. I can't even say growing up because you haven't grown up. You're like a giant two-year-old for Christ's sakes." Evonal's fingers went to his hair, yanked hard on it.

"Ouch!" he protested.

"Look at the gray," she said, dangling the hairs in front of him, and then, "Gray hair from your head, Jackie Boy. And you know the other thing. You think it's easier to pretend to love than to really feel it, but it's not." Her eyes, usually passive and warm, were hard as nutshells as she narrowed them at him.

"Are you mad at me?"

A long moment passed in which she just stared at him.

"Naw," she said finally, falling back into the pillows. "Naw, it's not you. I got my heart broke recently and just now, trying to pretend to love you, just about broke my spirit too."

Jack was shocked, jealous even, and then he felt he had something to overcome here. Evonal was supposed to be in love with him. He pulled her very near him so her hipbone nestled inside his.

"I'm gonna make you scream my name twice," he whispered hotly into her ear.

"Stop spitting in my ear!" She laughed, and rolled toward him.

"Tell me just one thing you want me to do to you," Jack whispered. The way he felt, he could be up all night giving it to Evonal, then climb to the top of that mountain, and come back and do it all over again.

Evonal took his hand and said, "Take that enormous thumb of yours, put it right here and rub it around in slow circles."

Their breathing intensified after only a couple of laps.

"Now you tell me something you want," she said.

"Put the cap on for me and then put your arms over your head, so I can get to your tits," he whispered, as she breathed deeply. Her eyes were rounder now and raisin brown, she always blinked very slowly. There was the smell of that tawl top in the ropes of her wet hair that energized him.

"It's good now, Jackie Boy, I'm ready." She sighed. And Jack drew into his nostrils the deep, rich scent of gold.

When it was over, they were both breathing hard and laughing a little. She didn't scream his name, though, until they'd separated. And then she yelled, "JACK! JACK!" just to make him laugh. It set the dogs off.

"Ignore them," she said, still laughing, but tussling his hair in a way he always liked women to do. When the dog yapping rose to a snarling, whining, scratching, yelping, cacophonous pitch, she covered her ears with a pillow bent over the top of her head and closed her eyes.

"Why do you have them?" Jack asked, once he'd pried up an edge of the pillow.

"My dogs?" Evonal sat up, tossing the pillow in his lap. "They need me. I got three left now. And I only got that third one because some asshole mailed it to me in a box. Just put the little guy in a box with stamps on the outside and mailed it to my doorstep with this crazy note that said he'd remembered me from stopping by here for gas and took down my address with a mind to mailing me that little dog when he got home. The note said the dog wouldn't be housebroke; it was too mentally ill. That man was too mentally ill to have a dog. What an asshole."

"Dog must've been hungry."

"Dog needed a bath too, but he's made it. Gonna outlive the others. He's just a little guy, you know." Her sigh belied her enthusiasm and for a moment Jack felt the weight of being so depended on. And then he could picture how she looked opening that box to find that miniscule, shit-upon, starving pup, pawing the box, all ashiver, its nervous eyes searching her for mercy.

"How 'bout that cup of coffee?"

"You hungry, Evon?" he asked. "I'm starving."

This set Evonal off into a burst of laughter. And then she rolled over so her back was to him. "Oh, Jackie. I've let you drag me into it full on, haven't I?"

"I don't understand."

"Listen, Jackie, you know how everyone in this whole town thinks there's somehow some kind of a conspiracy of all the others against them?"

Jack nodded uneasily. He could sense something he knew, but didn't want to hear, was about to be spoken out loud.

"Well, this time it's real and you're IT. Everyone promised your mom not to help you no more than what it took to keep you alive."

"Why'd they feed me at the barbeque, then?" he asked, offended, although he knew it all along. Still.

"They probably couldn't go through with it just then. You know them soft hearts. And that would've been downright rude to leave you out. Or maybe that weird fruit has them addled. Aw, but anyway, everybody likes you. They know what they know about—your mom. Her stuff. I mean no offense, but we all know she's a hard woman of, well, several minds all at once. And there were your illnesses when you were a little boy. It's why you get away with so much crap. 'Nin't it?"

His brows tweaked.

"Actually, it'd be my pleasure to make you a stack of grilled cheese sandwiches."

He pulled her close, two spoons resting together. They breathed together. And when she reached behind her back and ran her fingertips across his forearm, it came to him why people married.

"How come you never got married, Evonal?"

"Naw, Jackie. I guess I never thought I could hold up my end. You know?"

"Yep. Yow—married!" he declared, but now he wasn't so sure. Before he could put down his two more cents she'd already gone, stark naked, into the kitchen to cook his sandwiches. The long damp hair brushing the top of the two round cheeks of her bottom lingered in his mind for several minutes. He could hear her moving around in the kitchen, a place that seemed unrelated to this part of the house, it sounded so distant. Soon the smell of sizzling butter melting in an ironstone pan wafted into the quiet bedroom. The scent of sautéing onions made his stomach growl and he rolled over, thinking over what Evonal said. It was nice to be thought of, but he didn't want the good people of Foison keeping an eye on him, especially now. And before anything could come of it, he probably should work out what to do about it. Luckily for him these people were easily distracted by their own idiosyncrasies, so their attention could probably be easily misdirected too, should it come to that. If that weird vine didn't keep them occupied, then he was confident he could come up with something else. He mulled this over. There was an incident with a missing eggbeater from the now defunct Foison Surrounded Oddities Museum that caused an ever-erupting ruckus for six months before the next big brouhaha—over the county auction and removal of the little board and batten church—simmered it down with only the occasional boilover.

"What'll you have to drink, Jackie?" Evonal called from the other room, another world away. It felt good to be anchored right there by her voice. He sighed from contentment.

"Coffee!" he called back. If the good people of Foison were intent on watching over him, he would certainly find something to get their attention focused on besides him.

He stretched like a starfish into all four corners of her bed. Everything in her bedroom was pale blue, colorless glass, or white. He began to wonder why this color made everything so peaceful. Candlelight. Jack slapped his own face, sat up. He turned his mind toward his next climb to the top of the tawl. He would take a flashlight, just in case he needed to see, and then he remembered he didn't have a problem seeing at night anymore, so no need for a flashlight. Matches. He supposed a pack might be useful if he needed to start a fire. Jack dismissed the idea of matches; he wouldn't need to start a fire, and either way, he'd bring a lighter. Just then fire seemed dangerous, especially if stored in his pocket. Now that he thought of it, a lighter had usually ignited a string of events that went from fun to broken things and ended with a terrible hangover.

What he really needed were things that were going to help him move the lovely, but heavy, gold down that vine without dropping it or getting shot, or eaten alive by a rabid dog. He had no doubt he'd find the gold. Anything he brought would have to be small enough to fit in his pockets, or tied to his body; climbing that vine took both hands. Getting himself hung by a pair of binoculars wasn't in his plans. The gold was worth the risk although he wasn't certain why. He wasn't really thinking about what he'd buy with it, not once had Jack envisioned what he would do with the newly found riches. He just watched to get it into his hands, take a bite, and chew slowly.

■ ■ ■

Chapter 7

As Jack ascended the vine, he didn't pause once to catch his breath or to think through what he was going to do once he got up there. The moonlit night was his best cover. He wore black jeans with a black, long-sleeved shirt. It was hot, but so was everything, and the shirt soaked up the sweat. Oddly he needed the pale sunglasses to rest his eyes since they no longer got enough relief from the darkness at night. Binoculars were nowhere to be found in his house, Mavis must have taken hers, which wasn't surprising. The people of Foison were fond of their binoculars. Even though Evonal looked at him like some kind of asshat when he asked her if she had any she dug out half a dozen pair for him to pick from. The smallest pair was on a lanyard around his neck and stuffed under his shirt so they wouldn't bang around as he moved. They stuck to his sweaty chest on the way up, but he didn't mind.

Jack stepped onto the top of the tawl with an unusual lack of trepidation. All the way up, Jack had convinced himself there was only one old guy up there, and he could take him—though he'd never been in a real fight in his life. Surely he would have heard others. If there were more, they would have chased him down that shaft and killed him or thrown him over the side. The panic came on hard. The muscles in his back seized. He had to grab his knees, get a hold of his thoughts. Take a calm look around.

Everything around him smelled delicious, clean and fresh without the usual desert sand. The plants were almost lush, though of the desert variety: hardy, with hidden secrets no doubt. He counseled himself to stick with what he knew: the one old goat, giant as he was, didn't worry Jack. The guy seemed very much on the flimsy side, and a drunk. The first visit was easy enough; it turned out well. Look what he got! Jack could put up with a few bruises and scrapes—he'd get them anyway just making courtesy engine repairs around Foison.

The dog, however—he could still feel the slam of its forepaws against his chest and that whole tumble into that cave—Jack paused, said to himself: up the vine, grab some gold, down the vine.

Something moved in the brush, another thing skittered across the tips of the toes of his boots; his heart spazzed, buckling his knees. The brush rustled again. There was the flash of yellow flitting through the greenery. It was that dog, low on its haunches—watching him intently. He dropped onto his hands and knees, like a dog himself now, but with no tail to tuck in surrender. The dog seemed to make some sort of decision and trotted to Jack's side, slamming up against him, but not enough to knock him over when it certainly could've.

"Good doggy!" Jack's voice honked. He stood and began to make a careful getaway, but the dog followed, wagging its long feathery tail. They walked along side by side, almost companionably, with the dog occasionally rubbing itself against Jack's thigh. After only a few yards of scouting the place, he found he appreciated the company. The dog, at least, knew its way around.

The tawl was like the green, almost forested parts of the canyons in the desert mountain ranges where there was plenty of water. He thought he recognized most of the shrubs and what he could now see were dwarf trees, not bushes. Something caused fires in some of the clumps, they were blackened, maybe singed by lightning, or who knew what. There wasn't much sand, or it was hard-packed soil, and like Foison, littered with the colorful volcanic rocks of all shapes and sizes. There were boulders too, rocks more gigantic than he had ever seen down below, and many of these were cleaved in two as if a giant ax had split and left them. Plants grew thickly in there, but a man his size could easily hide there too, he noted.

When Jack started on a new path swerving left, the dog growled low and menacing. The dog turned, and Jack followed. Together they made their way down a sketchy, dusty, narrow path toward the acrid scent of an old campfire. Overhead the night sky twinkled with amber stars, and Jack realized that with his new eyes he could easily discern satellite from star, star from distant planet. If he'd paid attention in astronomy class he could be certain it was Venus he now stared at. He studied his own large hands surprised at the way they looked, almost capable.

And then without warning a stench of body odor punched him in the nose. The big, yellow dog nipped at his heels until Jack leaped sideways into the gap between a huddle of boulders. Jack flattened his cheek against the boulder, felt the rough grain sand away his skin even without moving against it, tried not to breathe through his nose, and waited to get caught. The dog froze.

"I know you're here!" the man bellowed. "I can smell ya', you filthy beast. Get out here and face me, you coward!" A large, grizzled hand gripped the rock while the stinky old goat wheezed. Everything inside Jack shrank toward the safety of his middle. The dog suddenly leaped to the top of the boulder where she stuck her snout into the sky and howled like a wolf.

"Get down off there, you stupid mutt, 'bout to give me a heart attack!" the man growled, but the dog wagged her tail and whimpered first, and then fell back on her haunches, pawing the air a few times before scrambling down. Jack heard them amble away, the gruff voice of the man swearing at the dog with a tone that spoke of begrudging affection. Wedged inside the boulders he waited some more until he became so thirsty he decided to risk leaving, squeezing out the opposite side.

And this was where he found the wonderland of water. The rain was already falling hard into the small lake. Lightning crackled above. The surface water shimmered with each of the drops. And then the rainstorm stopped as suddenly as it started, and the lake surface became smooth as a tray of gelatin. "Water!" Jack cried. He almost ran to the shore, but in his hurry to get to the edge his hand sliced against something that caused immediate and immense pain. "Please be cold," he begged the water. The minute he thrust his hand in, the water around his hand turned a ruby color, and sparkled and gleamed, making him as thirsty as he'd ever been in his life. He dipped in his good hand again and again to drink and drink while he kept his wounded hand deep inside the ice-cold water. Once his thirst was sated, and this took several more deep hard gulps, he gently eased his wounded hand out of the water, delighted that the pain did not reignite. There was a thin, pinkish line where the plant had sliced into him, but scars did not matter to him. He always thought they made him look like he'd been places, doing things that shook things up a bit, a good lie unspoken too.

The big yellow dog yelped, surprising Jack. This time the dog walked boldly to him, first wiping her nose into the palm of his injured hand before giving him a thorough going over, both back and front. Jack stood for it, but when the dog seemed satisfied with his scent and turned to offer its rear end to him, he shook his head.

"Naw. Thanks. I see you're a girl though so thanks for the information. Gotta get a good look around. Gotta get to high ground, Little Maid," he whispered to the dog as he tentatively swiped his palm across her forehead.

Jack stood uncertainly, looking around. He'd lost his bearings completely since finding the lake. Seeing everything in the amber tones during the dark of night was also confusing. The taste of gold remained in his mouth though; it was here, and he was going to get it. And then for the first time, the flicker of a thought about what it would mean to be a rich man made him smile. No, it made him horny, no impatient, no optimistic. He tugged at his chin. Would he ever know what was what?

"Which way is the gold?" he asked the dog.

The big, yellow dog responded to this question by nudging him forward using her nose, and when he paused, uncertain, she used her full body and soft growls, whatever it took to keep him moving in the direction she wanted him to go in. Since she seemed so certain, and he had no better instinct, he went along readily, but careful not to let his bare skin touch anything even though his hand seemed to be completely healed, the thought of that pain made his insides quiver.

Each step caused an uproar of lizards to scurry out and scatter in all directions. "There sure are a lot of you little guys," he told them, counting at least ten different types, which meant there should be a lot of bugs, but he hadn't noticed any. "Strange and mysterious place, please don't kill me," he whispered. "I mean you no harm. I just want another small pocketful of gold, and I'll be gone."

With the gentle guidance of the dog, he quickly got a better sense of the place. If there were anything more dangerous than the man and the shotgun, he had not seen these either, but he was certain there must be more dangers, both hidden and meaningful, because of the way his skin tightened over his bones. The dog traveled with her nose constantly snuffling along the earth, often shying away from certain spots, but he could not discern why. She ignored the lizards, but lapped up some insects. Jack saw no snakes anywhere, but he had rarely seen them in his own desert, he reminded himself, yet he knew they were there. And night was no longer night to him, not in the way he understood it, he also thought regretfully, so who knew what all this newly wrecked vision camouflaged. Jack reached a spot where he could see the lights of Foison Surrounded far below. It seemed so innocent, so still. A chill shivered up his spine and then all over. He realized he was going to have to take a piss.

As soon as night became black enough, Sam Skookum emerged from one of the roughhewn cabins some forgotten and now long-dead miners had built ages ago. His huge head pounded from the usual hangover, and he didn't see much more than ghostly shadows at night anymore so he felt around to his left until he took hold of the old weed, snapped off a branch and began chewing. It cured his headache almost instantly. Although he longed to go down to Foison and scare the bejesus out of those dolts, he really never had to leave the place; it provided everything he needed and he had his cache of thieved gold to console him. *Goldie, goldie, goldie, gold,* he crowed to the sky. *Every Jack wants ya, but none can have ya, only me.* Skookum felt like a dance, but instead he took a few shaky steps, feeling his hip ratchet painfully. Well, he was ancient by human standards so his body was bound to begin protesting at some point. Wading in the lake would help mitigate these troubles and he'd get to that shortly. Inhaling deeply he took in the minglement of odors expecting the usual, comforting mix, but what he took in made him stand stock still and sniff some more. "What the hell is that?" he wheezed, because if he didn't know better he again thought maybe another human had been about. He'd be certain someone was up there if he hadn't blown up the only way in and out in a drunken rage when he'd been so harshly rejected by that hard-crusted, stubborn woman,

Mavis. Skookum angrily kicked a rock hard enough to send it flying high into the sky. Screw any woman who preferred to live on ground with his son rather than in the clouds, with him, he thought. They could've been a happy family up there, slipping down to Foison to get whatever they lacked; rattle some nerves, get back. Well now she was trapped down there and he was trapped up here, happy as happy without her. It was his final bitter thought about Mavis for this hour. Now he needed to tend to his food and his drink, his aching hips.

The big yellow dog cajoled Jack along until they came to another mound of boulders and earth. This pile looked man-made; something like a slag pile made from the excess of any unwanted material created from the process of mining anything from anywhere. A hole can't be dug without leaving both a hole and a pile of unwanted earth. When you crack rock to get ore, the rock is left, also unwanted, and depending on the method used—also mixed in with the chemicals of that process, leaving something permanently scary. "You just stay right there," he told the pile. "And I'll make my way around you, thank you very much."

But the big, yellow dog seemed to want Jack to climb on top of the heap. "No girl, no way. This isn't a good idea."

But with the dog's persistent nudging, and a pretty convincing nip at his calf, he climbed up to take a good look around. This place was nothing like anything he'd ever seen. His eyes watered, and he wiped at them, embarrassed. The dog whined, then spun around as if chasing its own tail.

Taking a half turn, Jack realized he could clearly see several small shacks, and the miner's outdoor kitchen from where he stood. It was many feet below him and looked like a primitive campsite with a tall, square, very oversized table.

There was an enormous wood chair, and a couple of large flat rocks stacked neatly next to the table. Otherwise, the old giant was a slob. Both broken and unbroken bowls, plates and cutlery were strewn about. There was trash scattered everywhere. It smelled like the Ridgemont town dump, only worse; it smelled like the old giant guy, and he realized this was what made his eyes water. Off the center was a pit filled with a huge crackling fire that didn't seem to die down at all. He could not see any fuel burning within the flames, and nothing was being added. There was no charcoal odor. Whenever the wind picked up, it blew sparks and blossomed into an enormous, exploding poinsettia of flames.

The giant man—he had to be close to seven feet tall, maybe over—staggered into view. He was swigging so deeply from a large bottle that his head rested on the back of his neck. He straightened, and then wiped his mouth with the back of his hand before again placing the bottle to his lips, bending backward, easy as a young reed; it was the longest pull on a bottle Jack had ever seen. And then the man straightened and dropped the bottle, leaned back and clutched his stomach before vomiting it back out with such a force, he not only staggered backward and fell on his ass, but an entire bush was coated with the contents of his stomach, decorating it like some god-awful Christmas tree. Flinching—naturally, no one could witness that disgorgement without backing up some no matter how far away he stood—Jack knelt down, pretending to be part of the natural setting, taking his cue from the lizard that also sat motionless next to him.

Eventually Jack's back began to burn, and his feet went numb from being in the crouched position, so he lay on his stomach, moving slowly until he got to the very edge of the slag pile. The lizard slipped away. Night became a clouded amber, the big yellow dog leaped down and disappeared into the thick scrub brush, and still Jack waited.

A couple of hours later, the giant man stood, picked up another bottle, and took another hearty slug. In spite of the fact he was far out of reach and in the wrong trajectory to be hit by any vomited projectiles, Jack ducked his head down, covering it with both hands, in the same way his teachers taught him to prepare for a hit by a nuclear bomb. He lifted his head for a peek every few seconds. When nothing came back up he was impressed that the man was still standing, and again, taking another long pull from the bottle.

Jack waited, barely blinking while the crazy old man drank and wailed, decorated the bushes with what looked like partly digested cat guts, and drank some more. Normally Jack would grow impatient with this kind of waiting, but this time he knew for certain that if he just toughed it out, he would get his recompense. Of course, he'd also confirmed that the old guy was there alone with the one dog, and plenty of guns. And then, at last Jack did get his reward. The drunken, crazy old giant stumbled to a stack of wooden boxes and bags, opened an old gunnysack, and began to pull out handfuls of gold rocks, which he held up before letting them rain back in. Not ingots, not coins, but stubby thumbs of nuggets, just exactly as Trong Tri had described, a sack of gold rocks, each rarer than a five-carat diamond. Jack strained toward it, hungry, his brain chanting: golden nuggets, golden nuggets, golden, golden nuggets.

Jack's moment came when at last the huge, drunken man staggered back and fell down, spread-eagle and lay there without moving a twitch except to shove out hot blasts of stinky breath. Jack waited until he heard snoring before he made his move for the gold. It was easy filling his pockets with the delicious soft nuggets. The only thing that stopped him from taking more was their weight. There were smaller bags in there too, and when he held one in his hand he knew it was gold dust. Jack took the smallest one. He walked straight out of the campfire without fear of being caught. The giant man was plastered to the earth; his snores shook the ground while the fire continued to roar. Except for his footsteps, there were no other sounds.

It was easy finding his way back to the vine, and he climbed on without looking back. His pockets were much heavier than the last time—the time with the single ingot—but his body felt lighter. The sun began to push a new, glaring light into the sky with such a radiance of life that he had a hard time looking away. The breeze kicked up into a nice wind. Jack stopped halfway down to watch the muted colors of the desert floor slowly take on more depth. Daylight was now a relief to him, when his vision returned to normal, but he put on his sunglasses again, just to keep the glare down.

For the first time he began to think of being rich, he'd never dreamed of having such money before; what would be the point? His heart fluttered. Jack placed a hand over the nuggets that weighed down his pockets, and felt a weight crushing his entire body. Tears unexpectedly filled his eyes. The feeling of weightlessness vanished, his heart thudded. He considered flinging the stolen gold out onto the desert floor; could imagine the shimmering arc they would make as they flew out before dropping straight down into the soft sand, sinking in where they would lay undiscovered, perhaps forever. For some reason the image of Evonal flickered across his thoughts. He held onto her look of calm expectancy, the way she looked when she was waiting for him to finish a foolish sentence he wished he'd never started. Jack ran his fingers through the tight curls of his hair, and then he tugged on that imaginary goatee. He just couldn't tell anymore if he was on foot or horseback. And then he descended the vine. Those first steps into the desert floor sank in deeply, sand slid inside his boots. Jack plowed his way home and headed for his narrow hard bed, wanting only to sleep it all off, and awaken himself again.

Meanwhile the vine had taken notice of the sweet lake of water that rippled serenely on the top of the tawl as the wind whispered across. The vine knew it must tap this important source. It began its new course for survival with every cell in its being.

■ ■ ■

Chapter 8

The late afternoon found Evonal looking out her kitchen window as she washed the dishes, feeling stupidly brokenhearted, something she felt certain would not have happened if she'd had an occupation. There was only one cup and one plate to wash, and the dogs' bowls, but she kept washing them over and over in the tepid, soapy water. Although she always wished to be more, she had no idea of what to do with herself. Unlike the other inhabitants, she never chose to live in Foison. She was born and raised there, because that was where her wealthy, eccentric parents had wanted to paint.

Evonal wiped the plate over and over thinking about love, about the man who broke her heart. The racking crying fit came and went while she held onto the sink. It wasn't like she couldn't afford to move, her parents left her a fortune, and yet there she stood, leaning against their old sink, wiping their old dishes, frozen to the spot, still missing them.

Of course the rest of the family considered her parents' attachment to Foison, their art, and each other, a *folie de deux*, but Evonal knew they were not only happy, but abnormally certain about who they were, and what they wanted. Unlike her.

It couldn't have ended more tragically. They'd both died in a car crash on their way home from Las Vegas when she was only sixteen. It was to be one of those three-day weekends she'd been anticipating for months, for the time off from school and to be alone in their house. After they died, she never went back to school. High school was torture to her, just pure torture before she lost her parents and unimaginable without them around to cheer her on. Back then, she wasn't a despairing teenager—that came on just recently, and once she realized her full inheritance she'd no need to find an occupation, only a purpose in life. That was the catch. Evonal dried, put away all the dishes, and drained the sink. Then she went to get ready to take the dogs to do their business, thinking over those bad days as she gathered the leashes, water, and doggy rations, filling her pockets as she moved through the routine. The dogs excitedly circled her ankles; shivering, bulging-eyed pooches, ecstatic just to be going for a walk, something so enviable in its way, this also broke her heart.

"Come on, you little chippers." She sighed, and then right in the middle of fastening the last leash, the heartbreak once again knocked the wind out of her. Why did all the sappy promises keep circulating in her mind as if she was ever, ever foolish enough to want to believe them? There was nothing in that "love affair" she cared about, there never was, so why this time did she feel so bruised?

Walking several small dogs on their own leashes was like working a very large marionette inside a very small theater with a turning stage on uneven, shifting terrain. At the edge of her front yard, she stopped long enough to be sure no one was around before she chose a direction, but just as she turned east, she heard, "Hey, Evonal!" It was Vern, she knew without looking. She regretted how her body noticeably bunched up when it really was nothing personal; there wasn't a person anywhere she wanted to see just then.

"You got a minute?" he asked.

"Yeah, of course," she said; he wasn't a man she cared to wound. Vern was a spare man, covered in freckles. Although it certainly was of no consequence, he always struck her as someone who never knew his own worth.

Once Evonal faced him, Vern took a minute to settle his feet into a wide stance and cross his arms so his hands cupped his elbows before he started talking. "My brother, the butcher, I think I told you about him before, didn't I? He's coming on out and thought to set up a sandwich shop in your old building."

Evonal was taken aback. "Who would he sell to?"

"Tourists!"

"Tourists?"

"It *is* Vortex season, Evon."

"I guess it slipped past me. But still, the dozen or so what come, they bring their own stuff, don't they?"

This caused Vern to light up; his arms expanded to each side of him like wings, like he was getting ready to soar away. (She unkindly wished he would.)

"Why, Evonal, town's booming. Good god, that fruit, the juice from it makes this fantastical juice that everyone wants. We can barely keep up." And then, folding in his arms, he spoke in a quiet, confidential tone, "The other thing is my brother's mental health ain't so good, you see. He's taken a tumble downward lately. Wants a change of venue, from the big city, if you can catch my drift. He's sold his butcher shop for good money and wants to invest those dollars right here in old Foison."

"I can see a mental tumble from butchering," Evonal said over the thrumming in her own head. The dogs began leaping into her legs. Somehow she kept her fingertips from drumming her temples.

"I know you're one of those vegetarian types, but it isn't the butchering that's got to him. It's the city."

"Well," she said; it was all she had. The dogs yapped impatiently, now digging at her shoes to get her moving. When she took a step forward to get them to move away from her, Vern, misinterpreting, said, "You don't want to rent it to me? Did you have plans to cash in on all this?"

She didn't ask *all what*. Imaginations in Foison Surrounded were subject to great inflations, and even quicker deflations, which often brought sour tempers, and the eternal shifting of loyalties; the spats. Whatever the latest story was, it could wait. And she certainly didn't care about those damn buildings.

"I can let you rent it, of course. I don't need more than ten dollars a year rent money. You're the one always cleaning up after the demands of the county. Go ahead and get started however you want; we can talk terms later, whad'da ya say, Vern? I'm tumbling a little myself just now."

"Cadillac Man?"

"Yeah, Vern. Cadillac Man."

"Gotcha. It's a deal, then. See you tomorrow. You take care, Evon. Enjoy your walk with your little ones there."

They both turned in opposite directions, but while Vern was able to walk off quickly, Evonal found herself entangled in leashes. Of course the whole town knew about that wrong man even though she'd never introduced him to a soul and he'd usually come by late at night to pick her up and drop her off, or she drove herself to his place.

Once she got everyone straightened out the smallest dog kicked up sand and barked at the dust. The other two joined in with a frantic enthusiasm. The new pup tried leaping after a lizard. Evonal yanked it back with impatience before it came to harm and was a mite rough. "Sorry, Poochie," she whispered. These little Chihuahuas were noisy, frustrating ornaments. They were hers, but they weren't enough to make up an entire purpose in life, she'd realized a dog or two too late.

There was a subtle sweet smell to the wind, something that was never there before, it made the desert seem peaceful and the scent of the sand less arenose. The dusky sky was so beautiful; the brightest stars were already out, and from the sight of it she felt relieved that she would live after all. Cadillac Man. They all knew about him. Without warning, a new wave of hurt broke over her heart. So much for thorny, sweet-talking men in big, flashy cars, she told herself, sobbing quietly. She just could not understand what happened. There was never a time before that she was attracted to a loud man with a string tie and a big pinky ring. A turquoise dealer too, of all the ridiculous things. The first time they'd shook hands she'd actually coughed, his cologne had been so strong. And then he'd started giving her the rings, and she'd take each one knowing it was all wrong, everything about the two of them together, but she felt so happy anyway. *She had started to go along with it.*

While the dogs took turns lifting their legs on the same rock, Evonal twisted at the rings on her fingers. Far off, on the late evening horizon she saw Jack skulking from rock outcropping to yucca tree. Evonal let out a deep sigh, straightened up, and planted a hand on her hip to watch him. He would never see her; he was too busy trying to go unnoticed. Jack was like that. Always missing the forest for the trees. Shaking her head as she watched that huge frame bent in half in an almost cartoon-like tiptoe across the desert, she also worried some. There was no doubt he was mixed up in something he shouldn't be doing, but she knew it wasn't drugs or robbery or anything that would hurt another person. Going with him to sell that ingot to Trong Tri wasn't suspicious. People found small treasures like that all the time out there, and Jack just may've come across an old stash. Thieves, lunatics, and desperate people had been hiding stuff in the tawls and the caves in the mountains for over a hundred years; it was that kind of desolate place, perfect for thieves and the picked on. Anyway, she could never hold it against him whatever it was. She always had a soft spot for Jack. In grade school the kids were gentle with him, like he was made of glass, but they all avoided him out of fear too, and then when he'd bloomed into a sturdy teenager, well, they all depended on him to round up the fun. He'd joined her in bed three times now, and each time had been just when she needed that no-strings-attached lover's lust, tumbling-on the-mattress fun.

Whenever they met it was like they'd talked every day, but he knew how to leave her be too.

She watched as Jack paused mid-stride to pick up something, it made him look boyish and rather lost. There was a man would shoot himself in the foot with his own gun if someone wasn't there to take out the bullets beforehand, and she decided she'd best keep ahead of that gun. A sensation she could not identify caused her stomach to ball up. Men didn't seem to care that she cared for them because she was always reaching for the man that couldn't love her back. Evonal let her shoulders heave, let her eyes pour out the water, hoping, waiting for some feeling of hitting the bottom hard enough that she could begin that slow buoy to the surface.

Night dropped, completely surrounding them in dark. The dogs uncharacteristically begged her for protection, leaping at her knees, yapping pleas that intensified with each bark. Evonal knew better than to ignore a dog's sense so she scooped them up and set them calmly into her pockets, took out her flashlight pointing a beam at the ground just ahead of her footsteps, and headed for home.

The thick stench of his fat cigar reached her before her house came into view. Switching off the flashlight, she changed direction, moving to a vantage point where she could see the back fin of the big old-fashioned Cadillac to be sure it was him. At first her heart raced—she never wanted anything more than to climb into that car with that half-shit of a man, and yet Evonal turned away from her house, and him, and walked away. What felt like a band of thorns clenched her breast, and with each step tightened painfully, but she was walking away, she was walking away.

Evonal didn't stop to catch her breath until she reached the old train station and the adjacent storage depot she had been stuck with after her parents died. The buildings Vern wanted to set up shop in. The train tracks had been taken up fifty years before, but the railroad company had left behind the cavernous buildings, perfect for two artists who liked to paint large canvasses. She hadn't been inside in years. Twice she was fined because the rods of bamboo had grown into a thick, wild fence that collected desert scraps against it: tumbleweeds, empty potato chip bags, dried snake skins, dead lizards and even some paper money was found. In a very formal letter, the county called it a firetrap and an eyesore, and ordered her to clean it out or pay them to do it. Vern had stepped in, set everything to rights, and kept it up nice for next to nothing each month.

At one point, Evonal looked into having the buildings torn down, but this caused an uproar among the townsfolk that left them bitter for months; yet she couldn't give them up to the town either, because they weren't an official town anymore. And the county refused to take them. These were gray wood, unpainted buildings, except for one large area. Evonal went to see if the mysterious portrait was still on the back wall of the depot.

The most talked about person back then—before her parents died—was a woman named Tina Bell. "That woman and her intricate affairs," Evonal remembered her mother often saying with a laugh. Tina Bell was a licensed nurse, but also a palm reader and, it was rumored, liked to take lovers two at a time. She'd left a lasting impression on someone to be sure. A few weeks after her stormy departure someone had painted her portrait on the broadest side of the depot. Evonal rounded the side of the building and shone her flashlight on it. It was still there. That smile, wide and white, shone down bright as ever across that sexy, know-it-all face with its high, brightly blushed cheeks. The hair, a cascade of saloon-girl ringlets the color of ripe bananas, poured down on her left shoulder. Of course she had a white twinkle painted in each blue eye, looking mischievously heavenward. Someone kept that painting bright and fresh too, Evonal noticed with surprise.

The town rumor mill suggested that her father painted that ghastly portrait as a heartbroken lover's homage to Tina Bell. Evonal remembered how her mother lay on the floor to laugh a laugh that most certainly would have knocked her down anyway. The sting of the insult to her father was that he should be accused of painting such cartoon crap, and then they'd died before it could be sandblasted off. Her head began to ache a little; she laid a moist palm across her forehead. The stench of that cigar; it was perfume at one time. She thought her parents made loving look so easy that she'd learned nothing about the pitfalls.

Suddenly, the dogs leaped up to the top of her pockets and started barking. Evonal switched off the light and moved quickly to the side of the building. This was not always the safest place at night, especially during Vortex season. People changed when they got into the open space of the desolately remote desert. The visiting strangers brought their crazy notions of lawless freedom and their loaded guns too. Risking splinters, she stayed in contact with the scuffed-up old planks while trying to get the yappers pushed down into her pockets and quiet.

At the very corner of the building, she prepared to run. Releasing her grip on the building she broke into a hard sprint and slammed into the mass that had waited around the corner. The flashlight banged painfully into her cheekbone, the Chihuahuas leaped out, barking uncontrollably with their insane bravado. Evonal instinctively dived after the dogs, and while going down smacked the top of her head into something as solid as a boulder. The impact brought on a flash of light from somewhere behind her eyes, she bit her tongue, and cried out in pain, fully blinded.

"Ooomph! Jeez, Evon, take it easy!"

"Jack?" The dogs were trying to wedge their bodies under hers, looking for safety, kicking up more sand and clawing at her clothes.

"Come 'ere," she hissed.

He came into focus, a dark block of a shadow; she realized they were both sprawled on the ground, rubbing the top of their heads.

"Good grief, it is you," she squeaked.

"Evening, Evonal."

"Did we just knock heads?"

Jack got up and pulled her with him.

"You hit my hipbone. You haven't got a bottle of water, have you?" Jack asked.

Evonal fished one out of a pocket, settled the dogs back into theirs, and handed it to him, noting that he drank it in one long drink and still looked pitifully thirsty, sucking every drop off his upper lip.

"Here's the last one," Evonal said, holding out the second bottle.

"Ahhhh," Jack sighed before he sucked that down too. "That oughta do it. Thanks, Evon."

Jack wiped an arm across his forehead saying, "Went by your place just now. Some big car's out front with a bull of a man blowing big clots of cigar smoke out the window. He looked pretty much settled in to wait."

Evonal pressed her forehead into the flat of her palm as she walked to the side of the building where she leaned hard into the painted-on cleavage of Tina Bell.

"You OK?" he asked.

"Yep, never been better."

Evonal sat down, leaning against the building, wondering how long he'd wait for her.

"Evon?" Jack said, shaking her a little.

She left the smoky past, joined Jack in the present.

"Weren't these buildings your parents'?" Jack asked without looking at them.

"Yep, their art studio. Vern wants to rent them to open a store. He thinks there's some sort of boom coming over that vine fruit or some such."

"Or some such. Sounds like Foison. Did you let him have them?"

"Of course. The county won't let me abandon them. They're a sore spot for me, Jackie. Vern is welcome to them. Maybe they'll accidentally burn 'em down."

Jack chuckled. Evonal hated herself for wondering if *that man* was still waiting outside her door.

"Come on, snap out of it, Evon." Jack clamped a hand on her knee and shook it.

After that they talked about most everything except what was waiting outside Evonal's door, or why Jack kept both hands covering the front pocket of his jeans.

"Listen," Jack whispered. "You can hear the back bottle church moaning."

There were a couple of houses built with layers of adobe lined by hundreds of old wine bottles, used in place of bricks, but the maker of the church had turned half of the bottle necks to the outside, so whenever the wind blew over the necks, and that was pretty constant, it moaned like a dying animal.

"Whew! As a kid, the moaning used to scare me into sleeping under the bed some nights. And once, when I was about seven, I'd got parked in my wheelchair inside the bottle church while the town fussed over cleaning and repairing it. While the wind whistled around the bottlenecks outside, I counted every liquor bottle."

"How many are there?" Evonal asked, but she was picturing the old Cadillac parked in front of her house. She wondered if he was still there, hard as she was trying to forget it.

"I believe 3,087. All the same type of wine bottle too."

"That's a lot of wine."

"Whoever built that thing was pretty precise. You should see how the corners are worked. I think that's why he stacked those bottles one row out, one in, so they fit better. And the adobe that holds it together is smooth as cake frosting too. Now I only hear it when it's silent," Jack said.

"Well I could use a bottle of wine."

Jack chuckled.

The dogs got out of her lap twice to give a thorough nosing over of the few inches she let them out on the leashes. Evonal ate all the trail mix she'd left the house with and some old snacks she'd neglected to throw out. Then came the time after midnight, but before 3:00 a.m. when an opaque veil of sky fell over the area of the Numinous Vortex like a swath of billowing bridal tulle. They held hands as they watched it ascend, talking in soft voices about the people over there, sleeping in their elaborate campers, coming all this way, waiting for just this piece of time.

"Maybe it's a time of peace," Evonal said.

They spoke to each other in low voices about the visitors' expectations: trying to make a baby, hoping to cure depression, cancer, uncontrolled anger. Sometimes these wishes were boldly written on their camper shells, some wore T-shirts proclaiming their desire for a particular type of spiritual renewal they hoped the Vortex would bring them, others kept it to themselves, but they all wore the look of desperate hopefulness. The smell of the cigar; she wished the wishing away.

"Did you ever go there and wish for something?" Jack whispered.

"Yep," Evonal said. "Something for my parents. After they died. It was foolish. I just wanted them to be together wherever they were. Spent the whole night alone in a sleeping bag inside this tiny tent." She'd glossed over this; could not admit that she went there to rid herself of the fear of her being left behind, the heartbreak her parents left her with. And that all night she'd not slept a wink she was so terrified of all the nights ahead of her, alone.

"Did you have to stay in Foison?"

"My grandmother was dead. I just couldn't leave my parents all alone in the ground. Those three were all that was left of my family. I didn't know where I was supposed to be. Sounds so fraught, doesn't it?"

"Weren't you scared spending the night in the Vortex alone?" Jack asked, jabbing her gently in the ribs with an elbow

"Nawp," she said.

"I didn't think so," he said.

"Jack, you can't imagine all the places in a girl's body sand can work its way into."

Jack chuckled. "Sandy sand."

Those two words moved her thoughts to the past; a place at the beach, digging holes that filled with ocean water, her grandmother showing her a tiny crab. Jack knocked his head into hers, laughed with her. "They're together," he whispered, and she nodded, still catching ocean water in a plastic bucket, still an innocent child with muddy feet, overjoyed with the foaming sea, the love of her family right there at her elbow.

"Well," Jack said, pulling her back to Foison. "My mom used to take me to the Vortex regularly. Back when she had me in that wheelchair."

Evonal could picture little Jack, slump shouldered, passively waiting wherever his mother parked him, his small shaved head, those two ears like handles on a sugar pot, his hands dangling over the edges like empty gloves.

"What was wrong with you?"

"Oh, bad heart, water on the brain, glass spine, ratchet knees..."

"How are you still alive?"

"It was all her craziness. I was healthy as any other kid. You know how she is. I think she was actually trying to kill me, in her way. And some days seemed like she would do anything to keep me here—and then just, I don't know, can't stand me for it. When she took me to the Vortex she had it in her head that we were there for some divine purpose. She used to be quite a believer. I never understood. Ah, it was just more of her nonsense."

Evonal studied his broad profile, the way his eyebrow dropped just then, and his ear, how it wiggled before sagging. She thought about her own parents, and then finally decided to say, "We're both shaped by Foison."

Jack chuckled.

They both let the subject fizzle on what she thought was a rather peculiar high note. Jack leaned into her leg and breathed long, slow breaths. The fins on that old Cadillac, she thought, the smell of the cigar—why did she have to wonder if he was still there? Jack elbowed her again.

"I'd like to tell you something, Evon," Jack said, bringing her back again.

"So go ahead."

"There's a place I go that really makes me feel like I might amount to something someday. Don't tell anyone," he said, sighing deeply.

"This isn't a drug you're taking, is it, Jackie?"

"What? No! No, drugs for me, never again. I'm sticking to whiskey and beer. Seriously, it's a place I found near here. But, maybe I should keep my mouth shut about it for now. Do you think?"

Evonal shined the flashlight directly on his face. "You have a right to remain silent. Use it." She meant it as a joke, like in the old detective movies, but highlighted the bruises and deep scratches. His yellow eyes glowed like a cat's, but she didn't think they were as weird as she'd heard someone say.

"What happened?"

"I got a little banged up. Getting there and back takes some work," Jack replied.

"So what's the place like?"

Jack started telling her about remarkable rocks, crystal water, natural gas fires, and old mining equipment, but she found herself drifting off to the past, taking his hand in hers—hanging on to the present.

"So tell me what happened with Cadillac Man."

"He wants to get married, get set up in Chrysopoeia near to his family, blend right into their Sunday picnics. Expand his jewelry store, with me helping along at his side." Two-by-two tweetie bird, he'd said. Using her money he'd somehow found out about.

"You don't want that?"

Evonal felt like he'd jabbed a small pin in between the ribs nearest her heart. She flinched, even brushed at the spot.

"That's the problem, I do in certain painful ways, but in my heart, Jackie, I know he's the wrong man. I mean, I know it, for certain too. That's why I need the spell to break no matter what. I want to find my own place, finally."

"Do you even know what you want in a man?" Jack asked, but in a curious sort of way, no hint of a smartass at all. She didn't mind answering him truthfully.

"I'd like someone able to befriend an enemy. I'm tired of feuds. No mean streaks, no matter what. Oh, someone who can keep his place clean, wants to keep his place clean. I really hate dust."

Jack chuckled. Dust was the desert; the desert was dust, a popular saying.

"I'd like a man who's generous, but doesn't make it a fact, good to the weak, understands all life is as precious and important as any person's. Doesn't need drugs. No fancy tricks in bed; satisfied with the usual menu. Not too much liquor. No jewelry."

"A person can only remember about seven things," Jack said like he was trying to keep track. This made her laugh; started up her tears again. Evon laid her head on his shoulder, tried to cry without letting her body move.

"Here comes the sun, Evon. Come on now. Don't cry. We both know there's no such good man like that. Let me walk you home," Jack whispered, shaking her gently out of her stupor.

"It's a new day." Evonal sighed, one more to get through.

They walked slowly. She saw the Cadillac was gone. It was over. It was over. Think: yes, this is what you want.

"See you around, Jackie?"

"You wouldn't want to go for another drive, would ya?"

"Jackie, can you just take the truck and get it back in one piece? I need to shut myself in today."

"You don't mind?"

"Naw, I trust ya. I just can't muster up the strength to drive anywhere this morning."

"I was looking forward to your company. OK then, I'll borrow it. I can look into that rattling noise, and fill it with gas."

Evonal thought he seemed reluctant to leave. "Go on ahead, Jackie."

"Have a good snooze. Don't cry no more. I'll see you in a few hours."

"Just go on and park the truck in its spot when you get back. You know where to find the key. Put it back."

"You gonna be OK?"

She nodded. And they parted. It surprised her that when she got to her porch and looked out on the day that Jack was still watching her. They waved at each other, and she went inside her empty house still leaking tears, still looking for signs of that wrong man.

■ ■ ■

Chapter 9

Jack and Trong Tri made the exchange—gold nuggets for cash—while seated in his truck. The sun was still inching into the sky. Since Jack was walking back, he wanted to get on his way.

"I'd best get," Jack said.

"Call the store whenever you find another miner's stash," Trong said seriously.

"Hopefully, we'll be talkin' soon," Jack said, trying to match Trong's tone, dignity, and quiet.

"Seemed like an unusual amount of traffic heading into Foison this morning."

"It's Vortex Season," Jack said, quickly hiding the cash.

"You want to be sure you won't be followed. If you can get to the store, it would be safer. People have a way of knowing when someone has what you have. Take a good look around,

Jack. Especially here," Trong said. Jack swiveled his head for effect, but he didn't know what else to say. No one had ever bothered to follow him before. Of course he'd been tracked down, but only if someone needed a motor repaired right away or a refrigerator or such like moved. He got out of the truck, closing the door quietly.

Jack walked the long, roundabout way back to Foison, the thick stack of cash a thousand times lighter in his pockets than his beautiful gold. So light, in fact, it was depressing. Fingering his pocket, he started thinking about how all the gold had felt there. His mind ventured back to that place, the big yellow dog. A strong sweet scent gathered in his throat where it seemed to set claws in. He started clearing his throat to shake it loose.

"Hey, aren't you Jack?" It was a young girl's thin voice behind him. For a moment, Jack's insides jiggled. Throwing a wave over his shoulder, he didn't turn around. This was followed by the sound of feet running over desert rocks. Still he held his ground, pointed his nose forward and marched, trying to hack out the clingy dark taste from the back of his throat.

"I'm Linda Lake," the bright blonde appeared in front of him. Without meaning to, he leaped back, kept his eyes on the tops of his boots. He needed new laces. The shoes themselves were several colors of earth, none attractive. Hers were pink and glowing.

"Did I scare you?"

"I think those neon pink things did."

This made her giggle, a particular type of girly laugh that always grated on Jack.

"Nice to meet you," he said quickly, turning in another direction.

"Hey, wait! Meet my sister, Astrid!"

"You're Mavis's boy, Jack, right?" Astrid's voice was harder, worn by life, older, wiser, had the ring of someone suspicious of everything.

"So I am," Jack said, trying to keep his back to them, trying to keep his fingers off the thick wad of cash he had put in the inside pocket of his jacket. Somehow he'd have to get some of the cash to Mavis. Jack didn't treasure a meeting with his mother either; good as he was feeling, she would deliberately find a way to spoil it.

"Well come on by for a sandwich or a sweet treat! We have a nice store going now right here in downtown Foison."

"Thanks!"

"OK, we'll see you soon!" She giggled again and left on a streak of pink.

He put more power in his strides, climbing the small, rocky hill in the opposite direction of Foison, taking a rest as soon as he found a large enough spot of shade to cool off in. After draining his bottle of water he decided he needed to get back to the comfort of his empty house. He wanted to give Mavis some cash, but decided his encounter with the Lake sisters had drained all his energy. There was something about those two, he mused, something in that warning from Trong that made sense. Jack had nothing for them; didn't want to encourage anything like friendship.

When he looked up, he realized just how far off he had drifted. Outside her front door, Old Sylvia stood with both feet planted, a shotgun under her armpit, loaded for bear.

Jack backed up, waited to see if anything more was going to come of the situation.

"You OK?" he called. Generally, she was someone Jack especially avoided, but even he couldn't run off just like that. Vortex Season was a time of weirdos; the people of Foison looked out for each other.

"Aw, Jack! Yes, just getting loaded for target practice," she answered calmly, but he could see the aggravation in the way her eyes darted over the landscape.

"Good to know," he said congenially.

"Need a cup of coffee? I made some fritters too."

Jack's stomach roared, but he declined as politely as he could. "I'd best get," he said.

"Standing offer," she called back without a trace of sarcasm, causing Jack to believe she meant it.

After he heard the old girl's front door slam, he skirted around an old tawl until he got on the worn trail near the slit of running water they called the creek. Jack began to relax and look forward to getting into his dark bedroom, having a slug of whiskey, some solid peace to dote on his few remaining gold nuggets.

"Where is it?" His mother's voice hit his back like a hard fist. He stopped and turned around, his hand already fishing around in his pocket for the wad of money he'd separated out for her.

"I got some money for you right here," Jack said. He realized she must have been following him, as Trong had warned, so he really wasn't looking around hard enough.

Mavis looked at the wad of cash like he was trying to hand her some shit.

"Take it or don't," Jack said wearily.

"This ain't gold," she said, grabbing it and dropping the cash into her pocket.

"No, it isn't," Jack said.

"Well, I want some of the gold. Hand me over a piece." She held out a flat palm, vibrating it with impatience.

Jack fished a small nugget from his top pocket and dropped it into her palm. It was impossible not to watch how carefully she looked it over.

"There's more," was all she said, but he noted the satisfaction in her voice, like he'd finally, after all these years, done something right. "You gotta get it all before this whole thing goes up."

"Goes up?" Jack asked before he could stop himself.

"You always been so damn thick, Jack. Take a look around once in a while. I can't do everything for you."

"You're not gonna toss that?" He meant the gold nugget she had pinched in her fingers.

Mavis dropped it into her pocket, called out, "Yooo hoooo, Telly, I'm over here!" And left as abruptly as she'd come. He told himself to forget about that tiny nugget. There were five more in his pocket. But then, it was hard to get himself going; almost like he couldn't remember where he belonged.

The wind kicked up sand. Something flitted along on the current and became a sheet of paper that stuck on his leg. Lime green, a color that always galled Jack. He ripped it off, but couldn't let it go on its way without reading it. Jack stared at the advertisement for the Revival of Spiritual Voyagers. The first time he saw their tent getting set up in Foison he was a kid. He thought that the circus was, at last, at last, in town, but it wasn't nothing but crazed people infected with the jiggles, screaming and hoo-hawing over something they called the healing spirit. It was Vortex Season, and this year Foison seemed to be under special attack.

His next step wobbled when it hit the ground. Jack took a moment to collect his thoughts and reorganize them. After that he concentrated on getting to the tranquility of his rickety room. Jack tried to stop thinking about everything swirling in his head, calling on images of naked women to prevail, but his thoughts traveled swiftly over to the tawl, sparked around the thoughts of that cantankerous old giant guarding those sacks of gold. It had been so easy for Jack just to get the gold. A few cuts and scrapes. So easy. It was all he could think about.

■ ■ ■

Chapter 10

It hadn't occurred to Evonal that renting the stores to Vern would cause a controversy among the residents of Foison, but she'd been too caught up in her own silly melodrama with that wrong man. The simple truth slipped past her when of course she knew that everything usually divided the town into several camps.

The against group, Juanita, Sidus, and Old Sylvia, had got Evonal seated comfortably in Old Sylvia's tiny board and batten house, a smaller version of her own, to "discuss" it. Normally, she'd be squirmy and frantically thinking of ways to placate them, but her mind seemed to be clotted with the cloudy aroma of cigar smoke. She closed her eyes to ward off the evil spirits, barely listening to the usual chitchat about the weather. Finally, Juanita cleared her throat, ready to begin.

"Now, we don't blame you for renting out those old buildings just like that," said Juanita, reaching over to pat Evonal's knee. "I know Vern has been very good to you. He's the backbone of this community in so many ways. We'd find it hard to say no to him for anything too. We just wished to have had a say in it. Sidus here and Old Sylvia, there, they are worried about the environment, and so am I, but I think I should confess my reasoning is a little more selfish. I just do not like any change in Foison. I have lived here most of my life for a reason."

Evonal crossed her legs, and began wringing her hands in her lap.

"We don't want to make you uncomfortable," Sidus said sincerely in his deep, gravelly voice, like he was moderating rather than participating.

Evonal shrugged. "I just had no idea this could happen like this. I figured a couple extra Numinous Vortex visitors would show up, and as soon as the winds kicked up, it would fizzle out and that would be that." The truth was, she hadn't even thought about any of it. She was so overwrought at that point, that she wasn't thinking of anything but her own sad, broken heart and how she would keep what was left of it beating. And those buildings were always a problem for her alone.

"Well now that old revival tent is back with its new age kooks set out to convert this place into their own."

"They've always given up and left in the past," Evonal said. "Eventually."

"So if you'll just hear us out," Juanita coaxed gently.

"I'm happy to hear you out." Evonal folded her hands in her lap, prepared to hear them out, without apologizing, which would only open the door on getting her to try and—*heaven help her!*—evict those residents that had already set up shop in the old art studio.

"Well I was thinking if we just put our heads together, we could come up with something to do about this mess of people invading us. And that goddamned unnatural vine with its peculiar fruit."

Sidus cleared his throat. He had asked her to come, he and Old Sylvia being the seniors there. Both were dressed in jeans and washed-out pale-blue long-sleeve shirts, something Evonal thought of as quaint; the uniform of the people of Foison Surrounded, really. Juanita had her postmistress uniform on, but the colors still matched.

"Well, let me get the drinks and we can get started thinking aloud," Old Sylvia said. Everything went quiet when she left. Old Sylvia's living room was surprisingly cozy. On the wall, over the sofa, was a desert scene painted by Evonal's mother, a lone house in the winter desert: Old Sylvia's house alone. The enormous boulder that flanked it was left out. Next to that was a portrait of Old Sylvia, also painted by her mother. Portraits were something her mother rarely painted, and this was done with the precision of a Golden Age Dutch Master. Her mother must have thought a lot of Old Sylvia, and she tried to picture the two of them talking, wondered if the house looked the same back then.

Old Sylvia seemed to favor collecting broken things. The basic furniture was in repair and looked sturdy enough, but the corners of the wooden table were nicked up like they'd been dropped on their ends, the lamps were brass and dented, the silk shades slightly askew, maybe because the finial on one was bent, and missing on the other. The built-in shelves she recognized as Vern's handiwork, and these were straight, but there were no books, only more broken items. One shelf held half a teapot laying broken-side-up, a couple of sun-tinted, lavender bottles with the necks smashed off lay on their sides with silk flowers peeking out of the top, a headless doll in a bride's dress was on another, and other such ordinary things rendered odd. It was the framed picture of what looked like a young Sylvia, set off to the side that really got her attention. The glass was broken into several wedges, the points radiating out from the middle, like a crookedly cut pie; Evonal could picture the sudden smash of a small ball peen hammer right into the center. The house was neat as a pin and so well dusted the surfaces shone, but it looked like there had been a brawl in it and Old Sylvia put things back together as best she could, hung up some thick flowery drapes, and got on with things. Somehow this was terribly easy to imagine.

Evonal accepted the mug of tepid tea Old Sylvia brought her. Because it was made from her well water, it had the unappetizing faint odor of rotten eggs *warmed*, the typical smell of Foison water, and the reason Evonal bought bottled water for her kitchen.

"I made this mug myself," she said.

"It's so pretty."

"I learned the ceramics stuff in prison," Old Sylvia said, her voice spiking with pride.

"Ahhhh," Sidus said politely. Evonal pretended to sip in silence. Of course she'd known about the prison time, but Old Sylvia never said what she'd done. No one in Foison would ever ask. This was the whole point of the place.

After allowing for a few polite sips, Juanita waved a hand as if to bring them all back to the topic at hand.

"Well I suppose if there is nothing Evonal can do at this point, we'll have to take another tact."

They all glued their attention on Evonal who could only add: "The county may just shut 'em down. They like their permits and things in order. Otherwise, can't you all hold a town meeting and talk it out?"

They all chuckled like she'd just said the most preposterous thing, which of course it was. There were several long moments of silence in which everyone studied their tea as if they were actually going to drink the stink brew.

"Well, I don't suppose we can blow the old place up, can we?"

"Those are historical buildings. There's a government plaque!" Juanita cried.

"Never mind that plaque! People could get *killed*!" Sidus said, slapping his thigh with his flat palm.

"I meant when everyone was cleared out," Old Sylvia said, but, slowly, like she was mulling it over.

Evonal didn't mind the idea of destroying the buildings, if it could be done without harm to anyone. From her perspective those old buildings could've come down years ago, but she knew better than to even mutter such a thing. There was no explaining her personal frustrations over those relics; it just wasn't something she could make anyone understand, and no one really cared how she felt anyway: not these people, not the county. She pulled her lips together and kept them clamped shut.

"Well we'll just have to keep our thinking caps on," Juanita said.

Evonal set her cup on the nicked-up coffee table, "Well, I do believe it will all just blow *over*, like everything else does here. In time."

"That's all well and good and true too, but in the meantime just think about the damage that'll be done! Someone ran over a tortoise yesterday! Just flattened it, like it was an old paper bag! Do you know how hard it was to collect all those pieces for a proper burial? It broke my old heart," Old Sylvia cried out.

"Well," Juanita said, "maybe we could start there. We'll round up the tortoises we can find and take them to higher ground, as it were. It's a start."

"Yes," said Old Sylvia, sipping her tea with a growl. "It's a *start*."

The thought of the three of them rounding up the tortoises and moving those slow, ancient things off to safety; for some reason she pictured them pulling them along in her old red wagon, the tortoises stacked neatly inside like so many loaves of round, moldy bread. The thought pressed a new soft spot in her wrecked heart. Evonal couldn't hold back her tears.

"I've got to go!" She wept.

Juanita pulled a tissue from the box near her elbow and passed it to Evonal, who took several sheets with a nod, and left.

■ ■ ■

Chapter 11

This time when Jack set both feet on the tawl, he was wearing a special belt he stole off one of the dusty shelves of the now defunct *Desert Oddities Museum of Foison Surrounded*. It was an old miner's belt specially designed to hold nuggets of gold in thick leather pockets. The label he'd ripped off it said it was once sold by the name of *"California Saddle 1849" for the first gold rush*, the one in Sacramento, California, which caused all the ruckus. The thick belt cinched securely around Jack's waist and held fast, like it was made for him.

The big yellow dog was waiting for him, wagging her tail in slow, feathery waves while her front paws clawed at the air. In the last hour or so of the climb, he'd heard her calling to him in that deep-throated whine of hers. Once he got her head rubbed, pulled at her ears, and said, "Atta a girl, Little

Maid," she dropped half of a dead lizard at his feet, which he picked up and traded for a handful of dog treats he'd nabbed her from Evonal's small barrel of such stuff she had for her annoying yappers; dogs that were about the size of the turd of this big dog. Jack breathed in the clean air and listened. While he carefully smelled the air, his stomach growled, but he had his PBJ sandwiches packed in the side pockets of his pants for later. All had seemed peaceful, and when he didn't smell so much as a whiff of the noxious fumes of the old giant he went to the mound to check on Foison, which dotted its own small constellation of warm human lights on the vast dark tray of the desert floor, and it made him feel secure. Several dozen people were out with their flashlights. They looked like ants moving around their mound with high beams, something he found reassuring. And then it occurred to Jack that the total population of Foison was only around twenty people, yet there were dozens of ants down there. The arbor, with its festive lights, was distinct and out of place, and created a knot in his stomach too. The town dump was already twice the size it'd been just a few weeks before, and already reeked of decaying garbage, a growing carbuncle of filth that made his nose drip. He wiped it on his sleeve.

Beyond Foison, far beyond, looked like he could see all of planet Earth—flat and immeasurably distant in deep blues and purples, with sharp lines of light from strange cities. He believed if the mountain range hadn't blocked it, he could see clear to the ocean. Overhead the amber-colored, stellar lights winked at him. Unlike all his previous visits, Jack stood there unafraid, like he belonged to the ecosystem of the tawl as natural as any of the rocks or plants or even the oddly shaped lizards and small snakes. Jack picked up one of the smooth-looking rocks, and he rolled it around in his hand. Out of nowhere an uneasy tickle formed in his gut, and somehow it seemed to be connected to the foolish ravings of Mavis, so he let the rock drop with a thud, and he turned his back on it. That was when the odor punched him in the nose. He reeled like a tailless kite. A shotgun blast exploded into a bush to his far left, scattering both tiny birds, flying insects, and lizards. Jack leaped too. When he looked up, he realized it was a miracle that he hadn't been shot. The old giant was waving the gun, squarely facing Jack with puckered, squinty eyes.

"I know you're out there, and I'll kill you as soon as look at you." The old guy had his nose stuck in the air, sniffing snootfuls; his eyes squinted into folds of skin, Jack's first inkling the old coot might really be blind.

Quietly, Jack moved to his left, doing a knee bend deep enough to grab a stone, which he tossed to his right. The old guy's hips ratcheted as he twisted toward the sound, the deadly barrel wavered uncertainly in the air. The old fool couldn't see so well, but it didn't mitigate the danger of that shotgun. His heart hammered hard enough to move his shirt.

Be brave, he told himself. *Outmaneuver this old goat or die without another ounce of gold in your pocket!* Taking in a soundless, deep breath, Jack moved behind a stinky creosote bush. When the old guy dropped his shoulders, letting the barrel of the shotgun point to the ground, Jack eased away. If he was lucky he could find a safe spot to hole up and wait it out until the old goat passed out or fell asleep so he could steal another pocketful of gold and get down before he got hurt.

The next blast actually put some buckshot in his hair, but worse made him spring out of the bush like a scared jackrabbit. He ran blind like one too, eventually slamming into something rather solid and familiar. A crack of wood snapping in two sounded almost like another shotgun blast. A wall of some kind fell on him, trapping Jack beneath it; he was covered with a heavy pallet. The big yellow dog went wild with her whimpers of worry over him, but she shot off away from Jack, running a good distance before she started barking and howling like she was onto something deadly.

"If you're causing all this ruckus, I'll kill you dead, you big dumb dog!" the old guy hollered, blasting the gun three more times.

When the rush of fear wore off, Jack knew his arm was broken. It throbbed. There was a gash on his forehead that was oozing blood into his left eye. A nail from the thing that trapped him pierced through the upper auricle of his ear; a place he never wanted a hole, even during the peak of the piercing craze in high school. It wasn't exactly painful, at least not compared to his arm and forehead, but he knew if he moved he would pull it all the way through and have a rip instead of a hole. Once he got his breathing under control, he flattened his palms against the wood so he could push it straight off. His injured arm didn't have the strength of his good arm, but when he shoved, the thing lifted. Just when he had it upraised and got his ear free of the nail, he heard the old guy's footsteps approaching. Lowering it carefully, he closed his amber eyes and held his breath, waiting for the next round.

"Seems we got ourselves another fallen wall," the old guy screeched and guffawed. "A real fine bridge to nowhere, just like this whole goddamn place." Jack felt the old guy step on top of him with both feet. His full weight caused a new nail or at least something sharp to scrape into the flesh on the top of his head. For his size, the old guy was surprisingly light, but that didn't mean he didn't have an impact. Still, even as the breath was being slowly squeezed to the back of his lungs, he wondered if the old goat had hollow bones; the marrow seared out by that rotgut he swilled down. Whatever that old drunk ingurgitated got into his system, vented out his pores with the pungency of high-octane gasoline and sulfuric acid. Jack could hear him guzzling from his bottle, gulping hard and finishing each slug with a deeply satisfied *ahhhhhhhhhhh* while his disgusting body odor slinked down into Jack's throat, choking him as well as any garrote.

"Ah!" he crowed again. The weight on top of him shifted to his left, over his broken arm, and soon the sounds of a stream followed. The smell of his urine was caustic. Jack shoved with his right arm as hard as he could, pushing the entire wall.

When the old giant hit the ground, Jack rolled in the opposite direction into and out of some prickly brush, over rock shards, and some squishy shit that smelled like rotted fruit. He had no idea what all else, but he didn't care as long as he was moving away from the danger. Once he could no longer smell the old guy, Jack stopped rolling and got up. Alternating between holding his forehead to staunch the flow of blood and cradling his bad arm, Jack stumbled to the edge of the lake and slowly waded into the cold water. His left eye was closed from all the blood that poured into it, so he held his breath and dipped under trying to flush it out. Jack let himself sink, hoping to hit bottom, but even with the heavy clothes and miner's belt, he couldn't. Because he couldn't swim with his wrecked arm, he rolled instead, still deeply buried in the water, slowly exhaling the air in his lungs. Even in the pale moonlight he could see the blood bubble up, ruby marbles in the cold water, breaking at the surface with a red sheen. Jack was too afraid of drowning to put his head under water.

Once he dragged himself out of the water he went to a boulder sheltered by the berry bush that seemed to grow all over the tawl. Exhausted, confused, and soaking wet, he lay belly down over the boulder to dry off under the faint moonlight. The tantalizing scent of the fat berries sweetened the chilled night air. After the first taste, he knew that this was what the old guy made the moonshine from. He ate several handfuls with relish, feeling pleasantly full and numb. He laid his head back down on the rock, too drowsy to keep his eyes open.

Jack awoke just as the stars were beginning to vanish into the sun's dominating glow. After he pried himself off the boulder, he walked with aching determination to the stash of gold, stepped over the old guy—passed out prone on the ground, as usual—and resisting the urge to piss on him, he went to the bag and took as much gold as his miner's belt pockets would hold. Jack strode, well, rather staggered to the top of the vine. The big yellow dog was waiting. She ran her nose over his body, and whimpered helplessly.

"I'm good, Little Maid. Don't you worry none. I'll be back with better food for you. And if that fucker hurts you, I'll shoot his sorry ass and fling that bag of bones over the edge with his shotgun to boot."

The dog nosed his palm and then stepped aside. Quivering from exhaustion and pain, he bravely wrapped his good arm around the stalk, and stepped into the plant, slipping down the first few feet, barely hanging on. The sun appeared suddenly, bearing down on him with a blazing ferocity. The rest of his descent was a long, full-lunged screaming, slip and slide to the bottom, finally falling into a heap onto the desert floor. Somehow he was able to wobble to a standing position, and check the gold in his belt. "Fuck you, I'm alive!" he hollered to the top of the tawl. Jack began to stagger back to Foison, aiming for Evonal.

Once Jack got to the old highway, a car immediately stopped, the passenger window rolling down smoothly.

"Hey, buddy," the driver called, leaning across the seat. "You look hurt bad. What happened?"

"I took a tumble. Rock climbing."

"You need a doctor like right now, man," the driver said.

"Aw, I feel all right. I'm almost home. I just live in Foison," Jack said, flapping his good arm toward home. The car shifted into the parking gear. The driver—the kind of young guy that looked like that ubiquitous picture of Jesus with the sacred heart burning out his chest—was out of the car, and before Jack could process events, had him by the arm. Jack noted the guy's worn sandals, his long dusty toes.

"You're in shock, buddy. Foison's the other way. Let me help you get back there." He opened the passenger door, shoved the front seat forward. "Why don't you climb into the backseat where there's more room for you, and settle in. I'll give you some water and take you to the nearest hospital," he said.

After Jack squeezed into the backseat, he guzzled down the bottle of water the gentle-voiced man gave him and leaned hard into the seat.

"You OK back there? Need more water?" The man's light-filled eyes searched his from the rearview mirror.

"I'm good. I'm pretty tough," Jack answered, but the words caught in his throat, making him cough. The car began moving forward at a high rate of speed.

"You'd have to be, walking around the desert like that!"

When he caught his reflection in the rearview mirror, he could see what he meant. The wound in his head gaped like a pair of bleeding lips; his eye was bruised and swollen shut. The impression of the boulder he'd slept on was still pressed into his swollen cheek, making his skin look pitted, like a colorless, rotting orange. Looking down, his shirt was torn, smeared with blood, and mud; he could only guess what else. His knees stuck out of the rips in his jeans like two scraped-up, bald-headed men, old, old guys the both of them. Wedged in as he was, he couldn't see his boots, but his feet throbbed inside of them.

"Hang in there. I'm flooring it, man," the driver said he shoved the tiny car into gear.

Jack laid his head back and listened to the calming sound of a running car engine. "That sound you hear? People will say it's your transmission, but you haven't been rotating your tires have you?"

"Rotate my tires? Ah, no. What were you climbing?"

"Just some fool shit." Jack said, dabbing a finger at the cut on his forehead, feeling something sticky and different than skin. It was a big gash, deep. He wondered if he just touched the bone of his skull, or what else was under his head skin. He shuddered.

At the hospital, Jack's arm got x-rayed. After that, the doctor stitched his forehead, while the nurse cleaned all his other wounds, updated his tetanus shot, and probably because he wouldn't stop howling, gave him something for the pain. The moment Jack awoke, he automatically checked his belt for the gold. The doctor was singing under his breath, *How can you mend a broken arm?* Jack recognized the corny tune so he figured his head was clearing a little, the world came into focus, and he was shocked to find a hard cast on his left arm, freezing it into an engorged letter *L*. This made him misty-eyed with memories of the cloud letters they used to make with shaving cream in kindergarten, back when he believed his life would be easily escapable the minute he grew big enough.

"What the hell is this?"

"You dozed off. I took advantage," the doctor said. "I usually put a soft cast on this kind of fracture, but guys like you almost always take it off, and lose it, or just get too rough with it and that generally leads to more damage, a surgery you'll never agree to have, a lifetime of pain and arthritis and blaming me for malpractice blah, blah, blah—Do you have any questions?"

"You look familiar? Do I know you?" Jack asked him.

"You're from Foison," he said rather sadly, Jack thought. Jack nodded.

"Nurse and I are the med team that goes there once a year to check on things. I believe you call it Vortex Season. About this time of year, right. Any more questions?"

"Ah, yeah, can I have the soft one, to go?" Jack asked. The doctor heaved a sigh that could bend a tree, went to a cupboard, dug one out, and handed it to him. The thing was blue; a papoose cradle except with lots of dangling strips of hook and loop tape, and a flexible bend in the center.

"You also got stitches in your head. The ear will just have to heal with the hole in the cartilage, keep the ointment on it. Pick up the bottle of pain pills at the pharmacy, you're gonna need those. And take it easy for a few weeks. When you're up and moving, keep the arm in the sling to protect your shoulder. Sleep with the cast over your head to keep the swelling down." The doctor lifted his bent arm over the top of his own head, making a half frame of human arm over his round, flat face, before dropping it to write some more on the chart. "We'll check your cast tomorrow make sure it isn't too tight, check for swelling, and if all goes well, cut it off in six weeks, even though I know I'll probably never see you again. You can look for me in Foison in the next few weeks. Don't cut that damn thing off tonight!"

"Where do I pay?"

"Just follow the nurse."

Jack paid $100 for the huge bottle of pain pills; was astonished at the hospital bill. He paid in cash, counted what he had left, and called Trong Tri.

By the time Jack got back to Foison it was late the next night, he was driving a brand new truck, and in a box on the floorboard was all the stuff he'd need to get all that fucker's gold in a couple of swoops, enough food and drink to keep himself going while he healed in private. In his pocket were two twenties, all his bank accounts were empty, but he was not in the least bit worried, there was plenty more gold.

The whole drive home, he wanted to believe the teary-eyed longing for Evonal's company was from the painkillers, and his perpetual, lifelong loneliness. There were others he could be just as grateful to, like the stranger who had gone so far out of his way to save his life; he sniffled over that too. After wiping his nose on his sleeve, he told himself that he was stupid tired, and somewhat broken, but the new truck kicked ass.

■ ■ ■

Chapter 12

"Miss Evon Allison Hartley!" It was Juanita, Foison's only postmaster. Evonal dabbed at her eyes before she turned from her walk to wave at Juanita. Seems like she was never going to get much past her yard these days without someone stopping her. Usually this didn't bother her, but she was still having trouble getting the tears mopped up before they could be seen.

"You got another big fat letter here I need you to sign for," Juanita called, waving the large, thick envelope. Evonal was relieved she wasn't being called on for another serious discussion, over a matter that could now never be resolved to anyone's satisfaction. She gladly waited (it frustrated her, but she knew a part of her was hoping for a letter from the wrong man). Since her family had shrunk down to her, there always seemed to be some business connected to the family estate to make a decision about and eventually sign off. She appreciated that Juanita never told a soul about any of her letters.

"Here we go, my dear," Juanita said, having her sign the ticket before she tore off her portion and handed everything to Evonal. "You OK?" Juanita asked. Evonal nodded, but before she could stop herself, her finger tapped at her heart. Juanita nodded knowingly, cupping Evonal's elbow in the curve of her palm.

"Well, I'm sorry we were so hard on you the other day. Just forget it ever happened. If you want to talk, come on over to the post office. Although with the recent nonsense, I have been getting strangers in after lunch now; usually everything's quiet by three. And I won't never again needle you about renting out your buildings. It's like you said, Foison's gotta follow its path. You spilling more tears? You want to come on over now?"

"Naw, it's allergies. I'll be fine. I just wish none of it ever got started." Evonal sighed. Of course she meant the love affair with that wrong man, as she now called him, but she knew Juanita would take it as regret over the buildings.

"Well," Juanita said. "Don't go downtown. It'll only add to your misery. Just one look the other day and I decided I was drawing my own personal line in the sand I will not cross over there. People on that side will have to come to their boxes and pick up their mail. Period. I expected Foison to behave better than this, but people's people everywhere, I guess. Sorry. Did I just break my promise to you?"

Evonal shook her head, pleased no salty water was leaking from her eyes. Her nose began to run, and she dabbed at it with a fresh tissue from a top pocket.

"Is it so bad downtown?" Evonal managed to ask without her voice quivering.

"Bad? Oh, goodness no! It's pure *evil*! Used to be my favorite view was to stand right here and look out over the tawls, standing guard in front of our mountains. Now I can't stand the sight. Now I see what Sidus and especially Old Sylvia mean. I used to be able to tolerate the handful of them so-called Numinous Vortex kooks, but these kinda crowds is unnatural to the place. I hate to think about what our beautiful nature is being put through all around us by that awful vine. Now my favorite view is that ugly dry lakebed where Frank flipped his car and died that awful day. And I used to hate looking out there. Now, that death place is what I rather look than my beautiful mountains. I predict it's all going to go to hell in a blast before it's all done too. I mean this is Foison Surrounded, after all. What good ever come here that wasn't taken back, and then some?" She paused, Evonal sighed with her. She finished with: "I'd better be getting' back to the post office. Come on by soon, Evonal. You've got friends here!"

Juanita wiped her eyes, causing Evonal to tear up again.

Once she got herself and all the dogs back inside, Evonal sat at the small dining table to read through the letter carefully, and the news surprised her. The family house in Oregon, near the ocean, was hers now. She thought her parents had sold it years before.

Evonal's grandmother had died when she was thirteen, leaving her a fortune, and oh, how Evonal had plotted to tear out of Foison right after she blew out her eighteen candles with no plans to attend college, as her parents had expected. Evonal hadn't wanted to learn anything more from books. She wanted to *explore* the real world. And then her parents died. She was left to bury them here in Foison's cemetery along with Juanita's Frank, and all the ghosts of the dull past. Well now, finally, Evonal was tired of minding old graves.

Evonal kept reading. Seems the best friend of her grandma had been allowed to live in the house until her death. The woman, who Evonal vaguely remembered as Aunt Louise, never married or had children; there was no one else to contact. All the personal things of both women remained in the house for Evonal to dispose of: *Oh why me?* she thought. The lawyer advised her to go look over the house, pack up everything she wanted and to make a decision about selling, renting it out, or moving in. The lawyer advised her to consider its sale very carefully; it had been in the family for several generations. The place, he'd written, was quite special even for Oregon. She ran her thumbnail over and under that last part, trying to remember details of the house.

Evonal went to pack, thinking she'd have to get a rental car and drive the sixteen or so hours to Oregon, or drive down to Los Angeles, and fly back up. Driving would be her preference; Evonal had never flown before, and she didn't care for the uproar of Los Angeles.

After she got the dogs fed and settled in, Evonal walked to the post office, and once she got the door and pulled open a crack, she wiggled her finger at Juanita who came immediately from behind the counter.

"I wonder if you could keep an eye on my place, feed the dogs, walk them, like you did last time. I have to go see about my grandmother's house in Oregon. It's empty. Everyone's gone now. I'll have to leave next week. First, I need to go to town for dog food. The doggy treats all went to Ja—uh, uh, I also have to pick up the supplies for Old Sylvia, Sidus, and what all." Evonal's eyes leaked tears; she let them.

"Hush now, I'll take good care of your babies. You just go on without a worry. You can call me here every day, if you want to check on them. It'd be my pleasure to help you, Evonal. You and your parents have always been so good to me. Well the whole town really. They got us the school bus so the kids could go to high school in Edgecrest instead of the two-room here. I remember when your father sat and painted all of us. Two portraits each so we could keep one for ourselves. Oh, don't cry! I didn't mean to add to your misery, I meant to make you happy!"

Evonal nodded, dabbed at her eyes. "I'll leave next week. I just can't go sooner."

"Sure, sure," said Juanita. "You need some time to digest this. Get yourself set for it. I understand."

"Everything will be in the kitchen. If you think you need anything, let me know and I'll pick it up when I go—"

"Just you go on and get yourself ready. I'll stop by this evening to discuss the details and give them dogs a chance to remember me." Juanita gave her hand another tender pat before she let it go.

"Yes, I'll make us both something to eat," Evonal walked home in a daze, her closed fist fastened over her slowly disintegrating heart.

■ ■ ■

Chapter 13

Because of the hard punch the pain pills packed, once swallowed, Jack could lay down anywhere and instantly start dreaming. Usually they produced more nightmare than calming dream, but the pain was as bad as the doctor promised. The pills were like a friendly enemy and he'd learned not to swallow them until he was in his bed, on the sofa, or lying on the floor. His arm throbbed inside the cast, but not once did he consider driving back to the hospital to have it checked, he was just too defeated to leave his house. Jack lay angled across his bed and took two pills on an empty stomach, feeling them land and fizzle, before quickly pushing his newly warmed blood through every vein in his body. His lids snapped shut.

Inside this careening dream his mother had a good pinch of his underarm flesh, twisting it painfully. On the wooden pulpit the wild-haired minister, a rubber face like the evil old giant, exhorted them to *live the gospel! fight your demons!* The more the minister sipped from his water glass the more frenzied his speech; his tumbleweed of hair showered goat-head thorns over the congregation; they landed like glass confetti. When his mother's hands went to protect her face, Jack busted loose, but before he could pull up the tent stakes, the soft-spoken, light-haired Jesus appeared at his side, saying, "Whoa, buddy, let me take you out of here. I'm flooring it."

Something snapped Jack awake; he was relieved it was still daylight outside, and he was alone in his bedroom. The cast seemed to squeeze harder with each heartbeat. Jack worked his way out of bed, started to walk. Stopped. The house swayed, or his brain spun; he was confused, trying to decide on a direction. The tawl; he thought, a good soak in that lake, and some gold, if only a pocketful, enough to chew on. He needed more money. But, even in his painkiller haze Jack knew it would be suicidal to try to climb the vine. He doubted he could make the walk to the bottom. Exhausted he slipped a dream inside a dream.

In this dream a spike was being pounded into his arm; hammer blows through to his fingertips. Jack flailed against the pain, but nailed to it, he couldn't escape. His eyes clicked open, it was daytime; his throbbing fingers and thumbs were real, and a deep purple. Jack staggered to the bathtub, dropping heavily to his knees, making the floors groan and the house sway he fully opened the tap.

Once his cast was immersed in water, Jack forced his swollen fingers to keep moving while he tore at the softening plaster. When he got the whole sodden mess off, he sat on the wet floor holding his arm in his lap tenderly, like it was a fragile infant he'd just delivered. An hour, maybe more, passed before the pain spread to other parts of his body, starting with round, hard, pulsating knots in his shoulder. He wanted his head to clear, refused to take another pill or slug of whiskey, but the more he thought about it, the faster the pain began to intensify and then spread to the healthy parts; even his calves ached now, his Achilles tendons felt stretched to the point of snapping; the bottoms of his feet burned as if he was standing on a hot frying pan. And then his brain began hammering against his skull, a pain killer hangover, he guessed.

"Christ! Jesus! Aw right, enough is enough, crybaby. Stop your whining, and let's get out for a short walk nearby. Get these fat feet under control, and mashed back down to normal," he told the swollen balloons at the end of his legs.

Walking heavily toward the front door, he vaguely considered changing his shirt, but that was impossible without help. Nauseated, cross-eyed, and sad, Jack put on his sunglasses, got his arm in the sling, and left the creaking house.

Before he could get more than a few feet from the porch, he spotted the flutter of Evonal's long green skirt turning the corner.

"Evon!" he croaked.

She backed up without turning around. "Is that you, Jackie?" She bent in half and narrowed her eyes before running toward him with a smooth, graceful stride that surprised him. "My stars in heaven! What the heck happened this time?"

"Nothing!" Jack attempted to cross his arms, but just ended up cradling his broken wing under his good arm, causing them both to sweat. The buckle on the sling was bearing down on his neck joint painfully. By the time she was standing in front of him, he had more pain than pride.

"Can you fix that clasp back there, Evon? It's grinding against my neck bone."

"Hold still." Evonal gently worked at the sling until the buckle was fastened just below his shoulder and his arm rested at the proper height, neither too low or too high.

"Is that better?"

"Yeah, much," he said. Evonal eyed him carefully, but not unpleasantly before saying, "Mind just standing still right there another minute or two?"

Trying to hold his ground, he stood as casually as he could. Evonal took a couple of steps closer. Jack expected her to embrace him or at least run a soft finger around his stitches, but instead she took a pad of paper and a pencil from her pocket.

"I'd like to capture this on paper, Jackie, hold still. Jeez! Do you know you have a hole in your ear? That's cartilage, it's gotta hurt! What went through there? A nail?"

"A rusted nail. Aw, but not so big though. I got a shot from the nurse for it."

"I would hope so."

The swiftness and accuracy of Evonal's sketching amazed Jack, even though she spent a lot of time on his sore ear, he still liked the attention. "Now the other side," she said, walking around him, flipping open a fresh page in her small book. Another colored pencil was pulled from her pocket and using the edge of her pinky finger and the soft line of the purple pencil, she filled in his fading bruises. This was the time of year when the desert had the most distinct smell, some harbinger of happiness that never quite arrived. His heart fluttered anyway.

"You're amazing, Evon," Jack whispered, thinking the only thing that ruined this experience were those obnoxious rings she still wore.

"I am?" The crests of her cheeks pinked.

"You are. Listen. Where you off to today? Doctor said I should walk. I'll heal faster. Wanna come?" Jack asked hopefully.

Evonal tilted her head at him. "Doctor? Listen to him, Jackie, but don't go downtown neither; the way you look'll just create a new stir in that hornet's nest. You look near-murdered. They'll wonder what you've been fighting for. And they know you. And now there are plenty of opportunist types around, looking for someone to follow."

Follow. There was that.

"What types of people are those?" he asked, curious.

Before answering, Evonal put her pencil to paper. "Foison's buried under strangers these days. You won't recognize it. I've never seen a Vortex season like this, ever."

"Let's go look together. I got sunglasses and a cap," he cajoled, hurt that Evonal shook her head without even considering it.

"Thanks for the invite, but I gotta go take care of something for the next week or so. I'm finally ready. I gotta go while—I gotta make some decisions."

He did not like the penetrating sound of her sigh, the new authority in her voice, or that hint of leaving for good.

"Before I go I'm gonna send Vern over to check in on you, Jackie," she said. "Should I send Mavis over?"

"Why would you do that?" Jack asked, turning away abruptly, his feelings bruised.

"Let your arm heal, Jackie. Just leave things be for a while," she called after him. The lilt in her voice rankled him, and those awful rings! He flagged his good hand above his shoulder in a halfhearted salute.

"You go on! Don't worry about me!" Jack hollered without turning around. Forget the walk; he was going home to eat a few peanut butter and honey sandwiches, and all those bananas Trong Tri's wife said he should eat, plus a can of mixed fruit with the sweet pickled red cherries. He liked it with rice, which he could cook. And the nuts too, and then when he finally felt full he would gobble more pain pills and sleep off some of the misery.

The arm had a week and then it was back to normal. Jack needed to get back to his place on the tawl, the gold was calling him, Little Maid needed some tending, she needed him, and he needed—tears welled in his eyes. He had a dizzy spell that made his eyes roll in his head; he was so confused about what he needed that he almost threw up. Once Jack realized he was walking in the wrong direction, he carefully eased himself around and went back home, fell back into bed, throbbing everywhere.

"Jack! Jack!" The thin voice of Linda Lake filtered through his bedroom window.

At first Jack thought he was hallucinating through the thick fog of pain pills. From the wind blowing in from outside, he thought he smelled dawn. The strong welcome odor of cooked food wafted through the open window and so did her voice, saying, "Jack! Are you in there? Jack?"

"Who is it?" Jack called, trying to sit up. On his bedside were the sunglasses Trong had brought him. He carefully pushed them on his face.

"Hey, Jack! It's Linda Lake! Vern sent me over. He said you could use a bite of hot food. He sent some other things too. You didn't answer the front door."

Jack got to the window, pushed his hands through the opening, and felt the air. It was, as usual, hot and empty.

"Give it here," he said.

"Here you go. It's a lot," she chirped.

He took a box in both hands.

"You can pay me later," she said. "It's about twenty dollars, including the jars of peanut butter and jelly. My sister made them fresh. We saw the truck. Hey! Vern said it was yours and you were home. It's a great truck, Jack. Is it really yours?"

Her voice had a way of spiking at the end of each thought, something he might've found intriguing any other time. Just then the smell of food flooded his brain with images and thoughts he could not make sense of. It occurred to him that Evonal was good to her word about taking care of him. Tears burned his eyes. Then there was some sort of fistfight in his stomach—he didn't know if he was sick or hungry. He started coughing and couldn't stop.

"You OK in there?"

"Hold on!" he cried. Jack took a hundred-dollar bill from his drawer. It was the smallest he had, but he didn't want to owe her, and the paper bill seemed worthless compared to his gold.

"Put out your hand!" he yelled at the window, shoving his own hand out.

"This is one hundred dollars! Do you want me to bring back change?"

"No!" Jack called. "Just bring more groceries. Stuff that will keep. Canned stuff. Bread, bananas, rice, beans, shit like that! I'll pay!" He knew his voice wobbled.

"You gonna come to get it? Or do you want me to bring it to the window?"

"Leave it in a box on the porch!" And then it struck Jack that he might be over worrying this. "If it's hot food, come to the back window. I can't get out just now."

"Astrid said you should put something in the window when you're hungry for hot food."

So that was the back noise he was hearing. They were both there. He couldn't picture it, and this confused him more. Somewhere he thought he heard loud music blaring.

"Do you hear music?" he called, inhaling a small clot of desert dust from the curtains.

"That's the festival starting!" she yelled back, her voice high and thin in its struggle to get over the tuning of guitars.

"Festival? In Foison?" Jack asked the curtain.

"Yes, it's going to be wonderful!"

There was a break in the noise. The quiet burst in the room.

"Astrid said keep your door locked. These people just wander in looking for a place to sleep at night."

"What the fuck?" Jack asked, totally confused.

"So leave something if you want something hot."

"I'll do that. Thanks. Bye, you two! Bye!" Jack set the box on the bed, his insides twisting. He went directly to his front door and for once was grateful that Mavis was such a paranoid she had installed a series of locks. The problem now was finding the keys. The back door was nailed shut, but he couldn't do that to the front door every time he left. Resting his head against the back of the sofa, Jack wasn't sure if he was awake or hallucinating. A cool mist swept over him, and the pain left his body as Jack dropped into another dream.

Before he got to the top of the tawl he heard the dog whining. It kept him thinking he would get to the top when he was ready to give up and get down. Jack had to stop. His whole body vibrated, his back ached. If the dog was trying to hurry him, it was no good. When he finally dragged himself over the edge he couldn't move. The dog hopped to him, sniffed every inch of his injured arm, leaped away, and began spinning circles, letting a high-pitched whine escape every time her eyes met Jack's.

"Shhhh, shhhhh, calm down, girl! I'm good! I just smell bad from the pain. Otherwise, I'm good," Jack called. With sweat dripping into his eyes and his quivering body barely able to stay fastened to the vine, Jack paused in his comment to consider how hard he would hit the ground. He did not have the strength to hoist himself fully onto the tawl. Using great care not to tip himself off his perch he worked the lid off the huge jar of peanut butter and set it on the tawl. "For you Little Maid. I've been worrying about you. I know dogs like peanut butter."

Just as Jack would have done, she stuck her nose in and licked at it until it was clean.

"There, you go. Plenty more where that came from, girl." Jack whispered.

The dog spun circles again, disappeared, and eventually came back with a leather ball that he dropped near Jack, an obvious gift. He could smell the gold dust, and even in his delirium reached for it, pulling it to his chest while he panted. His broken arm throbbed painfully while the blood pulsed through it, but he managed to use it to pocket the small sack of gold while his good arm kept him secured to the vine. The big yellow dog whined worriedly. Jack reached to pet her, but she snapped at his hand before sticking her nose into his armpit, and pressing there, like she was nudging him away. Before he could make sense of it the sound of a rifle blasting off a shot startled them both. In that split second she leaped at him, sending them both over the edge.

Jack held her in his arms, certain she risked her own life to save his. But now they were both precariously suspended above the earth. The dog frantically pawed for the edge, and when Jack gave her a push he only stayed put long enough to see she'd made it back onto the tawl, before the illusion of safety was torn from his mind by his swift descent through the sharp, slapping leaves. A perturbed Old Sylvia wielding her shotgun flashed before his eyes; Jack felt helpless, and terrified in the face of *her*. The rest of the way down images of Evonal flickered through his mind. Most disturbing was the sound of Evonal's truck screeching its brakes. There was a long clarifying moment when Jack realized exactly what his life should be: married to Evon, taking care of her and the big yellow dog in a cozy house surrounded by trees and water. *Grow those delicious tawl berries in the garden, they will take*, a strange voice whispered directly in his ear. *Make a place that would satisfy her soul*; he was completely lost. Images like that tumbled on and on.

Hitting the ground was a relief.

When Jack finally awoke, he was sprawled on the floor of his bedroom covered in blood and gold dust. The rich scent of peanut butter seemed to be everywhere. A open jar of it was still by his bed. Getting up on his good elbow he could see he was in his undershorts, the sketch Evon had given him was crumpled in his hand. On the back of the paper he had actually scribbled the words: dog food, dog medicine. Jack could not remember the last time he had written anything, or if there was even a pencil in the house. A battered pencil lay on the floor. There were several gold nuggets on the floor. His fingers seemed to go to his head on their own, digging under his tight curls, marching around his scalp, finding only a deep scratch, and coming away with blood. The splotches of blood on the rug came from all the thin slashes on his body. He stank like the vine. After that, everything in his memory seemed to be thick lint.

Crawling on his good elbow, he got close enough to look under the bed. The few pieces of gold he kept for chewing on and turning in his hands were there, untouched. Jack added the nuggets to the stash. Once it came to him what it was, he added the leather bag of gold dust and hid everything in the box again. Falling back heavily, he thought he could remember flashes of the big yellow dog licking his face. Jack eased himself to a standing position, staggering into the bathroom where he was astonished to see the plaster mess was gone, but he didn't have the energy to go to the trash bin to look in there. After a shower, his insides quivered at the thought that he'd gone up and down that vine wasted on oxycodone. Or that he was doing anything outside the house in a drugged sleep. His arm didn't feel worse. The old bruises were tinged in yellow, but now his jaw was swollen and bruised. The line of broken skin under the old stitches appeared to be sealed closed, but the stitches themselves remained. The last thing on his list was drive to the doctor's to get them snipped out.

In the medicine cabinet he found a tiny pair of rusted nail scissors. Using the mirror was tricky, but by blocking his wayward jabs with his free hand, he eventually he got them out, dropping them into the sink, like a dozen dead flies.

Jack sat down naked on the floor, and even as he planned his next trip—sometime after he'd recovered, a time he could not imagine—he was thinking how that place would certainly kill him before he stole all the gold.

■ ■ ■

Chapter 14

Skookum peered through his binoculars at Foison Surrounded, wondering, not for the first time, what it would take to get their attention. Seemed like fun was brewing, and there he was helpless to help stir up an angry hornet's nest. The thought occurred to him that sending a bomb would be as easy as putting the catapult back together, and hurtling it so far they'd never guess where it'd come from. Skookum wanted to cause confusion and calamity, but he didn't want anyone on his tawl to see where it came from. The idea tickled him until he laughed so hard he had to take a piss, so he did. That left him feeling parched, so he grabbed up one of his bottles of moonshine, chuckling before he had a gulp.

"Get on there! Let's go rustle up some trouble, you mangy mutt!"

There wasn't any reliable way to judge time, but he'd got the sling up and going before sundown. Just to make sure it would cause a good ruckus when his bomb hit ground, Skookum added three gold nuggets to some twisted rusted bolts, broken glass, some sheets from on old ledger, a burnt matchstick, a torn-off piece of old newspaper, and he tied it closed with an oil-soaked rag, which he gleefully set on fire. Nothing started mayhem better than an old fashioned gold rush. He wrapped it all in some old hide, tied the ends shut and launched it, hoping to hit a human head, if possible. Once that was launched, he went to get a drink and go about making another bomb. He planned to give it time before he looked to see how well it went off. The fire went out in its first ten feet of flight. It made it inside Foison's boundaries, but no one was the wiser, not yet.

Jack wobbled on swollen feet, catching himself just as he pulled on the knob of his front door. Crazy fool, he thought. *Asshole. Assclown. Asswipe. Asshat.* He was all the *asses*. What was it about that place that he could not resist? He pressed the heels of his hands onto the sides of his head. He could not go back there like this, it would kill him. This time Jack nailed his front door shut.

The next time he awoke was inside a familiar cave, a place well known from a strange epoch that had occurred during his senior year of high school. In his right hand were a few sticks of dynamite. He could smell the sawdust and nitroglycerin the red tubes were packed full of. In his left hand were some ancient firing caps, the small spools of wick, all easily ignited by a match, just like the kind found in the best cartoons. Dynamiting was something he had intimate knowledge of. For a few weeks Jack worked with a handful of strangers blasting open caves in the hills. For a time these man-made dugouts were occupied by a group of crazy survivalists practicing drills. That was until summer came. Desert heat and lack of water will defeat any army no matter its cause or determination. The good people of Foison drew in ranks and stayed out of sight until the group packed their firearms and rations and left, never to return.

He carefully laid the sticks back in their wood box, out of reverence for their potential, not fear that they would go off. The blasting caps he put beside the box because he could not remember where he'd found them. These two were always kept separated, but Jack could care less for the safety of the creepy place. Anyway unless someone connected the two, strung and ignited the fuse, the explosives would remain dusty and impotent.

Already exhausted from just the thought of staggering back home, he tried to piece together what had happened this time. The last clear thought was in the kitchen over a cup of black coffee and soft bananas. His thoughts would travel only in one loop. Jack had wanted to end the constant, constant thought of climbing that vine. No, it had become more than a thought, it was now an impulse he could control when he was awake, but not when he was asleep or stoned. Jack knew he had intentionally gone for the dynamite, but he did not know why, exactly. And it actually terrified him to think he might've blown up his only way up the tawl *in his sleep*. It was apparent even to him that he was of some kinda crazed split mind these days: one half trying to save him from the impulses of the other half. The sides of his tongue stuck to his teeth. When he moved his tongue it felt like a roll of sandpaper inside his mouth; he needed water. Jack crawled out of the cave as best he could, craving gold.

■ ■ ■

Chapter 15

Evonal had driven her old truck to Edgecrest, where she'd rented a car to make the long drive. Driving a new car with power steering, windows, and something called satellite radio made her feel like a completely different person; her shoulders seemed to move more freely; she swiveled at the waist whenever she turned, light and free, her hair flying. The longer she drove the more distanced she became from her life in Foison; she could've changed her name and settled into the quiet car, driving away forever. Soon, the thick forests lined the freeway, overhead the clouds were as constant as the mountains, and even though she had maps she was able to drive to the house by memory. The miles slipped past, and then there it was, just as she'd remembered. She drove slowly down the long driveway, parking under the portico at the side. The house was an odd mix of styles, built solidly with a roof made to siphon off rain. Family legend was that the original house was only three rooms, with an outside kitchen. And then the next generation built another room, and once, during some sort of feud, a separate house had been built off to the side, and another room was added to it, making a shambling community of distinct abodes until finally the family had money, and an architect was hired to build it all into the one grand house, blending the exterior river rock with the perfect lines of unpainted clapboards. If it were true, the expansion was seamless. There was a cistern built into the house, Evonal remembered her mother showing it to her, but she had no idea if it was still used to capture and reuse the rainwater. It probably was. In the damp air her skin began to feel fleshy and smooth.

The key easily turned the lock. It was all still there, as she remembered it. As the attorney had said, her grandmother's house was filled with all the familiar furniture, but it was cold; she undid the sweater she'd tied around her waist and pulled it on. The entire house had wood floors the color of coffee, an anchor for the translucent color of the walls. She took her shoes off and walked barefoot through the house. Floors this old felt almost haunted. Babies had been born in this house, learned to walk on these very floors. People came and went, danced, shuffled their feet, crossed from room to room. They lived in this house for over a hundred years. The walls may have been just as old, but they weren't worn in the same way. The floors bore the people, as the sinks held their hands.

"Grandma!" Evonal called like she did when she was little. The sound of her voice settled into the furniture and rugs.

There was a blue sweater folded over the back of the sofa. She lifted it up gently. Soft as a kitten, it had tiny pearls stitched around the collar in a delicate pattern. Evonal studied it for a minute before she laid it back down and went to the kitchen, a capacious room with sixteen large windows where upper cupboards would usually be hung. Because it had two enormous pantries the cupboards were all below the countertops. The bead board island in the middle was at least fifteen feet long, and Evonal knew it was filled with every imaginable pan, gelatin, and baking mold. Real cooks worked here; every meal was prepared in this room for the family, including snacks. The old pale green-and-white squares of tile remained the same; the cracked ones were never replaced. The sink, large enough for her to sit in, was bone dry, while outside it poured rain. Evonal didn't bother checking the faucets, or refrigerator, or any of the cupboards. The electricity, water, everything was left on. Standing in that kitchen, she knew she never wanted to leave the old place. She could put a bed in the kitchen and still have more room in there than her little house in Foison; more room inside, the house, more room inside her mind. "Foison Surrounded," she said it out loud. The name sounded like the beginning of a limerick in this kitchen.

Impulsively, she wished she could show this place to Jack; him and his battered body and soul would benefit from this house. She could picture him lying across the sofa using that blue sweater to cover his face, as he liked to do sometimes with his T-shirt to get the light out of his eyes. Whatever he was doing was bound to kill him, she thought sadly; it'd be good to sweep him outta there. Not that he'd ever leave Foison. Not that she understood anything anymore.

For years the two barely encountered each other, let alone became anything like friends. What happened to change that?

Evonal shivered in the damp cold. There was a panel near the pantry that she went to and opened, and without thinking, she turned the heat on and closed the door, like she'd done it every day of her life. The old house hummed, she began to relax.

She went upstairs to her mother's old room, and once she made sure everything was exactly as she remembered, she looked out the window. The rose garden was below. In the summer, when the weather was perfect, they ate lunch there. Beyond that was the water pond, and berry bushes, and green upon green upon green in all textures of growing flora. The house and garages—converted stables—sat on several acres of land. There was an orchard of fruit trees somewhere, and another garden with an odd metal fountain made by a local artist from the beat generation. She remembered her mother talking about it. If it was still there, she would find it eventually.

This was her home if she wanted it, and she did, but wasn't this a house for a family? That wrong man always talked about getting married and having children, and she thought about how his large, squat, dimpled faced family had welcomed her with open arms, but that was his patter, she told herself, it was how he got over on women like her. And even back then, when he'd proposed marriage, she'd laughed. Now, she chewed the edge of her thumb, thinking if she had brought her dogs, she never would go back.

A bird landed on a bush outside the window, pecked at something before it flew away. The rain continued its patter without stopping. This was a house open to the world. The many windows framed the outer world like works of art. Here the plants had flat, soft leaves instead of the desert's modified version, the cactus needle. Vines grew naturally here, and did not entice people to make moonshine out of their fruit. Here was a fenced-in yard the dogs could run around in without supervision. The sound of the ocean roared at the front door. There was a river nearby, if she recalled correctly from her child's-eye memory. They used to sometimes go to a cabin inside a thickly wooded mountain area to hike and pretend to be the original natives. It was rugged, like camping in a wood tent, really. There, in those woods, life emerged from every corner. Trees grew tall, unafraid of the merciless sun, certain of the replenishing rainfall. But it was the ocean she thought of, mostly the beach, where sand was regularly flooded by cold, salted water, the color of steel, teeming with life from its surface to the very deepest, frightening, unknowable depth. Perhaps she would learn to sail; she could picture herself on board, scrutinizing the star charts, getting stung by salt spray instead of sand.

Evonal had replaced her practical pocket dresses with an old faded blue shirt, a jacket and jeans for the trip. They were probably ten years old; the regular uniform of Foison, she realized, too late. She went to her mother's closet, utterly delighted that some of her old clothes still hung there, just as she remembered them. There was a range of styles.

Her mother had been born in 1949. Evonal was born thirty-eight years later; she still had time, she thought, laughing at herself. It wasn't impossible to imagine anymore. Here, life thrived. And then Evonal wanted to try on everything her mother ever wore, and maybe even take back with her what she felt good in. The clothes fit her perfectly, even the yellow lace wedding gown. She kept it on while she searched the rest of the house, barefoot, and once that was done, she put on one of her mother's tulip skirts and over that a mismatching sweater with huge orange flowers and cowl neck, a product of the 1970s. Downstairs, Evonal pulled on a parka from the mud porch and the pair of rubber boots that fit her, grabbed an empty bucket and shuffled to the beach, ready to dig some wet sand in the cold, pouring rain.

When the sun hit its zenith, Skookum stood ready with his binoculars, searching Foison for signs of some fool what discovered his bomb of gold nuggets and was digging to China for more, certain to eventually turn Foison upside down. Nothing. This irritated Skookum. Foison was crawling with Numinous Vortex idiots these days; he didn't understand why he hadn't hit any. Already he'd tried sending out a stinker and a smoker, but he didn't see any signs of trouble from those either. It was hard to set fire to such a dull desert, unless he could get it to land on a dry roof. In frustration, Skookum put down his binoculars, adjusted his sling, loaded another small sack of shrapnel and hurled it out over the desert floor. As quick as he was, he couldn't get to his binoculars fast enough to see where it landed. And then his belly roared, but he wasn't about to give up. All this required was more thinking, a bit more Skookum ingenuity. The dog had already anticipated a deadly tantrum, so she took refuge in the very same cave Jack had fallen into, and once safely inside took special joy rolling in his scent.

■ ■ ■

Chapter 16

This time when Jack opened his eyes he felt unusually energized. He had a sense of healing, and a craving for cooked food and casual conversation with his neighbors. There was no unaccounted for gold, no added bruises or broken bones, no secret hidden messages on the backs of any kind of paper. At least none that had emerged yet. As he dressed, he did a rudimentary check of his body, finding no new injuries. There were no more blasting caps, except for the one he'd found in his hip pocket right after he had awakened from the cave. Then he set aside, strangely fascinated with it. Oddly, it seemed like a link to something. No matter. He was pretty certain he hadn't returned to the tawl or any other place in his sleep.

Time had become something different now. Jack had been living on the fringes of Foison, using the old routes to get out and walk a little while he healed. Under the cover of deep night he'd driven himself to town to get his own groceries, and taken care to hide his truck so no one knew if he was home. The pain pills were reluctantly tossed into the town incinerator, but they were gone now. These days he'd gotten used to the sight of Old Sylvia gliding by, waving at him, and even the occasional glimpse of Mavis shaking her head with disapproval. He was grateful she had kept her distance. With those exceptions (he knew those two old women were following him for reasons he did not understand; no one else gave him a second thought), he'd skillfully avoided everyone and everything Foison, but now he felt ready to face the familiar pack. First he peered out the bedroom window to be sure his yard was empty. On the surface, it all looked like it was supposed to. He got ready to go out into the open, looking forward to it.

Before leaving the house he stuffed his pockets full of all the cash he had left, all small bills, but they made a thick stack. Jack needed to see if he could tempt Vern into helping him with the house. A thick stack would seem more considerate to Vern. And then because he thought it might also help make his case, he tucked the soft cast under his aching arm intending to wrestle it on as he walked.

Outside he only got as far as the road before he heard the roar of Evonal's truck engine.

Smiling, he turned quickly and flagged her with his good hand. She pulled over, got out, dressed in yellow lace, and was striding toward him with uncharacteristically springy steps. The last time he saw Evonal he thought she looked flush and peculiarly out of sorts; now she displayed an uncommon giddiness. Although her arms were dropped at her sides, her fingers—still garnished with the hideous rings—rippled on the air, playing some invisible tune on an air piano.

"Hey, how ya doin'?" He asked. "I thought you were going somewheres."

Evonal hurried to him. "I just pulled in. It's been almost two weeks since the last time I saw ya. You're looking better, I see. Your color is almost normal. You can still pull a pretty good smile."

The sunlight radiated from behind her, shading her face. Jack reached for his sunglasses and found them already on his face.

"How'd it go for you?"

"I've made up my mind to be sure," Evonal said shifting her posture, but he wasn't certain what it meant. "Just how have you been getting along?"

"A couple of deliveries from the Lake sisters kept me alive," Jack said.

The ease between them shifted.

"I got some things to do." Evonal turned away.

"Maybe before you go, you can help me get this contraption fixed to my arm." Jack dangled the soft cast. Evonal wrapped him in it without a word.

"You take care, Jackie. I'm on my way to a different future," she replied with an odd quiver in her voice.

This time Jack walked away; looking back several times, he heard the truck start. He could imagine where she'd disappeared to, and although she was a free woman, he wanted to kick something at the thought of that big, fat cigar-smoking dick, diddling with Evon's tits. Or that she may be getting married. *Shit!* Next, he was haunted by the image of the sticks of dynamite in his hand. He didn't know why. He wiped his sweaty hands on his pants.

And then she pulled up next to him, leaning out the truck window.

"Want a ride, Jackie?"

"Where, to my future?"

"You have a future?" She laughed.

The future, he thought. The future. It didn't matter how much he thought it, the word was more an excuse for everything he didn't do. There was no sense to its meaning at all.

"I'd like to walk, Evon—"

She drove off before he could finish his sentence.

Catching his breath seemed to take him a long time. There were a few hours left of sunlight before he could get back to the tawl.

Jack went the long way to town, traveling by way of Vern's, thinking he could stop by and make a deal about fixing the house, or at least get some idea what it would cost. From across the highway, he watched someone with the same general size, shape, coloring, and posture as Vern filling an enormous bucket with water as he whistled an almost violently happy tune. This was the brother, he surmised. The man certainly didn't seem overly peculiar or anything like unhinged, but considering his competition here in Foison, that really wasn't a big blue ribbon. There was a crowd of children gathered around the well, the last thing Jack expected to see. The children were all in faded shorts, oversized T-shirts, and even the boys seemed to be shod in brightly colored plastic shoes, shaped much like the Dutch used to carve from wood. No socks on any of them; kids were lucky these days. They were in various heights well under five feet, every one of them had a hat on, and he could smell the sunscreen from across the highway. Some pleasant remembrances lingered and moved on, and then so did he. He'd catch up with Vern later. There were other things that he needed to take a look at first, and although the cast was gone, and his arm hung heavily in its sling, the rest of his body seemed to be reviving.

He was shocked by the carnival-like atmosphere that seemed to have sprung up overnight in the once dead town. The smell of ripe melon hung in the air; a severe odor that made him crave dark, bitter ale. Crossing the highway wasn't the easy task it once was; cars, trucks, SUVs tortoised slowly down the highway; some tugged trailers that were larger than his own house. Many seemed to be in no hurry to move at all. Everyone else seemed to be looking for a place to park. The gas station with its single ancient pump was stuck into the hip of a truck, filling its tank with the old-fashioned loud *ping-pings*. At some point in the last two weeks a tanker must've come to refill, and he'd missed it. He had to stop and rub his chin. With all of his nocturnal wanderings it was a miracle he never got run over. Then again, maybe he took an alternate route: maybe he'd again traveled on the slick surface of a crazy dream.

Jack strode quickly to what was considered the center of town. All along the way strangers greeted him as if they were his personal friends. "Heytherehowyadoin!" A twiglike man shot a two-finger salute off the brim of his cap. Jack nodded. He frowned at The Arbor, where there were dozens of people gathered around the tables eating and sipping on drinks with straws. It had grown the expanse of three power poles, making two enormous hammocks of shade. This time he recognized the plant immediately. His lip curled, his stomach tugged.

Jack hurried himself along to the row of once abandoned buildings that were at the center of town. They hummed with life and although the old wood sideboards remained dull and worn, there were bright new signs hung outside each doorway. He pulled at his chin. When Evonal had mentioned letting the town use the buildings, he didn't take it so literally, and nothing she'd said earlier prepared him for this. He'd no idea it had gone on like this.

Ahead there was a line of women wearing brightly striped tops and white sunglasses the size and shape of small toilet seats. Children were everywhere, clinging to their moms' hems, or eating—amazingly—ice cream or with chins tilted skyward, whining about something. Slump-shouldered, harried men were taking orders for, or returning with trays of food to their families. Jack wove around them, heading straight for the door marked, "The Lake Sisters' ~ Dessert in the Desert!" painted in wavy block letters in feminine purples, pinks, and sparkling silver. There were other distracting blotches of color in the corners, reminding him of sponge painting in kindergarten. The crowd parted for him, he felt suddenly enormous. There came an exasperating moment when Old Sylvia stepped into Jack's path, but she didn't block it, only gave him sort of a half salute, her bright eyes bearing down on him. After that he spotted Mavis too, so he went over and pressed another bundle of bills into her hand. It disappeared into her pocket and she let him pass without comment. Of course her glare said it all.

Inside the building Jack was surprised at the change. Instead of being slapped together and slipshod, like he'd expected, it was well built and finished like any other town eatery. The big space of the old depot had only been loosely divided into individual stores, which all flowed together with a zigzag of countertops that ran almost the entire length of the first floor. This was a huge building, he thought, tilting his head back. He recalled the paintings, Evonal's parents. Here was what made her different from the rest of Foison, Jack thought, somehow in awe of her.

Overhead, enormous fans lazily turned, but the breeze they stirred was too high up to cool anything but the broad beams. The assorted people in line were either tugging at their shirt collars, or blowing air down them or fanning themselves with anything that could stir a breeze, but no one left empty-handed.

At the largest, busiest counter, pretty Linda Lake with all her golden perkiness was busy reaching into the glass case retrieving the sugary baked goods people were pointing at.

"Hey, Jack, You're outside!" Linda called, fluttering her hand at him from inside the cookie case.

"Yeah, hey!" he responded, but turned to find the exit. The place made him sweat.

Behind him a few steps was Linda's sister, Astrid, dressed in her usual flurry of scarves and flowing skirts, busily dusting off an array of candles lined up row after row on wooden planks held up on each end by wooden folding ladders. Several tourists were holding the waxy replicas of the Numinous Vortex, studying each carefully. Astrid, in her flowing garments, was telling someone how she made the candles. An odd thought about Foison struck Jack just then. There was now a butcher, a baker, *and* a candlestick maker. There was a ferry too, if he counted Sidus's place. Fairytales, limericks, nursery rhymes; not stuff for Foison Surrounded.

Jack turned back around to watch perky Linda Lake with a blatant intensity. He pushed back his sunglasses to get an unfiltered look. These two seemed to somehow hover lightly around Foison, never quite fitting in. Desert butterflies, Vern called them, but Jack could never read his tone. The two sisters showed up one day, at their aunt's funeral, and surprising everyone, moved into her old bottle house. Colorful birds for that drab town—all of Foison imagined them on some sort of prolonged vacation, but never as permanent residents, and yet they seemed to be here for the long run, making a living now too. His hand covered the thick fold of bills in his front pocket.

Again, she caught his eye and radiated her golden essence toward him; her cheeks blushed a warm pink, she batted her eyes and smiled like a baton twirler about to make the big catch. Normally, he would leave it at this passing glance. But now he had cause to reassess. Her golden hair was braided and wrapped like a crown at the top of her head; she looked dipped in sugar.

The idea of a princess putting him through his paces gave him pause, when there was never a time in his life when he ever wanted a woman to play hard to get. Now he couldn't wait to see how a princess actually put a man off. Jack had the foolish notion that she was a virgin. Jack watched her tiny hand encased in a nearly invisible plastic glove, flutter, hover, and capture small and frilly decorated cakes that she flicked inside a filmy bag with ease. Their eyes met again for the briefest moment, in which she pulled up her lips into a tiny V before looking away. He thought he had enough for one of her cupcakes anyway.

He walked to the front of the line, "Hey, Linda," Jack said.

"What happened to you?" she shrieked with a kind of amused giggle.

"Knife fight," Jack replied.

The mouths of all the onlookers gaped, but no one gave up their place in line.

He slapped a wad of cash on the countertop.

"What's this?" She squealed, again and again smiling at him with her perfect row of pearly teeth.

"I want everything," he said suavely. Princesses adored gold, everyone knew that, and Jack had gold. "Put it in a bag. To go."

"I can't sell out now! I would have to shoo everyone out while we baked more—it would upset them." When she giggled this time he almost backed out, frightened.

"When's your break?" he asked.

"'Bout two hours. You want to take me for a drive in your new 4X4? Everybody's talking about it."

"Wait for me out front," Jack said taking the cupcake she held out to him and jamming it into his mouth whole, paper and all. Leaving a ten-dollar bill, he stuffed the wad of cash back into his pocket, while he chewed and swallowed the entire cupcake, especially enjoying the sweet, sticky paper.

Later, when they were parked in his truck, he was disappointed with the ease he got her top off. He'd said, "Take off your top, princess." And in a whoosh! The shirt, a pink confection that matched her cupcakes, was flung to the floorboard. Two lacey swirls cupped her breasts; the fanciest bra he'd ever seen. While Linda seemed to get caught up in giving his earlobes a serious massage between her thumb and forefingers, Jack leaned the seat back, rolled down the window. The wind wafted over his truck making him long for the earthy odor of campfire, lighter fluid, Marlboro cigarettes; the carefree age of seventeen all over again.

They were parked out in the boonies, where he used to go as a teenager to make out. The stacks of rocks and boulders had a way of capturing the sunlight. Heat and glitter, green shoots made it through the cracks. It was such a perfect hiding place behind the half ring of boulders that all the teenagers in Foison had actually trucked in hard dirt to make a solid parking lot and to fortify the mile-long rudimentary road, making the spot unnoticeable from the main highway. The work had to be done under the radar of parents. Luckily, as a rule, the parents of Foison weren't very watchful. The task had been gut busting, but nobody quit. Every time they got a section packed, they clanged shovels—a noisy high five. Chugging a quick beer was a given. His nostrils flared.

Finding real dirt, not sand, was the real work. It all came from Edgecrest, back before anyone gave a shit if you took dirt out of the local park. Burt, Mathey, Stubs, Tenny-Bird—who else? Everyone wore those big belts with trademark buckles the size of a deck of cards. It was like an ongoing competition trying to find the biggest buckle, the next coolest logo. Girls wore them too, with their tight hip-hugger jeans. Girls, Jack thought, girls, girls, girls. His mind flipped to gold, gold, gold, but he managed to work it back: there weren't a lot of girls his age in Foison, maybe Evonal was the only one, now that he thought about it. The girls they partied with all came over from Edgemont in their fathers' faded old pickup trucks. The old high school crowd. Evonal came along once in a while, but she didn't mix with the guys; never paired up with any of them. Not from Jack's group anyway. She was different about everything she did, and she didn't care. From way back, she was always someone who became something like a best friend when they were alone together, but she always broke herself off from him. She became someone he ignored. Now, he wondered how he could make as strong an impression on her as that old joke that was parked outside her house in that boat of a car that night. This was the first time he had a real sense that his life had changed. Forever. And he had a sense of some power over it too. This was like a wet slap on the jaw.

"Jack!" Linda Lake's voice swam to him from a distance, and then her tiny hand cupped his jaw and shook it playfully, saying, "Tell me what you want."

"Uh?"

"Why did you bring me here if you are going to ignore me?" she teased.

Jack realized his sole purpose for getting Linda Lake to go out with him was to escape his own confining thoughts. Now he realized he'd just added something to the pot he ought not of. It tasted bitter already.

"Why don't you take out your braids?"

"Like this?" She giggled, pulling on the nubs of glitter. It was shiny and golden and by all standards, quite lovely the way it tumbled around her shoulders in those kinky springs and curls. Somehow her bra had come off without his noticing. She took his good hand and placed it over her ice-cream scoop of a breast. It was shockingly warm; her heart beat under his fingertips.

"I like it when my boyfriends bring me gifts," she whispered.

"Like what?"

"There's this precious pillow-shaped diamond pendant in the window at Paymein's. It's sitting on a silky nest in the very first window by the front door. The chain is gold and very delicate, like a spider web. Don't you think it'd be perfect for me?" She tilted her head back, so he could appreciate the long, smooth line, and when she petted her throat, it became a strange turn-on, but one nonetheless.

"Gold, delicate as a spider's web."

"Oh, Jack, push the seat back, and let me make you feel really special."

He lowered the back of the seat all of the way down, felt the weight of his own head drop too quickly, making him dizzy, slightly nauseated, and his arm felt like it was a pinned-on substitute. She leaped on him. Jack closed his eyes, and thought of the way Evonal grabbed his hands and squeezed whenever she was on top. The end came quickly. While Linda Lake dressed, Jack had the feeling he somehow missed the essence of the whole thing.

"I got a long night of work ahead," he told Linda, starting the engine.

"You're gonna to think of me, right?" she asked.

"Of course! And get you that necklace."

"With the real diamond. Pillow shaped. Set in gold."

"Quick as all that," he said, trying to match her overblown, off-pitch exuberance while his mind turned on climbing back up that vine.

The roots of Jack's vine pushed at the confines of the water source and realized its limits. There was only so much time to get to something deeper, more reliable. Already the water was running out. These roots were vulnerable. The vine would need to get to a better source. And as surely as it grew toward the sun, so it grew toward the water on the top of Skookum's tawl.

Meanwhile, blind to all that was right underfoot, Skookum fumed and fumbled. After several unsuccessful attempts at blowing the town up, he began hurling things at Foison in an impotent rage.

■ ■ ■

Chapter 17

As the sun began setting, Evonal was laying on the floor of her front room, the dogs playing nearby. The radio was on, and she even sang along, but the effervescent feeling she drove home with was steadily evaporating. She fingered the acrylic fabric of the wildly paisley dress she was wearing, feeling its vague connection to the drain on her optimism. Then she twisted the turquoise rings before polishing the stones with the soft pad of her right index finger. The world was getting away from her again, she thought; like in the nightmare where you can never get the phone dialed or run away fast enough. Seeing Jack when she got back made her feel so confused. Of course he was busy with those Lakes, she'd heard blatant gossip as soon as she arrived at the post office. Tears flooded her eyes, her heart constricted. This was the way of her emotions in Foison: tide in, tide out.

Thoughts of that wrong man began leaking in again too; all the sweet sentiments and buoyant moments began flitting through her mind again. "You and I are birds of a feather, tweetie-bird. We belong together," he'd said out of the corner of his mouth, steering into a wide turn with one hand, squeezing her thigh with the other. It had turned her on; she couldn't lie to herself about that. She started to imagine things she never ever wanted.

The letter he wrote said it all: *it was all a misunderstanding.*

And every time she read it she tested herself to see if she could really believe that maybe she'd been wrong, misunderstood what she herself had seen.

"You are such a dope, Evon Allison," she told herself and then exhaled so loudly, it set her dogs barking. The dogs nuzzled into her side, sniffing deeply. "Hush there," she whispered, stroking each of their small heads, the man's rings rough knobs on each finger. She sat up. It was time to repack her bags, but this time she would take her dogs so she could slip out of town unnoticed. It was time to close that tweetie-bird door forever.

■ ■ ■

Chapter 18

The moment Jack awoke he checked outside his bedroom window for signs of anyone. That afternoon it was the backyard of his childhood: empty and cheerless. Happiness broke over him, he felt pretty good. Jack thought he had been a model of patience while he waited to heal, but he'd had to sell more of his precious gold, to buy dog food, and the equipment he needed to move the gold off the tawl. He drove to Trong's during the night, feeling energized, but lonely. Jack needed Trong to help him come up with a way to get more gold down at one time. Now on his way home, while the odorous dry dog food wrapped itself around him, he felt he'd had it. There was a box of stuff secured in the locked toolbox, the instructions rolled around in his head, step-by-step as Trong had laid out the plan. The long round trip gave him time to think free of

Foison. There was only one rough patch when Trong's wife had inquired after Evonal in that way that women did when they meant to hint at something for your own good. He'd flagged it away with his least nicked-up hand. And she'd politely let it drop.

The string of traffic back into Foison barely registered, his mind was so busy zigzagging over his big plan to claim his tawl. The lake, the dog, and all the gold, of course. Sometimes Jack found himself daydreaming about living up there; this brought a sense of profound peace he'd never before felt, until he thought of the one obstacle: that drunken blind old fool with all his big scary-ass guns.

Linda Lake had taken to tacking notes each morning to Jack's front door. Bright pink or yellow, he could see them from any approach. In his pocket was the folded sheet of Evonal's drawing of his bruised face; on the back his crookedly written store list. He fingered it gently before pushing it back to the bottom.

The note that afternoon invited him to "come on over for something scrumptious." The usual. It was signed with several curly hearts and her looping initials. With a swipe of his paw, he tore the note off his door, wadded the scented, pink sheath of paper, and when he couldn't decide what to do with it, he opened the door and flicked it back inside. He'd been avoiding her ever since that uncomfortable parking incident, after which he'd been going to get his own groceries. It occurred to him that she must have spotted him on the way in and flitted over. His stomach rumbled; he rubbed it sympathetically.

Trouble was, Jack didn't know how to stop Linda Lake. Managing women was never his suit; this was why he usually avoided them, kept to the *anti*-relationship types. Also somewhere in his head he thought he should keep an eye on those two, keep them in full view whenever possible. He didn't trust Linda or Astrid; they seemed to know he had gold, although he wasn't sure how they could know. They were smart. Anyway Astrid was smart. Trong had sold him a necklace that he hoped would satisfy Linda, but now he wasn't certain it would be wise to give it to her. All confusing. He might need company if Evonal was true to her word and left. Jack didn't really believe she would; why would she? All confusing, unwanted thoughts.

He left the truck running while he unloaded everything into his house. The odor of dog food made him crave gold. Jack decided to drive over to Evonal's, to ask her some doggy advice—it was an excuse to see what she was up to—and he was sorely disappointed to find her gone. He pulled his truck it into her carport where it was hidden from view, locked up, and dropped the keys in her hiding place before he started to walk home, turning once to look at the small, white house. Unlike the other houses of Foison, for some reason hers had subtle details worked into every line and corner; it was like the carpenter couldn't bear to stop. Although small, he realized for the first time that it was a particularly rare house for Foison, except now the picket fence was leaning in one spot and a mound of tumbleweeds had gathered like thorny clouds against her small porch. It didn't sit right. And he didn't like that Vern would be tending to it either, although he couldn't think of anyone he liked more than Vern.

After he straightened up the fence, hacked out the ubiquitous rods of bamboo that were trying to get a start, he cleaned out the weeds, raked her yard clean, even moving the sand into swirling designs around her three cactuses. There were three large rocks that he repositioned so they looked more natural. Then, he put the tools back in her shed, and got on his way. Soon the sun would begin to set. Jack jogged home, grabbed his stuff, and got on his way.

He rounded the Bottle Church—it was out of his way, but the sight of it always reassured him. Of what he wasn't certain, but he liked the way it made his heart feel bigger, his head clearer. When he looked up, he was only half surprised to see Old Sylvia appear on the mound of hill in the near distance. The butt of her rifle was tucked under her arm, the barrel pointed down. It looked almost like a crutch. Her free hand sliced through the air as her fingers trilled. Jack had come to realize that she was waving, although he wondered if it wasn't also an attempt to send him some kind of signal. This made him nervous. To keep her from approaching, he waved back by chopping at the air, then he slowed down and backtracked a few paces. There was a good chance Mavis was lurking somewhere in his shadow too. The two women wouldn't speak, but they always seemed to travel as a pair. He stopped, pretending to tie his boots, so he could take a stealth look around. The world was empty, and yet he knew it wasn't. Where was that old twat coming from? Jack asked himself. The thought was rather random, but it occurred to him that Old Sylvia also knew where that stash of dynamite was. This almost troubled Jack, except he refused to dwell. He had things to do now.

Setting the eyebolts into the sides of tawl was easier than Jack had thought it would be, holding the drill came naturally as holding a wrench. Soon he had fixed an eyebolt at the points where he usually had to stop and rest. Because the compound had to set for twenty-four hours, he wore his California saddle, not wanting to waste a trip.

It was a pretty straightforward system, according to Trong; as long as the ends of the cable stayed fastened Jack should have control. The eyebolts would keep the one loop of cable from getting hung up on the vine so the heavy bags could travel smoothly over all the uneven edges of the tawl, on the free line of loop. There was a special clip that could stop the momentum of the sacks, but if everything went to shit, at least they would go straight down and stop just short of smacking the bottom. In theory anyway. Once back on the tawl, he planned to rig pulleys so he could move the heavy canvas sacks of gold to the vine without breaking his back. Jack was stronger than he'd ever been in his life, but gold was heavy.

The sweat ringed his hairline, and by the time he got to the top of the tawl, his muscles were quaking like gelatin; his bad arm ached. Dropping his tools before falling to his knees, he just let go and collapsed to the ground. The big yellow dog appeared from nowhere and began licking his face, and then with unrestrained glee, she leaped into the air, like a cat, landing on her huge paws before rubbing on him and licking his hands. "Gawd! Dog! No one has ever done a backflip when they saw me. Let's go take a swim and get a snack."

Unfortunately he was so single-minded about getting to the lake, he missed all of Little Maid's signals and stepped right into one of Skookum's snares. Fortunately, Jack was too heavy to be dragged off his feet. Unfortunately, he was the perfect size to get flipped into bush of stinging nettles instead. His skin was immediately outraged pressing up a rash immediately.

"Yayyy!" He swallowed the outcry of curse words so hard they dropped into his belly, which swelled, causing him to burp long and low instead.

After three hours in the lake watching the night sky, Jack felt revived enough to swim out and dress. That night, the sky crackled with lightning, turning bursts of air to whiffs of cinders. He found the old crankass standing on a small boulder swigging his moonshine out with one hand, while reaching the other to the sky, daring the lightning to grab him. The rain fell gently for a few minutes. Jack settled into his rock cave to wait out the old goat, eating his lunch, scratching the new rash the strange nettles had just given him. "You don't look so bad," he told the red bumps. When he got bored he went and got some berries. When dawn threatened, and the old giant was still going strong, Jack snuck around and began throwing rocks inside one of the old cabins until the old crankass heard the racket and went in to check it out. Jack moved swiftly to shut the door and barricade him in by using a couple of wood barrels half-filled with rocks, and then he went to grab some gold before he battered his way out.

The gold was gone. There were a few minutes where he actually went blind staring at the empty space. When Little Maid banged into him and pointed with her nose, Jack followed her to a big metal box locked shut by a rusted metal lock. The gold was inside there; he could smell it. While Jack scowled over his bad luck, Skookum groused and sang and howled over old enemies, some old lost love, and then finally realized he was shut in some place he could not define. The force he used to batter against the wall began inching the old cabin off its foundation. It wouldn't contain him for long. While Jack's mind raced, the big yellow dog started digging under the box, backing out only when her nose had a nice coating of gold dust.

"You *are* a good old girl!" Jack whispered. He collected as much gold as his leather pockets would hold, backfilled the hole, reaching the top of the vine at about the same time Skookum broke down the shack and freed himself, crowing like a rooster at the sunrise. The big dog whined and rubbed against Jack.

"You wanna' come?" he whispered. She backed away from him, like she understood.

"You can trust me, girl. I'll take good care of you. You'll have plenty of places to roam. You don't ever have to come back here."

When he opened his arms, he expected her to go to him, but she didn't budge. When he took a step toward her, she shied away, sitting on her haunches an arm's length away, regarding Jack, with her great big smile, her tail swooshing against the ground.

"Come with me, girl!" he hissed at the dog, slapping his upper thigh.

From somewhere in the distance Skookum whistled, sharp and shrill. The dog whined worriedly. She walked cautiously to the top of the tawl, and took a few sniffs, before she turned heel and ran into the dense chaparral, that long yellow tail waving like a flag before disappearing inside the greenery. Perplexed, Jack took a look. The dog had more common sense than he did. Given her physical limitations, she couldn't climb down; there was no monkey in a dog. He couldn't carry her, he needed both hands to get himself down, and he sure couldn't stuff her in his pocket; she was about the same size and weight as Evonal. It was a problem he'd eventually solve, because he was now certain she'd like to go with him as much as he'd like to take her. He climbed down the vine, sinking into the soft sand at the bottom, itching all over. Jack meandered toward home wondering how miserable the new rash was going to make him.

The shots of gunfire caused Jack to recoil and double back. The wind was blowing steadily, but not enough to hide his tracks. Jack stood next to a creosote bush trying to decide which way to get. The gunshots came again in that certain kind of rapid fire that Jack decided it was some asshat at target practice, plinking bottles. From the sounds of it, there was only one shooter.

"Hands up, Jack!"

Jack's hands shot to the sky, the fear shocking his fingertips.

"Keep 'em up there, young man!" Old Sylvia ordered.

"I hope you're kidding me," he croaked. He couldn't actually see if Old Sylvia had a gun on him, but could smell the oil, the residue of smoking gunpowder. His arms relaxed into soft Vs over his shoulders. Somehow Sylvia holding a gun on him seemed normal. He certainly was not surprised to see her.

"Oh, I'm not gonna hurt ya. Go on now, put them down." Sylvia's voice shook, like she might be laughing a little. "What you doing over this way, Jack? I said, put your hands down and turn around. My guns are down."

Jack shrugged and reluctantly turned. Her face was in shadow under an enormous flying saucer of a hat. The holster held two guns, one on each side of her narrow hips. One hand held an old bottle, the other bony hand rested on the hilt of a gun. This was the gun that had his complete attention. He was certain he could sketch it down to the broken nail on her pinky finger.

"You see the damage that vine's caused Foison? Have I been exaggerating?"

Jack nodded, still watching the gun. Her stance and the curve of her wrist seemed to suggest she was prepared to draw and shoot, like the old Western movies.

"Can't you take your hand from the gun?" he whined. She dangled it near her side.

"It's bringing all manner of unwanted persons here. Did you cause it?" she asked, rubbing her fingertips together like they were itching to get that gun again. "Cause if you did, you should help me get rid of it."

Jack shook his head almost violently.

Old Sylvia stepped close to him, dragged something out of his hair. After examining it closely she put it to her nose and then took a small nibble.

"Where you been?" she asked, but this time it wasn't a command. Jack thought he'd heard a quiver of fear in her voice.

"Just out walking," Jack said.

"Listen to me, Jack, I know what can become of a man in these parts. You don't want none of it. You're a good kid, always have been. Stay down to earth."

"I am!"

They stared at each other. Both of Old Sylvia's hands were on her hips like she was trying to decide something.

"Do the right thing, and help me kill the vine. It's settled in the town well, draining it dry. Next it'll be something worse. What is all over your skin?"

For reasons he couldn't fathom, the thought of that stash of dynamite flickered into his mind. Sweat began to bead on his forehead. They weren't too far from his vine, the important one and he certainly didn't want that killed, but of course she would if she found it. His skin began to itch like the fire was beginning to burn under it. It was hard not to scratch it. Resisting seemed to be closing off his throat.

"We could blow up that well. These days everybody has their own well."

"I'm not sure I can help you." Jack scratched at his arm.

"You're the only one that can do it. You have all the qualities."

"Like what qualities?"

"Big, strong, no politics, loyal to Foison. You're about the only person in Foison that can keep his mouth shut. You know how to handle the TNT."

Jack shifted under the rare praise. "Don't you think blowing shit up is usually connected with insane, crazy folks?"

"Maybe I am crazy," Old Sylvia said taking a breath. "But I'm right too. And you know it, don't you?"

Jack scratched a patch on his neck. It was like igniting something, his whole body began itching. He wanted to get out of there. "I'd have to think about it. I got other things on my mind just now."

"Yes, I can see that. Gold fever. I can spot it a hundred yards off. Believe me, it'll lead you to ruin without you ever knowing it. Nothing I say will stop you so before you forget right from wrong, help me blow out that noxious weed! I don't have the strength in this old body anymore." She closed the distance between them and grabbed his arm. "Promise me!"

"I can't promise you anything!" Jack jerked his arm away. "It's something to think about. I got to get going."

"Stay off that tawl, Jack! You don't need gold; it'll only lead to your ruin! You need to set things to right for Foison. That was the place, all the people in it, what kept you alive when your mother refused to! You owe us!" In one swift movement she launched three empty bottles into the sky, and shot three times. Each shot plinked, hitting its mark.

"I never miss," she called out in triumph.

Jack turned to hurry away.

"Wait, Jack! You're gonna have to help me back. I hurt my knee over there. I stumbled on something I didn't see. Look! I can barely move. You can't leave a woman stranded in the desert." She lifted her skirt to show him, but all he saw was a shadow. He had no interest in verifying such things.

"You're not going to leave me, are you?"

The accusation in her appeal sounded so much like Mavis he almost kept going, but then he stopped, went back, and stood with his hands on his hips, studying her. If he didn't get her out of the vicinity she might happen upon the real vine, the important one. His vital connection to the tawl, the gold would be known. Also, no decent human would leave another stranded in the desert like that, especially an old woman.

"Well?"

"You got any water?" The energy was draining quickly from Jack. Old Sylvia reached into the folds of her skirt and produced an old-fashioned canteen of water. Like Evonal, she also had pockets worked into her skirt, but hers were harder to see. Jack drained it and gave it back.

"You got more?"

"Of course I have more!" She started to reach into another pocket.

"I meant for you."

"Well, I'm set for the walk back," she said.

"You got the safety on those fuckers?" he asked.

"There's nothing I don't know about a firearm. Y'er safe as long as I want it."

"That's what worries me," he said.

The sun reached the spot where it began its slow, hot burn through the day. Jack started to sweat, causing the rash from the nettles to begin digging down into his bones. He wanted to run for a cold shower, to get the poison off his skin as quickly as possible, but Jack lifted the old woman into his arms—she weighed less than a blanket. Together they started to trudge home.

"If you won't see to blowing it up, digging that vine out of our well would be nothing to a big, strong boy like you." She started up only ten steps into their journey.

Jack shook his head.

"You were always a good boy, when your mother wasn't around, especially then. I know you want to help. You try to hide it, but you're the helping kind. Everyone looks to you when they need a heavy, dirty job done."

"Look, old woman, I'm only gonna carry you as long as we go in silence," Jack said. Old Sylvia pulled an imaginary zipper across her lips.

They went four or five more paces before she said, "I see no reason why a big man like you can't help me dig—just dig—that infestation out of that damn well!"

"You sound just like my mother—anyone ever tell you that?"

"No. Because it isn't true. Her voice is more melodious, but that only led to her ruin. Listen, Jack, I can tell you things about your past. There are many other mysteries I can solve for you. Ever wonder about your father? There're things you should know. You'll need to prepare for your future. All you gotta do is help me get that vine out. Your father would've done it for me. He would've done anything for me."

He didn't like the mention of his father when Jack had believed there was no such man. Sylvia kept rambling on and on, Jack helpless in the face of it until he smelled the town dump, took a turn toward it, and marched until they stood on the rim.

"You say another word and I'm tossing you in," he told her.

"You aren't going to put me in there. You smelled it; you had to come see for yourself too. It shocks you too. The stench! That's why you walked over here. And just look at this dump. It's almost as big as Foison!" Old Sylvia started to cry, something his mother never did.

"Don't you have your own son to make help you?" Jack asked weakly. This made the old woman howl all the harder.

"Listen, I'll think about it. I promise to think about it. Now stop bawling."

"Take me home, Jack," Old Sylvia howled in a new voice, a kind of giving up, he thought hopefully. Jack walked swiftly toward her place, feeling the handle of her gun bang on his soft belly, the burning rash searing into his skin, the lousy sense of guilt draining every ounce of his energy. Under the burning stare of several strangers, and someone clicking a camera, he deposited her at her front door.

"Come on in, get some beer," she said. "That rash is getting worse!"

But she didn't have to tell him. An odd sense wafted through him, he turned and made for home on a full run, before anyone else could call him. Jack felt eyes on him everywhere.

At home, once he got his gold stashed, he ran and stood under a cold shower with shaking hands, trying to rub off the rash. He could add his odd encounter with Old Sylvia among the dozen he kept having—and wanted to forget.

The rash had been a thousand pinpricks when he got into the shower, but now it seemed to spread into one mass of thick scaly red. By the time he got out, his eyes were virtually swollen shut. Somehow he got dried and dressed blind. Following the hard glow of the brilliant sun, he got himself going in the direction of Foison, banging blindly into solid objects and people. Kids squealed in horror. Something hit him across both thighs. He backed up and veered off into unseen space. Jack thought his throat was closing in on him, his lips felt too swollen to press together. Exhausted, he sat down where he was, prepared to accept his fate. Then he let his body fall into the ground. Someone grabbed him by the arm and shook it.

"Whoa there, big guy, you gotta see to that rash! Did you get stung by a bee?" It was a woman's strong voice. Jack went limp under its command. He thought: I may live.

"What are you allergic to?" she shouted directly into his ear.

"I don't know. I think I fell into some kind of stinger bush out there."

"You look to have anaphylactic shock. Is there someone I can call?"

Jack thought of Evonal, Mavis, even Linda Lake. He shook his head hard.

"Well, I'm giving you a shot of epinephrine, I'm allergic to bees. I carry an EpiPen everywhere I go. From the looks of things, you should have one too. After this we're going to have to get you over to the doctor's. SOMEONE CALL THE DOCTOR FOR HELP!"

"Is the visiting doc here in Foison?" Every so often one of the local doctors came to Foison with a nurse to check on the people, bring medicine, give flu shots, and vaccinations to whomever would take them. Generally they focused on the old frail people, but Jack had gotten his shots too.

"Yes there's a doctor here. He's set up in a tent, like the ARMY. This is going in your thigh right through your jeans. Got anything in your pockets that might break the needle?"

There was a crowd gathering, he could tell by the conversations, their smells. He didn't know if he had underwear on, but Jack stood enough to drop his pants. The shot jolted into him, and then it was gone. His heart began to hammer.

Someone said, "Is that a desert monster?"

Another person said, "I think you should stop taking pictures of it."

By the time the doctor saw him, his eyelids had opened enough for images to barge painfully through. His heart was still slamming against his sternum.

"Just lie on there for a while," the doctor said. His voice sounded familiar.

"Do I know you?" Jack asked.

"I may have patched your arm, although I don't see a cast. You seem determined to break yourself into a million pieces."

"Listen," Jack said with a sigh, "I'd really like to live."

The doctor chuckled. That was the last sound Jack remembered.

■ ■ ■

Chapter 19

Somewhere inside this dreary, near-sleep he heard a scratching sound at his window that was followed by a familiar, high-pitched female voice calling, "Jack! Hullo, Jack! It's me, Linda. You in there? I come to see to you."

Jack emerged from his coma to see the golden crown of Linda Lake's head come through his open window first, but that was all. "What're you doin' here?" he called, trying to make his voice sound pleasantly surprised.

"I saw you go in, and thought I'd bring you breakfast. Just stay in bed while I—oops! Sugar! Darn!" Linda's voice dropped off and her head disappeared from the window. "Don't get up!" This came from outside; Jack waited pensively, hoping he was not turning into the type of person who liked to see how things might unfold.

A minute passed and her head poked through the window again. "Stay there!" she commanded, radiating a quick smile at him. "I want to give you breakfast in bed. I thought this would be cuter, this way, through the window. Your door is always locked. I wanted to surprise you in bed. Wake you. Anyway, this'll work like this too. Just give me a minute. Just settle back and wait."

"I can go open the front door," he said, his brain thinking: food, food, food.

"No! Just lay back! Astrid is here to help boost me in. Just relax and be patient!" Linda's blonde head dropped out of sight, and then it reappeared as a pinch of bright green ass sitting on the sill. Food, food, food, his mind hummed, as he watched her lean back , like a gymnast, touching the floor with both palms before tucking in her peachy knees and tumbling gracefully in. Landing on both feet she sprang up and flung out both her arms, her hands two bright stars tipped in pink.

"*Tahhhh-Dahhhhh!*" she cried jubilantly. Her belly button winked at him from under the tiny shirt she was wearing, its bottom edge barely skimmed her tiny green shorts.

"Hello, Jackie!" she cried, before bending at the waist and leaning back out the window. "Ready," he heard her say, and then from the outside he could hear Astrid's similar voice talking, but he could not make out a word. They were discussing something, and then, he watched her angle an enormous tray through the window. When the tiny vase with the single flower started to tip, he briefly got a glimpse of Astrid as she jiggled through the window enough to help right everything that was tipping over on the tray.

He wanted to ask her what she was doing there, but he wanted the food.

"Wow! What happened to you?" she squealed.

"I had an allergic event."

"You sure are accident prone. Look what I brought you!" Linda called sweetly, the weight of the heavy tray swinging uncertainly in her hands. There was hot coffee on it, his rumbling belly contracted to his spine in fear.

"Yayayaya! Let me save that for you!" He grabbed the tray, righted it. "What's this?"

"That is a dish of our own very special Foison fruit. Astrid made jelly from it."

"No! I'm allergic. Throw it out the window."

"I don't know, Jack. I mean we depend on that. Gosh if we didn't have that vine, Astrid and I would have to go back to the city and—"

Jack threw it out the window, flowery dish and all. Holding the tray with both hands he stepped back until he was once again lying back down on his bed, but now with the thick tray on top of him. He kept it balanced, realizing it felt as light as holding a piece of cardboard level. There was an array of colorful food.

"You don't like the vine fruit?"

"No, I'm allergic to it. Did you see how it made me swell up the other day?" he lied. "I don't ever want it near me again."

"Well, OK. Sure. I'll remember that," Linda said uncertainly.

"You know this thing has gold in it. It looks silver but it must be white gold," Jack said to the tray, really, surveying the dainty, fluffy, lacey food he was certain could never fill him up, but still filled him with joy. Hunger, he realized, was a terrible thing. He thought he might actually eat the tray itself, he was that hungry.

"Doesn't it all look so yummy? Ast—I mean, I cooked all morning for you, my big man," Linda Lake cooed. "Do you like it? It's my way of saying I know you've been busy, but I've missed you! And the truth is, I have so much on my mind these days. Running our business is more work than I dreamed, but Astrid is so focused and happy about it."

"*OooohhhGhhhhh*," Jack grunted before he grabbed the tiny rose out of the vase and ate it whole, washing its delicate bitterness down with the hot coffee before reaching for more food. Linda looked shocked, but then quickly covered this with an approving smile.

"You like to eat flowers?" she asked, as if making a mental note.

Jack stuffed more food in his mouth and grunted. How could he explain to her what he liked? He had no idea himself. His belly roared.

"Here, let me tuck this napkin right here before you spill, my big, hungry man!" Linda Lake seemed out of breath, and excited, but she sounded like she was talking to a baby, or maybe some sort of confused idiot, but he was too hungry to look up to check on her expression. Anyway, he didn't really care; he was both.

"Here, I brought this new hot tea we're making, it's really sweet, so I was certain you would…ooops! Sorry!"

"Yow!" He took a direct hit on the belly. "Ah, OK. It wasn't that hot. Thanks. The tray's good too. Nice I mean. Nice touch. Great food. Tiny, but you brought some great snacks here."

"You should slow down, Jack, you're going to make yourself sick eating that fast. Anyways, I thought I'd feed you some nibbles before you came over for your big meal. Here, let me feed you."

"Naw, too hungry, I might bite off one of your fingers. Did you bring ketchup for these scrambled eggs?"

"*Frittata*. And, um, no, sorry, I didn't think of ketchup on a frittata."

"*Oghgh*, frittata, piñata, whatever; it's food, and I'm fucking starved!" Jack had no control now, the first tiny bite of food opened the hunger switch, something he couldn't turn off even if he wanted. And he didn't want to. She giggled, but he was just too hungry to think of anything but the food. His stomach rumbled so hard it caused him real pain for a very long moment. And then it let up and he gobbled down the rest of the food, falling back into the mattress heavily, not feeling at all full, but no longer starved either. At any rate, he could think of other things; he began to notice the details of her. She went from faint shadow to beautiful female.

"Thanks, Linda, I needed that. You must be some kind of angel or something."

Linda was standing in the center of the room, examining everything with rapidly moving eyes.

"The floors really creak when I walk," she said to the ceiling. "And it's dusty. Maybe I should go grab something from the kitchen and get started here." When she wiped a finger across Jack's dresser, he pushed the tray aside.

"Naw, I'll do my own dusting. You're much too pretty to do anything like housework. 'C'mere, kitten," he said, patting the bed next to him. He was pretty certain he could discourage her from ever wanting to bother him again. She leaped next to him, hunkering down on his broad shoulder.

"I think you may need a wife," she purred.

A wife? Suddenly it was imperative to get her out as quickly as possible.

"Aren't you busy? Don't you need to get back to work?" he asked.

"I've come for something that only you can give me. And I'm not leaving until you deliver, Mister."

Jack grabbed Linda and playfully threw her on her back making her squeal, and the house creak too. Linda Lake found the center of the bed and stood on her knees to pull off her tiny top. The bed sagged miserably and when she flopped on her back with a little too much enthusiasm, even with her puny weight, the house moaned, and the ceiling sifted a light dusting of plaster down on them. Looking up at the ceiling with wide eyes, she said, "Get on your back, Jack," and although he wasn't certain, he thought she straddled and dry humped him to see if the house would hold up for the real thing. The house moaned and creaked threateningly, the ceiling let go of another fine coating of white dust, but this did nothing to deter her.

"Is it safe in here?" Linda Lake's voice came out thin, and for once so filled with genuine emotion it caused Jack to find her almost irresistible.

"Probably not. You're safer out of it than in it. That's got to be certainty."

Her face crinkled, but she shimmied out of her shorts. "You live here."

"That time in your truck was fun, but this will be better. Do you want to be on top or the bottom?"

Jack lifted her up off him, got a condom—it took him a few minutes to find one— and once back at the bed, rolled her under him. Linda didn't waste any time.

Every time the headboard slapped the wall before he could brace a hand on the wall, the house shook and creaked. In his mind, Jack viewed every naked centerfold he had ever moaned over. By the time he let go, he was winded from the exercise, not the feeble, half-done orgasm, while Linda was misted with sweat that smelled like cake batter. He could feel a fine layer of plaster dust all over the back of him, and began to feel desperate for a shower, alone.

"What is all this white stuff?" she asked, brushing the plaster from her arm.

"It's desert dust. I could use a screen on the window." He tried not to look up at the ceiling, her eyes were sure to follow his.

"No, I think I was right before. What you really need is a *wife*."

Jack was thinking what he needed was a big yellow dog, a new foundation for his house, and a stack of Evonal's grilled cheese sandwiches with a side of her genuine affection for him.

"Don't you have people waiting to be fed?" he asked her.

"Why yes, I do!" she chirped, getting her clothes on.

Once Linda was finally gone, Jack went and got the hammer and some four-inch nails to permanently seal his bedroom window shut. The nails cruised into the old wood like it was refrigerated butter. About a hundred yards outside the window, Old Sylvia appeared and waved before she marched off. Seeing her at random moments no longer surprised him. It was a small town, and she was another woman in it with a mission that had somehow ensnared him. The old girl was right about clearing out Foison. Message received, he thought. But he had no idea what to think after that. Jack locked up and headed to Evon's to see if she'd lend him another meal.

Evonal's truck was not there, but that didn't mean she wasn't around. He regularly hid his just to discourage visitors, a tactic he would need to employ every day now, he thought wearily. And she would lend her truck to about anyone. He went directly to Evon's back window where he could easily read the message she left on the window in blue marker. *Jack: I'm over to Chrysopoeia. If it's food you need, get the key and help yourself to the pantry and refrigerator. The dogs are with me. ~E* He rubbed his thumb against the letters, clearly they were written on the inside, all formed back in her neat handwriting. Jack could easily imagine Evon standing there at the window writing back on it with no more effort than writing any other way.

At sunset Jack put on his gold collecting belt, and headed out. Once Jack got outside Foison proper, but still a good distance from his tawl, Old Sylvia glided past on the near horizon in an odd kind of getup that glowed around the edges, like she meant for him to spot her. Doubling back, he wrapped around an old trail and struck a new path only to spot her again, this time waving at him outright. This went on for most of the night, until Jack found a good place to ease down into and wait her out. He awoke to the sound of half a dozen three-wheelers, tearing up and down the dunes. Sand encrusted his eyes, the sun was scorching his skin. Morning already. He wouldn't climb the vine in daytime; there were too many freaks visiting the area. Worn and irritated, he dusted himself off and headed back for home.

■ ■ ■

Chapter 20

The bustling town of Chrysopoeia was the one Evonal favored over all the others she regularly visited. It was large enough to have interesting stores, but not dizzying, and it was far enough away from Foison that none of them went there. Its industry was now evenly divided between tourism and the large mining company that recovered a unique, but caustic, mineral from the quarries. From the time she was a little girl, she'd watched Chrysopoeia flourish from a stark company town with only a post office, a school, and a general store that ordered art supplies for her parents, to a place she could go around as a stranger and never be bothered by anyone who recognized her. This always gave her an incredibly happy mood.

Most of the businesses ran down both sides of the major highway. East of the highway, in what were called the Flatlands, were several blocks of small homes—the old company houses—the locals now lived in, remodeled, and expanded as it suited them. In the foothills of the mountains were the luxury cabins used during the rather robust ski season. Adjacent was the Indian gambling casino, a small concert hall, a modern museum of natural history, a lovely natural lake, and parks with several playgrounds.

Of course this town also had Mr. Archie X. Helms, proprietor of the Archie X. Gems & Jewelry Store just a few doors down from the kennel where she now stood, certain she never wanted to see him again. More puzzling, she had chosen to arrive at this odd point in time, dressed like her mother. She was wearing her mother's lapis lazuli necklace, her creased slacks, silk shirt, and a long vest, left open. And for the first time since high school, she french braided her hair, and put on the emerald earrings, feeling as buoyant as she had at her grandmother's house.

"Miss?" The chirpy, young assistant at the Artful Dogger and Pet Hotel broke the spell. All her dogs were seated on the counter, but quivering so nervously Evonal dropped her arms around them, afraid they would shiver themselves right off the slick surface.

"I was asking if this is your whole group."

"They're all I brought with me today," Evonal responded brightly.

The girl narrowed her sharp blue suspiciously. "You haven't left a pet in a hot car, have you?"

"No!" She waved her hands at the small pack of jittery pups, with their bulging, anxious eyes.

"I have to ask if I have the least suspicion. It's a national campaign to save our precious pets from being roasted alive by their thoughtless owners..."

Evonal didn't respond. The girl had an annoying way of swinging her head so her long, beautiful ponytail swished over her shoulder flirtatiously before she swept it back behind her shoulder with an impatient flick of her slender hand—that looked staged.

"I've used your services dozens of times, at least. They'll be here two days at the most."

The girl plucked an artificial flower out of a pot and pointed it at her. It took a moment for Evonal to realize it was a pen attached to the end of the stem by green florist tape.

"Can you write your address on this card?"

"I'll be staying at the Miracle Spring Hotel."

"Nice place. Real comfy beds," the girl said, and then her cheeks glowed hot red. "You meeting someone?" the girl said, quickly, keeping her head bowed.

"Nope." But as she said it, Evonal's skin tingled maddeningly at the thought of running into Archie. Evonal twisted at the rings nervously. Clearly, she was struggling with cross hopes. And now she couldn't remember why she thought it was so important to come. This was not going to be something easy. She considered scooping up the dogs and driving home. She suddenly wondered how battered-up Jack was getting along, feeling just then that she'd abandoned her friend when he needed her the most. But, that wasn't it, not really. Jack didn't need her, no one did. The dogs collapsed on the countertop and dozed off.

"OK," chirped the girl said. Let me take 'em back." She scooped up the dogs like so much laundry and disappeared. "You're free to go!" she sang from the back of the shop.

Dropping her sunglasses from her forehead, she hooked a thumb through the strap of the purse that swung from her shoulder, took a deep breath, and stepped onto the sidewalk with embarrassingly shaky knees. If she couldn't avoid him, she wanted to see him first.

Just three steps out, and she did see him barreling down the sidewalk, coming toward her. He walked like an overfed bulldog, huffing and puffing, his shoulders pushed back by his massive chest. The enormous, half-eaten sandwich he carried was dripping yellow goo, and was no doubt a hot pastrami, his daily lunch. He stopped long enough to slam the second half of sandwich into his mouth, wiping off with a wad of tissues that he then tossed in the trash receptacle at the very spot he had first introduced himself to her. He stopped to fish a cigar out of his top pocket and put a flame to it before he took up his pace again. In a feeble attempt to act like she hadn't recognized him, she turned away slightly, but he'd already seen her; his eyes bounced all over her as he approached. Without warning, her hand shot up a flicker of a wave, before she could get it under control.

"Good day, Miss," he grunted, walking right past, puffing on his cigar. Evonal stared at his wide back. A car pulled to the curb, scraping its tires as it parked. In its window she could see her reflection, a woman she didn't recognize. When she bent down to get a better look, the man behind the steering wheel waved at her tentatively, snapping her back to reality. Embarrassed, Evonal backed off. At another store window she surreptitiously studied her reflection with her sunglasses on and found herself bumping into the glass. Not quite drowning in her own image, but still she liked looking like a woman that didn't attract the likes of Archie X. Helms.

She turned and called after him.

"Archie!"

Evonal prepared her speech.

"Evon? What did you do to yourself?"

This took the wind out of her. She met him halfway, talking before she stopped.

"I came to say good-bye. Face-to-face. I just wanted you to know. You'd best stop driving over to Foison. I'm moving away," Evonal opened her purse, to retrieve a photo and offer it to him.

Archie didn't say anything. When he didn't reach for it she stepped forward and pressed it into his hands.

Something stirred him. He whispered, "We can work this out. You love it here. Let's go get a beer at Foghorn's and discuss this. With what you have we could build—"

"No, I don't have nothing for you to build with. I don't belong here. I certainly don't belong with you. Furthermore—" Evonal's resolve stumbled here. She gave herself a minute to regroup her thoughts. "What do you want to keep bothering me for anyway? You have another girl."

Archie twisted first right and then left before he seemed to decide what he should say. "Listen. You misunderstood. I am true blue, tweetie bird. Let's go over to Foghorn's and sit down."

A woman's voice called, "Hoo-hooo, Archie, where have you been?" She came out of the door of the hair salon, went straight for him, and hooked her arm through

Archie's as if it belonged there. In truth she looked like she belonged with her arm locked through his. In her free hand was a leash attached to the familiar overfed Corgi doing his best to climb up to Evon's knees with his stumpy legs. Evon let a hand drop long enough to scratch its head. This caused him to begin leaping frantically on her leg for more.

"Get down, Pretzel. Goodness, climbing on a stranger!" the woman cried, swiping a hand at him before yanking on his leash. It didn't deter him.

"Pretzel, sit," Evonal commanded. The dog obeyed, his tail lazily sweeping the ground, while his forepaws pranced in place.

"You know my Pretzel?" the woman asked.

So this was her, thought Evonal, crossing her arms. And Pretzel had been her dog, all along.

"Pretzel and I have met before! I'm Evon. And who might you be?"

"Meg," she said. Ginger-colored hair puffed up attractively around her small face, held there by some hairdresser's magic. White pants, orange lipstick, tiny gold slippers. All looked good on her. Evon felt oddly cheered by this turn of events: There was no way but out!

"I'm Evon," she said, bending enough to scratch the dog's head. Pretzel jittered and frantically leaped up for more, most likely expecting dog treats, but she had none.

"Sit, girl, sit!" Evonal ordered.

"Evon? Evon? Evon?" Meg began chanting to herself.

"We're like opposites attracting," Evon said directly to Archie, but he was waving his cigar between the two women like he was wishing it were a magic wand.

"Opposites attracting?" Meg said. "Well that only works with sex! I'm sure you don't mean you and Pretzel?" The woman placed her fingers at the corner of her sunglasses like she was threatening to lift them and get a really good look at Evon.

"There you have it," Evonal chuckled. The sex with her and Archie X. was hit and miss, she thought, but didn't say anything. Sweat was springing off Archie's head; he was having a difficult time getting it mopped off with his bare hands. Smoke plumed from the chewed cigar, but wherever his right hand went so did the smelly thing.

"You two look like the perfect couple!" Evon found herself chirping; she meant it.

"Well, thank you! See there, Archie, we look like the perfect couple!"

"Good day to you all!" Evonal said. She stepped back, turned around. Snapping her purse shut, she headed for the only boutique store in town on a hunt for some more new clothes.

Inside the hotel room, and still exhilarated from shopping, Evonal settled her packages near her suitcase. There was a copy of the local newspaper on the bed, with a headline that immediately caught her eye: *FOISON SURROUNDED GUARDIAN OF THE FOUNTAIN OF YOUTH?*

She read that bona fide scientists had tested a sample of water from an undisclosed source in Foison Surrounded. This was the real juice, the report confided. If it didn't allow you to live forever, it declared unequivocally, it would at least slow the aging process. It was preposterous, of course, but unsurprising; every resident claimed to be healthier just from living in Foison. Everyone had a well, and the water all came from the same place, somewhere underground. Although she had a well that she used for washing and bathing, it stunk like rotten eggs. The water she drank was bottled. The one resident that had been there for years before anyone else was Old Sylvia, and she only used the well water, yet she was wrinkled as a white raisin. Mavis Stanger, Jack's mother, looked incredibly young and pretty, once you got past that steel-spiked veneer of hers. Jack looked his age though: seven going on thirty-whatever.

Evonal leaned her elbow onto the edge of the small desktop, cupped her chin in her palm picturing Jack. Now whenever their eyes met, his right brow crinkled affectionately. She wondered what had changed between them, after all these years. And then Evonal became weary of thinking of Foison Surrounded, even Jack. She was going to move to Oregon where she could live without absolutely everyone knowing which mood she was in minute by minute.

No matter what that tiny voice in her head kept whispering, she was going to have to go alone; she would be alone for a while, but she would make new friends in time. First thing in the morning she was going to collect her dogs and drive home to tell Jack good-bye, to pack, and quit the stalling. Picking up her purse, Evonal decided to treat herself to a drink in the bar downstairs, and a big steak dinner with rolls swimming in real butter.

■ ■ ■

Chapter 21

At her driveway, Evonal stopped before turning in. Jack's monster truck was parked in her covered carport. There was a nice moment of exhilarating happiness that caused her to spring out with her motor still running, but he wasn't in the truck. Evonal's disappointment surprised her. The only thing left was to park at the fence, and face her empty house.

Once she fixed the dogs in their room, she peeled off her clothes and took an ice-cold shower. Getting out slowly she toweled down the goose bumps, buttoned on her granny nightie, opened the window for a breeze, and dropped into her bed, awakening when she heard Jack call, "Evon, it's Jack! Don't freak out."

"Jack!" she echoed.

He slid in through her window and plopped his enormous butt on her bed.

"Didn't you see my truck? I thought you might drive it back over to me. I left you the keys in the hiding place."

"The thought never occurred to me. I thought you were hiding out from someone."

Jack frowned. "And you thought I'd lead them right to you? I would never do that, Evon. Hell, no! And, you shouldn't sleep with your windows open nowadays. These people are likely to take it as an invitation and just barge right in! Where've you been?"

The silence became a hammock slung between the two of them, ready to either entangle them or throw them both off.

"I liked the note on the window. I swung by to see if you might've left another. You shouldn't leave it open like that anymore."

"Are you doing any better?" she asked.

"Not really," he replied.

"Why can't you ever stay out of a mess?"

"Why don't you ever take those ugly ass rings off?"

"Have the pests chewed the house in two yet?" she countered.

"Is that your way of asking me to leave?"

"Don't you have a girlfriend? Or three? Or what is it, four now?"

"I thought you didn't care about that stuff?"

This caused a lump to gather under her heart. "I was just asking about your poor ramshackle house," she said.

"I haven't done a damn thing about the house; there, you caught me. I need Vern. He's been busy making millions of tourist dollars. I can't do it on my own. I was injured, remember?" He let his head thud into the pillow, taking up most of it, letting out a deep sigh.

"You have an enormous head," she said by way of apologizing, liking the way he lifted up one of her fingertips and gave it a good polishing with his big thumb.

"Been downtown lately?" he asked her.

"Naw. I've spent the last few days out of town, getting things organized so I can move on with a clear conscience."

The sides of their faces were against each other, but they both kept their eyes on the ceiling.

Jack sighed a few times before saying, "I like it here with you."

Evonal felt a drop of pure joy buoy up. She rolled on top of him, laid her head on his huge chest and listened to his heart thunk around inside.

Jack wrapped his arms around her, before he started talking. "People are over there drinking that strangely glowing brew, buying all manner of goofy shit, including candles that look like the old tawls as if they are holy relics. That Old Sylvia is out doing target practice like she's about to put up a gunfight any day."

Evonal laughed. "I'd heard she was walking around trying to warn people away, ringing her bell, playing her small harp, and giving speeches on the damage to the ecosystem. She is determined to clear out Foison. A lot of people probably are siding with her now."

"She might need those guns if she keeps up irritating everyone," Jack said with a hint of uncharacteristic irony.

Evonal had a vague recollection of some kind of silent feud between Jack's mother and Old Sylvia. She could not recall why, and yet she thought it had something to do with

Jack's father. Whoever that was. She lifted her head to take a good look at him. He couldn't be Vern's son; Vern wasn't the kind of man to ignore his own son. Sidus could fit in the timing, but he was black as wrought iron, and although Jack had all that curly hair, Mavis Stanger gave Sidus jars of preserves; she was certain if it'd been Jack's father they'd been hurled at him, but she didn't know why she believed this.

"I feel like a bug under a microscope," Jack said.

"Your amber eyes suit you." She sighed.

"Old Sylvia's been pestering me to help her. Lately I've been thinking of helping Old Sylvia clear out that well. Just to keep her from hurting herself."

Something in his tone or set of jaw gave Evonal the inkling that there was something larger going on there.

"That sounds like a Trojan horse idea," Evonal told him.

"What kind of idea is that?"

"A big, formed idea hiding many smaller, deadlier thoughts. Is it so?"

"Where the hell did that come from?"

She gave him a quick outline of Helen of Troy, and the Trojan horse. "I used to read the Greek myths. They were big on philosophical teachings," she explained. "I started in with them after I got over the bible stories. After my parents…"

They let the subject drop.

"And I know you are trying to get my nightie off—don't pretend you're not."

"*Shhhhh*," he told her. "Rest your head back here. This time of day you should be out of your nightie already."

She put her ear back on his chest to let Jack fumble with her gown. He worked at the buttons, humming the way he did when he was fixing her truck or replacing a light bulb.

"Jack, you're pulling my hair out! If you want my clothes off, why don't you just ask me?"

"Shhh, you speak nonsense," he replied, but his hands kept working.

"Uh huh. Well, Jack, if you can get it off without my help I'll be glad to have sex with you."

"It's coming off, Evon."

He kept humming while slipping her arms out of the holes, moving her up and down like a rag doll. When he got the best part of it ringed around her neck he said, "You're losing too much weight. Maybe you should start eating meat," he said before he stood, removed his own belt, pants, leaving his underwear, T-shirt, and socks on.

"Your big fanny is glowing white in those shorts, and it's daytime!" She laughed.

"So you find me sexy, do you?" he asked, working his eyebrows comically, shaking his ass at her.

"Jeez, Jack the backs of your legs are just covered in a rash!"

"I fell into a nettle bush. I got some shots. Something called an IV. It's healing."

Evonal studied Jack. "You haven't been going hungry. That's for sure."

"Those Lake sisters also deliver. Good thing, I have no one else."

"You're a grown man. You have to take care of yourself."

"I pay for all of it," Jack said. "I drive to town for my food, mostly."

"Good to know you drive yourself for your own food," Evonal countered.

"Calm down, Evon."

This really made her bristle. "Where's your cast? It hasn't been six weeks."

"I'm healed. My arm's good. I could use some help with pulling my T-shirt over my head. It's the only thing I really have trouble with now. By the way, did you notice your yard? Out front."

"Did something happen?" She started to get up.

He pulled her back down. "Naw. I just been keeping it clean and I fixed the fence."

"I thank you, but I don't understand."

"Vern's been busy. Aw, just let it go," he said it like he was teasing her. "Come on, back to me."

The shirt seemed to be stuck to him in several spots, making him flinch as she gently peeled it away. "The rash covers your back. And all these cuts and scrapes?—good lord! Is your paradise fighting back?"

"Shhhhh," he whispered. "Please, Evon. Please, do not mention it. Let's not fight!" Tears seemed to well in his eyes.

"Yes, OK," she answered quickly.

When they got to the part where they were like two spoons set together on their edges, she started to tell him about her grandma's house.

"Shhhhh, let's just shut the whole fucking world out," he whispered.

"Yes, but this is the last time for us in the bed. I'm really moving. Soon."

She waited to hear what he wanted to add, and when he started to snore she rolled over. For several minutes she let her thoughts wheel around how the Lake sisters should relieve her of her last bit of worry over Jack, not that she should have any. Rumors, rumors, and more rumors; she would not miss these.

Moving as carefully as she could, she got up. He unfurled across her bed, a giant X, looking larger than she remembered, but he was too old to be growing. Because he made her want to stay, and watch over him, she dressed, leashed the pooches, and walked them toward town, thinking how she used to be able to transfer any emotion she had for a person to a painting on small drawer knob.

Jack got up as soon as he heard Evonal shut the front door. All along, he'd been pretending to snore, hoping she'd fall asleep, or paint his portrait, or do whatever she did when he wasn't around. There were sides of her that he wanted to know. It cut him, the way she'd slipped out without saying so much as, "I'm going for the mail, but don't wait in case I get hung up," or any sort of lie to smooth it over. He had to lean out the window to see her walk toward town, those little dogs prancing under the hem of her skirt. He promised himself from that moment on, he would leave her be, stop this foolishness, and get back to his old self; concentrate on getting his gold. He would only complicate her life, not add anything to it. Jack stroked his aching head, rubbed at his heart. He had to leave her be, get back to being friends, help her out of there if that was what she really wanted.

The room seemed to shrink without her. The blue color, darker. Jack's eyes blurred and clotted. It took a few hard rubs with his thumbs to get them dried out. Then he went back out the window, got his boots on. There was no more putting it off, he would have to head toward the place in Foison he dreaded the most, but could never avoid: Mavis's new sleek silver trailer.

The door banged open before he had a chance to raise his fist and knock. Mavis crossed her arms.

"Did I see you carrying that old bag of rags, Sylvie, the other day?"

"Here's your cut of the money. What do you have to say about my father?" Jack said calmly.

This ruffled her feathers enough. She took a few short sweeps at her shoulders before she took up the next topic. "My house is slanting, Jack. What are you going to do about that? Every time the wind blows I wait to for someone to come tell me it's collapsed into a pile of sticks with you under it, dead as all that."

"I'll bring you more when I have more," Jack said, but her remark hit home. He needed the house, he certainly wanted to live. Mavis went back inside. Jack headed for Vern's.

"Hey, Vern, need a hand?" Jack called to his backside. The man had his head inside his workshop, his legs coming off the ground every few seconds like he was trying to wrestle something out.

"That ain't a wild animal you're pulling out, is it?" Jack never knew what to expect from Vern.

"No, that'd be easier. It's my saw. Ah! Christ on the cross, this is heavy!" He emerged grunting, but an old radial saw was emerging in measures. Jack grabbed hold and pulled it out like it was on wheels.

"There you go, Vern!" he said, delighted with himself. Vern nodded his appreciation but then immediately crossed his arms, studied him.

"Are the rumors true, Jack?"

"Which rumors would those be, Vern?" Jack found himself unprepared for the lie. Vern would be the only one to ask him outright where he was getting all the money.

"You engaged to that little Linda Lake? The smaller half of the Lake sisters, the one that glitters."

Jack coughed until tears came to his eyes. "Now that is the last thing I'd thought you had as a rumor about me. How come you thought of that?"

"You seem to be over at their restaurant all the time."

"I'm hungry," Jack said. He didn't want to tell Vern that this was his strategy for keeping the pink notes off his front door, and her "pop-ins" with food at his bedroom window. "And naw. Never have been, never will be. I ain't the type."

Vern clapped his back with approval, "Atta boy, Jack! Good to hear you're still one of us confirmed bachelors."

The expression confused Jack, but he didn't ask for elaboration. Jack wasn't that either, but this wasn't a point he was about to argue.

"So what you up to here?" Jack asked.

"Aw these goddamn tourists think nothing of peeling off whatever they can get their fingers on. I'm about to shore up the Oddities Museum, and then the roof on our little bottle church."

"The saw's making squalling noise. Maybe you can take a look while you're standing there."

"Step aside, Vern." Jack said.

While he went about tinkering with the saw motor, Jack continued to listen to Vern tell him all about the ins and outs of the new Foison. Jack didn't ask him about repairing the house. Vern had his hands full. Jack would have to help him, and he didn't have time just then to shore up that rickety old house no one really wanted, including him.

"Good as new!" Jack said, starting it up.

"I can't make up my mind about this place anymore," Vern said. "It's filling up with people and sure, they bring their money, but all the same they're choking the place off."

Jack had to agree, he put himself in the direction of his own home, ready to have a look, see if it wasn't something he could fix on his own, but first he wanted to see the Bottle Church. He loved to catch any of those outside asswipes screwing with it, Jack was pretty certain it could be moved and hidden. As a kid he'd spent a lot of time hiding from his mother inside it, and it seemed to him that it was built on a pallet, meant to be a transportable type of church.

But of course he didn't get much farther than the rock formation they called the hunchbacks when something landed on his back. Bright pink legs wrapped around him.

"Jack, where have you been?"

"Jeez us, Linda. What did you do, leap from the top of the boulder?"

"Yes, I set a trap! I was out getting my exercise and I spied you over there with Vern. I couldn't hear what you were talking about; it just made me proud to see you talking with Vern like two big men…"

Jack's thoughts turned to getting Linda off his back, in every way. There was a moment while she was chattering on and on that he realized why Evonal was so desperate to get out of Foison. Then his thoughts turned to his tawl, the dog, the peace to be had.

"I just knew you would like that!"

Jack hadn't kept up with her, except she always seemed to use the words *I knew you would just like…*

"Linda, we don't really know each other at all," Jack said, pushing her dusty silver shoe off his belt.

"I know you like to eat." She laughed, playfully trying to lock her pink legs around waist. Jack wanted to set her down and run to his tawl. Maybe he could live there.

"Where you headed?" he asked Linda. It occurred to him that there was no escape. If Evonal left Foison he'd have to get along without her just as he always had. When he thought about it, the idea that he had come to some sort of reliance on her might just be a response to all the other changes his body and brain had been undergoing since all this started. Taking Linda to see the bottle church might be a way to show her who he was.

"I'm gonna show you something," Jack said.

"Giddy up!" Linda said giving his thighs a little kick.

"It's like our house!" Linda squealed. "It's getting hot, Jack."

All Jack could see was the damage. He turned around and took her back to her restaurant, waving to Mavis, who only shook her head. It looked like he was doing a lot of carrying of women lately. He didn't see Evonal striding past, stopping to watch him pack Linda to her front step. There was just so much giggling and small talk to keep up with.

"Come in for a sandwich! I had such a great time! Quality time!" Linda cried. It worried Jack that he'd made just almost intentionally made her feel "they" had made some kind of progress. Jack went in, but before he took a sip of coffee, he ate a small piece of gold as an appetizer to the meal, longing for the simplicity of getting his ass kicked robbing the gold from that angry old coot.

■ ■ ■

Chapter 22

Evonal found Foison just as Jack promised, a circus of people. The vine now stretched across all the telephone poles that marked the beginning and the end of Foison. There were concrete slabs under three of the vine-covered sections. Each of these had tables and chairs full of people, and lots of children. Townspeople were busily picking the fruit from the vine, which seemed to never empty of the globes. No one seemed to notice her. Evonal put the dogs in her pockets so she could walk through the throng more easily.

Sadly, the old church signs that had weathered decades of desert storms were now freshly painted advertisements for the benefits of Foison's Fruit of the Vine. There was a stemmed glass of the glowing orange wine with ribbons curving around it, containing words like "magical properties" and "restorative powers." Evonal crossed her arms, and wondered how the crazy people always seemed to know where to gather. The sun reflected off the silver of her thick running shoes. Her pink socks glowed just under the hem of her awful dress patched with pockets that were full of all sorts of things, including tiny, fidgeting dogs. Evonal realized she could be the ambassador for Foison, a bronze statue should be made of her waving these people in. Exhausted, she wanted to go home, but didn't want to wake Jack. Her heart was already a glob of warm butter ready to melt all over him. She vowed to avoid him until she was packed and about to drive out of town.

Old Sylvia emerged from the crowd, wearing a large piece of plywood that hung from straps at her shoulders, like a long stiff bib. Her long hair flowed down the sides like holiday tinsel. Naturally, she held a miniature harp under her chin like a violin, strumming a nerve-wracking tune. The board read: *People Out! Nature Stay!*

"G' day, Evon," Old Sylvia sang as she strolled—and strummed—past, the beat kept by the knocking of her knees against the front board.

"G' day, to you!" Evon chirped back.

Evonal was unsurprised to see that Old Sylvia was naked under the boards although she was wearing her usual sturdy shoes and neatly cuffed, white socks. The septuagenarian had a surprisingly well-toned body, though mapped with veins. The backboard read: THE DESERT WILL BE AVENGED.

The crowd of people closed around her. The dogs went wild, Evonal panicked, but as she turned to sprint home, someone grabbed her by the elbow.

"Are you Evon Allison Hartley?" he shouted. A short man wearing a Mounties hat and a shirt creased like a uniform gripped her. She yanked her arm away.

"What do you want?" she cried.

"I was told you were the mayor!"

It took a moment to sink in, and then she doubled over with laughter, as stupidly uncontrollable as her sudden bursts of tears had become. By the time she could look up, he had his sunglasses off, his eyes beading down on her like she was the lunatic.

"Well?" he cried.

"Foison doesn't have a mayor. I just live here. Ordinary citizen."

"Don't you care?" He waved his hand at the crowds of people colliding into each other, their noise, the lines of vehicles farting invisible gas into the once clean air.

Feeling the fear well up, she said as coolly as she could, "This place comes and goes."

"You have to understand what's at stake here. There are elements in this desert that are found nowhere else on earth."

"That's very true, sir." Evonal was thinking about the people of Foison.

"Well, the government feels it's worth protecting," he said, quieter now.

"Mister, you might as well press your shoulder against an elephant's rump, and try to get it to scoot over when it's comfortable where it's standing," Evonal replied genially.

When he tipped his head back his face came out from under the shadow of his hat. She thought his chin looked larger than the rest of his face and with a dimple so deep it was like someone had stuck a finger in a ball of soft dough. Somehow it made him look vulnerable and childlike. She was certain he wasn't a real government anybody, just another tourist in a costume.

"Good luck," Evonal added sincerely.

The man shook his head gravely and stalked off. When a jeep drove by, painted like a sunburnt zebra and advertising *Illuminating, Numinous Vortex* tours, she ran after it, found the business stand and bought passage on the next tour. Taking a hat from a pocket she settled the dogs down, and boarded last.

On her tour there were two couples and another man, plus the driver packed into what looked like a small bus with the top removed. She sat in the third row. It was a flat, slightly padded slab with seat belts. The ride was bumpy. Fortunately, there was no roof to bang her head against, and she could get a good grip on the roll bar to hang on. The man next to her murmured *"juck!"* at each rough bounce, causing her to warm to him immediately. As they bounced along, the guide called out the names of the old tawls—newly named by the tour group after their vague representation of kitchen items: Johnson's Tawl, according to this tour guide, was now Teapot Butte; Honaria's Sacrifice was now simply, the Salt Shaker. There were more; this group seemed to favor kitchen items. Evonal wondered what Jack would say about all of this.

"First stop, everybody out," the guide called cheerfully, shutting off the engine. The spot had been prepared over the years for the heavy vehicles of the regular visitors of the Numinous Vortex; it was a campground of sorts, anyway, it used to be.

"This is the heart of what we call the Numinous Vortex," the guide said with authority.

He was a middle-aged, self-assured man that Evonal had never seen before in her life. During the first part of his speech, Evonal learned for the first time that there were masculine and feminine "vortexes." It was like a joke to her, but everyone else took it all in with an anxious earnestness that worried Evonal. Home was under three miles, she estimated, an easy walk, if she had to.

"Let's all move over there, and form a circle," he commanded, and the group went where he pointed. One couple looked like a brother-and-sister team, but they were married: drab blonds, lanky, long faces with features that seemed to melt down into pointy chins, almost identical clothing, white shirts, and baggy shorts that hung off their skinny frames. The other couple was more compact, and they wore similar outfits too. The woman's dark curly hair drifted around her shoulders under the baseball cap, while her husband didn't seem to have any at all under his. The single man stood opposite Evonal; she noticed he had incredibly large feet with knees as hairy as coconuts. He crossed his arms over his chest as if to keep it in place. The tour guide was dressed in that khaki African safari costume made popular in old movies and certain theme parks.

When the guide cleared his throat, they all looked at him.

"Now the first thing I'm going to explain is how these strange volcanic rock formations were called tawls by the indigenous Native Americans."

While the others nodded, Evonal had to dip her smile into her collar. The tawls were a Foison joke. The early pioneers just called the rock formations *talls*; they weren't mountains, they weren't hills, they were useless, but tall. Of course someone making the Points of Interest plaques spelled the name tawls, after their "Native American" name. She caught herself thinking how she would describe this tour to Jack.

Someone asked a question Evonal didn't quite catch. Their tour guide answered by saying, "Now the next thing I want to say is that you're gonna hear many things about what people have reported experiencing here in the Numinous Vortex. Let me be the first to say that many of these tales could be filed under the *weird and whooo hoo!* But you are free to make up your own mind." He said the last part as if he really expected them to believe the weird and *whooo hoo;* the theme of the tour.

The first story was a retelling of how a crystal was laid onto the upflow of a masculine vortex and was immediately charged into a dust cloud that whipped itself into a giant Indian warrior dressed from head to toe in beaded, golden buckskin. While Evonal wondered why the American Indians were always dragged into these types of delusions, the dark-haired woman nervously fingered the crystal she wore around her neck.

And yet, even with her skepticism, she was certain that she felt something. All around them it seemed like the tawls were leaning in, the thin desert air grew denser; her fingertips tingled. For a moment she had the unusual sense that it was about to rain, but overhead the sky was bright and the two puffs of white clouds looked a hundred miles away. Her dogs became so still she reached into her pockets and felt the heartbeat of each one. Evonal could not remember a time when she could breathe so easily, but it didn't last. Someone began shaking her arm.

"Didn't you say you were a local girl?" the tall woman asked.

Evonal nodded politely, wishing they would not speak. She felt she was on the edge of the cold sea on a hot summer day, about to jump in and swim the whole length in one breath.

"What do you know about that Skookum ghost we keep reading about?" The woman persisted.

The name snagged her, pulled her back to them. Skookum? Ghost? No one talked about ghosts or spirits in Foison, only God and UFOs, an equal divide. They were all looking at her now.

"A ghost? Here in Foison?"

"Named Skookum."

"That's not a ghost I've ever heard about," she said.

"What are the ghosts' names, then?" someone else asked.

Evonal was taken aback. "I meant I've never heard talk of any ghosts."

"But it says this is a likeness of the ghost of Sam Skookum. It's a painting titled *Sam Skookum*." The woman pressed a fingertip to the nose of the image she held up. On the cover was a three-quarter-view portrait of an old man, painted by her father. His art was often featured in books and magazines, but why here, why now? It pierced her. And then there was a crystallizing moment when she was certain that this Sam Skookum had been alive and well at some point in Foison Surrounded, her father had painted him, and that he was also Jack's father. Their curly hair, square chin, and brow ridges were the same, but especially those ears, the same sharply curliqued pinnas, thick lobes the shape of Illinois. The painting hung in her mind now as clearly as if it were on the wall of her bedroom.

"We'll get the greatest benefit if we all connect our energy," the guide informed them.

Evonal had just made up her mind to walk home when the big, single man crossed the circle and took up her hand, the woman next to her grabbed her other hand. A crackle of energy snapped through her; every inch of her skin felt like some kind of wildfire was burning off the tiny hairs. Evonal squeezed her eyes shut and let her head fall gently forward, planted both feet onto the ground, and felt more grounded than a century-old oak tree struck by lightning. The others in the circle were chanting, jittering, and twitching; the handholding became hard to manage, but no one let go.

That feeling she had at the beginning returned and intensified. Tears came to her eyes; she felt the sensation of jumping rope, climbing a large leafy tree, playing on a beach, the ocean, she thought, the sea, and then she could smell the heavy, salty air. And rain, beautiful, cold rain soaking umbrellas, filling the cups of flowers with its fecundity. She believed in spirits, she realized, and now she felt the three trying to guide her home.

Evonal opened her eyes, ready to go home. Her breaths came in deeply relaxing inhale-exhales, she felt wonderful. The rest of the group, however, seemed to have jittered themselves into some sort of quaking frenzy. All six had their faces tipped skyward as if trying to press them onto the sun, their hats lay crumpled on the ground. She hoped they had put on strong sunscreen. When the tour guide whooped a war cry as he fell to his knees, he dragged the people on each side down, half and half: each had one knee and one foot pressed into the ground.

Snapping her hands away, she clasped them in front of her, a shield to protect her own heart. Once the connection was broken the change was instant. They all stared at her, six children who'd just had their favorite toy snatched away.

"Take us back there," someone cried.

On the ground was the book with the image of her father's painting. It had fallen facedown, but wide open. The pages were crumpled, and worse, there was a coating of sand on both the front and back covers. Grabbing it up she rolled it enough to tuck it into a pocket.

"You don't need me," she said. Turning on her heel, she pointed herself in the direction of home and walked.

As soon as she got inside her house, she put the dogs away before going to her bedroom. All the way home she had avoided people and hoped Jack would not be there when she arrived, yet Evonal felt her heart ache at the sight of her empty bed. Sitting on the very edge of the mattress, she gently smoothed her hand over the impression Jack had left in the sheets. Next, she touched the pillow. On the nightstand were her miniatures turned awry; Jack must have been looking at them before he left.

Evonal stared down at the faces looking back at her. They were good and she was proud of them. There was life in her artwork, she took after her father in her penchant for portraits and her use of color; she didn't want to ever stop painting, but now she wanted larger canvases and new landscapes—her own landscapes. Suddenly she wanted children, an unending line of artists, bridge builders, hotel managers, even thieves, she didn't care. She wrapped both hands at the back of her neck and waited out the emotional storm.

Finally, she stood, stripped off her clothes and threw them into a wad on the floor. Evonal began to empty her small closet of clothes, keeping only her mother's things and the new clothes she'd bought in Chrysopoeia, two pair of socks—actually, she would keep all of the socks, she decided, retrieving them and putting them in a pile on the bed. They made nice sweaters for her dogs with just a couple of snips with the scissors. Everything else was quickly bundled into bags, which she would throw into the bed of her truck. On the way to Oregon she would throw her old clothes into a thrift store collection bin, and be done with Foison.

Even though she knew she would never sleep now, she stretched across her bed, and stared at the ceiling. When she felt her hands for the rings, she found them gone. The next step seemed obvious. She got up, got a thick red marker this time and wrote another sign on her bedroom window. *Jack, this room is closed now. Do not come in.* She didn't like the looks of it, the letters were crooked, and went at an angle up the window, shaking because she was, but she couldn't clean it off. The message, though in shaky handwriting, was important, and she meant it. For his sake, she thought, he had to stand on his own, because she was going to be fine.

■ ■ ■

Chapter 23

When dark night had finally come, Jack emerged from his front door, wary, but ready to go. This trip Jack was trying to time his arrival on the tawl with the old giant's hitting his limit and passing out. Just to help cut down on injuries to himself. Holding off was difficult, while being there made him anxious, and being away made him apprehensive. Acting on something less than instinct—maybe he was propelled by guilt or curiosity or he was edging toward accepting responsibility for the plight of Foison—he found himself walking toward the town well. Just when it came into view and he'd decided there was nothing he could do, he almost turned back when he saw Old Sylvia at the well climbing in headfirst with not so much as a rope around her slender waist to hold her back should she slip. Both her feet disappeared inside. Jack ran.

"You in there?" he called down the well. The stench of the rotting vine mixed with the sulfuric water began jabbing his nose.

"I'm hung up on the damn vine, it stings. I don't believe there's any water left." Her voice still quivered with old age, but otherwise sounded nonplussed. There was no room in there for an echo.

Jack fished his hands around until he got hold of her ankles and lifted her out as gently as he could. Besides her hair being tussled, she seemed the same. "I need my backpack," she ordered. Curious, he picked it up and handed it to her. She pulled out a large sheet and spread it over the ground like she was readying for a picnic. The pack still bulged.

"We're going to have to rip it out by the roots." Old Sylvia said like that was the purpose of their meeting.

"I'll be on my way, now," he said.

"I got something I'll trade you for your help. I got a safe."

Jack stopped. He could really use a safe.

"You can take it home tonight."

"Why would I need a safe?" He said as slowly as he could, just to throw her off his scent.

She laughed. "You need a safe. You go right in there and rip the whole mess of vine out by its roots. I can't get much. I'm just too weak, and shooting it won't stop it. We'll roll that stink vine up in this tarp and take it to its pyre. Once it's burned, you can have the safe."

Jack wanted to walk off, but he could use the safe. And he felt an obligation to her, though he certainly didn't want to.

"How big is the safe?"

"It'll do, and a big man like you can move it by yourself. The only hitch is you'll need to load it on your truck."

He had a truck, so he missed her point, but he wanted the safe. Maybe carrying her way back when had been his surrender. He leaned in and started ripping the vine out by the armfuls, eventually climbing in and handing the reeking bundles up to her.

"This well isn't as deep as I always thought," Jack called up to her.

"Yes it was a good well. Destroyed now. Keep yanking on it Jack!"

"It stinks like it's dying already. And it stings, too."

"Remove every leaf, every piece of it. We'll burn it over the Wad's Hill. No one goes there these days."

When Jack couldn't find any more vine, he climbed out. After sending him back in for green shreds about six times more, eventually her search with the flashlight left her satisfied. Jack didn't think this would ever be the end of that vine, but he said nothing, afraid to get the old girl started on a new quest she'd somehow hook him into. He knew better than to mention the other one, the stronger one, his vine. She'd climb it, clobber the old goat up there, maybe even insist on rescuing him, and then root out the vine. Nevermind all that gold, she already made her position clear on that. It would be lost forever. Old Sylvia just didn't understand everything.

"Roll it up and follow me. I got its funeral pyre all ready."

Jack carried it, stumbling over the rocks and bushes silently while Old Sylvia talked.

"Looks like you're growing."

Jack grunted.

"Could be a tumor on your pituitary gland. You might get that checked. Of course, it could be you're taking after your father." She seemed to think that settled it. They walked on in silence over Wad's Hill.

"Throw it in that pit and throw on that gasoline. Get way back and I'll strike the match."

Jack complied, moving away until she nodded. The thing went up in a thick flame.

"Die!" Old Sylvia commanded it. "Don't go, Jack. I got something else to show you. You just follow me."

"You're not secretly my mother or anything scary like that?"

"Your mother? No. I'm your aunt. You know that. I do have two boys, your cousins. Bad, bad, bad. Their father took 'em, turned them against me while I was in prison. I robbed some banks, to feed them, but I never hurt anyone. They'll be the death of me so I'm trying to make the most of my time I am left with. Fix something. Do good. Listen, let's walk very quietly, just in case that fire brings some of those idiots around. They believe this thing is some spiritual ladder or some such bullshit." His footsteps sunk in the sand while hers seemed to glide across the desert. Finally she shone her flashlight on a spot.

"Look," she ordered. He tasted gold.

There on the ground were some gold nuggets, an old rag, and some rusted bolts. Enormous rusted bolts: all very familiar. He was shocked she didn't move to pick it up.

"You know anything about this?"

"No, do you?"

"Not a clue."

They both turned toward the tawl.

"Shit!" she said, kicking sand over all of it before jumping up and down on top of it. Her actions puzzled him, but he didn't ask. "Stay away from gold. Some people think I got a stash, but they're wrong. There's no convincing them though; once they believe you got gold, they want it. They'll kill you for it. Even your own boys."

"Is Mavis my mother?" he asked.

"She's your mother all right, but not a reliable woman. You were always a big strong boy, something your mother wanted to suppress. Sad thing, Jack, not all mothers want their kids. The one good thing is she didn't want you to grow up like your father. The rest I don't know about. We had a tough life growing up, poor. Fending for ourselves at every turn. We farmed a farm like grown women when we were just small girls, then we lost everything. Seems to me, looking back, she was always a bit off, but who wasn't? Then she got the gold fever too. I tried to help her with you, but neither of us were equipped to be good mothers. Picked bad men. Unlike my boys, though, you were a tender kid so maybe I'm just wrong about who your real father is. I don't know." She kicked more sand, and again Jack was amazed that she didn't dig out the gold, pocket it, and run away. It's all he wanted to do.

"Was my father some sort of healing preacher?"

"Preacher? Oh no," she replied.

"I just remember the tent revival."

"I don't know who that was. Those tent revivals come and go around here. Listen, you're gonna need to get your distance from this place. It's closing in on you."

"Now just where the fuck would I go?" Jack asked. The beam from her flashlight went off. They stood in silence.

"That's always the question," she said finally.

He spent most of the rest of the night moving the safe into his bedroom. Once he got it in place of the dresser, he nailed his bedroom window shut, closing the curtain. If he'd had paint he would've painted the glass out. After that, instead of going to the tawl, he went back over Wad's Hill, locating the gold by smell alone. Once he secured it in his pocket, he dug out the bolts, burned the paper and the rag. On his way home he went in an arc so he could hurl the bolts into the dump. After that, he deposited all the gold he had hidden in the house into the safe, closed and locked the door. His plan was to sleep through the day and get back up there for more gold to fill the safe. This is what he intended to do until he had it all. And then he'd blow that vine up, rid Foison of it once and for all.

■ ■ ■

Chapter 24

While the drunken giant was passed out, Jack had spent the night moving gold from the box to a stash closer to the exit. His back and shoulders throbbed, but nothing seemed to be trying to kill him. The big yellow dog followed him wherever he went, guided him just as strongly as before, but it was obvious she was sick.

"I'll get you better food and some medicine, Little Maid. I'll get you down. I know I've been selfish, but I get it now. You're the gold. I just need help saving you so I don't get you killed on the way down. I'm going to get you down."

The big yellow dog, lay on her side, exhausted. The good sign was that whenever Jack put food into her mouth, she gulped it down, and she opened it for more. Jack used his shirt hem to mop the goo from her eyes, clean up her chin. Now as Jack spoke she waved a paw, like she agreed.

"So you'll come, won't you?"

She waved a paw. They went on like that until he could picture her living in Foison with him, frisky with good health, the two of them side-by-side everywhere. It felt like the first time Jack ever let himself imagine the future at all.

Before he went back, he moved her to a comfortable bed of leaves in the shade and fed her until she refused to eat more.

"Rest, girl, and hide. I'll be back really soon. Stay away from that old goat."

Jack stood up, but warily. This place didn't seem to ever want him to leave in one piece, but so far nothing had happened. As usual his feet were throbbing inside his boots; his clothes felt too tight, like every muscle in his body was swollen from exertion. Gold was so heavy, and so worth the pain, he thought, taking a nice chunk into his mouth.

At the bottom of the tawl, early morning cracked open like a fresh raw egg and spread its blinding light across the desert quickly, catching Jack outside with his pack of gold when normally he got himself inside his house before the dawn broke.

"You're out early, Jack!" When he turned toward Sidus's voice, he could see two figures; his good mood deflated. Just when he was congratulating himself on a clean getaway, there was Foison already on his heels.

"Hey, Sidus! Lenora, I can't remember the last time I saw you!" Although he'd just eaten, his stomach growled a noise more embarrassing then a prolonged, blasting fart.

Lenora smiled at him like she was forgiving a small child for announcing at a stranger's house that he was hungry. "I've been in Reno visiting my sister. Sidus and I came out to get a good look at everything before it got too hot. The stench from the town dump is so bad these days. Gawd, it'd gag a maggot. Things have changed since I've been gone. I might have to just move in with my sister for good. Foison's gone, isn't it? And just how've you been faring, Jack? Your mom moved into that nice trailer, but you're still in the old house? I heard it's tilting some, but haven't gotten by to take a look yet," Lenora said.

"Yeah, I'm gonna get it fixed up." His stomach growled again.

Sidus cleared his throat before saying, "Is Jack growing, Lenora? None of us can be sure, but you haven't seen him in a while."

"I've been working out. I eat too much."

"You were always a big man, Jack, but it does look like he's growing, Sidus. I think you're right," Lenora said.

"Hiking, climbing, trying to get into shape. And, I've got to get on my way. I'm late," Jack said lamely.

"We'll let you get on your way, then. You take care, Jack," Sidus said slowly like his words would settle over Jack and stay there, a protective coating, a caution sign.

"I'll tell your mother I ran into you!" Lenora said, formally releasing Jack.

After that encounter he took care to get home without being seen, but of course that was impossible. Vern was already out. He waved, and to his surprise, Evonal stepped from his shadow, and waved too. "Vern!" Jack shouted, when he wanted to say, *Evon!* Jack quickly hiked over. Once they were close enough, his and Evonal's fingers reached out and brushed against each other's, interweaving just the tips like they were finding their way in the dark; like they wanted to snake into each other and hold hands, but then they both let go, embarrassed.

"What're you two doing up so early?" Jack asked.

"Oh, couldn't get my old hay mower running so Evon here is taking me to get my brother's medicine, and to drop some stuff off at the thrift store donations."

"I'm just cleaning things out a bit," Evon said, her eyes signaling Jack to drop it. Both his shoulders sagged, letting the backpack drift down toward the back of his knees. They dropped their eyes at the same time, said nothing else.

"I'll see you two later, then," Jack said.

"See you later," Evonal called. And Jack nodded woodenly.

The house creaked and moaned its usual greeting, Jack scuttled inside the dark, quiet of his house, thinking about Evon making grilled cheese sandwiches in the nude. His stomach growled, and his brain spun. Inside his bedroom he went right to the safe. A fine layer of dust already covered it like a warm, furry suit. It caused a noticeable dip in the floor where it sat, but then the floor hadn't been a level plane in years. Jack went to the safe. After working the combination, the door opened.

"You are one well-oiled beauty, and I thank you for your protecting my goods," Jack said, finishing his daily tribute by whistling it a love tune as he quickly transferred the gold from his backpack to the safe, locking everything up tight, giving the top surface a good rubdown before he covered it with the old rug. When the wind started kicking up outside, he braced his large feet for the reciprocating sways of the house. He'd come to like that too, as soothing as a rock-a-bye-baby hug.

Jack's stomach growled, but his pants felt snug. Of course he was getting bigger. All he ever did was exercise and eat these days. Jack was going on a diet, a strict one that started with a fast, like one of Mavis's treatments when he was a kid.

The sudden picture of a large jar of peanut butter slipped into his head, making his mouth water. Next he thought of spreading it on soft white bread, covering the smooth creamy surface with coins of very sour dill pickle, and topping this off with freshly crushed peanuts, like he used to eat as a kid. Or, he thought, melted chocolate on a hard roll with chopped fresh jalapeno confetti, the way Evonal did it.

His stomach growled. "I can't feed you so much anymore!" But he thought of cooked carrots smothered in mash potatoes and gravy with meat, any kind of meat. Jack sat up sniffing the air; he could smell the food cooking in every kitchen in Foison.

The next deep rumble from the bottom of his stomach was so strong that it brought acid up to his throat. He swallowed it back down with a grimace, and rubbed his belly with his fist. He studied first his right and then his left hand, opened and closed them into tight fists. He was stronger than he'd ever been in his life. Just that morning he'd dangled off the bottom lip of the tawl, before he let go and landed in the soft sand below.

His stomach growled again. There was a ringing in his ears; he began to shake slightly from hunger. Jack rubbed both hands over his face and then his belly in frustration, before he turned the backpack over, dug into its special pocket, took out a small golden nugget, and ate it slowly, like a pebble of chocolate. After a quick shower he lay across his bed, doubled in two. If he could, he would fall asleep and stay asleep forever, like in the fairy tales, awaken in a thousand years, to a strange world he would never expect to adjust to. Jack fished a bottle of whiskey out from under the bed, twisting the top off with his teeth.

"Bottoms hatched," he said. His gurgling stomach appreciated and thanked him for by sending up a nice flush of head-spinning warmth. Once he settled his head into the pillow he drifted off, wondering why he wasn't happy; he was rich.

■ ■ ■

Chapter 25

Skookum, having given up on his rage toward Foison, stopped lobbing his stuff at him. It was feeble, and a waste of stuff he just might need in the future. That morning he was on his way back from the lake with his jug of water and shotgun—in case he wanted to shoot some annoying birds, foolish enough to flit around his tawl—when he felt a splat of water hit the bridge of his nose. He grimaced. Overhead the usual rain clouds collected, loomed, and leaked the precious water. The flowers opened and reached expectantly toward the heavens; once filled they would snap shut and hold onto the moisture better than any clamshell making pearls. The big yellow dog turned her head skyward and opened her mouth, yipping and prancing at the large splats of rain; her renewal dance. Years before, some oddball artist that used to like to hike up there and make paintings of him liked to wiggle his brush and talk of ancient jet streams, rivers in the sky, and microclimates. He put it out of his mind: everyone, all the people what left. Lately his mind had been turning on the past more often than usual. Skookum feared it was the signal of some kind of end, and this scared him.

The minute he stepped into the rock-lined thicket, a tingling sensation enlivened his ear lobes. He went to take the flat bottle of booze from his belt to get a bolstering swig, but found it missing.

Planting the shotgun into the pit of his arm, he slapped at his pockets, his belt, his chest. Nothing. This set him off into a foul mood immediately. And then he remembered that he's set the bottle on the lakeshore as he squatted down to fill his jug.

Sam had a decision to make, go back for it or go on to his camp to get some more. When the breeze shifted, he paused to sniff at the air again. Wet dog and something else, he thought, immediately suspicious. There had been some weird goings on recently, whether the cause of dreams or the booze-fueled hallucinations or real, his gut told him to get ready. Skookum sniffed at the air for clues. Sam Skookum had a keen sense of smell, but fortunately for Jack, who was hiding in the rocks just to his right, it was dulled by the scorching booze he drank regularly, and thanks to the big yellow dog, Jack was downwind.

Smelling nothing threatening, or even discernible, Skookum needed a drink, but then decided only a namby-pamby couldn't wait until he got all his chores done first. This morning he was on a treasure hunt of sorts. This tawl top had hosted fugitives since the beginning of time: ancient, indigenous people hiding from warring tribes, old miners, violent outlaws, a large family of Japanese-Americans unwilling to be interned in an American prison camp—who could blame them? Some Japs were smarter than they looked, to be sure. Most of those people liked to live down in the caves they dug, so they rarely crossed paths, and when the war was over, they'd left behind things that were often very useful to him. Since he couldn't get down the escape route anymore to steal what he needed—and spook some of the crazy townsfolk in Foison just for the fun of it—Skookum paused, resting a hand on a grainy rock, regretting that explosion that closed him off.

"Awk!" he cried. He needn't ever go anywhere to get what he needed. There was his sparkling, clean lake of water, the old gardens never stopped producing some vegetables, even with his earnest neglect. There was even an old lemon tree; it could be counted on for a couple of yellow sours every couple of months. In all his years there, Skookum had come across perhaps a dozen different types of wild berries and hard seeds. One seed, once dried and pulverized, became a rich, bitter-flavored coffee he'd come to prefer over the stuff in the cans of MJB he had rusting on the shelves. The making of it was simple—pick the seeds, throw them onto the tabletop until the thin covering came loose, smash them flat, let them dry some more. After that, boil them hard, gulp it down, so he could feel the scorch down his throat and boil a little in his belly. The lizards were easy to cook on a spit over fire. Crisp and black, cooked through and through with just a bit of soft squish in the middle was his favorite meal. Plenty of other stuff to be had too, although he wasn't a man what craved variety. The stupid dog fed, watered, and bathed itself, or it died, pure and simple.

The clothes were becoming a problem though. They were tattered, shattered, and threadbare in all the important places. Some days he feared they would fall right off him, split open, and be gone. He did not favor the idea of roaming the tawl naked as a portent of what was to befall, on into eternity, or whatever time he had allotted to him by the almighty asshole swinging the ax so very slowly over his grizzled head. Skookum glanced cautiously at the sky above, hoping he hadn't just sent up some kind of invitation.

The whining of the big yellow dog alerted something from the deep recess of his mind. Skookum wasn't sure what it was, but he didn't like the feeling, like death was on the march; a thought that made his skin crawl. The dog whimpered and whined, shaking her rear end.

"Hush up that whining!" he hollered, grabbing up the shotgun by the stalk, slipping his fist over it so his fingers locked firmly around the trigger. Sometimes the old things misfired, but they were deadly, all the same.

The clobbering he took came out of nowhere. The gun went off with a satisfying *bang!* He heard shuffling, a flutter of birds' wings, and more goddamn dog whining, but he laid low. He briefly wondered if it was the Almighty Ax come at last. The world shimmered and went black.

Throwing the rock Jack had smacked the old goat down with, Jack felt good. More rain fell. The lizards lined up on the rock faces, heads flung back, mouths gaping, all hunting temporarily suspended for this time of worship and renewal during the light shower. If he'd been in a safe place he too would stretch his arms out, tip his head back, try to catch some droplets in his open mouth, let it bathe the lids of his closed eyes, crown his curls with the sparkling droplets.

After helping himself to another bag of gold, Jack took long, swift strides to the lake to fill his water bottle before heading down.

At the lake's edge he crouched, settled his large feet firmly in the smooth, moist bole, and once settled, he drank deeply from the bowl he made with his hands. Because everything had gone so much better than planned, he was feeling confident, expansive in his mood. He wanted to enjoy the tawl before he had to head down to dreary Foison. He stripped off his clothes and stashed them in his usual hiding place before going into the lake for a quick bath.

Shaking himself to dry off, the dog actually pranced to him, and he rubbed her down, feeling her bones under the thinning fur. "Man, you need help, Little Maid." She gobbled down the food he brought her, but none of it seemed to be adding any meat to her bones.

Before he got dressed he grabbed a handful of round, purple berries off a nearby bush. The dog also loved the berries, and he scooped a handful for her, let her eat them off his palm, and then got another handful for himself. When he reached for more, it sounded like a gun exploded in his ear, knocking him onto his back, naked. Jack wanted to run, but was paralyzed from the neck down. Little Maid began spinning in circles before licking him all over his body. He knew he'd been hit by lightning. He felt ridiculously relieved to see his penis was its usual fat snail, curling into his hairy bush, his feet were still attached, and so were his toes. Overhead fingers of lightning stabbed toward him, crackling in the air. Jack believed that lightning would strike the same place twice, and he closed his eyes and actually prayed it would kill him all at once. "I'm OK, Little Maid. I got cocky," he whispered. He wanted to tell her he deserved whatever he got. The big yellow dog lay next to him, resting her muzzle across his belly, growling at the storm. Jack reread Evon's window note to himself over and over in his mind like some kind of torturous punishment; he could not get it to stop. After that he swore to God that if he lived he would root out the vine wherever it anchored its nasty roots, and live a clean life of doing good.

The amber moon and stars began fading toward daylight before the feeling returned to his body, and Jack could finally work his way up to his feet. Once he did, he still felt a little electrified, like his hair was standing on end, his vision was clouded some, his fingertips were numb, his knees trembled, but otherwise, he felt like he might live. There was a sore, black spot on his hip and one burn on his heel, the entrance and exit wounds. Down his arm was a white tattoo of what looked like a multi-branch spray of lightning following his own network of veins. He knew it would be permanent. Walking came easily enough once he moved around in a few circles, and he was oddly gratified to find his clothes were where he'd left them. After, he ate handfuls of berries until he couldn't get more down. They quenched the taste of burning metal in his mouth, and when full, he quickly dressed. Stuffing his swollen feet into his boots became the real challenge. Little Maid disappeared, no doubt to check on the old giant, who Jack could hear snoring from where he was. His stomach roared from hunger, and he thought of Evon sitting on the edge of her bed, braiding her hair.

The sky was a shocking blue, one flat plane of solid color so simple and clear he could not stop looking. And then something else caught his eye. On the bank of the lake was a bottle of Skookum's booze, the rag stuffed into the top made it look like a Molotov cocktail ready to be ignited. Jack picked it up, and finding it pretty full, he worked it into his back pocket.

At his cache of gold, Jack hesitated to reach in and take more. He wondered why it was so important to him. Most of the stolen nuggets still remained locked in the safe, unspent. The last time he'd taken some cash to his mother, she looked at it like it was a meal she didn't order, before she reluctantly took it into her boney hands. No words were exchanged, but Jack had left feeling his debt to her had finally been paid. And then, because he couldn't stop himself, he took more. On the way he tripped, looked down and noticed that the vine had crept onto the tawl top; it blended in quite well, but the lizards on top of it were dead.

At the exit point, the pain in his back was searing, and he decided to again try his pulley system. Jack had changed his system and added a mechanical ascender that locked when he pulled down on it so he could lower the bags as he went down. Now, the difficult part was lugging the gold home in his heavy backpack. The thought deflated him; he was tired, wished he could abandon the gold and quit the place forever.

The dog showed up to say good-bye. Jack knelt down to pet her gently.

"I got an idea how to get you down, but it's gonna take a little planning, and a simple sling thing, like they lift horses with. Then we ain't never coming back here," he told her. She was also panting wearily. Jack gave her one last good pat, reluctant to leave her.

"I'll be back, and then we can put this place behind us," he told her, climbing onto the vine. As he descended the plant his body kept twitching, sometimes for long minutes, like it was trying to reset its own electrical current, causing his grip and step to be shaky.

When Jack got to the bottom he sat on the ground, in the shade of the vine, and panted some more. It felt like the pull of gravity had doubled. He took the bottle of moonshine out of his pocket and pulled the rag out of the top. The smell alone suggested something caustic, but he took a swallow anyway. It burned his teeth, mouth, and all the way down his throat into his belly, but this searing pain was swiftly followed by the sweet sensation of cloudy, heavenly happiness sweeping his mind clear. Jack let his body fully relax against the stalk of the vine and took another burning swallow. Everything seemed so majestic. His life expanded and became meaningful; the point of it was entirely clear. When he thought about it, he realized he had finally done many things right. He was deliriously proud of himself. There were so many people he would like to thank for making all this possible, he thought gleefully and then laughed at himself. Why shouldn't he feel gratified? He'd been struck by lightning and survived.

Time began slipping away. And then the usual feeling of despair began to grind him down. He thought of Evonal and how she so generously ignored his asshole qualities, and even seemed to like having him around, but had locked him out and was leaving him anyway. He did not think he could forgive her. Jack sat down, leaned against the tawl, and wept uncontrollably. When he finally got on his way home, the weight of the backpack pressed unusually hard on his kidneys. Everything about the light felt wrong; he started shivering. When he removed his sunglasses, he realized it was night; somehow the day had slipped away. Goose bumps rose on his entire body, and when he rubbed at them, his skin burned. The lightning strike must've caused his feet to swell; he could barely walk in his boots now.

During the trudge home, he crossed a newly made wet streambed, shallow but at least five feet across. The water was only a trickle inside one of the tracks made in the wet sand, but it was obvious that a flash flood had washed through fairly recently. When the effort to lift his boots seemed too much, Jack wobbled in the lonely desert, thinking he should just lie down and let nature take its course. But, he kept on.

When he finally caught sight of his house, every muscle in his body felt shredded. His wet boots were coated in sand, his feet throbbed, but he knew if he took them off, he'd never get them back on. His head hammered. To take the edge off, he decided to stash his gold and then make a beeline into town to get some hot food, oatmeal, something bland, but sugary, washed down with a few pitchers of dark ale, enough he hoped to wipe out his thoughts of loneliness, Evon, crazy old coots, lightning strikes, aching bones, throbbing feet, constant hunger, luckless love, helpless dogs, and fucking gold, gold, gold.

When Skookum awoke covered in dirt, cactus pulp, and shivering, he decided it was high time he got off the ground. Once up, he took measure of his surroundings, including several deep, long sniffs of air. The smoky scent of another human hung in the air, and taking a good look around, he decided it would be quite impossible to get up there without a flying machine, and he would've noticed that. He could not conceive of how another human could get atop the tawl without his knowing about it. However, since he had time on his hands, he was going to set some real traps this time.

■ ■ ■

Chapter 26

The Lake sisters had now expanded their enterprise into Vern's old territory in the rambling depot. They now included a large menu of cooked food, along with the bakery. They had added a complicated menu and more racks of goods to sell. Jack ordered several turkey sandwiches, and several sides. His thirst seemed unquenchable even after drinking a gallon of liquids.

"Gosh, Jack, you ate an entire turkey in all those sandwiches. I'll have to get another one in the oven tonight if we're going to have turkey on the menu tomorrow! But, I'm really glad you stopped by. Did you get my note?" Linda Lake cooed and batted her eyes a lot, he noticed. This confused him.

"I don't like those notes, Linda."

When she started to cry, heads turned and all eyes bore down on him.

"Go for a walk?" Jack asked.

"In this heat?" Linda's nose crinkled.

"Just some place we can be out of earshot, only for a couple of minutes."

Linda looked uncertain, but she signaled to Astrid to take over her food station, and followed him.

They got as far as the edge of the shadow of the building, before Linda's tears started flowing out of her eyes.

"Are you crying?" Jack gasped.

"I'm just really scared right now, Jack. My heart is pounding! Are you breaking up with me?"

"Breaking up, what?" Jack asked nervously. "Whoa there, Linda."

"Yes, but you never even got me that necklace! You are breaking up with me! You never want to see me again, do you?"

"What? Never see you again? How's that possible? We live within half a mile of each other! And what necklace?" He lurched his brows at her like this told her everything she needed to know.

Linda's eyes continued to pour tears, drying on her cheeks and blouse in huge stains. "Do you ever think about me? Because I think about you, about taking good care of you." She sniffled.

"Right. Of course I think about you," Jack mumbled. "Listen, kitten, I've got to get to work on some things right now. I'll be back around to eat. Constantly. I'll be over to visit without the pretty pink invitations. You needn't bother with those."

The new flood of tears made her eyes sparkle. His heart softened unexpectedly. Unlike all his past women, Linda Lake was a soft, white dove of beauty whose unexpected prettiness always took him by surprise. Really, it frightened him, and he didn't want to break this up. He wanted to go back in time and delete the whole episode so they could be passing acquaintances. Before he realized what was happening, Linda kissed his cheek tenderly, laying her head on his shoulder, both her arms clung to his neck. They were out in the open; he was paralyzed with fear.

"I like gold," she whispered.

"So do I!" Jack said, trying to back out of her grip.

Linda finally let go of him, wiping her tears, "I'd better get back. Astrid will be swamped. We do all our own cleaning to make sure it's done right." She sniffled, walking off.

"I'll let you get to that," he said lamely, hurrying away.

Unfortunately he didn't get far before he heard, "Jack!" Astrid's voice caused a spasm of pain to shoot through his shoulders and down his spine. He halted and turned to look at her.

"I need a minute. Over here," Astrid said, her voice and her manner rather stiff, contradicting the clothes that freely flowed around her, ruffled now by the hot breeze.

Jack reluctantly followed her behind a natural outcrop of boulders.

"There are a couple of things you need to know about Linda and I," she said, placing her hands on her hip.

Jack sighed.

"It's like this, Jack. The reason Linda and I came here was to get away from her ex-boyfriend. He was brutal. The last time he put her in the hospital so badly beaten that brain fluid leaked from her ear. So we moved, and he found us. And we moved again, and that bastard found us, we moved a total of five times all over the eastern half of the USA, quaking each time that he'd catch up with her, and then our aunt died, and we came hoping to settle in and get enough breathing room to make a plan."

Jack shifted his weight. "Are you afraid he'll find her here? You need help?"

Astrid, with her hair bundled at the back of her head, had taken her hands from her waist and folded them under her meager breasts. Her weight shifted to her left hip, she stuck her right heel into the sand. "Maybe he did show up. And maybe he'll never show up anywhere again. This desert swallows the dead in no time at all. Doesn't it?"

Just beyond the two of them the sound of a crowd of voices, and engines starting echoed out of the empty desert. The air was soon filled with dust, like when a dozen dune buggies are going at once; it stirred memories of past carefree days, he wished he could leap back into and just be the asshole he grew up thinking he was meant to be.

"Astrid, you don't need to try and scare me, I'd never lay a hand on a woman," Jack said. "And secondly, jeezus, I like your sister, but I barely know her." He turned and started walking away.

"I just need to make sure you won't hurt her," Astrid said.

Jack said over his shoulder. "I enjoy your food. I'll be back for more. You two take care of each other."

The dust continued to blow, all riled up, like Jack.

■ ■ ■

Chapter 27

evon heard someone on her porch, knocking on the door like they weren't going to stop until she answered. She ran to the bathroom, snapped on her battery-powered radio, turned on the shower and started belting out "Nessun Dorma," the only aria she could sing along with the words without patching in made-up sounds. She stayed in there until her skin could not absorb another drop of water, and then she got out and naked, dripping with water she wrapped on a towel to tentatively check to be sure she was still all alone.

Disappointed that his bombs got nothing stirring in Foison, Skookum spent the first couple of hours of sunrise surveying his tawl for signs of interlopers. He was certain no other human had been up there since the big blow up of the tunnel up. Just giving up didn't seem like something he cared to do, so he got busy putting together a new trap. If it were human, he'd kill it; if it were a ghost come back to haunt him, well, he'd sure welcome the sport of all that. Skookum had no intention of going on to the devil without a real hard fight.

The vine paused in its relentless growth spurt toward the lake of water. Its ability to prosper in virtually any ecosystem that had enough water came from its clever adaptations acquired during millions of years of some very trying circumstances. It had evolved. There was no thinking involved; environmental events stimulated its cells to make the necessary adjustments. In order to survive in this arid climate with its ravenous lizards, a toxic resin would have to be forced to the surface of its cells. This would protect it from the strong sunlight, and from the attacks by ravenous insects and those curious, hungry reptiles. Because this adaptation required so much energy, it would take longer to bear fruit. And when it did the skin of the fruit was the only part of the plant that would not undergo this molecular change; it was what it must be.

■ ■ ■

Chapter 28

On the way up, Jack pulled the cable through each of the eyebolts taut and snapped the loop closed. It pulled through more smoothly than he had hoped. Strapped to his back was a bag of dog food, and small dolly he'd fashioned from his car repair days. This would be simpler than trying to make the more complicated pulley system work. The bags of gold would get wheeled from where he'd stashed them to the edge where he could attach them to his cable, and lower them down, saving his aching back every step of the way.

Jack climbed onto the tawl, his good spirits dropping when there was no sign of Little Maid. It meant Skookum was up and about doing something that no doubt was worrying the poor dog. From somewhere an unfortunate breeze got the task of carrying the old giant's stench to him, causing him to gag before he doubled over. Jack whistled softly, hoping Little Maid would appear, or at least give him some sign that she was still alive, and after several tense minutes she finally did answer with a yelp from somewhere near the ever-burning fire. He headed for the lake to take a swim and eat, wait until the old goat passed out, and his furry companion could join him.

The sight of the lake always made him happier than seeing his own house. He wished he had someone to show it to, like Evonal, but that was a bad wish, he told himself, selfish, wrong. When his stomach growled, he found a place to sit and took the food from his pack. The lasagna he'd bought before coming had congealed perfectly, he'd wrapped it in bread to keep his hands clean, and his stomach rumbled as he chewed. He brought a block for the dog, which he put down on a flat rock. After that he filled up on the berries, putting a handful of these down for the dog too. Before he went down he would tear the dog food open for her to nibble on while he was away. The bag of chocolate chips he emptied into his mouth in one long drain. Finally, he stuck a sliver of gold into his molar. And then he lay back on the boulder, crossing his legs at the ankles, sifting through the various scents, smells, and odors. The lake water was perfume, the air itself was spent firecrackers because of the recent storm; he hoped it wouldn't return. Lightning was his latest fear. There was one plant that carried the scent of steamed asparagus. The gold was still like food to Jack; it lived in the hunger center of his brain and kept it wide-awake. It was still the most delicious dessert he knew. And then he smelled the moonshine cooking. The still must've been just heating up; it had a distinct aroma of the berries he enjoyed from the bushes that grew everywhere, so nothing repugnant about them being cooked down at all. Jack eased himself off the cold stone to go to find it, arrogantly, with a hand tucked into each of his front pockets. Luckily, he could not whistle, or he might of.

The magic feeling didn't last long. He took only a few more arrogant strides before he got tangled in some fishing line or something that took him a few moments to get a hold of, because he couldn't really see it, but it felt like that plastic Easter grass that you could never get off you once it stuck. This piece of line seemed to be a mile long. Unspooling it turned out to be easy once he caught on to the trick of holding the stuff and spinning his own body out of it. It occurred to Jack that the rope must be tied to some sort of trap the crazy old giant laid out again. He wrapped an end around his fist and pulled as hard as he could. His shoulder clicked; the pain was a temporary pop. Beyond him he heard some clatter, but whatever it was, fell out of his line of sight. And then he heard Little Maid yelp like she'd been kicked. Jack walked quickly toward the sound, ducking just in time to miss the boom swinging at his head. Jack was adapting.

From his vantage point Jack watched as Skookum dangled a cooked lizard on a stick to get the dog to jump up after it. It was like a sad lion tamer's act. At any time the dog could surely attack and kill this man, but out of some sense of pity or loyalty or maybe just plain civility he jumped after it as if he needed that morsel of food, from that man's grizzled hand. In the end, when Skookum tired of the game, he ate the lizard and whipped the stick at the dog. She shied away from the blow, already anticipating it, and Jack realized she knew this game well, but still went along. There was not a single person in Foison that would allow even that battered old coot to treat the dog like that. He didn't move to stop it. The big dog could go with him, and he would take care of her, but Jack could not kill on her behalf. There was no way of knowing but he didn't think Little Maid would settle for that trade-off either. The whole scene made him feel like he might never get things to right.

Little Maid seemed to be limping on her one foot, and her tongue lolled far outside her mouth when she sat back and rested. When Skookum grabbed up his binoculars from the rickety table and wandered off, Little Maid laid down at once and laid her long snoot on top of both her outstretched front paws, panting in rapid bursts. The poor dog was sick, Jack realized. Time was running out for her. And it was obvious she needed good food. All things he could give her if they got to Foison in one piece. Maybe she was the gold he was after.

Backing out, he came across a net Skookum had mangled into some sort of almost-trap with one end tied into a U bolt that had been fastened into one of the leftover contraptions from the early days. It would never work the way he had it, but it became clear to Jack just exactly how to make it work for him. He got to work spreading it out as flat as he could on the ground while leaving the fastened end fastened, and taking the free end with him behind the boulders. Eventually the old goat would step into the middle, and then Jack would only have to pull to have him slung into a nice cocoon of rope net. Little Maid finally struggled up and rubbed against Jack, wagging her tail.

And when Skookum reappeared Jack held his breath.

"I smell ya!" the old giant declared to the sky, stepping right into the middle of the net. Jack pulled hard, scooping him into it. His shoulder twinged again, but Jack hardly had time to think of the pain. Watching Skookum twist and turn, trying to get out until he was in a cocoon of rope was impossible to look away from. It worked better than Jack could have imagined. The dog whined, her loyalties split, or maybe her sensibilities were just more refined than Jack's; he wouldn't doubt it. She followed him, whimpering some while looking back, like she wanted Jack to go back, and free the man, do the right thing.

"I know, girl. He's bungled up in there good, but I'm sure it'll only take that old goat twenty minutes or so to chew himself out. And I gotta move some gold, get back down there, and get you more food, dog food, the real deal. My friend Evon says a dog needs a proper diet, and some medicines to clear the bugs out. She also says never make a promise to a pooch you can't keep. I'll keep my promise. I'll get you some good food and all you need. You aren't feeling too good now, are you? Aw, come on now, he'll be all right. He's tough as old shoe leather, and besides, it gives him something to do." Jack gently patted the dog's head. She leaned into him for more, but still looked worriedly back where the gruff old giant could be heard swearing at the rope that held him.

Favoring his aching shoulder, Jack overloaded his dolly with two enormous sacks of gold, anxious to get back down before something got him too. Both sacks were larger than he should ever consider taking down the vine, but his victory over outwitting that old goat puffed him up, and he became fully confident of his new pulley system, thinking how he'd lower the bags and then maybe rig the dog and just take her with him then too. He was certain he could rig something up, maybe using his jeans somehow. Maybe he could put the pants on her and hook her in by the belt. Lowering her down would be a snap on his ingenious system.

He got the gold into the bucket and the bucket hooked to the cable and gently pushed it over the rugged lip so it wouldn't snag on the vine or the wall of the tawl. Before he could stop it, the bucket tipped, the bag of gold slid out and disappeared. Jack stared into his open hand. All thought of trying to rescue the dog with some makeshift sling left his head. He'd kill her with his brand of genius. Just then, Little Maid came into view and ran to him, ramming him gently with her nose.

"Aw, it all went to hell." He petted her gently. "I'll be back with food for ya. If the old goat is still stuck I'll get him out. Don't worry, girl. It'll be OK. Just a dozen hours, no more. I'm certain I can fix this. If you want to come down with me, I'll find a way." This wasn't arrogance or bullshit; he believed he could save her, but not by himself. The dog whined all the harder, nudged her head under Jack's hand for more scratching. He hugged the dog. "It'll all work out," he said the way Evonal was always saying. "Go on now, go watch after him. You'll see; he'll chew that rope off in no time. And I'll be back with food for you so go on now, stop worrying. I can fix this."

For the second bag, Jack hooked it to the cable, and then stepped into the vine, and carefully brought it over the lip, like fragile glass. It weighed much more than he expected, but he eased it down slowly with one hand on the cable. Twice it slipped and he caught it quickly, but it took all of his strength, his muscles began quivering with the exertion, and he worried he might not be able to pack it home. Then it got away, Jack flicked the nearest hand to it, caught it and wrenched the shoulder bone from the socket. His howl was so deep he could hear Little Maid howling her sympathy.

At the bottom, he knelt in the sand to feel his shoulder. Dislocated, yes. The knob of his upper arm was in the wrong place. He sat there for a while whining into the crook of his good arm, afraid to move. He wished he'd stolen another bottle of that hooch, one good slug, and he would feel no pain at all.

Determined to have it all, Jack sucked up a deep breath and set to organizing the gold into his leather pack so he could bear the weight across his broad lower back. After he got the pack pulled on, he covered a fifty-yard radius kicking at the sand, searching for the lost gold, knowing it was futile. That was the way of gold: you let the fortune slip out of your grasp it went to whoever found it next, down through eternity. A shadow of the figure of the future discoverer moved along the bottom of the tawl, kicking up the first nugget, bending in half, finding first a yellow rock, soft from the hot sand, and wondering if it could be gold, rolls a pinch of gold into a thin string yards long. Next, the figure weighs it in its hand; it is ten times heavier than the same amount of sand in the opposite hand. The gold fever excites the finder's senses all at once; the only smell on earth is gold, from that moment on. The figure bites into it: its taste is smooth metallic, and sweet to the tooth. The figure examines the color: no one can guess the color of real gold before seeing it, not in its natural concentration; it is deeper and brasher than the diluted gold of jewelry.

It looks *earthy*. And then because almost no one can keep a secret, the others will come and at last bring down the ancient tawl, a natural edifice that was created over thousands of years first by a violently spewing volcano, and next the fickle ocean flood waters, wind, rain, and ice, in cycles until it was crushed into its independence from all of the other mountains in the range. Yes, because Jack once carelessly dropped a large bag of gold into the sand, the tawl will one day be leveled by humans determined to find the strike, missing its real treasures, the lake, the magic berries, the multitude of lizards; the history of all its residents will be never unlocked by careless, gold-fevered humans digging for heavy yellow metal.

Jack looked up at the tawl, and regretted its future demise, his greed, his stupidity, the overinflated ego, his clumsy science; his poorly built system that would someday destroy a place that he only stole from. He pulled on his hat and went to get the big yellow dog some food, some medicine. For the next two miles, anyway, he had to keep his head out of the distant, unmanageable future. He wondered if he might be hallucinating too. When Jack stood up and walked, the strap of the backpack became a misery. His moans seemed to echo off the low clouds that hung overhead.

"You OK, kid?" Old Sylvia called. "Don't look so shocked to see me. You know I've been following you. Which brings me to, what are you doing here?"

"I think I broke my shoulder," he cried, keeping his pace steady, moving Old Sylvia away from his vine.

"Let's see it," Old Sylvia said. Jack dropped his pack instantly, but she had to remove his shirt.

"Dislocated." Old Sylvia *teeched* and *teeched* and shook her head. "All right, something's got to be done, and it's going to hurt, Jack. Brace yourself."

"Wait!" Jack cried. Suddenly it became clear what he had to do. "Listen, I need your help, and in exchange I'll help you destroy that vine."

"You mean the one in the town or the one you keep going up and down? Uh huh, don't think you're so clever. I've lived in this place many years, Jack. Many long, long years."

Jack gulped.

"What do you want my help for?" she asked, busy taking things off her person, including her hat and guns.

"I need to bring this big, very big yellow dog down off that tawl."

Old Sylvia stopped. "It's still alive? Is there anything else still alive up there?"

"Oh sure. Lizards, birds, bugs, and a dangerous fuck of an old coot torturing that dog."

"Yeah." Old Sylvia sighed. "I'd best help you get the dog."

"Think you can climb it?"

Old Sylvia's face lit up in an unexpected smile. "Brace yourself, Jack, this is going to really, really hurt for a few minutes."

Before he could ask another question or even back up she jumped on his side, planting both feet on his waist, she was that tiny. Her stiff body made a neat angle off his, the wind blew through them lifting her long loose clothes like they were about to set sail. The dusty wind soothed his burning back. She pulled hard and pushed. The pain knocked him on his knees. The pleasure of the cooling breeze crossed somehow with the pain; for a second Jack went blind, deaf, mute. Old Sylvia stepped off his hip.

"It's back in place. Now that's going to pop right out again if you aren't careful. Drink this water. Once you get home, you're probably gonna want some whiskey."

While Jack moaned, she helped him dress. "Kneel on the ground. I'll hold it up and get the traps onto your arms." Together he got the heavy pack onto his back. "Yep, I can climb it, but not in this skirt," she said. "Now you tell me what your plan is to get the dog down, and I'll tell you how to fix that plan so none of us dies. And after that, you tell me where that vine is getting its water so we can root it out. I'll find it sure enough without, but what if it gets to the lake, Jack? What if?"

"There's a place inside an old mine near to here. We used to dam it up so we could light candles and swim in the dark, eerie place. It's got to be there. No telling how it got there."

"It travels underground. We'll never find all of it. Just have to cut off its water wherever we can. I read up. You're going to need a few days to rest that shoulder. You going to get the dynamite or am I?"

"I'll get it."

"It's a deal, then. And listen, Jack, you're gonna need some new britches. You're busting out of the back of those."

For the entire walk back they talked about many things Foison, but they didn't exchange any other particulars about what they knew about that old goat up there, which was fine with Jack.

Once home, he put his pack away, grabbed some cash, and just out of the corner of his eye, went to see if Evonal was home. When he saw her truck gone, he headed to the Lake sisters' restaurant.

■ ■ ■

Chapter 29

Jack's shoulder seemed to be healing quickly, but he was careful not to get it snagged on anything. He could feel the tenuous connection of the ball and socket. The thought of it coming out was second only in dread to the thought of it getting snapped back in. Using the reliable sand sleigh he'd built as a kid, he got the dynamite OK and stashed it and the caps in his tool shed, all awaiting Old Sylvia to make good on her promise. Fearing the demise of his vine, he didn't rush out to find her, but he knew Little Maid was pining away. All that gold; how much time would it take to bring it down? Once the vine's roots were destroyed would it hold up against the tawl long enough to keep his coming and going ladder secure? Old Sylvia might have some plans of her own once she got up there; he couldn't know. Mixed with those fears he fidgeted with the thought of the big yellow dog waiting in vain for him all these long days. Although Evonal wouldn't talk to him, her words still came at him, but without the warmth. She once told him that dogs needed friendship as much as food and medicine. Whenever they started losing hope they just lay down and waited for the person to show up, make good on their promises, or for the broken heart to take them to heaven.

Downtown Foison was still busy with strangers weaving around him. Free of the weight of gold, his shoulder repairing itself, Jack walked more easily, but the tight clothes were having their say now too. In spite of having very little room, his stomach roared.

With nowhere else to go, he wandered over to the Lake sisters' restaurant.

As soon as he entered, he slid into a booth, melted down into the chair, and buried his face behind a menu. Linda appeared immediately. "Jack!" she yelled, making him flinch.

"Pancakes and eggs with all the sides you got, and honey, syrup, and jam."

"What do you want to drink?"

"Water, lots of it. Orange juice, half a gallon, and a pot of coffee with a quart of half and half."

"I'll be right back!" Her eyes twinkled, like he was kidding.

"I'm serious. I'm starved!" It was the best he could do, considering what all he had on his mind. When she skipped off, he began to eat the sugar by pouring it into the spoon before dumping it onto his tongue.

"What else can I get for you?" Linda whispered into his ear, startling him. That girl needed a bell around her neck, he thought, but he said, "Just hurry it along, please. I gotta get into town and find bigger clothes. I can barely move in these, let alone work."

"Jack, you should spend here. The people of Foison Surrounded need you to shop local."

This only widened the chasm between the Lake sisters and Foison. Jack knew none of the locals needed cash from him. All his life, they'd been on the bartering system. Anyway, they were in their own world spinning up a cyclone of emotion that now crackled through the air, another thing about real Foison the Lake sisters didn't notice.

"There's no one here that can make clothes."

"She means I can make your clothes for you. I got some boots in the house I'm certain will fit you, Jack." Astrid spoke from behind him, also startling him, but at least she set three large glasses of water in front of him, a jar of sugar, and the juice. It took a second, and another heaping teaspoon of sugar to steady his nerves and make sense of what she'd just said.

"Hmmmmmm," Jack mumbled gulping down the water, one glass after another, thirsty, but also stalling while he thought it through. "I doubt they'd be big enough. Where'd they come from?"

"I have no idea where they came from," Astrid replied. "They were there when we moved in, in a metal box, locked up tight to keep the mice out, I'm sure." Astrid went on to explain that soon after finding them she'd stuffed them with paper and oiled them and saved them on a top shelf back in the sealed metal box, a pair of boots way too special to just get rid of. He asked Linda to bring him some milk, and he was glad to get her big, round eyes off him.

"I could only imagine the owner of those, and wished he'd of come back for them." Astrid said this with a sigh that expressed both acceptance of lost love and longing for more, something Jack understood completely. Then she disappeared.

"I'm certain they will fit you perfectly, they are gi-gan-tic," Astrid sang putting platters of food on the table. "I brought you some whipped cream too."

Jack began inhaling the food.

"Finish your breakfast, and come along and try the boots, if you want. I can measure you for the shirts and pants so I can get started on those tonight. I have a power sewing machine. I can get something done for you by tomorrow if I start now. Juanita can probably knit you some nice, thin socks too, if you can't find any to fit," she said pleasantly, like she was certain. Jack knew Juanita would be politely outraged at the thought of this interloper making such a suggestion on her behalf.

"I'll follow you over," Jack said, popping the last bite of food—the size of a small woman's fist—into his mouth and washing it down with a full quart of hot coffee in a series of gulps. "Ahhhhhhh!" he cried happily when the liquid hit his stomach and the caffeine zinged to his head. But before he could wipe his mouth on his sleeve, Linda swooped in with a napkin, and mopped his face for him on his way to another table swinging her ass with a motion that kept him oddly transfixed, yet also feeling a bit let down too. Jack wiped his own mouth with the back of his hand, threw down some cash, and stood up.

Astrid and Linda Lake lived in one of the oldest dwellings in Foison, one that had been lived in by several families before their aunt bought the place a few years back. Like the old church, it was constructed of hundreds of old glass bottles that had been layered into the thick adobe walls. Unlike the old church, the builder had done it right, putting the necks inside, decorating the outside with the bottle bottoms, leaving hundreds of glass circles in staggered rows from bottom to top, and no whistling when the wind blew. It was often called the polka-dot house.

At certain angles, the house looked like it was falling down, but that was part of its sheltering, enduring design, having the east roof drop lower than the west, protecting it from the sun.

"Nice cactuses, Astrid," Jack said. The place was surrounded with them.

She surveyed everything with a steady, stern glare before saying, "They help keep the creeps out, you know. I'd prefer dogs, but Linda's highly allergic."

"Aaa."

"Low ceilings!" Astrid called as she pushed the door open and waved him in. Jack bent in half to get himself through it, entering with a vague sense of apprehension that had nothing to do with banging his head.

"Let me just run to the powder room. Have a seat."

Jack felt self-consciously huge in the place, but he enjoyed seeing it again.

The familiar house was made of a conglomeration of materials. Most of its walls were the thick adobe mud found locally and mixed with crushed sagebrush, a common building material for underground homes out there, but this one wasn't underground because there really were no hills in Foison proper to dig into. It was trussed like a rambling, horizontal shaft, sturdy as a steel cage. Of course the necks of the bottles stuck into the house about an inch;

just that part where the cork fit inside. Here, these had been methodically stopped-up to keep critters out. As a child, he must've spent a lot of time in the house. It all came back at once. The builder's large handprints could still be seen in certain places in the plaster on the ceiling, as if they held the house up.

There was plenty of natural light because of the thoughtful placement of the windows. Although the temperatures were scorching outside, the bottle-long, thick walls kept it cool and dry inside. The floors were made of rows of more mine timbers set closely together, but with a strong wire mesh over it with one-eighth-inch grids, probably to keep mice out. There were small rugs covering much of the floor, no doubt to protect bare feet from being shredded by the mesh. This was the type of place that was destined to crumble over time, but it was obvious that all of its residents had taken good care of it. He wondered who all the past tenants had been. From the date scratched into the front door timbers it was easy to calculate that it was well over one hundred years old; one of the originals.

He took a seat in the largest, sturdiest looking chair. There were flowers in several vases, of course quilts, and more; all the layers of stuff women found essential for their peace of mind. The potbelly stove was bright red enamel. The entire place was in perfect repair and absolutely spotless. Jack pressed himself as deeply as he could into the chair, feeling weirdly young, yet also bone weary with age. His shoulder stopped aching.

The scent of lavender soap wafted in before Astrid appeared. It was obvious she'd brushed her hair out; it fell in smooth waves over both her shoulders. "What would you like to drink?" she asked, still wiping her hands on a small pink towel.

"Something with sugar in it."

"We don't have ice. So hot or tepid mango tea?"

"Tepid. And sugary."

"Don't get too comfortable, Jack, we need to move back to the sewing room so I can take your measurements. Take your old boots off, I'll get the new boots and the tea." Astrid disappeared again.

Prying his boots off using only his good arm made him light headed and he had to sit back and heave heavy breaths while his feet throbbed. Once his feet settled down, Jack relaxed some.

"It smells like new timbers," Jack said loud enough so Astrid was sure to hear him.

"Well, we added some in the back, but the rest has held up just fine," she called from another room. "They don't seem to age much and even the mice don't chew on them. We got an electrician to drive over and fix the wires inside steel tubes so the mice can't get to those anymore either."

The new steel supply lines had been skillfully strung along the supporting timbers. Astrid entered the room still talking about the electrical stuff so he did his best to make the expected appreciative sounds. The topic only reminded him of everything he wanted, but could never have.

"Well here's the tea. Ooops! Sloppy me." Astrid sloshed tea on his foot. They both looked down, but she spoke first.

"I think your swollen feet could use a soothing soak and a nice penetrating massage," she said. "Wanna try?"

"If you think it'll make 'em go back to normal."

"I'll get everything."

Jack closed his eyes and waited. It wasn't long before Astrid returned with a tub of hot water. It smelled of salt and vinegar. "Just tip your head forward," she said, tucking a pillow behind his head before kneeling down to roll up his pants leg. Once she had those out of the way, she gently smoothed the hairs back down on his legs before planting his feet in the heated water.

"Epson salt bath," she murmured, like that said it all. "I'll just massage the one while the other one soaks. We'll do a couple of cycles until the swelling is gone down."

He felt the warm oil ooze over his skin and her strong fingers begin to dig into his swollen flesh. Working himself deeper into the chair, Jack took the delicately embroidered pillow from behind his head and held it in his lap. Really, it repulsed him; he wanted to throw it off him. He drifted off into some new misery, awakened when a pillow was clamped over his small face; his frantic pulling at her hair until she let up, and he could roll under the bed. He snapped his eyes open, looked around, recognized the dream, thought about the way his head floated on top of Evonal's plump pillows, next to her dark hair, the way she told him about her day, like he'd lived it with her and she was highlighting the best parts for both of them to think about again; the delicate scent of her oil paints; the big yellow dog's silky fur after he'd given it a once over with his pocket comb, getting all those burrs out.

It occurred to him that Astrid worked at his feet, humming a tune with a strong march beat to it. The next time he awoke his feet were dry and the boots were next to him. Astrid was not in the room with him so he bent down and tried them on. They were enormous, and to his relief a bit large, which he thought was good in case he continued to swell, or when he needed thick socks in the winter. When he laced them up and stood, he felt like they were made for him. And then he was seized with a peculiarly enveloping sense of claustrophobia.

"Astrid?" he called.

"Follow those red rugs to the back," she answered, like she'd been waiting to hear from him.

He'd only walked a few feet when the floor changed to thick, cemented-down tiles of a pale brick color, which did not move, even under his weight. He found her in a room with both sewing and laundry things, the obvious recent addition to the house, and although it wasn't made with adobe or old wine bottles, it was nicely fashioned with the thick plaster walls of old-timey forts and those deep-set windows that opened into the sill, but the ceilings were higher. He could stand up fully; his sense of claustrophobia eased.

"Great room. I bet Vern built these windows from scratch, didn't he? Is that a cactus forest in the back there?" he asked, looking out the back window where rows of large cactuses stood like armed sentinels.

"They look natural, huh? None are really native to this place, but they don't jump like that wicked bamboo someone cursed this town with. Those boots look made for you. Now that we got your feet shod, let's see what we can do about the rest of your clothes. Stand over there near that table and let me get you measured. I'll start tonight. Don't break wind, Jack, or your pants will split right down the back."

Astrid and Linda Lake apparently used glass jars of all sizes for storing thread, snaps, zippers, buttons, colorful powders in small, knotted bags, thousands of jars of colorful indiscernibles. When she turned, they made eye contact as long as it took for her to slowly pull the measuring tape apart. Confused, he picked up a jar of red buttons, screwed the top off and began shaking red disks into his mitt.

"Jeez! There are sure a lot of ways to make a red button," he said, studying them.

"Well the trick is finding enough of the one you need. I think you should stop fiddling with those buttons and come stand here so I can measure you. I've got to get started if you want something to wear by tomorrow."

"I need bigger clothes," Jack said, clumsily trying to get the small buttons to spill from his thick hand back inside the small mouth of the jar. Most of them tumbled to the floor.

"Sorry."

"Just leave them," she said, but as Astrid knelt down to retrieve them, Jack automatically bent over too. The small nugget of gold that he kept in his top pocket dropped into her long hair. They both stood immediately.

"What is this?" she asked, threading it through her hair until it landed in her palm. "Gold?" When her twinkling eyes met Jack's it was like one addict meeting another.

"Take a bite of it," Jack whispered.

Astrid took a nibble, seemed to be savoring it like he would.

"Just tuck it into your molar, like a filling," Jack advised.

"A nugget for the boots," she whispered.

Jack fished one out of his hidden pocket and laid it in her open palm where it set like a quail egg. Astrid closed her long fingers over it and then her eyes and savored it there before dropping it inside her bra.

"I think we should see about getting you into some comfortable clothes," she said, with a new huskiness in her voice. "Do you want jeans exactly like these?"

"In as thick a fabric as you can manage."

"I've got a strong canvas I was going to use for a patio cover. It has some stretch in it too."

"Canvas," he repeated, like it meant something to him.

Astrid wrapped the measuring tape around his middle, pulling herself tightly into him. "Do you plan to marry my sister?" she said, the gold on her breath wafting to his nose, tantalizing him.

"Marry?"

"You heard me."

When she tipped her face toward him, the angle forced the soft chin into a strong point, her wide eyes turned to his, sparkling blue and reflecting no pretense, her faint smile causing her smooth cheekbones to rise like two opalescent hills. Astrid Lake was dangerously beautiful, Jack realized with a start, feeling a renewed power surge. He could smell the gold on her breath; closed his eyes and inhaled; felt a sudden urge to get to his tawl so he'd have another handful to share, but it was Evonal's open palm that he saw in his mind's eye, dropping the gold into and covering it with his own hand. The two of them stood together, he could see it like a moving picture, and all around their feet were golden puppies, big-footed dogs with long ears and sweeping, feathery tails fanning the dust out of the room.

"Do you plan to marry little Linda or not?"

Jack backed up a few inches, coughed a few hacks just to settle himself back in the room. "Don't you think she's kinda young?"

"Yes," Astrid said. "I do think." She moved the tape to measure his inseam. And then she worked her hands up Jack's legs. She cupped his knees, one in each hand, giving him a sly look. "I'm not too young," she said. And then she gave his balls a gentle caress before releasing his crotch.

To his surprise, Jack pushed her hand away. The only woman he wanted was Evonal. Depressed by the thought of wading through a long life alone, Jack began to fidget, ready to escape Astrid, the cozy cute-ass house, the clever women, the gold fever, the one woman he would never have: everything. Just get the dog and get away to his own foreign land. That was always the big question, but how hard could it be to answer it?

"Cat got your tongue, Jack?"

"Uh, Astrid, didn't you once go to the trouble to make me understand how dangerous you can be? I mean, I don't want to dig my own grave or anything."

She laughed at him, twisting her tape measure over her fist, chewing the tiny ball of gold in her mouth.

"Do I need to find another pants maker? I'd like to keep my balls attached to my underside," Jack said.

Astrid quickly shook herself out of it. "No, Jack. I'll make up your shirts and pants while you and I both think this over."

"Thanks," he said.

Astrid looked pleased—and ordinary again. He stood still for the few minutes it took to finish measuring his large frame. When he left the Lake house he didn't know which direction to turn in. The dusty smell of a desert storm filled the air, and although Jack could see the dark clouds on the far-off horizon, flashfloods were washing through somewhere, and they'd be hitting parts around Foison soon. Well, he thought, a good flash flood or two, a couple sticks of well-placed dynamite, and Foison might be free of that vine and everything associated with it.

During that first visit to her new seaside home, Evonal had discovered photo albums with dozens of photos of Foison, a documentary of sorts that her parents had taken for her grandmother. Looking through them she couldn't help but feel that they must have made her grandmother a little sad. Before she left, Evonal was trying to document the changes, if any, in Foison. It was a more painstaking project that she'd dreamed, requiring a good camera and binoculars to help spot landmarks to set up accurate shots. Photographing the dry lake was the most heartbreaking. There was still some water in it when her parents had first photographed it. The surface had shimmered like there was a film of silver over it. Now the surface was cracked and peeling topsoil, death white. There were other changes too, but nothing as soul wrenching as the ugly arbors formed by the errant vine. Evonal begrudgingly photographed it too, because that was what recording a place in time meant. The cloying scent of the vine was something she no longer noticed; for that she gave herself a personal reprimand. She walked until she could glimpse Jack's house. It was leaning a little, it made her heart ache, then she returned to getting a long view of her own place with the mountains and tawls in the background.

Wearing the new shorts had drawbacks; the back of her legs were getting sunburned. She didn't let her deter her. She patiently searched for the same landmarks that were in the old photos. It was through the binoculars that she watched Jack walk up to her porch and clip a letter to the screen door. In itself it wasn't such a strange event, although she couldn't imagine Jack writing anything, let alone finding an envelope to stuff it into. That was a side of Jack she would love to see. And then a few minutes later, Evonal's mouth fell open when she saw a shimmering-haired Linda Lake sneak onto her porch, and snatch the letter away.

"You see that?" Juanita's familiar voice asked. Evonal had seen her earlier, out with her binoculars, spying on Foison "across the way," as she'd come to call it. Like the rest of wary Foison, Juanita had a gun tucked inside her belt, inside her shirt, hidden. Evonal remained unarmed. The two women had their binoculars trained in the same direction.

"Did I see that?" Evonal echoed by way of encouraging Juanita to tell what she was looking at.

"That damn Linda Lake just stole something off your porch!"

Evonal nodded. "Yep, I saw that."

"Those two sisters need to win the lottery and get on their way out of this town. They do not understand Foison at all. You going to do anything about it?"

Evonal thought it over. "I'll ask Jack what he wanted."

"He wants someone to take care of him."

"Well. Well," Evonal said, and she thought sadly, I can't do that. "Listen, Juanita, can I get a photo of you in front of the post office?"

"Now wouldn't I love that?"

"You lead and I'll follow!" Evonal chirped, but she was thinking how later she would wipe that mean note off her window so Jack felt free to come around again. She missed him, and now she knew he missed her too.

■ ■ ■

Chapter 30

In only two days the big clothes had been delivered. When Jack tried to take them, Astrid held on to the stack like she was parting with things that were actually keeping her alive. She had charged him more than she'd first quoted. A hundred dollars for each pair of pants, the shirts had been sixty. Giving Astrid that tiny bite of gold had been a colossal mistake, but this dawned on him about ten minutes too late. Of course all she wanted was more gold. "That's all I got," he had told Astrid, flapping the bills. The sidelong look she gave him was feline, like he'd just become her prey. She took the cash.

Having clothes that weren't about to tear off him gave Jack back his freedom. He was doing his best to creep around the side of his house, trying to make a clean getaway to where he'd parked his truck. The two Lake sisters were doing their best to follow him, and it wasn't paranoia. Suddenly Astrid was pretending to get her exercise run in wherever Jack happened to be going. The saccharine perfume Linda Lake wore was as aggressive as gasoline, so he didn't need to see her shadow to know where she was. It was a good thing they were busy running their sandwich shop.

His shoulder was flaring up; he thought he might have rolled over and slept on it. Every time he overreached, it clicked, giving him the chills. Since he hadn't heard from Evonal, his plan was to get to town, get the dog food, some drive through a gooey pancake breakfast where he didn't have to talk to nobody, beer. Get back, climb the tawl one-armed, and at least feed and brush the dog. Maybe she'd bring him another bag of gold dust. Jack hit himself in the head before hanging it in despair at his gold-fevered, greedy self. This seemed like a good moment to stop and wedge a bit of gold into his molar.

"Jack, where you going now?" Old Sylvia hissed from somewhere behind him, like she was hiding out from someone too. When her footsteps got closer he half raised his good arm over his head, waiting for the feel of the gun stuck into his back.

"Relax, kid, I'm not holding a gun on you. Don't act so guilty." She chuckled, and for some reason, it made Jack laugh too.

"I'm trying to escape to town without those Lakes tailing me," he said honestly.

"Now you're thinking on your feet, Jack."

He loved the way she said that, like he was smart enough to actually think at all.

"I see those two shiny girls following you everywhere, now. Why is that?" she asked like she already knew.

Without thinking he confessed the events that led to his most recent situation.

"Then we'll have to distract them."

Jack half stretched by taking a deep twist to the right to ease the pain in his sore back, but he was also careful about doing any uplifting of his dislocated shoulder.

"Is that shoulder still giving you trouble?"

"Yep."

"Can we get to that vine today?"

"The one in town? I don't think we can pull it off with all the people downtown."

"I mean the other one. The one you need to get rid of."

Jack took a couple steps back. "I don't see why that one matters."

"Yes you do," Old Sylvia said. "And you promised."

"I just mean it can wait. Right?"

"Not if you want my help getting that pooch down to safety."

Right, Jack thought. Little Maid. How long could she last? He could hear her heavy breathing, her lolling tongue. Under all that fur: skin and bones. The cruelty she was living with every day. Yes. This rattled him, the trade-off. Was it really going to be the dog for the gold? His heart began pounding, but he nodded.

"You got the dynamite?"

"Listen, that stuff's got the crystal crud. It's old. We have to be careful."

"I'll pull the sled, then. Don't look shocked. I saw you taking it to your shed," Old Sylvia said. "But first give me an hour to make sure those Lake sisters are good and tied up."

"Tied up?" Jack liked the sound of that.

"I'm gonna distract them. Don't be so literal."

A couple of hours later, as they trudged along, Jack was whispering to the dynamite sticks. "Be calm," he whispered. "Don't blow your cool." For a change, Old Sylvia was completely silent.

"We'll stash it here and I'll show you the spot where I think it's getting its water. I'll have to think out where we're gonna blast." His voice quavered, the knot in his stomach growing until it felt like something was gripping both his bowels and lungs. The end of the vine was the end of everything Jack was pinning his future on.

"Relax, Jack, it'll take weeks before it dies. The thing is huge. We can get up and back down with the dog before it knows it's dying. After that, you take your chances, but you probably have enough time to steal all the gold you want. Once you're satisfied, cut it off the wall. I made a brew to pour on it too."

Jack couldn't listen to that anymore. He decided to worry about the dynamite. Climbing into an old mine shaft was lunacy for teenagers. What was the word for someone like him with funky-ass dynamite in a leather backpack?

"I think we'll stash the dynamite out here."

"Don't we need it in there?"

"Let's go in, take a look, and see what we come up with."

"You scared, Jack?"

"Obviously. That shit's pretty powerful. When it goes off, it's a gigantic *Kabang!* and not just in a cartoon bubble," Jack said seriously.

"That was clever. Hand it over. I'll carry the pack," Old Sylvia said. "I'm old, I have this one thing to do and then God can sweep me into her arms."

"Look, old woman, if you go, I go. That explosion causes the air to fold and suck and push out to get away too. And it breaks up all the rocks and makes them go flying with it. We gotta be real far back before it goes off."

They picked over the piles of long-ago chiseled-out rocks moving through the dark mine slowly, their way lighted by the powerful flashlight Old Sylvia had dug out of her pack.

"Stop here, let me get my bearings. I don't want to stumble down the shaft."

Old Sylvia shined the light around, illuminating the walls. When the beam hit a wall of graffiti she ran it over all the scrawls, over and over like she was searching for clues. "Did you kids really misspell swear words?"

"Keep the light on it a minute," Jack said.

Old Sylvia chuckled. Truth was, Jack remembered them painting the walls, but now he was unable to decipher it. It felt like he'd lost some special powers.

"Ready?" she asked. Jack motioned her to start again.

"Stop! It's just off this cliff, here," Jack cried. Old Sylvia shined her light down on the pool of dank water. Great clumps of the vine rose out of it like an ancient serpent.

"It's worse than I thought!" she cried.

Jack shuddered.

"Our best bet is to blast it out and drain the water, but we can't do it inside here. We'll get killed."

"What's your best plan?" Old Sylvia asked.

"It's a sin to poison water, but maybe pour your potion in there for starters. I'll chop at it. Outside we'll blast a hole and try to drain the pool. This once drained down into a dammed area we built way back when. It can't be much these days, but will give us our bearings. I got more dynamite in my shed if we need it. We'll come back if we have to, once the dog is off that tawl and seen by the vet. I ain't exactly anxious to kill my route up there either." His voice cracked.

"Once you are away from that poisonous gold, you'll get over the fever in a few months. But you have to get away from it."

Jack imagined himself in a sweaty delirium craving a bite of gold.

"You'll have the dog to help you. She'll make a difference. You'll see."

Hacking the thick growth in half took Jack the better part of three hours, with Old Sylvia mainly getting in the way. It was night when they got outside, about the time he usually climbed up there. Jack tipped his head back to look at the night sky, imagining himself up there, feeding Little Maid. Was she worried?

It took another two hours to locate the outdoor pool.

"Here it is."

Old Sylvia studied it. "That pool we were just looking at is above this?"

"Yes, that spout of water comes directly from it. We had to bring the water outside using an old pipe. The girls wouldn't stay inside the mine and swim."

"I can't imagine how they didn't find that inside utterly charming," she said sarcastically.

Jack frowned at her. "So we built the pool. It was a great place. Under the stars. Shine the light around see where that vine went." They couldn't find it.

"It must be under there, come out the bottom. That thing likes to travel far underground. This might take years clearing it all out."

Old Sylvia circled the pool with her light again and again.

"You kids were certainly ambitious!" Old Sylvia said.

"Gave us something to do. Gone days. Just gone now. Took all the best people with it."

Her light shined over the area, falling on a clump of green near their feet. "I see your pot plants have made it."

"I'll have to remember those," Jack said seriously. Another thing he'd forgotten.

They discussed how to set up the two sticks to get the wall to give way and release the water. Time had helped erode it. Eventually Jack settled on a plan, got the caps on and with shaking hands, tamped the leaking sticks, reeled out the old wicks. Picking up Old Sylvia when she protested leaving, he set her down a good distance away and gave her the matches.

"We light and run," he told her.

He carefully wound the fuses out until he thought they might be far enough away.

They lit the fuses, which sizzled a bright glowing line, and waited and waited and waited for the explosion.

"I'll go blast it with one good clean shot," Old Sylvia declared, running toward it. Jack had to run faster to grab her up.

"Noooo. You have to get too close to hit it. It's certain death. And you promised to help me! I'm sure I can smell the burning fuse. Just wait."

"Let me go look!" When she tried to break away, Jack ran after her, knowing they were already too close. "Wait!" he called, struggling to catch up with her. Grabbing a flap of material from her dress, he was able to whip her off the ground, and at least keep her feet from moving across land until he could get a better grip.

The blast broke over them like hell had arrived. Jack went ass over tin cups watching the soles of his own boots churn air, but then realized they were not his. The whole world seemed to be up in the air—sand, rocks, shards of concrete. Old Sylvia had flown out of his arms, tumbling in the air with her flashlight lighting her ballooning skirt, like an umbrella in a lightning storm. When she landed, she collapsed into the ground without a sound. Then the world settled back down around them, only newly arranged. The ringing in his head promised to be painful and prolonged, steady as his beating heart. Jack got up to see if Old Sylvia was still alive, expecting every bone in her frail body to be broken, but she was standing by the time he got to her.

"I think my shoulder come out again, he shouted, trying to hear his own voice above the ringing.

Old Sylvia took her time checking it. Jack knew she was trying to find her bearings as much as he was trying to find his own. Her fingers shook as they kneaded his arm.

"It's just sore. You're scared. It's good. Just be careful with it. It'll never be like before. Just don't go up that vine tonight. I know you want to. It'll hold if you rest it."

He wasn't certain if he could hear her or if he was somehow reading her lips.

"Your ears ringing too?"

"Hell, yes. Now let's go see what happened," she shouted. Jack hesitated, uncertain if both blasts went off.

"We best check in the daylight when we can get to a safe vantage point and use the binoculars. For sure the wall has a hole in it. Tomorrow we'll put a blast in the water pipe, take out the wall so the water can't pool, after that we can start rooting it out."

"Think that brought the wall out?" Old Sylvia asked when they both stopped.

"We'll know tomorrow," Jack shouted over the ringing in his ears.

After that, they hobbled to the highway, Old Sylvia leaning on Jack like she might be really hurt.

"You gonna be OK?" Jack asked.

"I just need to rest this old body. You can let me go here. I'll see you tomorrow. Get about a hundred feet of strong rope, like the kind you use to tie down a load on a truck. Not too thick, but not clothesline either. I'll tie a sling we can use for the dog. We'll meet at the tawl, just before sunset. I'll have whatever else we'll need to get the dog," Old Sylvia shouted. Jack, still stunned, possibly deaf, and uncertain of who he was exactly, nodded dumbly.

He hadn't gone five feet when he heard Old Sylvia whistle. "Jack! Don't go yet!"

A pickup rolled past, Old Sylvia jumped behind Jack forming herself into his frame.

"Can you see your way to taking me over to Juanita's?"

"What happened?"

"That truck. Those two are my bad boys. I want you to avoid them. I'll bunk at Juanita's tonight. They'll leave in the morning after they see I'm not there. On the way, I'll need to stop at Evon's for a minute."

Jack, now oddly caught up in the strange life of Old Sylvia, took her there and waited at the fence, thinking over Evonal and Old Sylvia, two women he'd known all of his life, but really had intentionally avoided. Now every day they seem to somehow sustain him. And then his thoughts went back to the gold, the dog, that lake. How much gold could he bring down before that vine had to be chopped up and burned? Jack was beginning to see a larger picture in his own tiny life, it made his stomach churn and his muscles ache.

"She's not here, I'll leave a note," she hollered across the yard.

Jack had no doubt she carried everything she needed in one of her pockets, he went back to pressing the heels of his hands into his ears, trying to suck his eardrums back in place, and hear the world without the ringing. After that, he deposited her at Juanita's, watched Juanita guide her in, and went home feeling hungry and alone. The thought of having Little Maid keep him company at night while he counted his gold was the only thing that kept him working toward the future.

■ ■ ■

Chapter 31

Early the next morning, Jack, his ears still ringing, and as usual, starving, got up and showered, noticing even through the thick fog in his brain that the shower water had a slightly different odor, but he wasn't up to analyzing it. There was no more instant coffee; the cans of condensed milk were empty. After getting his truck out the stack of tumbleweeds he had artfully arranged, he trolled slowly past Evonal's to see if he could talk her into coming along. It hurt him that she didn't respond to the get-well card he'd left her, but she probably thought he was teasing her. Maybe he was; he didn't know anything anymore.

The plan was to drive into Edgecrest to get dog food, vitamins, and more food for his house, and the rope, as Old Sylvia instructed. He was also going to bring along an ax. On the way, he'd convinced himself that he'd enjoy a few hours kicking up his heels in Edgecrest, away from Foison, but the minute he arrived, he became anxious to leave.

Jack parked at the front door of Merry's Market, the only store he ever went in from the time he was a kid. He hurried into the store, feeling like he was in a time zone he didn't belong in anymore. The liquor and tobacco were locked up tight in glass cases at the front of the store, within easy reach of the cashiers, but out of the pockets of the shoplifters, he guessed. Like most of the big towns near to Foison, Edgecrest was also a fly-by town, sprung up on each side of the one highway that travelers used to get to skiing towns, or just to cross the great state of California. No doubt some shoppers flew in and out without paying. There were still three checkout stands, but only one was open this early. That morning he was grateful that the two people working in the store—withered, sagging, but not old, not really, simple folks who no doubt lived on eggs and beef poached in grease with buttered white bread—were taking turns going outside to smoke, so were not concerned with him at all, the lone shopper. When he saw he was going to have to ask for the beer, he decided to cut down the amount by half, and he pushed his sunglasses on; avoided looking up at the clerk by fiddling with the bills in his wallet.

Outside, the hot and dry morning indicated that a hotter and drier afternoon was coming. The gray storm clouds were hovering in the far-off distance just beyond Foison; Jack knew it was raining on his tawl. He thought of Little Maid, and knew she'd need to go to a vet right off to get checked and vaccinated. Jack stacked the bags inside the cab of his truck, planning to drive straight back, stopping only for four cups of coffee and breakfast at the drive-through, anxious to get to the sanctity of his place, and rest or do something to untie the knot that now pulled painfully at every joint in his body. At the Burger Fast, built weeks after Merry's Market, he actually ordered four of their largest breakfast trays with orange juice. As an afterthought he asked for a couple of cups of ice water. Lately Jack had spells of unquenchable thirst, and he could tell by the way his tongue flattened, and every taste bud grated like sand across the inside of his mouth, that another was coming on. After he got everything settled so he could eat while driving without spilling too much, he put the truck in gear and began rolling out of the parking lot. There, crossing the highway was Crystal, the car thief.

The highway at this hour was mostly deserted. There was the sound of a car that had already passed, but his was the only moving vehicle just then. Her platinum cap of hair was now dyed a brilliant red, the color of his sudden anger, red. Jack blasted his horn at her and she jumped, but glared at him before flipping him off, her usual come-hither enticement whenever she saw him. There was a time when Jack would have wrecked his truck to get to Crystal. He let the truck roll toward her just to get a good look at his past; it came as a shock. She held her ground, there in the middle of the highway with her middle finger still in the air defiantly, the other hand cocked on her hip, like she could stop wind if she wanted. On the opposite side of the highway, a huge semi thundered passed, tooting its horn, twice, like a trucker driver's how-'d ya do. The way she shook her ass at that driver, said it all, but when she turned her attention back to Jack, he knew it was only then that she recognized him. Crystal valiantly—he had to give her credit—stood her ground for another split second, before she ran to the nearest sidewalk, like that would stop him. Jack drove up on the sidewalk and kept her running along until at last, she stumbled, and fell to the ground where she cowered into a ball, barely hiding her head under her arm. Jack pulled up next to her, rolled down his window with a single press of a button, and thought he would throw a cup of the water on her red hair, just a little; something to put the flame out. Maybe she'd melt, or that ridiculous color would bleed from her hair into the back of her snug shirt. The impulse reminded him of the high school days when they used to throw Kool-Aid at each other right before they were all to shuffle in for the patriotic "wear white" assembly on Fridays.

"Don't kill me, Jack! I'll pay you back, I swear I will!" Her voice was muffled under her arm. He was certain someone would murder her someday, but it wouldn't be him.

"You look good, Crystal!" Jack yelled, backing up enough to turn away without touching her.

After that he drove toward home, eating the breakfasts, drinking all the water, orange juice, and finally four of the beers. Nothing settled him down, but he was full. His thoughts kept turning around when and how he'd get the vitamin-enriched food to the yellow dog. He slammed on the brakes and turned around; he had to get the ax and rope from the hardware store.

Jack swung the last turn to the old highway with one hand on the wheel. In the near distance were all the landmarks he knew so well, and now anticipated, even leaning forward on the steering wheel to see them sooner: the tumbling-down old stone house to his right; the landmark plaques, markers for old, dead pioneers of note; the black, purple, and red hills on his left; the first tawl, and then, at last, the highway sign that read, *Foison Surrounded, ten miles*. Sheriff cars began passing him with their lights on. Jack slowed his speed and drove toward home.

Even on the approach, he knew something bad had happened. There were sheriff cars and an ambulance. Everyone in real Foison was out clutching their own bodies with crossed arms. It was Vern who flagged him down, pointing to one of the dirt turnoffs that led to a hard patch behind his house.

Jack rolled down the passenger window, dreading the news.

"What's up, Vern?"

Vern broke down, laying his head on the window frame to weep. It was his brother who told him. "That old, friendly gal Sylvia was found murdered." Vern sobbed harder, a sister lost. Jack imagined Old Sylvia, parachuting through space, and landing on her own two feet. He could still hear her voice in his head, "Don't never give up, Jack." And he had the ax, the rope, ready like she said to be!

"Where's Mavis?"

"She found her. She's like the rest of us, torn up." Vern sobbed.

Jack could not picture his mother crying on her arm, like Vern.

"Where's Evon?" Jack choked, his tongue deadwood in his mouth.

"She's out of town. Drove Sidus to town yesterday for some reason or other. She'll be back soon. We'll tell her."

Jack leaned toward the window to say quietly, "We was out walking last night. She saw her boys drive by in a banged up '90 Ford. She asked me to walk her to Juanita's, so I did."

Vern lifted his head, studying Jack. "Where were the two of you?"

Jack told him approximately where they were.

"Now that I think of it," Jack said, "I saw an truck parked in Dun Flats. Hood was up, looked like two men working on the engine."

Vern narrowed his eyes. "Where in the world could you have been standing to get a look down on Dun Flats?"

Jack had been on his tawl, but he shrugged and lifted his brows.

"OK, don't say nothing. Listen, Jack, those aren't boys. I know that's the way she told of them, but they're grown men older than you. And dangerous, the both of them. You steer wide clear of them. We'll catch 'em."

"Not by yourselves?"

"Should've done it long ago. Goddamn it!" Vern kicked the side of the truck, and started weeping again. Jack said nothing about the dent he was certain to have in that panel.

"I'd be glad to help," Jack said.

"You keep out of this one. The best thing you can do is nothing. Say nothing. Forget we spoke of it. But thanks for the tip." Vern's look meant nothing more was to be said.

■ ■ ■

Chapter 32

The only time Jack ever went barefoot was inside his own house, but the soles of his feet felt scorched, like he'd been walking on coals. Walking on the edges of the sides of his feet, he got up, pulled the safe from the closet, and began pacing morosely in front of it. With each heavyhearted step, the floorboards moved like sticky piano keys, but it just seemed natural to him now.

He pulled the safe to the center of his bedroom, studying it. Rubbing a flat palm over the surface of the old safe, he thought about Old Sylvia's neat and tidy house. Her odd expressions; he could still hear her voice clearly. The way she chuckled when they were talking. That she was willing to bring down the dog, no questions asked, seemed to mean she understood something about him that he didn't really.

Jack wished he could cry, but he didn't want it to be about self-pity.

When he thought he heard footsteps outside, he blocked the safe with his body, throwing his arms around it protectively. Jack held his breath, hoping Linda would not appear; he didn't want to go through all that right now. And when nothing came of the sand-crunching noise, he let his breath out slowly, but his heart continued to hammer. Today, he felt like he was the one locked in that safe. There were things he should see to, but he just didn't want to ever leave his house.

Under the sink in the kitchen, in a small plastic bucket, was where he'd kept that old giant's Molotov cocktail of booze. Grabbing up the bottle of hooch, Jack went and sat on his bed and rolled it in his hands again and again. Two, three, scalding sips of this stuff and he would be gone for hours. Jack rubbed his chin, pulled on a tuft of hair; examined the old bottle. The purple glass meant that it was old and sun colored over time. It was scratched up and obviously used again and again, probably never washed, but that wouldn't matter; this stuff would fry germs off wet wood, he was certain. The smell made his tongue curl; his nostrils closed like shutters in fear and disgust.

Squeezing his eyes shut, he began counting to ten. He counted fast, slamming the bottle to his mouth on six and swallowing whatever made it in. It was hard to keep it down, but he did this three, four, five more times, but could not do it again. He belched painfully, as the newly swallowed liquor welled in his throat blistering his uvula. He swallowed another pull and held his breath. Once he was certain he was going to keep it down, he drank swallow after swallow, and when there was only an inch of moonshine left in the bottle, a loud burp blasted out of him, scalding his throat. A headache began crushing his brain—his thinking wobbled, his vision blurred.

Feeling suddenly euphoric, Jack fell hard back onto the mattress, the bed slamming into the floor from the reverberation. The underpinnings of the house squalled as if in pain. The room spun wildly, causing Jack to cling to whatever his hands closed around. The bottle fell to the floor, draining its caustic liquid out of the stubby neck, but Jack could only watch it wet the dirty clothes. Outside the single bedroom window he thought he heard everything on his tawl. That place, he thought. Special, it needed him to take care of it. There was a lot of stuff wrong up there. Jack had the sudden impulse to gather up his things and get up there to protect it. Dig in. He'd need weapons. Somewhere in the house he thought there was still a gun and some bullets. Mavis was an excellent shot too; she often cooked wild rabbit, and lots of snake too. He'd need that gun. Kill the old giant and throw that bag of bones over the edge. He was certain he would disintegrate before he hit bottom anyway so it wouldn't be murder. What had Old Sylvia said, "Some people deserve their life sentence." Old Sylvia, Jack thought, she'd advise him to take a gun. The idea wavered, hung out a little, while he tried to remember where that gun was kept, and then from somewhere inside his dull brain he knew there was a flaw in this plan, but couldn't decide what it was. The dog would have to be taken care of, that much was right. Jack squeezed his eyes shut to stop the spinning. Get a sling from Trong Tri, get the dog down to Foison. Keep feeding the dog. His brain began to calm down. He relaxed into the soft mattress, absently petting it, thinking of the faithful dog that he needed to protect. Fuck that vine. It would thrive or die, like old Foison Surrounded, so maybe it did fit right in. Jack needed something to protect him too, staunch the terrible loneliness.

Soon he found his mind drifting across the contours of Evonal, her voice coming to him in that easy flowing way of hers—like he was a part of her—talking about the rain. No. She was talking about places that rained. Rain, he thought. Nice. The flashfloods had been washing through on his trek across the desert, changing the monotony of things. He liked thinking about storms. Lightning too, especially after he'd survived a hit of that too. He wanted her to know he'd made friends with Old Sylvia. She was his aunt. His aunt! There was other things he meant to tell Evonal about, but where had she been? The world shifted under him, but he couldn't move.

Someone once told him that lightning snapped up a charge from the ground, and then all of a sudden the thunder was the clouds tearing. Jack smelled the lightning, heard the thunder crash so loud that the house shook. Somehow the noise banged into him. He rolled into a ball, covering his head with both hands, dropping to the floor helplessly. Another loud crack roared and the house split in two, right under him. Out of some sort of instinctual reflex, Jack's arms released his head, flying into two stiff splints they went to his sides, like a wooden soldier. After a brief, hard drop his straight arms and balled-up fists pegged into something soft and caught his fall. The landing felt cushioned, but it wasn't from the mattress. That had slipped out from under him and rested, folded in half at his feet, bowing to him. Somehow he had landed in cool sand, thick with dust. And he was in full sunlight. There were several moments of disbelief as he tried to piece it all together, and then he got it. His house had indeed broken into pieces. Mavis was at last right about something!

The safe now rested squarely inside the earth with only the top protruding from the sand. The metal top of the safe glinted in the bright sunlight. He crawled to it and curled into a ball on top of the hard, narrow surface. There was no way this would go unnoticed for more than a few minutes in Foison. They'd all been waiting for it. Staggering on drunken, wobbly legs, he managed to drag the old mattress onto the top of the safe. Jack fell on the mattress. Before he could do anything more, he'd have to sleep. After that, when it got dark, he'd have to bury the safe but good.

"Jackie Boy! You alive in there or ain't ya?" Sidus's voice came across to him the loudest and clearest. There were other voices too.

Jack stretched an arm full length over his head, waved his open palm like the flag of plague, calling: "Fine. Just sleeping it off. Don't worry 'bout me," he said it three times, barely lifting his head, on the fourth try he couldn't get the words out again so he let his arm drop heavily.

"It's not safe where you're at, Jack, Old Man," Vern's voice was coaxing.

"'Be all right." Jack lifted his head to yell over to them. "Just gotta' sleep some right now. Just too fuckin' drunk to get up."

"Yeah, we got it, Jack, but we're gonna move a few things out'ta the way to let you sleep out'ta danger for those couple a' hours. When you're ready, come on over for a bite to eat." Vern's voice sounded far off and strained, like he was already lifting something heavy. Jack heard the creak of old nails being stretched out of wood and then the sound of very hollow wood being thrown into a pile. That was the last sound he'd heard until he awoke several hours later under a makeshift tent.

Jack noticed right away that it was Evonal's blanket that protected him with a clever lean-to made of a simple wood frame, rope, and a blanket. There was a pile of his clothes neatly folded inside a cardboard box, with his shoes on the ground next to it. Evon had thoughtfully stuffed his shoes full of his paper and thick white socks to keep the critters out. Near those she'd left a gallon-size insulated cooler that he knew was filled with water; he could smell it.

Unfolding himself from the crinkled position he'd passed out in was an achingly painful task. Once accomplished, he sat up, grabbed the cooler so the spigot went into his mouth, and pushed the tiny button so he could suck the water straight down into his stomach and didn't stop until it no longer flowed. Still thirsty, he shook the container a couple of times, didn't hear anything slosh, so he took the lid off and had a look. The inch of water at the bottom would have to do, he lifted the container and poured the last tiny stream over his head, letting it trickle through his bush of hair to his head. A single drop reached an eyebrow. Not at all satisfied, he ran a hand through his hair with the hope of getting some water down to his burning scalp; it did nothing but stir the grease. Jack wiped his fingers off on his underwear, rested an elbow on each knee. Through the clot of hangover, Jack thought: bury the safe, put on clothes, go into town so no one comes back. Jack set about each task like a man struggling through chest-high wastewater, but he got the safe covered.

Once in town, people moved around him like he was a building in their path.

"Jackie!" A chorus of voices shrieked. The group of his neighbors, Fisher, Telly, his mother's best friend, and Mackson, were waving him over. The thought of having to talk to anyone in Foison made his head pound with a set of newly minted hammers.

At first he tried giving them a friendly salute before heading off, in that way people trade a wave for a wave and keep going, but when Mackson stepped out of the pack with his arm extended as if he was going to pull him in no matter what, he wandered over trying to muster up a good-natured greeting.

"Hey, Mackson, thought you were moving over to Eastridge permanently," Jack said, even though he wasn't certain he heard such a thing at all.

"Old Sylvia's been murdered."

The news hit him this second time worse than the first. He let his chest support his chin for a few minutes. Sweat beaded on his upper lip, tasting of the moonshine. Jack licked it off, felt an instant lift of his headache. His heart thudded down to the inside of his boots. His feet wanted to run.

"I gotta go," he said.

"Stop! We got important ground to cover here. You're Foison too, and we need your voice."

"Kill the vine, before it kills you," Jack said, walking off.

■ ■ ■

Chapter 33

Evonal learned of Old Sylvia's murder at the post office. Juanita, clutching the telephone, yelled, over the heads of the line of strangers, "Oh my God, Evonal, Old Sylvia's been found murdered!" Everyone turned to look at Evonal.

"Are you sure?" Evonal yelled in disbelief.

"Dead! She was just over visiting last night," Juanita cried.

Evonal sat on the floor butt first, but didn't feel the landing.

Juanita climbed over the countertop, wove through the people.

"Let me help you up, Evonal. I shouldn't've shouted that out like that. Sidus had just telephoned when you opened the door!"

Evonal stood on wobbly legs, "What happened?"

"That poor frail old thing fighting so hard for us all, and look what happened. Shot right through that brave heart! Evonal, I have to set you down in the lunchroom. I can't lock up here for another hour."

Inside the tiny lunchroom Juanita said, "There's gonna be a town meeting, just Foison, at the old schoolhouse. It's time to make some hard and fast decisions."

"Old Sylvia is gone!" Evonal cried over and over.

Two hours later they all crowded into the old school room, kept the door shut, and the lights low so no one outside of Foison folk would get suspicious and poke their nose in.

"First off, let's take a good look at just who isn't here," someone said.

Evonal was thinking about her last visit with Old Sylvia, when she went to tell Old Sylvia she was moving away. The old woman had clasped both her hands together and declared, "At last! At last!" After that she had talked on and on about her childhood in New Hampshire with her own grandma. "Hard, Evon, but glorious while she was still alive to guide us." Evonal began sobbing.

"She put up a good fight. I just got there too late. I shouldn't of left," Sidus said, between sobs.

"Don't go blaming yourself!"

"We'll give her a good send-off, Foison style."

"Here. Here."

"Now let's get down to brass tacks. Isn't it time to get these strangers out of here?"

"Things are getting stolen all the time. Yesterday we caught some of their idiot kids trying to climb to the roof of the bottle church by standing on the necks of those fragile bottles. No one can fix this stuff back!"

"The garbage is taking over. The stench! The car-sin-o-gens are sneaking into our bodies!"

"That vine is starting to wrap around the old building. Won't be long before it's swallowed up too."

"Old Sylvia was right-on! Oust this crap. Now!"

"But some of us need this money!" a voice cried out. The room erupted. It was Juanita who tried to get things organized by bringing out a stack of worn, numbered cards. Those that wanted to speak, took a number. Someone else rang a bell, a fragile tinkling that persisted until the room finally went quiet. Evonal slipped out, but her walk home was spooked by shadows, her heart hammering, her fingers bunching the hem of her new shirt. For the first time in her life she imagined criminals lying in wait inside her house. She veered off and went to Vern's, where she found him tinkering on his latest sculpture, using the light from what looked like a metal hat on a cord, while his brother stretched out on a battered chaise, drinking from a tall can of beer.

"Hey, Vern!" Evonal called bravely. "I didn't see you at the town meeting."

"I meant no disrespect, but my mind is made up especially after this tragedy," Vern replied, shaking his head. The torch poured white heat into the sky. He shut it off, and set it down. "How you doing, Evonal?"

She shook her head, holding back the tears. "I came to check on Jack."

"Aw, he's fine, sleeping in my camper shell over there, unless he took off already. Guess he's a man alone these days, now homeless too." Vern's chuckle sounded like he was chewing on pebbles.

It occurred to Evonal that she could let Jack live in her house, he'd fit in it comfortably, and he'd keep trespassers out too. She thought of her huge grandmother's house and her alone in it, and then of Old Sylvia defenseless against a slap, let alone a bullet, lying naked in some refrigerator drawer with a tag on her toe.

"Hey, Vern, can we talk for a minute?"

His brother said, "I'm going in for another beer," and got up and stepped out of the meager light. The sounds of gravel crunching under his feet made his leaving seem ghostlike. Vern lowered the drop light to the ground. The desert night closed around them and the two stepped closer together.

"I came to talk to you about the buildings, the future, but you have to promise to keep it a secret."

"Of course, you got my word."

"I'm keeping my house. I want to be able to come back and visit from time to time, but I'm moving away, Vern, back home to my grandmother's house in Oregon. And I want to give you the buildings and the ten acres of land my parents bought here. I'll be sure to pay the taxes each year, but you'd be the rightful owner. All of downtown Foison would be yours too. You can do what you want with the land and the buildings—keep 'em or sell 'em."

"Or vacate them," Vern said, rubbing his hands together. "It's a beautiful gift, Evon. I accept!"

They shook hands on it. "The attorney will get the papers ready. You'll want to read them before we legally fix the signatures. I'd like to get it settled soon."

"Man, Evonal! I feel like I just got crowned king of Foison Surrounded."

Evonal started sobbing.

"You sure you want this?" Vern asked.

"Yes! I'm just shook up. Part of me wants to hide in bed and the other part wants to get in my truck and drive over to Ridgemont to look in on Old Sylvia. Make sure they know she has people. Pay for her funeral." Evonal started sobbing.

"Let me walk you home."

"I'd appreciate that, Vern. I really would," Evonal sobbed.

"Listen, Evon, this is a secret you can keep. I don't know where he got the money, but Jack paid for Old Sylvia's funeral, even a nice ride home. He don't want nobody to know."

"I'm gonna miss everyone," Evonal sobbed. After that they walked in silence.

At her house, Vern went in first, checked over the place, got the dogs barking, which helped fill the house with noise, and made it familiar again.

"Noisy little guys!" Vern scolded the dogs. "Hush, there!"

He appeared in the living room, going directly to the front door. "It was her sons."

"Whose?"

"Old Sylvia had two no-good boys. Always trying to get her gold."

"Gold?"

"Just leave it at that, Evon, but don't you worry. A group of us will be patrolling at night. You can feel safe. We're well armed. Just don't drive anywhere tonight, promise me that?"

Evonal nodded. "I'll wait for morning," she said, waving him out, and closing the door.

Vern must have jumped from the porch into the yard, she heard him land and walk off, the gravel crunching under each confident step. Evonal took the note out of her pocket that Old Sylvia had stuck into her screen door. "*Be sure you help Jack if he asks. In case I can't keep the promise I made him. I'd like to ask you to do it for me. I'll see you soon, dear girl.*" It made her cry again.

Old Sylvia used to tell Evonal tales of her life. She wanted to picture her friend in heaven, looking out over them all, but what came to her mind was Old Sylvia as a young girl bundled up for the snow in an old coat and belted blanket, her long braids frozen into icicles stuck to her back, stumbling over boots three sizes too large, as she frantically gathered the chickens into the coop before the Nor'easter hit.

■ ■ ■

Chapter 34

Before Jack got to the top of the tawl, the big yellow dog was waiting for him. They met nose-to-nose, like a hello kiss, before the dog leaped up and danced back, almost doing a backflip from joy. And then she stopped suddenly to whine low in her throat.

"I can smell him, girl, don't worry. I don't have the energy today for any of that, and I banged my elbow coming up." Jack twisted his shirtsleeve over so he could see if there'd been more damage to his elbow than the ringing in the bone. Of course there was blood. Nothing could sink his mood lower than it already was. The old girl's murder seemed like a separate tragedy. He was sad to be there without Old Sylvia. The more she had talked, the more convinced he had become that she looked forward to climbing the tawl with him. He had wanted to see what the yellow dog would do when the two met again.

"I'm gonna get you fed and give you your vitamins then we're gonna get you down to Foison." His stomach rumbled; he hadn't brought anything but the dog food. Little Maid shoved her big head under his hand. Jack petted her, reaching deep behind her ears like she liked, and then she laid on her back exposing her belly for him to scratch. He ran his fingernails up and down her long belly several times, like he was polishing them before he stopped and got back to work. "Let me get your food," Jack whispered. It took some time, kneeling and reaching down some while he hoisted it up. "Look at this," he told her. The smell of the dog food made his own belly rumble, as all food did, but the dog pawed the air nervously and then shot off. He sat on a chunk of smooth rock to wait. The singing for Old Sylvia's funeral was still going on. He'd heard it start while he was climbing, but he couldn't bring himself to go watch it from up there. Their voices echoed through the desert valley and up into the tawls in individual strains, Jack could probably identify each singer by name if he wanted to. They were a unique choir, voices that would never harmonize. The hymn they sang was sent up to warn God that a deserving, but strong soul was coming. *She is coming, she is coming, open your arms, plant your feet,* or something like, he couldn't remember the words exactly, and couldn't make them out. It was sung at every funeral Jack ever attended, and there'd been several. The last had been when a six-year-old, Luke, accidentally shot his brother, Mark, with the father's hunting rifle. The family buried the boy and moved away that same day. A couple of years later all the kids were gone. The music became stronger now in its echo. Someone was playing a guitar. This time the words rang out clear and mournful, so maybe someone had passed out hymnals. *Our friend and sister, lo! is dead, her cold and lifeless clay, has made in dust its silent bed, and there it must decay.*

In his pack he had dog treats and water. He snapped the top off three of the water bottles, and guzzled them down before crushing them flat against his thigh and putting them back in the pack. The singing grew more discordant, but stronger. He knew the emotions were building, could envision Evonal with her wad of tissues held under her nose to catch the flow of snot and tears. He wished he was there, but knew Old Sylvia would expect him to see to the dog, finish the business they'd started. Jack lugged up a sling he'd put together out of a piece of old tractor tire, chain, and rope.

Evonal had caught up with him that morning. He was just making his way around the old church. "I knew I'd find you here," she'd said almost cheerfully, or maybe (and he could be reading too much into this) she was glad to see him. "That blanket of flowers over the coffin, everything is so beautiful," she'd said. "Will you come over later? I want to talk to you."

He'd just stood there like a standard issue asshat, unsure of what to say.

We will meet you in the morning, where the shadows pass away; we will meet, we will meet, we will meet over there. He hoped not, he thought.

The dog appeared and dropped a small sack, the size of a child's fist, at Jack's feet. "Whatcha got there, girl?" It was a bag of gold dust, he knew without even bending close to it; for him the scent was strong as a freshly cut lemon.

The sack of gold dust fit into the palm of his hand like a softball. The dog's saliva dampened one hand and smelled of chewed, dead lizards, her staple diet. He gave it an affectionate squeeze before securing it inside his backpack. The dog already had her nose inside his pocket, trying to get to the treats. "Whoa, girl, let me get those for you." He fished them out, fed her a large handful of treats, letting her lick them out of his flat palm, and continue to lick even after they were gone. This is a hunger Jack understood, the tasting of the food long after it was gone; the smell moved into the nose and hung on.

"Listen, Little Maid, our friend Old Sylvia, I think you knew her. Well, she was going to help me haul you down, but that met with tragedy. But I haven't given up. I got a friend named Trong Tri. He's making you a sling I can fix you into to take you down safely. I know I keep promising and then I don't show up, but things keep coming between me and you and that promise. I can help you get some meat on your bones, and take good care of you. You need a vet. Just a few more days." Jack sighed, stroking the knobby ridge of the dog's back as she dipped her nose into the tub of food and chewed into it like she was crunching down small, but delicious rocks.

"You're gonna need some water after all that!" Jack whispered, patting her gently. Far down below the singing finally hushed, leaving a ringing silence, although he knew someone was most likely starting a eulogy. Foison would drag this funeral out for the rest of the day, and maybe into the night too.

The sound of an explosion shuddered up the great tawl. Skookum pulled back; reminded of war. He moved his binoculars over to see if he could spot the cause of the blowup. It was the first time he'd shifted his posture since he caught sight of the banner strung across the graveyard entrance announcing Sylvia's funeral. Now there was a beautiful woman whose history went back with his a ways. He knew who'd killt her, those no-good sons. He moved his binoculars back to Sylvia's gravesite.

The turnout satisfied him. They'd all shown the proper respect for Silver Sylvia. There wasn't a grave marker yet, but someone had covered her small patch with something green, and no one rushed off.

Then an engine's noise boiled from above. Shocked, Skookum bent down, searching the sky. The thing was a gleaming white, giant insect. It slowly dropped down between the tawl*s*, neat as can be, landing on the pad. When it occurred to him what had just happened, Skookum chuckled, slapping his thigh. At last the stupid-shit landing pad's goddamn prophecy had been fulfilled. And then it sank in, *the prophecy had been fulfilled*: hoo-hooey. Skookum got serious. His binoculars stayed focused on the activities surrounding the whirligig. A couple more idiots were added to Foison. It occurred to him that the flying machine could have easily landed right where he stood. He collapsed into his hopelessness, standing there alone, alone, and then letting the binoculars dangle around his neck, he went to get a hard, scorching drink, decide on another suitable trap for anyone landing on his tawl.

As Skookum watched out over Foison, Jack was already chopping up the vine that had begun snaking along the top of the tawl. Battling the stink and the newly sharpened edges of the leaves, he chopped until he couldn't lift the ax again.

Then he straightened up, and hid the ax. The sweat poured off him, pooling at his feet.

Little Maid wagged her tail as he slipped the makeshift harness under her and fastened it. Jack didn't think it was big enough, he led her over to a cluster of boulders, and saying, "Stay put," he got on top. Even lifting her a few inches off the ground caused her to tip forward. The dog whined, but trustingly allowed Jack to spill her on her nose. He made some adjustments, and tried lifting her again. This time she got spilled on her tail. Jack jerked on the rope, but he wouldn't be able to keep the balance and get down the vine. Some common sense crept in. Jack got down and tried to rearrange the sling, cinching it tighter, but when he lifted her, she pawed the air frantically.

"Goddamn it!" Jack swore, tired of failure. "OK, girl, let's eat something and think this over." He'd never get her over the lip without it tipping too far over with what he had, though he already knew he'd need a bigger sling. When the dog darted off, it didn't concern Jack until he heard her cry out, like she'd been hit by something. He looked up to see her lying on her side, panting heavily. At first he thought this time she'd been hit by lightning.

The stench and weight of Skookum slammed into Jack at the same time, knocking him off his feet, churning him into a tangle of arms and legs.

"What the f—" Jack wheezed while the dog barked and barked.

Jack tumbled around with the stinking old goat until he got him near a nettle bush. The old giant wrestled himself on top of Jack. Using his legs as springs, he catapulted the stinking man into the bush, and rolled away. The big dog panted wearily.

"Don't give in, Little Maid," Jack whispered, petting her quickly. "It's best I get down before he sobers up and really goes nuts. I'll be back quick as I can, and when I do, I won't fail you!" The words were an echo of every promise he'd ever made to her, and then she nudged him toward the exit before scooting off, disappearing into the brush.

■ ■ ■

Chapter 35

During an abnormally cool and pleasant day for the desert, Jack sat pensively under the breezy shelter of the new Lake Sisters' Food Pavilion, trying to feed a hunger that would not go away, lonely, homeless. Earlier he'd gone to Mavis, just wanting to see how she was holding up over her own sister's death. His mother must have sensed his despair. She wouldn't open the door.

The day of Old Sylvia's funeral news people had arrived full force, even a camera crew in a helicopter, reenergizing the surge of curious people to Foison. Today, while he awaited a sling from Trong Tri, he watched the protesters gather, literally, under their individual umbrellas: green for those who wanted the vine removed and orange for those who wanted to keep it. This was no longer a Foison fight. The outsiders had taken over, but this was another event that had brought everyone out, except Evonal, Jack noted, rubbing his heart.

Seemed Jack was sitting in his own peculiar Switzerland. The rest of the people there had no interest in Foison, but had arrived nonetheless. Invariably they arrived with a larger party, took a seat, said something like:

"I'll be right here while you look around."

"You have four hours, then I'm driving back to the hotel."

After that the parties splintered off, orders were placed, they settled in to wait for the leaving hour. Jack was astonished at the patience of these people, and it again stirred the idea of true love.

No one made eye contact or commented about the destruction of a delicate ecosystem by greedy people. They all sipped their drinks and read or just plain daydreamed. Jack drummed his fingers on the table. Trong Tri was due to deliver the larger, lighter sling anytime now. It would do no good to worry until he could get back up there, but stopping one worry only started another. Jack worried over the soul of Old Sylvia, like the god he'd learned about as a child might not know enough about such a mortal to admit her into heaven. He missed talking to the old girl. He was homeless, but didn't want to get another place in Foison, but if not there, where?

Someone had left a book on the table next to him. On the cover was a portrait that looked like one of the miniatures that Evonal painted on the wood knobs. He got it and read the title: *The Artists of Foison Surrounded.* The old guy on the cover looked familiar, Jack thought, feeling like something loathsome just landed *hot* on his belly. And then he recognized who it was, so he flipped through the book until he found out his name. Sam Skookum, giant asshole at large, Jack thought, so that's your name. The painting was by Evonal's father, so no wonder it looked so familiar; she painted like her dad. This thought both astonished and deeply concerned him because of its reach into his own life. There was nothing about his mother Mavis that had been passed on to him, he was certain. He glared at the old guy's portrait. Something very unpleasant lurked in his thoughts. He flung the book back to the empty table, and didn't watch it land. Letting that old guy catch him up there had been a terrible mistake; he'd gotten careless. Now he'd be on the lookout for him, when he wanted to slip up there, grab Little Maid, if she was still alive, and get the hell out, a task that seemed to get harder with each try. Each damaged place on his body throbbed, as if to remind him.

Someone began talking excitedly about the news team that had arrived in the helicopter. The reply was a flat, "Really?" And the area went back to peaceful quiet.

Grumpy, Jack gulped down the glass of beer. "Do ya need more beer, Jack?" an effervescent Linda Lake called from some far corner of the patio behind him. He pretended he didn't hear her. Within two seconds she was standing before him. Jack regretted he no longer had his own kitchen to prepare his own meals.

"The news people interviewed us. We are very excited. Astrid and I stayed up all night sewing. Do you like my new uniform? Cute, huh?"

"What's that kind of outfit called?" Jack asked halfheartedly, but he was still thinking about how that book had blown a spindrift across the surface of his already corrugated life.

"Dutch girl," Linda was saying as she sashayed around the table in her short skirt, but his eyes locked on the sweets on the tray. He'd come to absolutely love the heavy scent of white sugar, and especially the feel of powdered sugar on his tongue.

"What you got there?"

"Chocolate drip cake." Linda handed him a small, sugary block that fit easily into his mouth. Inside the heavy white cake were drips of bright goo so delicious he wanted to keep chewing it forever. He ate ten more before feeling he could now start eating on a full stomach.

A chair scraped. Just beyond Linda's ruffled shoulder, a tall woman with large hoop earrings and copper hair piled on top of her head was lowering herself into a seat next to one of the contentedly silent men. The way she propped her elbow on the table and fanned herself with her floppy hat reminded him of the first time he'd felt true, burning love for a woman. That pain, he thought was like eating cake this good, but then biting hard on his tongue. It drew blood.

"Jack, you in there?"

It took an effort to drag his thoughts back.

Linda's tray of sweets sat on the table, her bent knee on top of his thigh, applying pressure. To keep Linda off his lap, Jack reached for the farthest thing on the table—the sugar shaker so he could subtly turn his whole body in. There was growing tension between the sisters that made him edgy. He was a jack-wagon for getting involved with either of them, yet he couldn't seem to back himself out of it. They wanted his gold. He wasn't stupid. Jack began slamming the small cakes into his mouth whole. Linda took a seat in the chair closest to him.

"Are they good, Jack?" Linda hummed her words, resting her cheek against her open palm.

"Mmmfff!" Jack nodded.

"Here's a cold beer and more of your favorite mixed nuts!" Astrid called.

She had to set her tray on the table and use both hands to place a full pitcher of beer in front of him, but instead of pleasantly blinking as she used to, she pulled her lips into a sly smile before she went to the next table. Linda began fidgeting in her seat, unfolding and then smoothing the edges of a paper napkin until a bird with a surprisingly sharp beak emerged.

"For some reason, Astrid is just glowing these days, isn't she?" Linda sighed, but her eyes bore down on Jack, the bird beak pointing toward his heart. After he turned it away, he turned to watch the cleverly camouflaged, multifarious Astrid.

Wherever she passed, the men shifted in their seats and lifted their heads out of their necks to watch her. She certainly gave them something to look at. Fully illuminated by the bright sun, her flowing dress became see-through; there was no denying she had a willowy, yet shapely body. She did glow, but Jack alone knew it was from gold fever. Linda Lake watched the men watch her sister. This time she made another bird, its beak pointing at the sun. And then, as if pulled by some invisible thread, Linda slipped out of her chair and went to her sister, leaning in to whisper something the moment she got close enough. They didn't touch. Astrid smiled directly at Linda's shoulder, nodded, and swung away with her tray. Both sisters flickered their eyes at him. From what he knew about women, their silent feud would have to play itself out; he could only make it worse. Linda came back first, carrying a tray of cupcakes.

"Scoot back, I want to sit in your lap," she ordered, narrowing her eyes at him. Something like fear made Jack pull back. She did the rest, curling her body and arms around him like a monkey might, except her one hand rested on the top of his head where she drilled her fingernails into his crown, tapping out some sort of drum warning. Jack sipped his beer, kept his eyes on the aluminum napkin box nailed to the table to withstand the desert winds, the heavy salt and pepper shakers, the tray of luscious cakes, the nearly empty pitcher of beer, his glass of beer.

"Here's another glass of rose petal lemonade, sweetie! And another nice pitcher of beer for our Jack," Astrid sang— Jack hadn't seen her coming and he shifted uncomfortably as she set the huge mug with the dripping pink goo on the table, wiping her hand off with a rag she seemed to pull out of the air.

"You look good today, Jack. How are the clothes fitting?" Astrid asked.

Linda immediately sat up and started pulling at the seams on his shoulders. "Are they too tight?"

"I can always have him over to measure again, and make a fresh batch, if you think these are too small," Astrid stated without a single note of question in her voice.

Linda narrowed her eyes over him, ran a flat palm over his broad chest. "I think Jack should decide."

"Well, Jack?"

Instead of answering, he picked up the full pitcher of beer, and held it on his open palm.

"You are so strong, Jack!" they both squealed.

He set it back down, trying to decide the best way out of there.

"Well you come to my sewing room whenever you want," Astrid said, patting his hand before she turned and left. Linda busied herself, working her hand inside Jack's shirt.

"My sister really adores you, Jack, but I love you!" Linda whispered.

He pulled her hand off his chest, thinking how one Lake sister was as good as the other, but neither could be trusted. What he had to do was save the dog; the one who would be completely faithful to him. Of course, Jack would have to find a place to live. A dog that size would never be comfortable in that tiny camper; he barely fit inside that soup can. The image of Evonal's tidy house popped into his head, making him feel even more out of sorts. That little house would be too big without her. He shifted his legs and groaned.

Linda slid over to his other knee. "What are you always thinking so hard about?"

He looked at her. When she smiled at him like that, a light seemed to turn on under her skin, making her luminous and pink cheeked.

"You are so beautiful," he said wearily, looking away.

An attractive woman, curiously familiar, dressed in shorts and a bright T-shirt walked breezily toward him. The sight of her put him on some kind of alert; the force of emotions confused him, but when he felt more elated than alerted he grew all the more tense. When he realized that it was Evonal, Jack bolted up, ejecting a squealing Linda. Racing around the tables, he waited where it would seem they were accidentally running into each other.

But Evonal breezed right by him, looking at something far in the distance, smelling of fresh lemons. The bounce in her step had an unmistakable air of contentment; her long strides certainly indicated a sense of purpose. Evonal looked sexy too, or anyway if not that, then it was something even more powerful. Jack glared at the strong calves that dropped into her slender ankles; her long, slim feet attractively wrapped in Roman-style sandals, for all to see. Although she hadn't said hello to anyone, not noticing him left Jack feeling like a small boy abandoned in a familiar place, but still unable to get home.

■ ■ ■

Chapter 36

Evonal stood on the edge of the highway on her way to see Jack. She wanted to tell him about the note Old Sylvia left her. There was no good reason not to, but every time she'd gone to find him she just hadn't wanted to. When the long wall of purple trailer passed by, it took a moment for Evonal to put it together: Tina Bell was back in town. The same portrait that for years was kept fresh and bright on the back of her parents' studio was also on the side of this trailer.

"Evon! Will you look at that?"

Evonal turned to see Telly shaking her head to the spectacle. "Let me wipe the goose bumps down."

"I wonder what she wants."

"Money. She's here to cash in too. I heard tell the minute she learned of the murder, she was determined to take control of Foison and run for mayor, or I don't know what all goes on in a mind like that one. Old Sylvia wouldn't've let her near this place again after what she'd done. Gawd, I know Mavis couldn't stand her, but I miss her," Telly said. Loud, hallelujah music began pouring from another van.

Once it passed, Evon asked her how Mavis was doing these days.

"She's good. We just spent a couple of days in town shopping, getting a good stretch."

Evonal had never understood the friendship between the two, but what did she know about friendship?

Telly, still shaking her head said, "You look like you've lost half your body size. Aren't you eating anymore?"

Evonal looked down at herself. Now that she wore form-fitting clothes she supposed she did look much smaller. "I think it's just the change in clothes style."

Telly *tsked*, "You're shrinking, Jack's growing. Old Sylvia murdered in her own sad bed. Sidus's place was ransacked over a made-up treasure map from some poem in a kid's magazine because some yahoo at the magazine used the photograph of his place to accompany the poem. At least they've been caught, those log heads, but Sidus took his tent and headed for higher ground. He wants to be alone 'til things blow over, which may be never, or any minute, who knows anymore? I'd like peace again too, especially if Foison's attracting the likes of Tina Bell again."

"Yeah, I can see that." Evonal turned to leave.

"Where you off to? Come over for some coffee. You haven't in ages."

"I'm just on my way to see how Jack's faring—"

"Aw, honey," Telly said, gathering the edge of Evonal's sleeve into her bony hand. "Not only is Jack fine and dandy, but, sugar, he's just been as busy as ever plowing the fields with Linda Lake. His mother is furious how that girl keeps hinting at a big, white wedding. Jack married! It's not even to be imagined. And my God, is he growing. Have you seen him? A barn on keg legs. Don't know what he can be eating…"

Evonal stopped hearing Telly and just studied how the lines in her face were beginning to intersect. All around her mouth were thousands of them, from the old days when she smoked. This old weathered woman was not someone she would ever miss, Evonal thought sadly, and it scared her too. She wanted to get out of this harsh weather immediately.

"Telly, that's just fascinating to hear, but I've got to get on my way," Evonal said.

"Come for coffee!"

"*Sure, soon!*" Of course she should've never considered Jack as anything but a friend and a flaky, stupid one at that, but screwing Linda Lake when he'd been sleeping with her? It made her head spin, but then she began to calm down. If Jack was getting married, she would only believe it if it came from him.

A few minutes later, she found herself outside the tiny camper Jack now holed up in. His snoring echoed off the small canyon of desert that was Vern's land, so there was no doubt he was in there. The tin camper shell used to fit on the back of Vern's old truck, now abandoned in his backyard with the hood removed, and the metal sculpture he'd been working on now exploded from where the engine used to be. The truck bed was filled with cloudy broken glass that had its sharp edges worn off in an old cement mixer Vern used regularly to polish his glass and stones. Well, he'd always been an inventive, intuitive artist.

A few raindrops fell on the crusted sand around her, leaving small rings in the pale earth. There was nothing like the scent of rain in a desert. Evonal studied the door to the tiny dwelling, and could not imagine how Jack fit inside it. When she thought about what Telly had said, especially the tone she'd used, like Jack was some good-for-nothing, well, she couldn't wait to leave. After a few more minutes of listening to Jack snore, and imagining how it would feel never to see him again, she decided to go see if Vern was ready to go sign the papers, and wait for Jack to come to her.

If a plant could be frustrated, the vine was. It was genetically stalled on the tawl, wrecked and running out of water. To save itself, it was bringing forward different forms of adaptation, but this was sapping its strength. The vine was dying. The promise was the water. If it did make it, its growth would be unstoppable. The vine began to grow much thinner with a thick under covering that would protect it from the repellant soil, much like a boot on a man's foot kept it from harm. If it made it to the water, it would claim this place as its own dominion.

■ ■ ■

Chapter 37

The activities of Sam Skookum preparing to build another human death trap were frightening in their manic verve. His mission to trap, and destroy another human being was terrifying even to him. The exhausted big yellow dog wisely stayed tucked under a thicket of bushes that she could easily back out of.

Sam Skookum thundered around as he picked up and threw things into a fast-growing pile of wood, old metal parts, and whatever else he could find. Much of the stuff that landed on the heap had flown a good distance, even for its weight. Skookum was old and certainly not as strong as he'd been as a young man, but he was still huge and powerful. He found it very satisfying the way he easily grabbed up and flung the lengths of board, landing exactly where he'd intended. The big yellow dog nervously inched back, deeper into the thicket. To mollify her, Skookum took a dried lizard from his pocket, snapped it in two, tossed the dog's moiety at her feet, before stuffing his share into his own maw, swallowing it after only two hard bites. He washed it down with liquor, and once swallowed, howled with great content. This time everything stayed in his stomach even with the force of that whoop-cry. Sam Skookum patted his giant, bloated stomach before resuming his frenzied search-and-throw activities.

Sam Skookum had lived a very long and peculiar life, one that ruined his eagle-keen eyes and damaged his hearing, but refined his sense of smell to an animal's keenness. Sticking his nose into the air, he sniffed. There were traces in the air of the scent of another human, he was pretty sure. Course he didn't know what the wind might blow up and over from that stinking town below. After that flying machine, and then a fight, he didn't know if he'd dreamed it. He believed in ghosts—who didn't? Now, everything confused him. Either way, he thought drunkenly, he was going to lay a nice trap, and if nothing got ensnared in the trap, what had he lost?

Tipping his head back so he saw only the very apex of the sky, he hitched up his worn pants and searched it carefully.

"Bring 'em on!" he screamed at the brilliantly blue sky. The sky stayed where it was, bright and unchanged, and this made Skookum feel foolish for letting such crazy notions get in and knock around his addled brain. A crazed man again, he got back to work.

The brainless, genetically programmed vine that after Jack's savage attack now fought for life, but went undetected by him, was a far more insidious threat to his way of life than anything that might fall out of the sky—including highly intelligent space men or the one earthling of very average intelligence that had robbed him of all his gold and was now trying to get his dog. Skookum knew none of this.

The contraption he built quickly collapsed. "Goddamn it all, and shit to all hell!" He had a hammer and no nails, a good sturdy hand drill with rusted bits. He slung the hammer as high and hard as he could toward a distant cloud before taking a deep swig off his bottle. Little Maid raced for the safety of the caves.

Skookum drained the bottle of booze, but threw it gently toward the pile of other empties, watched it land just short of another bottle, and then roll in to join its kin. Calmer, he kicked at the dirt, some bushes, a spiked cactus before sitting himself down on a rock to think. There was little choice but to change his original ingenious plan to something simpler. After ten or so minutes of turning it over in his mind, he decided to go get a pick and shovel. Skookum was going to build pit traps and cover them with the flora of the tawl top; catch the interloper like a dumb rabbit. Maybe he'd skin 'em and eat 'em too. Skookum's stomach rumbled hungrily just thinking about it.

■ ■ ■

Chapter 38

Evon sat up in bed the minute she heard Jack tapping at the window. Before she could warn him about the moved furniture Jack fell so heavily on the floor that everything on her night table clacked, rattled, or fell over. Something tinkled like broken glass when it landed on the floor.

"Evon! It's me. Don't freak out!"

"I'm over this way. I moved everything. Be careful," she called him to her from the center of the bed. There was a hard bang that caused real crashing and the breaking of something glass.

"Oompf!Shithellchristfuckinhellgoddamnitmotherhum personofabitchjeeezzz!" Jack cried out.

"Don't move!"

The light snapped on as soon as she twisted the switch. She frowned and blinked from the glare. "Watch the broken glass," she said. And then, once her eyes had adjusted and her head had cleared, she said, "Good evening, Jack. I've missed you."

This seemed to please him. "I noticed you took the sign down, so I came right in."

"I'm glad you did."

"Where you been?"

"Oh, here and there, trying to get things ready. You seem bigger every time I see you," Evonal added seriously.

"It's not fat though, it's muscle and bone," he said, sitting on the bed, tipping everything in his favor with his weight; Evonal had to struggle to stay balanced.

"Do I look freakish?"

"Let me have a good look, take your clothes off," she ordered, making Jack smile at last.

"I'll do it the way you do it," he offered, standing up. And then, he said, "Watch!" As if she could look anywhere else. And then he mimed her undressing, first pretending to fuss with his hair to get it out of the way before taking off his shirt, after which he smelled both underarms before wrinkling his nose and letting it flutter to the floor. When he got to his pants he leaned over enough to brush a hand across each thigh before he removed them and then carefully folded them over the back of the chair.

"Enough!" She laughed.

"Well then, off they go!"

At the first flash of his brilliant white undershorts she got unaccountably embarrassed and looked away. He wrapped himself around her.

"You smell good. Nice toenails. Flamingo pink, right?" Jack whispered directly into her ear, which made her flinch.

"You really do smell nice," he said into the back of her head. "Like happiness or something. Is it true?"

She started to ask about Linda, and then decided she didn't care. Evonal laughed. "What've you been drinking?"

"A little beer is all."

"Maybe you should take it easy with the alcohol, Jackie."

"And maybe you shouldn't be so prissy, missy. I remember that time you got stonking drunk on the local beer fest that one spring. I remember the table dancing. Christ, you were lit. You had short hair back then. Old Sidus took you home in a wheelbarrow arms and legs dangling over the edges, passed out like a drunken fool. Jeez, I wonder if someone's got a picture…"

"That was so many years ago. I'd forgotten."

"I'm guessing you never remembered much of that night at all. Aw, there was more than once, and you know it, don't ya'?"

"I didn't think you thought much about me, Jackie-Boy."

"Lately I've been remembering a lot of things about you. When my house split in half I found a box of old photographs. You were in a short—"

Evonal turned around to plant her mouth on his. She was bored stiff as a rod of bamboo replaying the past. By the time they started kissing in earnest, he had her pants off, was working his way down, dragging his tongue across her belly button.

"Your hair is thinning on the top of your dome here." Evonal laughed as she pulled her fingers through Jack's curls.

"Thanks for noticing."

"If you were doing a better job down there, I couldn't have noticed."

"When did you get so hilarious?" Jack said before he wrapped his enormous hands around each of her calves and in one yank, pulled her under him. By the time their noses banged together, they were both laughing hard, breathing hot air in each other's faces. The cold desert night air began blowing steadily in through the window, cooling the room ten degrees in a matter of minutes. And in only a very few minutes it became hot enough between them to create a little wind in that tiny bedroom.

Later, when they were resting, draped across her bed and eating the chopped spiced fruit recipe she was experimenting with, she finally said, "Old Sylvia left me a note the night before she was murdered. She said I should help you. Now you tell me, with what?"

Jack said, "I left you a note once. You must of tore it up."

"Jackie-Boy I heard your girlfriend Linda Lake stole that right off my porch before I got there."

Jack sat up so suddenly, the shifting of his weight made her roll into him, pinning her arms between the both of them. "Kindly help me out of this ditch, please." Jack set the dish on his broad chest and lifted her out with one hand.

"Evon, maybe it's best left unopened, then," he said, disappointing her a little.

"You know you can move in here," she said.

"You think I should stay in Foison?"

"Wouldn't you rather live in a house by the sea?" she asked him.

"I've never been to the sea."

"Wouldn't you like to?" she asked.

There was some kind of nod, but nothing she could easily discern, and he kept his eyes on the dish.

"I know you're just killing time with me," he said. And then, holding the rim of the bowl to his bottom lip he shoveled it all into his maw, chewed a couple of times before swallowing it all in one gulp. "Listen, Evon, I do need your help. But I need to take you someplace that is weird, strange, and kinda dangerous."

"With sex?" she squeaked.

Jack laughed hard. "Naw. And anyway it's the place I often go to. There's this dog I need to help out. Like I want to adopt it. But I can't help her out by myself. I can't balance the sling and get her down. Will you trust me to take you there?"

"Trust," she repeated. Her mind began snaking around those words: weird, strange, dangerous: *will you trust me?* It tickled some uncomfortable memory of a long night with that Wrong Man. She started humming so it could not get further into her heart and mind. There was a long moment of quiet panic, because she was certain she had all this behind her, and yet here it was again.

"You humming?" Jack asked.

"Yes. Humming. By the by, Jackie, I went by your new place the other day. You were blowing the windows out of that camper shell."

"Why didn't you wake me?" he asked.

Evonal shrugged. "You sounded like you needed the nap. Aw, the truth is, I'd heard something about you and Linda and it hurt my feelings."

"What did you hear?"

"There's a rumor you're marrying Linda Lake."

Jack shook his head. "Don't believe that nonsense. I can't trust her not to slit my throat in my sleep. I want real—" He cleared his throat. "Right now, time's running out for my dog, and I need your help to save her. Will you come?"

"Where is it?"

"High up. You have to make a long climb, but you can do it."

"Where?"

"To the top of the tawl?"

"Where Lenny Keeny broke his leg?"

"No, this place is worse."

She made a face.

"You're the only one I can trust. And the dog, I call her Little Maid, although she's huge, she'll trust you. You're a dog person. So?"

"I'm not sure why you want me to go, but of course I'll help you." She shrugged. Evonal's idea of danger were the flash floods, rattlesnakes, being chased by a sidewinder, and certain strangers she'd encountered in Foison over time.

"We'll have to go tonight. You coming?"

"OK."

"Wear long sleeves, pants, boots, and gloves." Jack sighed mightily, letting all of the air out of his lungs, sinking deeper and deeper into the mattress. Evonal began to think about what it meant to climb to the top of a tawl with her crazy friend, and lover, Jack. Lover. Love. Was this love?

"I'll go with you," she said, nodding.

"Well, Evon, we'd better get some sleep. We're gonna need our strength."

He flipped off the switch on the lamp. The room went dark, but she could see his great head pressed into the pillow, his legs crossed at the ankle causing his feet to take on the shape of a large pinniped's.

Jack tipped his head into hers, and said. "I know you'd like me out, but please, just give me a couple of hours to sleep some. It comes so easy to me here next to you."

"Please stay, Jackie."

When he offered his hand, she tucked hers inside his.

"Don't worry, Evon. I'd never let anything happen to you." He sighed, lacing their fingers together before he began snoring. Whenever he moved it rocked the bed.

Jack shifted positions, turning onto his slide. If he stretched out, Jack's huge feet would dangle off the edge of the bed by a foot she thought, trying to guess in the dark by judging where the bulb of his knee hit her own bare leg. The phrase, *the lightning of God* surfaced.

There was a year, right after her parents' death that she delved into religion, something she would occasionally return to when she was feeling especially sorrowful or terribly lonely. The book was good, she'd read several versions, several times, because the stories were so incredible, but the religion part never really took hold except in a slanted, pre-dawn light sort of way that vanished in the full light of sun. Thinking it over, Genesis, Numbers, Deuteronomy, Joshua, Judges, Samuel, Chronicles, Nehemiah, Job, Psalms, all contained descriptions of a giant of some sort. All of whom were met with a tragic, biblical ending.

There was a collection of cold minutes in which Evonal worried that Jack was the victim of some errant gene awakened this late in life by some force that surrounded even her. With her one free hand, she covered her own womb protectively when she realized they had sex more than once that night without so much as a worn raincoat for protection. In mild shock at her own uncharacteristic irresponsibility she imagined a baby with six-fingered hands, double rows of teeth—never mind that Jack had neither, but who knew what evil lurked in the tiny heads of his loaded sperm?

But then the light in the room shifted to that soothing first-sign-of-sunrise light she always found so reassuring. Jack snored a loud, snozzling growl that boiled in the back of his throat and when it blew out, she wasn't at all worried about herself or any future child that may or may not come to be. She bent his arm at the elbow, and he turned toward her in his sleep, snoring softly now. His enormous face looked boyish and helpless, round as a handless clock.

■ ■ ■

Chapter 39

After their shower, and breakfast, Jack left Evonal singing while she cleaned a kitchen she said she was moving away from. He climbed back out the same window he'd come in because he had to fish his boots out of Evonal's small manzanita tree, where he'd always hung them before coming in. It kept them free of small animals, but the fruitless tree grew leather hard spikes that jabbed at him so relentlessly, he came close to setting it on fire. That morning he felt especially clumsy and irritable.

Exhaustion was part of his irritability; he slept, but he didn't rest. He was nervous about taking Evonal to the tawl. The air stirred, and soon sand blew straight up his nose, he began sneezing so hard, he thought he'd lose his scalp. His hand went to the bald spot Evon joked him about, but he couldn't feel anything, but the usual thick, curly hair. It was a relief when he could see the door of the camper.

"Jack!" The voices of the Lake sisters jarred him. He'd decided food or not, he was going to carefully avoid them. He kicked at stones in frustration.

"We both saw you coming out of Evonal's window, Jack. You need to tell us what that's all about."

Jack shook his head, "Evon and I go way back. Long, long before the two of you."

Linda started to cry. "I believed you loved me!"

Just looking at them sapped his energy. They were too complicated, too smart, too beautiful, too calculating, and too desperate. Rocks formed in his stomach grinding against the walls, a hot spike was now resting in his lower spine. While he was with Evonal he believed he could get exactly what he wanted. Now he needed to stay focused, but he needed time to pull it all together.

"Go home, you two. Linda, I am not the guy for you. For either of you, and you both know it. If I could, I would love you, but I just can't. I have tried and tried," he told Linda, but his eyes also flickered to Astrid.

"Listen, Jack! Please! If you can't decide on one of us, you can take us both. We can rotate, get two houses, we don't care. We both want you." Astrid called this out dramatically, waving her arms like she was trying to summon a storm.

Jack laughed. "There's only one woman I care about," he said, and as soon as he said it his backache left; he felt his bones slide back into place. At last, he fit inside his body. His ears stopped ringing, his headache went away.

"It's Evonal, isn't it?! Evonal?" screamed Linda. "That skank? I wish her dead. Dead!"

Jack grabbed Linda by her golden hair and shook her, "Take that curse off her, you fucking witch! If something happens to her I'll kill you myself."

"Let go, Jack!" Astrid cried. "Enough is enough. No one is cursing anyone. Especially Evonal. She's good people. We don't want to live in a world where we are hammering on one another. Now let go, Jack."

Jack loosened his grip. "Take the curse off her, Linda."

"Come on now, Linda. You can't wish death on people. It ricochets! Tell him you didn't mean it," Astrid coaxed.

But Linda shook herself free, giving him the finger for several long seconds before she turned, and sprinted away. Astrid's hands fluttered helplessly. She looked at Jack like she wished she had the words to explain before she turned to follow her sister.

"Astrid!" Jack called. She stopped. Her shoulder blades pinched, like she was dreading a blow.

"I'll do right by you both. I get it. Just give me the space to work it out, and I won't leave you two in this desert without water," Jack said.

Astrid nodded, "I know you won't Jack. That's why we love you."

■ ■ ■

Chapter 40

Evonal was dressed in long pants and sleeves with an old pair of boots on, ready to meet Jack. Her long hair was braided and pinned tightly to her head so it would not snag on anything, as Jack had also suggested. Outside the small window of her kitchen, day was coming to an end. The time was nearing. She thirstily drank water, wrung her hands, thought of excuse after excuse to stand up Jack. Although she would never consider herself superstitious, she had planned to stay inside her house until the next morning when she was driving away, to Oregon. It was with a sense of foreboding that she stepped out onto her porch. Feeling clumsy in the big, hard boots, she panicked, went back in, poured the dogs two more bowls full of kibble, threw them a couple of knotted socks and then decided they might need more water too, so she filled a large, shallow plastic tub of water and set it over the gate she kept locked across the doorway to keep them in their room. Water sloshed on the floor so she went and filled the coffee pot with water to refill the tub completely. The dogs raked their tiny claws on the gate and the wood trim. They whined and wagged their tails, begging, for her to stay.

"Aw, Vern'll be by to check on you if I'm not back. In a few days!"

"Evon! Let's go!" Jack was calling as he knocked on her door while opening it.

"I thought we were supposed to meet at the landing pad," she said weakly, joining him on the porch. He pulled the door closed behind them and they started out.

"I was afraid you'd stand me up."

"Me?" She could barely look him in the eye.

"I got the sling and everything we'll need. It's going to be rough climbing," he told her. "But, I think you're going to be amazed by what you see up there. I mean it isn't anything like another world, it's real…"

"The dogs aren't barking for me. I can't hear them."

Jack squeezed her hand, switched his conversation to the life inside of Vern's old camper, what he'd heard, the pros and cons of owning a truck versus a car. That got her to talking about how she wanted to buy a new car for her new place. Once she and Jack skirted the town she felt more united with him, more of a team. They held hands as they walked. And somewhere beyond them there was the noise of a large gathering.

"Do you hear that crowd?"

"These days I always hear that crowd," Evonal replied. "Even when I have two pillows covering my head, and the dogs are whining."

"Yeah, but it sounds like it's coming from the landing pad this time."

They stopped to listen. "Let's go have a look," Evonal suggested. At the UFO landing pad, they found a large crowd of people who looked like they were setting up to give speeches. One end of the pad had a podium, and two banks of lights ran off a portable generator. The rest of the space was taken up with several rows of chairs. No one noticed them, but they stayed at the fringes anyway, shadows in the growing dark.

"Good grief," said Evonal, pointing. "Look at that Tina Bell taking charge. Doesn't she know it's all about to collapse?"

When Jack turned to her, his eyebrow arched. She'd accidentally revealed too much of Vern's secret plan to destroy the Foison vine. But then he pushed his nose toward hers, and kissed her lightly on the lips. Such a soft kiss, it seemed to mean so much.

Jack said, "Let's get."

They began walking. It wasn't long before Jack stopped to drink a bottle of water, which he squashed flat against his thigh and tossed like a coin into the air before he caught it and put it in his large pack. She found herself studying the curve of Jack's jaw and then oddly, the shape of his nostrils. The hole in the auricle of his damaged ear had a hair curling through it. She brushed it out.

"Why are you staring at me like that?"

She wanted to say, *you mean something to me*. But instead she said, "Why would I stare at you? Of all people." And then a thin wind threaded around the two of them. Jack put his nose into the air with his eyes closed, like he was transfixed or paralyzed.

"Jack?" Evonal gently shook his arm.

"Flashfloods. Can you smell 'em? We gotta stay alert."

"Yikes!" She kidded.

Jack shined his flashlight on her face. "For or against the vine?" He made his brows quiver comically.

"I'm not in the mood for this."

"I'm just nervous. Sorry. Let's go."

They started off again.

"Why are you nervous?"

He pulled at his chin, turned to study her carefully.

"I'm nervous about this place we're going. It's a dangerous place. A crazy old coot lives there. I've been stealing stuff from it—gold—his gold and lots of it. I'm afraid you might think I'm a thief, but can you steal what's been stolen?"

"Jack!" Evon cried. "You can't keep it!"

They stopped and stared into each other's eyes.

"Right. I can't keep it. Maybe it's wrong taking you there. Maybe I'm about to get you hurt."

She stopped, looked toward the opposite horizon. Somewhere miles away her new home awaited her, she could clearly picture it, her grandmother's gorgeous piano in that elegant little room. She was going to take lessons.

"I can't die tonight," she whispered. "I've recently realized I've done nothing to recommend myself to death. I need a bit more time here."

Jack shook his head, placed an arm around her, and pulled her tight against him. "I won't let anything happen to you."

"Maybe some things can't be stopped. Let's go," she said.

Jack's strides were longer than hers, but because of his weight he sunk into the sand deeper. That backpack added weight too. The force of his breaths worried her some, her own heart rate had barely increased and Jack was wiping sweat from his brow every fifth step. The night became ink dark when Jack turned off the flashlight.

"We're here," Jack announced, panting.

The stars glittered. While her eyes adjusted, there was only the sense of something mountainous beside her, that and its pull on Jack. His whole body leaned toward it even as they stood there. Overhead the sliver of moon glowed a brilliant crescent in the sky, but reflected no light on them. Evonal felt resolved now, strong, and willing to follow Jack.

"Follow me up the vine, don't take your gloves off, and don't give up," Jack said. And then added, "I'd shove you up first, but I need to step on that place ahead of you. Check on things. That old coot is armed. I can see in the dark pretty good with my funky eyes."

Evonal fished out her miniature flashlight, shined it around her feet, found the bottom of the vine, then ran the flashlight up until the light grew faint.

"It looks like a lot of climbing," she said. When she reached out a bare hand to touch it, Jack slapped it away.

"Don't touch this fucker. It's sharp and the cut is so painful it'll make you piss your pants. Put your gloves on." Securing her flashlight into the deep well of her jeans pocket, she put her gloves on with shaking hands.

"Listen, before we go up, I want to explain something about Old Sylvia. She was gonna help me. She knew this place. Told me the gold was stolen, and cursed. That's all she said. Jack, it's stolen and cursed, you best blow it all up and find another way to get your life right. She was gonna help me get the dog, and I was helping her kill the vines. I was with her when she left you that note. Those boys of hers had spooked her. I didn't know they were trying to kill her! I didn't know what she wrote to you either. And, Evon, I just wish—"

When Evon saw him wipe tears out of his eyes, her eyes teared too.

"Let's hope Old Sylvia is right up there watching out for us," she said.

Jack cleared his throat and said with difficulty, "I've stashed bottles of water in the vine. You'll want to drink a lot as we go up. It's going to take a couple of hours. Follow me," Jack said, with assurance.

The protective clothing made her hot. The climb was much harder than she had expected; sweat dripped in her eyes and was hard to wipe out. The gloves were hard to keep on when her hands got sweaty, and this slowed her down. She could imagine Old Sylvia, ancient as she was, climbing up the vine without breaking a sweat. The thought got her to push on.

"I don't think I can go on, Jackie! I'm gonna have to go back," Evonal conceded before hanging her head through two enormous leaves, ready to vomit.

"I'm at the top," Jack said, panting hard. "Just give me a minute."

Evonal could only nod. It felt as if she'd just climbed into heaven against the wishes of all the gods; her heart pounded like it never had before. She thought she would never be able to catch her breath.

"OK, Evon, come on up," Jack whispered now. "And hold onto me. There are pit traps up here. That crazy-ass lunatic is trying to snare me. Jeez us!"

Evonal crawled onto the top of earth clinging to Jack's calf, trembling. Using his back pockets for handles, she pulled herself up his backside. Once on firm footing, both of her hands clung to his belt and she breathed hard, leaning against his back. Jack reached both hands around her and gave her a squeeze. "You all right now?" he whispered.

"Where are we?"

"Shhhh, Evon, let me listen. There's a crazy old miner up here," Jack whispered, setting the pack on the ground. "He's idiotic, dangerous, and armed with a shotgun. He's made pit traps all over the place. I can see the coverings clear as day. What an asshat."

"Good grief, Jackie, look at all those dead lizards," Evonal whispered. The vine was snaking several feet onto the tawl top now. There were dozens of dead lizards on or near the vine, curled up as if they took one bite, had an apoplectic spasm, and died on their backs.

"I gotta put a stop to that thing," he whispered. "Listen, I'm gonna leave the harness here and hide you too. I gotta go make sure that old fucker is passed out or locked in his shed—"

"OK, Jackie, you gotta slow down. Just who is this old coot?"

"It's this old fucker that lives up here, all alone. I've been stealing his gold. Well not really stealing, just following the golden rule. Now we're here to get the dog and get down forever."

"The golden rule is to do unto others as you would have them—oh never mind, you're not leaving me here alone nowhere! I have a bad feeling about all this. And now I've got to pee bad!"

Jack mopped his forehead. "OK, let's go very quietly down by the lake. You follow me, but hold on at all times. There's a safe spot you can pee in and wait for a few minutes while I get the situation in hand."

Evonal clutched the back of his shirt so tightly in both her fists that the front pulled taut across his chest. All the while, Evonal kept whispering one incoherent phrase over and over, something that sounded like *hum-da-da-hum-da-da-hum-da-da-hummmm.*

"I'm going to hide you inside this clump of boulders, while I go get the dog. You can take a piss, drink water, get comfortable. Once we get the dog rigged up and back on the vine, we'll be fine. It'll be over. I can't hear or smell that old fucker yet so he's probably still passed out."

Once they got to the lake, the clouds seemed to meet them there. Rain began drumming on the tawl, and in this microclimate, the private storm shimmered onto the lake.

"Look at that!" Evonal cried. It was a thing of beauty, hard to stop watching.

"OK, Evon, see that crowd of boulders? There's a pocket inside, a nice cave where it'll be safe. Just wait for me quietly, will ya?"

"Is that a lake? Oh my stars, is that a night rainbow?"

"The rain'll keep up for quite some time, maybe all night, but just let me get the dog—"

Instead of working her way inside the boulders, Evonal stood shoulder to shoulder with Jack.

"It is amazing. Just like you said," she whispered.

The slender moonlight was reflected as a wavering parenthesis on the surface of the lake; each drop of rain was a silver bullet shooting deep inside it.

"Those willow-like trees ring the back half. You ever go back there? I swear I can hear water falling," Evonal whispered.

"Listen, Evon, just tuck yourself in there and I'll be right back," Jack pleaded.

"What do I do if you don't show up? I'll have to wait for dawn to get home for help."

"I'll be back. But, yeah, OK, if the sun comes up, and I'm not here, don't try to find me. Get home and put me out of your mind. But, listen, I can get us all out of here quick as a wink, so if you'll just hide out right in that cave in there and be patient. I'll go scope out where that old fool is, and if need be, lock him up so we can avoid his hellfire," Jack spoke as quickly as he could.

"Lock him up how? He could die up here," Evon said.

"He's a wily old fuck. Don't you worry none about him. He's tough as train tracks. We gotta worry about him killing us." The words barely left Jack's mouth when Evonal coughed. "Jeez! What is that stench? Ag!"

"Aw, Christ! Get behind me, Evon!" Jack cried.

"JAH! Got you!" Skookum hollered, seeming to jump out of nowhere. The two barrels on the shotgun looked like two cannons, pointed too near his head.

"Run!" Jack shouted to Evonal, but she crushed herself harder to his back.

"Don't shoot!" Evonal screamed, twisting Jack so his legs were corkscrewed around each other. He began hopping first on one foot and then the next, trying to stay up.

"Run, Evon! He can't see you." Jack made himself a steady shield for her to escape behind.

But when Evon hopped away, Skookum wheeled around, pointed the shotgun and fired, but Jack wasn't certain he heard the *bang!* of a shotgun or the *ka-pow* of the usual thunder. When Jack spun around to get a look at her he accidentally clobbered Evon in the head with his elbow, knocking her to the ground before he tipped over on her. The crush under his foot was her foot, bones cracked. Once he got to his feet, he kicked Skookum so hard in the knee that the weathered giant buckled like he'd just smashed a paper bag. Jack took the shotgun and hurled it as hard as he could, certain it made it over the edge of the tawl.

"You stupid idiot, I got plenty more of those and dynamite too!" Skookum hollered.

"Evon! Are you OK?" The way she folded into him, like a book closing shut, he was certain she'd been shot in the gut.

"You shot my girl!" Jack cried, scooping up Evonal.

"I didn't feel no kick! It didn't even go off!"

Evon howled. "It's my arm!" There was so much blood he had no idea where it was coming from so he placed the arm against her stomach, gently folded her in two and squeezed, hoping to keep the blood from flowing faster than he could travel.

"Oh my stars, I regret this. I haven't done anything to make my life matter," she whispered, and then went limp in his arms.

"Evon, hold on. Please! The water'll take out the burn, and stop the bleeding. Just lie in there and once I take care of him, I'll get you home in one piece."

"You're not going another inch onto my place!" Skookum bellowed, grabbing onto Jack's ankle as he stepped over him.

"Let go, you old fuck!" Jack stomped at his bony fingers with his free foot. Skookum would not let go, so Jack dragged the huge, bony man along with him.

"You ain't staying on my land!" Skookum belched from below, clinging on.

"She dies and I'm going to stomp your head into this earth, and throw the rest of you into that fire pit," Jack wheezed, traveling as best he could with the old man clinging on, his human ball and chain. He was perhaps ten feet into the struggle when the big, yellow dog came charging into the fray, snarling and snapping. Jack could see she'd pulled a huge stake from the ground to get free, the heavy chain dragged behind her, the thick collar kept it all fastened to her neck.

"Get back, Little Maid!" Jack cried, but the dog leaped on Skookum and clamped down on his ankle with a hard crunch and wouldn't let go.

"I'm gonna kill you too, you furry bitch!" Skookum screamed, but stubbornly clutched to Jack's leg with both hands, kicking at the big, yellow dog with his free foot.

Jack dragged the parade along. Evonal barely breathed.

"You won't die," he reassured her. "Breathe, please breathe."

When he reached the shore of lake, the lightning crackles were like spider webs being ripped from the surface of the earth. A white light flashed in front of him, something shot him from the soles of his feet, but he stretched up, far above the world, where he could see the line of them struggling along. When he snapped back, the hard tingling in every cell of his body started. It felt like the dog and giant were fused to Jack's ankle. Evonal became light as air.

"You won't drown; just swim when you hit the water." And Jack threw her as hard as he would any normal-sized basketball.

He watched her unfurl and float like a feather on the air, hover over the water, and then fold in half and drop like a stone. Jesus! Jack had not expected that. He turned to free himself from Skookum and was surprised how easy it was to unlatch his bony, cold hands from his ankle.

"Keep him there, Little Maid," he whispered, running to Evonal.

He watched the brilliant, ruby red bleed into the lake top, rippling to the outer edges, knew from experience how the pain just left her body.

"Swim, Evon!"

He called as he ran to the lake's edge, hitting the water all at once, digging in hard to try to reach her before she drowned. The lake was deeper than Jack thought. The harder he swam toward the bottom, the farther away it went. And when he finally back-paddled a few strokes, something underneath him released millions of tiny, blood filled bubbles that shot around him like a violent snowstorm of rubies, glowing more as they neared the surface. He held his breath and looked for her far below, all of his hopes sinking into those depths. In the time it took him to swim another seven feet he was cured of the greed of his gold fever; his lust for the big nothing he never wanted. Slowly, he emptied his lungs of air, mixing his own clear bubbles of air into the crystalline lake, hoping to sink and die quickly. Wherever Evonal had sunk was where he was headed, because he just wanted to be there with her. When he ran fully out of breath and began to kick—against his will—toward the surface, he saw the outline of Evonal floating peacefully on her back, just above him. When he broke through the surface of the water he found her gazing at the thousands of stars, gently breathing.

"Am I going to live?" she asked the stars.

"Yes!" said Jack, as he treaded water, towing her to shore. He scooped her up and ran. The dog was lying on the giant, her jaw clamped over his ankle.

"I'll be back for you, Little Maid," Jack yelled. "I promise. Just you hide from that old coot so he won't kill you. I'll be back." Evonal was in a stupor he could not shake her out of. Jack struggled to get Evonal's gloves back on and fix her into the harness. Hooking her up, he slipped into the sling, making sure it was secured to the line. Balancing her weight against him he lowered her over, and using the untested contraption he'd meant to lower Little Maid down in, Jack and Evonal began the slow descent back to earth. It went smoother than he'd ever hoped, but when they got to the bottom he lifted her out and carried her toward home.

Jack had no way of knowing that the old shotgun smashed into the top of a passing camper. The driver, convinced that the dent in his roof was caused by an asteroid, decided to take an iffy side road to have a good look around, an action that would help Jack immensely. Once the owner got his rig stuck deep in the sand, he unhitched his dune buggy, getting it mired in a deeper drift. He left it abandoned only a few feet from the road, and he walked back to his wife to wait until dawn.

Finding the dune buggy stuck, did not surprise Jack. Many a non-village idiot tried to drive through this desert at night, taking a paved road that worked until it gradually—or suddenly, it was impossible to predict—fizzled out into soft lake of sand. The keys were still in it, which surprised Jack, so he seized the moment, got Evonal inside, and easily shoved it free. "We're good now!" he assured Evonal, heading for the hospital.

■ ■ ■

Chapter 41

The doctor recognized Jack before Jack recognized him.

"This your wife?" the doctor asked, again examining Evonal, who was comfortably sleeping on a gurney, while the nurse got everything assembled.

"Yes, Evon Allison, uh…my wife," he was frightened by how natural it sounded.

"Just what is this place that is worth all this damage?"

"Just take care of Evon here."

Evonal sat up then, "I was shot!" she cried.

The doctor and Jack exchanged a look.

The doctor spoke first. "No, you weren't shot. You got a nice slice down your arm from something very sharp. Not much swelling though."

"There's some strange cactus she fell against."

"Aw," the doctor said. "This desert is full of surprises. And this is going to take a few layers of stitches too. You might want to go out and get some coffee. It's going to take awhile."

"I'd kinda like to watch," Jack said. Evonal sighed and squeezed his hand.

■ ■ ■

Chapter 42

Evonal's eyes fluttered open and she looked around her own bedroom carefully before examining her arm.

"This is a great scar!"

"You want a scar?" Jack asked from somewhere on the floor, where he'd been sleeping since he'd put her to bed, dead asleep from the pills the doctor gave her for the drive home.

"Well, a scar shows a storm you've weathered. Better than a tattoo."

"Whatever you say, Evon. I'm just glad you're stitched up and feeling OK."

"The funny thing is, I thought I got shot, Jack! My body felt like I was burning from the inside out. And then when you cannonballed me into that lake, and poof! I was cooled right down, but by degrees. My arm stopped burning, my foot went numb. I'm surprised it's just a deep bruise. Anyway, I don't remember anything after that except this peaceful floating sensation. Better than the peyote that time. It feels like I'm still floating in it, kinda free from my body. But, I realized things in there, beautiful, meaningful things. Like where we all belong, what I truly feel. But now that I'm starting to feel normal again, it's getting away from me. Pretty soon, it'll be forgotten, so I'd at least like the scar! You still have my clothes, right, Jackie?"

"Yeah, Evon, and I didn't wash them. Just like I promised. I hung them on the hook in the bathroom. Are you gonna be all right now?"

"I could eat a horse."

"You're a vegetarian," Jack said.

"I just feel so wonderful, breathlessly wonderful."

"I'll get you some food right now. Can you keep it down?"

"Peanut butter and dill pickle sandwiches, *mmmmmm*," she breathed. "I'm so hungry."

"No harm in trying," Jack said softly. He was up and peering down at her. "Can you get yourself to the bathroom? Do you need to go?"

"I think you can stop worrying 'bout me."

Jack hung back in the doorframe.

"Just say it, Jackie. Stop stewing."

"Nothing. I'm so glad you're here. Alive. I almost got you killed, and you're still talking to me."

"Say, your eyes look normal again."

"Yeah? I'm having some problems with 'em—everything is fuzzy. Let me get you those sandwiches."

Evonal sighed as he left the room. She breathed in deeply, so happy to be alive. And then her nose wrinkled, "It smells like gasoline in here." When Evonal lifted her head she saw the chain saw gleaming from the corner of her room, next to the small wood chair she was leaving behind, it looked evil, that long jaw and its hundreds of banded teeth.

"Jackie!" She yelled his name up to the ceiling before she turned her head toward the doorway. "Jackie, why do you have that chain saw?"

"You know I gotta go back and kill that thing, once I get the dog safely," his voice came from the kitchen.

"You can't do murder, Jack!"

"That *vine*. That old coot will do himself in soon enough. I gotta go get Little Maid, she's waiting for me," he said quietly from the doorway now.

"She's a good dog. She loves you too. Listen, I was thinking if the sling scares the dog, you can give her a doggie sedative. In the kitchen cupboard there's a bottle of pills I give the dogs for the Fourth of July fireworks and banging Foison craziness during the Spring Fest. Give her the pills that are left and she'll relax enough to go. Just wrap the pills in the dog treats. The other thing is, Jackie, you two have to move in here. It's a great house. Built to last." She closed her eyes. And then she heard him walking to the kitchen again. She thought of Jack all alone there without her, and she cried until she slept.

■ ■ ■

Chapter 43

At the first light of dawn Jack jingled the key chain at the dune buggy. "Thanks for all your help, but you're not quite done yet." He told it. Jack stashed the chainsaw on the backseat, the plastic containers of herbicide, a reserve of gas, and a few other things he thought he'd need. There was a new urgency to his trip to the tawl this time. His plan was to get to the top of the vine, and destroy it by chopping it with the chain saw and soaking it in the potion Old Sylvia had concocted. Once that was done, he would grab Little Maid, strap her in, and go right back down, chopping the vine away from the wall as he went. Once he hit the base, he'd hack the shit out of it, douse it with more potion until it let go and died. And in case that wouldn't kill it, he brought along gasoline and wood stakes to drive into it and smoke it out.

The sky was filled with clouds, far off, flashfloods in the making. He'd made an attempt last night to get up the vine, but couldn't do it. The wind blew, creating a haunting hum, and there was a good stream of stinging sand. Everyone knew twilight was the best time to be stealthy in the desert, but Jack needed daylight now. He could no longer see well at night, and he had a lot to do. The dune buggy started with the first try, and in spite of his size—overwhelming to the small buggy—it sailed over the desert floor like sand riding a light breeze.

Jack got there sooner than he'd expected, but had to take an about-turn, so the owner didn't catch him. Their motor home was still mired in the sand. There was a clothesline set up on one side, where a series of shirts dried stiff as bark, so they were prepared for the duration, he thought.

There was also an enormous gash on the top side of the camper. Jack wondered what had hit it as he quietly parked the dune buggy, got his things, and left it. He pitied he owner, but couldn't offer to help him just yet. It would take several men to push that camper out of the sand and get it back to the road, and this would take negotiating with half of Foison to round up enough willing participants. Later. Later. He left the key in the dune buggy and got his stuff, strapping it all on as he walked toward the bottom of his tawl.

Halfway up the vine, Jack stopped to look back over the desert floor. The colors were a muted blue, making it seem like a vast portion of thickly salted water rippled out there instead of dry sand. Jack could smell the rain coming, taste the lightning. The dark clouds were still piling up; it had been raining for days out there, but he was high enough to stay out of any flashflood, for now. He again shifted all the tools he had strapped to his body and began to climb as quickly as his strength and clumsiness would allow.

Even with his normal eyesight he could tell where the pit traps were, because the vegetation they'd been covered with was dried, making them obvious. He didn't smell that reeking old man, not that he was afraid of him anymore. Jack crouched low and whistled.

His Little Maid ran out of the brush, waving her tail.

"You ready to go, girl?" he whispered, freeing her of the collar and heavy chain.

The dog wagged its tail, spinning a circle.

Jack took the chain saw out and started it with a flick of his wrist. He cut into the vine in several spots. Once it was hash, he poured the herbicide over it. A whiff of smoke came up and the interloping vine wilted in a dramatic mush. It was a very satisfying sight.

And then he bundled the dog up into the Evonal-tested sling, and with some clumsy maneuvering, got Little Maid latched on. Like Evonal, the dog went limp once she got put over the side.

Jack stepped onto the vine and began to chop away as he descended. His hope was to make sure none of it clung to the wall of the tawl. After a couple hundred feet, he could see it was stubborn, so he decided to hack at it as best he could, and if it didn't fall on its own, he would hitch a rope to the winch on his truck and drag it off. Even if his truck got mired in the sand, he could deal with that once the vine was killed. But first he wanted to set Little Maid down at the bottom, on solid earth, and give her a good drink of water to celebrate.

Sam Skookum had just rounded the bend when he saw that two-bit punk asshole step into air and disappear with a large sack of his stuff strapped to his back. No one would ever accuse Skookum of being cowardly. He lay on his belly and crawled to the edge and looked down. Well. That pip-squeak seemed to have disappeared down a stack of leaves. He crawled back and went to get his old, razor sharp, hunting knife. Before he descended, he laced his boots tight, rolled down his sleeves, and stepped down into the stinking leaves. When he felt the enormous plant begin to crack a bit and sway, Skookum tried to climb back to the top, but he was too precariously balanced in the vine to do much more than hang on tight and hope it would quit quivering long enough for him to get back to his roost and maybe make a new plan. The wind kicked up, and he hung on with all his might, one foot batting at the edge, trying to make contact.

■ ■ ■

Chapter 44

The next time Evonal awoke, she felt stronger and could sit up. There was a sandwich on a plate; the slices of bread were stuck together crookedly, and it was obvious there was at least peanut butter in it. On the small table, sat a pitcher of what she thought might be either dark iced tea or warm cola; neither appealed. The house was unusually quiet; her dogs were not there, she thought, but was certain she could hear them scratching around. Still, she wasn't certain, she was so darn sleepy. The odor of gasoline merely lingered in the air now, dissipating out the open window. Evonal sat up, alert. Jack was gone. The chainsaw was gone. Her heart began hammering the warning. Evonal buried her head under the covers. The images that formed in her mind as she floated on that life-renewing lake came back like inner music. A fisherman's net of living things;

a delicately knotted web that held together whole worlds, secret, and vital. Nothing in the world existed on its own, she thought. And no one, even her. Love expanded inside her until she felt she might burst out of her own skin. She loved Jack.

Ten minutes later, she was up on wobbly legs getting dressed. Another ten minutes after that she stood in front of a cringing Mavis Stanger, who stood with one foot fastened to the top step of her silver bullet trailer.

"You're coming with me to save your boy. You cannot shirk this. He needs the both of us right now," Evonal bluntly insisted.

Mavis Stanger wrung her hands before dropping them back in her pockets. "Jack gets himself in and out of scrapes all the time. He always has. He don't need me."

"He needs you to tell him the truth. And you're gonna do it before real tragedy is done. I know that crazy lunatic up there is Jack's father, and Jack's gone back to take his revenge without knowing a thing. And we're going to help him before he gets hurt. Now get in the truck, Mavis. We'll drive as far as we can to that place and then we're gonna run to save him! And, Mavis, if you don't come with me now, I'm going straight downtown to tell every soul we know this whole sordid story."

"It's nothing but a fairy tale!" Mavis declared, but her chin quivered and her eyes stayed downcast.

"Mavis! You know some will remember when. No one will ever forget or forgive you if you deliberately let something happen to Jack. I've been up there and so have you. I know who that evil old stinker is. And Jack's on his way back there now to do I don't know what!"

"You can't've been there! We blew up the mine shaft years ago."

"Jack found a way, and you must've known it all along. Now what are you going to do to save your boy from all that evil?"

Mavis's hand trembled as her bony fingers moved back and forth over her puckered mouth. After a few swipes, she dropped her hand back in her pocket and said, "I'll get my things."

The petite woman flew into her trailer and back out again, carrying a purse. She climbed into the truck, and settled in by strapping the seat belt.

"Best be getting to it," she ordered, pointing a finger in the direction of the tawl.

On the way over, Evonal had to take the long way around to have a road with substance; her foot pressing the pedal to the floor, as hard as she dared, the back end still slipped around, Mavis's tiny hand clenched on the dashboard, her arm a rod, pinning her to her seat. When Evonal turned the truck around the bend she noticed, too late, a flash flood was washing through, cutting an uneven diagonal line across the old road, the brown churning water still flowing fast in the newly carved ravine.

"Brake! Turn!" Mavis cried.

The truck stopped at the lip of the wet ditch, which immediately crumbled under the weight, and before Evonal could make sense of things they landed in the newly made flood channel, brown water gushing up to the lower edge of the windows, but they were upright, at least. The heavy old truck began to float, slamming first on the right and then the left sides of the ditch, before it turned to an angle sweeping down until it got pretty firmly wedged while the water poured in.

"Climb out the window!" Mavis shouted already mounting the frame.

Evonal scrambled out after her.

"Run, run, run!" Mavis hollered, scuttling across the hood of the truck, dragging that huge purse after her. Evonal was amazed by her agility and strength. They ran until the flooded channel was far behind them, and they felt safe enough to stop to catch their breaths.

"Don't do nothing foolish, Jackie, we're almost there," she whispered, planting both hands on her hips and searching the sky for the top of the tawl.

"Let's get, let's get!" Mavis urged, looping her arm through Evonal's, tugging her along with the oversized purse like she was dragging two heavy kites by the strings. The sand was soft there; walking in it was like wading through knee-deep water, but Mavis easily treaded over it. And it made her heart thump all the harder for Jack—she wasn't sure why.

■ ■ ■

Chapter 45

"Thank the stars! There you are, Jackie!" Evonal called, taking him completely by surprise. The big yellow dog ran to Evonal and gave her a good nosing over as she pat the broad head, talking in her mysterious dog talk that made the tail wag even harder. And then there was his mother cradling one arm in another like a baby rested there, her big purse dangling down. Mavis was tapping her foot, like she was impatient to get something started. The big yellow dog shied away, taking a safe distance from his Mavis. It gave Jack the uneasy feeling that they'd also already met.

"I've come to tell you something," Mavis said, lifting her chin. "Important."

But before she could finish, the vine cracked over their heads like thunder and then the sound became more rapid fire, like someone letting off a string of firecrackers.

And then a loud cry filled the air, "HOLYSHITMOTHERHUMPERPISSON—"

The vine dropped like a rope that had been cut down from its hook in the sky. The minute Jack smelled the fumes of Skookum, he shouted, "Get back!"

Skookum came careening toward earth, facedown and spread-eagle. His mouth was wide open, a cave, his tongue an evil snake looking ready to strike. They all watched with their own mouths agape. It seemed like he'd never land, but once he did, he disappeared into the earth with a *whomp!*

They all looked at each other and then back at the landing spot. Little Maid cried out and pawed at the air. It seemed to Jack that Foison's UFO had finally landed. He looked as tightly fit into the earth as a worked jigsaw puzzle piece.

"Help me outta here, you fucking nitwits!" Skookum's voice was muffled, but strong.

"That old asshole can't still be alive!" Jack shouted at the sky, stomping a foot into the earth. The rain fell steady for a long minute.

Evonal had begun backing up at the sound of Skookum's voice, and when Jack looked back at her, she held the chainsaw up ready to strike. Jack smiled, just a little.

"Give it to me, Evon, I'll kill him for you," he said.

Evonal shook her head. "Nobody's going to die. Now we're going to have to fish him out of there and see to him. Somehow we're gonna need to get him someplace. To the hospital..."

"Naw, he's evil. And he stinks like the devil's shit. Leave him in there. Let's go call the sheriff, and let him take care of it. And I need to finish that vine off before it does untold damage to this place, like I promised Old Sylvia."

"Jack," Mavis said evenly. "You're gonna have to help him. He's your—"

"Stop talking!" Jack commanded. "I'll fish his ass out. Evon, get me the rope over there. I'm gonna have to tie him up so he can't hurt nobody even though he's a goat that'll get it chewed through in no time at all. And, Ma, run around the bend there and see if that camper is still stuck. We're gonna need a ride to the hospital."

Skookum was too busted up to need tying. And the couple with the camper—a tall, gangly pair of soul searchers who looked like button bucks in broad-brimmed sun hats—agreed to take him to the nearest hospital if Jack could get help to dig them out. Jack did that by the force of his shoulder against the rear of the camper while the deer man stepped lightly on the gas. Once it was on solid ground, he carried the old giant into the camper and laid him on the floor, face up before going about the business of getting all of him in so the door could be shut. The awkward angles his limbs took couldn't be helped; he just wouldn't fit in there any other way.

"Whew!" Jack cried, wiping the tears from his eyes. "He's gonna need a hosing down with scalding lye before anyone can work on him. And don't let him have anything with a point on it, not even a plastic fork. This is one angry, evil ugly here."

When the couple looked alarmed and maybe ready to change their minds, Mavis put her hand up.

"Let me in there with him. I'll see him through to the hospital at least. He won't do nothing to no one, just look at him. Besides, I've got my big gun in my purse right here." Mavis patted her purse and asked Evon if she wanted to get dropped off back at town on their way through.

Evonal shook her head. "I'll stay and help Jack finish up here. We can walk back together. I'm footloose now. I wrecked the truck on the way here," she explained to Jack.

The big dog pushed its nose in Evonal's palm and licked her wrist.

Once everyone was packed in and sent off, Jack said, "OK, let's see what I can do about killing that thing for good."

"Jackie, let's go point those government people at this thing, and let them have at it. They know what to do about this plant devil."

"It's probably best," he said.

They both deeply inhaled.

"Are you really moving away?"

"Yes."

"I'd like to take you to your new place. I just got to take the big dog with us. What do you say?"

"I think I'll let you," Evonal said.

"I've got to set a couple of things straight before I go, pack a few things. Take me two days." He wiped an arm across his grimy brow.

"I'll wait."

Skookum rumbled painfully along in some kind of vehicle that he did not recognize, and didn't like the pleasant smell of neither. As if his pain weren't bad enough, whenever he opened his eyes, there was the hawklike woman, glaring at him; something else lingered there, but he wasn't quite sure what it was. No doctor needed tell him that every bone he owned had some kind of crack in it. The pain was already seeping into them. He could also feel a cloud moving into his brain, popping off hot noise like thunder on a cold December morning. And then he decided he was done, so he took one last deep breath and while he let it out, he died.

"It's about time," Mavis said, unfolding her arms and settling back into the seat so she could look out the window now, at last, free.

■ ■ ■

Chapter 46

With Little Maid's help, Jack spent the night digging out the small pile of gold he'd intended to keep hoarded near him for the rest of his life. Mavis was set for money, he was taking a small bag of gold dust with him; he just wanted to have it, and his cash was packed, but there was a goodly pile that he had carefully hidden in an old cave in a nearby tawl that wasn't frequented by tourists. The safe was still somewhere under the rubble of his old house. He figured it was rightfully Mavis's once Vern and his crew came across it. Jack wasn't going to claim it. He was done with that stuff. Drawing the treasure map for the Lake sisters was pretty straightforward, and he wrote on it four cautions: keep the find a secret, sell it only to Trong Tri, burn the map once they were set, and never again bother Evonal, not with words or deeds. Better still: move out of Foison for good.

Wanting to avoid all types of tears or recriminations, or worse, those long, sorry apologies he was so used to delivering to women, or any combination with Linda Lake, Jack got the map to Astrid by waiting until she jogged by on her early morning run. He held it out like a baton, she took it, and kept running without exchanging so much as a g'mornin'. Jack watched the soles of her feet take turns kicking up dust, and he realized this was the first time he'd ever seen Astrid in short pants, and a snug-fitting top. She was terribly skinny, he thought, and the way her shoulders were falling in when they should be straight back and squared off, and her fists seemed to bounce off the thin air, he realized she was really struggling through the run.

Next, Jack fed Little Maid and himself, and then he rounded up a bouquet of metal flowers, thanks to Vern's artistic talents, and went to pay a call on Evonal, who he'd found outside, sweeping her porch. These days her old dresses were gone. She was wearing regular jeans and a white shirt with the image of an ocean wave on the front.

"All packed, Evon?" Jack called. He was pleased the way her back straightened just a bit between her shoulder blades at the sound of his voice, but she kept the broom moving.

"I'm just cleaning up a bit. I've got a few things left to do before I go," she said, looking up. "What you got there?" She laughed.

"I'm bringing you flowers, for your new place," he told her, handing her the bouquet. If her first expression over the flowers was any indication—a flush in her cheeks, a wavering smile she tried to tuck away quickly—he thought he might have a chance.

"Did Vern make these of empty soda pop cans? Or what? They are so delicate. Beautiful, like irises. So detailed too," she said, examining them like she might make some herself. They were light, the stalks were long, the bouquet shifted with the breeze.

"And they come with their own vase," Jack said, pointing to the heavy metal disk they were somehow fastened to.

"Thank you! I am truly amazed, Jackie. I never got flowers from a man before," she said.

They stood together on the tiny porch, while Little Maid smelled every inch of the ground in the small front yard.

"She looks nice and healthy, Jackie. You have to brush that long coat, help her get the old hair off so she doesn't rub on things or start scratching too much. That is one big, big dog. Has anyone said anything?"

"I haven't really seen anyone lately except Vern, and Astrid when she was running by on her morning routine," Jack answered.

"I haven't been out either, but your mom stopped by." Her pause made him regret the day, but she kept on gently. "Seems that Sam Skookum character died on the way to the hospital. She had him cremated, and plans to scatter his ashes over the cemetery," she said with a softness to her voice that shot into him like the tip of a spear. Pulling it out would be agony, so he just left it be.

"Want to go for a walk?" he asked. "Take a good look at the downtown before we leave?"

Evonal turned to him. "I'm not so sure of it myself, but I don't love it here like you do. I never felt I belonged."

"That's why we belong together, Evon."

"We belong together?" Evonal repeated.

"Put those metal flowers inside before they blow away, or rust, and let's go see what Foison is up to today. It doesn't seem near noisy enough lately. Bring the little pups, if you like."

"Yes. Let's do just that. I'm not bringing the dogs, but I'll put these inside," Evonal said, taking the broom with her inside. Jack sat on the porch to wait. Little Maid at once went to him to lick his face. "There's a good girl. You're going to a good vet in Oregon," Jack told her, scratching behind her ears, feeling comfortable, and satisfied for perhaps the first time in his life. When Evonal came out wearing a soft blue shirt halfway buttoned with a snug white T-shirt underneath, he was uncommonly pleased that she went through the trouble to change.

"Wow," said Evonal when they arrived. There were people about, but not the big crowds. All the posters were gone. The poles were scraped clean. There were some uniformed workers, about, taking measurements and samples. The government people, Jack surmised. A woman Jack didn't know sat in a deep plastic chair with a small umbrella, eating an apple, a small computer resting in the crook of her arm. She looked prepared for work in the desert. This warmed his heart.

The stores were still open and people were filtering in and out.

"Jack! Evonal!" called someone Jack thought sounded familiar, but when he turned around and spotted the man, he wasn't sure.

"Is that Mackson?" Evonal asked, squinting her eyes at him.

They stood together and waited for the balding man. It was Mackson, who once had so much hair it seemed to flow out of the top of his head.

"I didn't recognize you at first," Jack spoke first.

The lanky man ran a hand over the top of his head, "Stopped wearing the wig. Time to be the real me. Tired of grooming the sand out of that hot old thing." His attention flickered to Little Maid. "Say! By god, that is one big yellow dog you got there!" He began cooing at Little Maid, who shied away behind Jack and Evonal.

"What's been happening over here?" Evonal asked politely, reassuring the yellow dog with a hand on her head.

"Aw, the government convinced us with their fancy Power Points why we should get rid of the noxious weed, so we voted to let 'em eradicate it. They're paying us. Anyways, we woulda done it for the good of Foison. It's a rare and delicate ecosusskind, like Old Sylvia said. Anyways, once Old Sylvia got murdered, everybody that was real Foison Surrounded all lost heart for that GD stuff. I surely miss the old girl too. She would've loved to know she won. Would've been proud and rightly so that she done the right thing, stickin' by her guns, when everyone ran for the greed of the thing. Now we're all just waiting for normal. Us desert rats like the quiet alone." He took a deep sniff of air, noisily, through his nose, puffing out his chest before he let it all go. "Smell that? Just desert. The way I like it. Just good old Foison."

"Looks like the jeep tours are still going strong," Jack said, when he really wanted to smooth down the few strands of Evonal's hair that were still sailing on the static electricity.

"The Numinous Vortex, eh, all the tawls, really have always attracted the outsiders. Since the wave of craziness, even more people have experienced the spiritual healing qualities, and they want to come back. It is beautiful, and business is good enough for who we are here. There's talk of Vern building a small motel on his property. Only twelve cabins, and some RV parking, a nice campsite with shade from the mesquite trees and maybe outdoor showers. And now that the German tourist trade has come on in, we'll have more than enough to keep ourselves going without all that other fuss. Those Germans are nice folks too, respectful. They apparently like to hike in the hottest time of year, so we expect 'em next month, and they love their beer, so we have that stocked in the new bar Astrid and Linda Lake have put together with their sandwiches—over a hundred different types. Did you know there was so many kinds of beers?"

"Jack certainly knew that," Evonal said.

Jack and Mackson watched her. Silence dropped on them.

"I heard you was leaving too, Evon," Mackson said.

"Yep." Evonal nodded. "I'll come back from time to time, but I'm moving to Oregon, where my family is from. Originally."

"It rains there," Mackson said, obviously disheartened by her leaving.

"Yep," said Evonal. "It rains. And there's all that cold ocean too."

Jack detected an almost imperceptible smirk, surprised at how well he knew her. Mackson only shifted his posture so now his right hip jutted out and his left arm came on top.

"What about you, Jack?" He asked, his voice pitching up high.

"I'm taking Evonal to her new place."

"But you'll be back, Jack, won't you?" Mackson asked. Both his brows shot up to his hairline, clearly shocked.

"You'll see me when I'm here."

"We'll see how long he lasts," Evonal said.

Jack studied her, thinking about leaving for the first time, with her. Little Maid wagged her tail slowly, causing a draft of cool air on his back. Leaving Foison, Jack thought, for a strange land. A sharp, tingling sensation ran through his body, a feeling he thought might be a good one, but he wouldn't know yet, not 'til he got there, just like Evon had said all along. Jack studied her profile, the way she protected her upper lip by pulling it under her teeth and wrapping her lower lip over it made him want to wrap his arms around her. He tried to imagine her as an old woman, himself as an old man. Evon was saying something to Mackson that he didn't quite catch.

A sandstorm began blowing hot air on them. The three of them began walking.

"I'll say good-bye now in case I don't see you before you go." Mackson screwed up his face, wiped a hand over his balding head, "Hey, Jack, you got any herb?"

"Naw." Jack couldn't remember the last time he'd smoked weed. The gold had been his high; even the beer he drank was only to keep the gold fever from jangling his nerves so much—he barely felt the effects of liquor. Just then he felt he could use a deep drink of cold water, but he didn't crave anything other than that. He stretched, feeling free, really free for the first time in his life.

"Here, take what I got left," Evonal said, pulling a wad out of her shirt pocket, handing the bud to Mackson. While he pocketed it, they turned and left him.

■ ■ ■

Chapter 47

It was early morning when they arrived. The sun burst out of the clouds, the rain they'd been driving in for the last five hours had stopped. The heavy scent of the sea covered everything, and made them cough when they tried to inhale it too deeply. Although Evonal offered out the key, Jack took her hand, and they walked around to the back of the house, smiling at everything. It was good. The small dogs, newly relaxed and oddly quiet since they licked the water off Evonal's lake clothes, jumped down from the truck with the big yellow dog to nose the ground as thoughtfully as their golden companion.

"This is the original part of the homestead," Evonal said.

At the center was an old brick kitchen, and surrounding this was a small orchard of fruit trees, each already holding the promise of a thousand small, autumnal miracles. The earth here smelled differently, of moss and other living things Jack knew nothing about.

"This place is gonna take some getting used to," Jack said.

Evonal was looking at the treetops, spinning slowly around with both her arms straight out. The scent of the sea made the pungent smell of the trees richer, almost edible. The wind picked up, rustling the leaves, louder and louder, a frenzied crowd. Jack laughed. "Take a bow." Evonal did, the applause of the leaves grew to a crescendo; her clothes blew away from her body, sails on a ship out to sea. And then it stopped. Everything resettled except for her hair. It stayed blown away from her face, a crooked cape at her back.

When she held out her hand, he took it. Together those two hands formed a pretty tight bond.

The end.

Made in the USA
Charleston, SC
19 October 2013